The WEIGHT *of* SMOKE

In the Land of Whispers

———◆———

BOOK ONE

The WEIGHT *of* SMOKE

———◆———

a n o v e l b y

GEORGE ROBERT MINKOFF

To Lenny,

A new world in its
new poetry rises .... yea !
right ! you better read
my little book .... or, !!
nothing !

Best
George

Mℱ

McPherson & Company

For Nancy,

Because...

Published by McPherson & Company
Post Office Box 1126, Kingston, New York 12402
www.mcphersonco.com
Manufactured in the United States of America
DESIGN BY BRUCE R. MCPHERSON. TYPESET IN GARAMOND

FIRST EDITION

1 3 5 7 9 10 8 6 4 2   2006 2007 2008 2009

Library of Congress Cataloging-in-Publication Data
Minkoff, George Robert
 The weight of smoke : a novel / by George Robert Minkoff. — 1st ed.
   p. cm.   —   (In the land of whispers ; bk. 1)
 ISBN-13: 978-0-929701-80-6 (alk. paper)
 ISBN-10: 0-929701-80-1 (alk. paper)
   1. Smith, John, 1580-1631—Fiction. 2. Virginia—History—Colonial
period, ca. 1600-1775—Fiction. 3. Jamestown (Va.)—History—17th
century—Fiction. I. Title
 PS3613.I64W45   2006
 813'.6—dc22
                                     2006026371

Publication of this book has been made possible, in part, by a grant from the Literature Program
of the New York State Council on the Arts, a state agency. Grateful acknowledgment is made to
the editors of BOMB magazine, where a portion of chapter thirteen first appeared.

One hundred copies of the first printing have been specially bound,
numbered, and signed by the author.

O for a Muse of fire

KING HENRY THE FIFTH

ADVERTISEMENT

HE saved the Jamestown Colony. Of that there is no doubt. This Captain Smith, whom I knew, this Captain John Smith. So little his reward for all his luck and for all he survived. How small the blessings for one so blessed. For all the pain he suffered and the neglect—and now he is forgotten but for a few.

Most called him mad, but I am not so sure. I will not condemn with such easy certainties. Captain Smith before his death sent me his one last book, this manuscript which would tell the tale in full. All the truth is held now on these scrolls of ink. How dark its flesh upon the page in thins of plate, as the skin of Eden's apple, this book is the measure of our fall.

How many works did Smith's quill produce? Six, eight, a dozen to sentinel the path to this final hope. How many unrequited visions whisper in the passions of this, his only epitaph?

I think of that time before the colony, when all for Drake, our youth and prideful joy were set to destroy the Spanish empire to save the stricken world with benevolent English law, our bodies given as sacrifice to the task, our wealth in pledge, to free again the free. All the conquered of the New World, enslaved and destitute of hope, we would cradle in our might and the sanctuary of our law. To us a vision of all nations of the world, all in equal partnership in a greater England. No masters, no seekers of gold.

All failures are failures of the soul. Smith's narrative is the breath that holds the balance, that assays the history of a hope gone to ghost. It is a justice held to judgment in the imagination. When Sir Walter Raleigh wagered Queen Elizabeth that he could know the weight of smoke, the queen laughed. Raleigh weighed the tobacco on a balance, then tapped it into the bowl of his pipe, lit the weed to enjoy the smoke. The pipe finished, Raleigh weighed the remaining ash. The loss of weight, the weight of smoke.

If thought be smoke evaporating in the wind, what ash is left is our estate. To know the loss from the confections of the fire is to know our plight. Our world is a dry leaf. Palm-veined our hands as the tobacco weed. All is mother to the ash, its smoke the measure of our loss. To weigh our failures is to weigh the smoke.

This book is the ash and the smoke, together it is the tobacco leaf. The words are Smith's, tracing him through the genealogies of an idea from May of 1607 through the finals of his revelations. I give it to the public now, as he wished.

GEORGE SANDYS, *London 1632*

PART ONE

The Coming of History

THE ALCHEMIES OF THE RIVER

*I cannot remember when they came in their boats. I did not
know them. I could not remember them. I only flow. I am only
a present. I flow constantly and everchangingly in my banks.
I think others had come before. My memory rots in their debris.
My past is my inner eye, watching beneath the surface.
It sees the dissolving mist of their bodies rising
moments of time before my present. They flow away.
They disperse and I am again the same.*

Chapter One

E WERE ALONE. The Chesapeake Bay held us in its cup. Under the moon the water ran milk white. I touched its wetness, mesmerized by the surface. It shattered into darkness, the pellets of light now reforming the confused image of my hand. Someone groaned.

"Quiet." My order was a whisper.

There was movement in the barge, a voice. "What, Smith?"

"Nothing, go to sleep."

I watched a wisp of cloud pass, darkening the land in its silhouette. I could almost taste its vapor. I closed my eyes, searching my brain for a memory of light. One of our gentlemen was smoking a pipe. Its smoke glowed as if born to ghost above the river. Its whiteness flowed beyond the barge. I smelled its sweet sting.

In the morning, our backs were bent again against our oars. There were twenty of us in the barge, heading north up a river of no name. Weight upon weakness we pulled upon the heave of waters to explore for a few days into the west. The scintillations of the river glowed in a golden mirror. We to discover perhaps the passage to the western sea. Our orders to make good prospects in trade and alliances with the savages while the other eighty-seven of our company unloaded our small fleet. Those three ships our only protection, their cannons our sentries, their wooden hulls our forts, and they soon to sail for England. It was May 1607. Only three days earlier we had landed in Virginia and founded, at great expense and not inconsiderable danger, Jamestown. The name of our king to grace a flat of sands now strewn with the barrels of our supplies. Soon the river too would bear our sovereign's name. We had come as England, and England was not another Spain. Sweetly we had brought our salvations to these shores. Spain had come to the New World to find slaves and easy wealth. We had come to build a single nation from the nations. The enslaved would be our allies; we would war against a heathen

Spain with kindness. I throbbed with mission. All human enterprises are enterprises of conversion. I wished to be the expedition, to be transformed, to live action without thought, to become one with this great enterprise, to be its instrument. What need I of thought, I am of Drake.

In our barge for one day and already we were anchored in a brew of uncertain consequence. Fatigue was upon us. It was hot. One sailor chewed a dried tobacco leaf, brown like a fouled breath, its fabric cracked as it disappeared between his lips like the wings of some great bat. The sailor smiled and licked from his own hands the white powder of a crushed seashell, a physic known to clean the teeth and ward off exhaustion. Several of the party pruned each other, adjusting metal and belts, shining pistols. They looked like monkeys at play, groomed and self-absorbed. A gentleman lit a silver pipe. Almost all of our crew were gentlemen or their lazy servants, easily exhausted at just the thought of work. And so they brought their patriotism to puppet before their own eyes as a dumb show in the wilderness.

"The savage admires a well-turned-out gentleman," said one, extending his cuffs down to his wrists.

"I doubt a savage knows what a gentleman is." There was laughter from the crew.

"To them savages a shiny piece of metal is a god. To them it does not reflect light, but is its natural prison," said a youth, Thomas Mutton, shining the metal of his arrow, kissing it with his breath as he had done every day for months at sea and now on the land and in his dreams.

"Every nation knows a gentleman, even if it has never seen a proper one," said another youth. "It's in the cut of his coat, in the gesture of a hand.... Even in the wilderness there is protection in a noble nature, is there not, Smith?"

"The wilderness has its own gods...gods who never suffer fools lightly. You better know what you're about here." I am a fragile iron, but the crew cleaved to me as a shield because they knew I had fought the Turks and, though small in stature, had traveled all of Europe and survived Eastern slaveries.

"Said right," sparkled one who had returned from his business at the edge of the boat. "And that's how it's to be here. We English know how to manage and how to think. A day of English thought is worth a year of others' burden."

"English thought and to hell with the burden," yelled the gentlemen of the company. The enthusiasm of patriotism over, the side of the boat was again populated with bobbing heads and retching.

"We better get to it," I said, picking up my oar again, looking at Captain Christopher Newport, the admiral of the colony, a man of fractured shadow, having lost an arm privateering in the West Indies. He of hollow eyes, and of cautious action, a sometime follower of Drake, who had fought under his command against the Armada in 1588. How great men spawn lesser minions in their tread. And I am not that, no matter what the wreck. The puppet is not the apostle, no matter how he loves his strings. But still our admiral was one of the few men among us who was used to a day's work. Newport nodded to me slightly, as if his mind were perched on a nervous authority. And how eager am I to hide with determined voice my own misgivings? I have lent myself to consequence. "Let us not order the men, Smith. You are not of the council yet." Though I was younger, the men looked to me. Newport would not yield an easy equality. For the moment we both served on the leash of each other's will.

The water moved in serpent's coil at our passage. We headed north again. The land seemed heavy with thought. The English backs bent and rowed and cursed their servants, some of whom were left behind unloading the ship. An oar floated past me. I pulled it back to the boat, handed it to its owner who refused it. "I was not birthed for toil. We gentlemen afford the colony protection by our presence. Manual labor for us is a waste of our inherent talent, and a sin against God's order." I pushed the oar back into the man's hand. He refused. *We believe those beliefs our comfort can afford. I am a beggar*, I thought, *my hope spends its only coin.* I rose slightly, smiled a terrible silence, and said, "Either you row or you swim."

"Damned English savage…" He continued for several miles to mutter. I didn't care what he said as long as he rowed. The man adjusted the armour around his neck and was silent for a moment. "Work is nature's burden for the poor. Gentlemen by birth are removed from such labor, held in reserve for command in war and government." *Yes, idleness is for a gentlemen a signpost of great promise*, I thought, smiling to myself. *If we work, who will recognize who we are?*

"Hear… Hear." There was general agreement among those agreeing, pleasure in shared pleasantries, certain certainties certified in affable affirmations of affirmative formulations, all of which left gentlemanly smiles on the gentlemanly lips of the assembled but overworked gentlemen. Wounds of pride now bled speech to purpose cures in easy philosophies. The gentleman at his oar now spoke.

"As in heaven where spheres are assigned by nature to unique and separate runs, never colliding, always reconciled to their task, forever affable in their distant intercourse, and so there is in man an orbit, an assignment, a rational order, certified by natural law: the poor to work; the worthy to think and govern; the savage to be lifted from his naked state, protected and taught the true and noble use of civilized tools; and the plenty to be won from the earth by English farmers under the guidance of English law, a law so perfect in utterance that it is from nature's own only once removed."

The crew murmured its approval. Chests swelled in pride. Armor strained at its buckles. I'd seen it all before: soldiers filling the prisons of their fears with the alloy of dreams. Someone wiped his eyes. The terms "a natural leader" and "golden tongue" floated around the deck. The boat moved more smoothly now, on hopeful waters. A deer sprang up the sandy bank. "Should I take a shot?" someone said. A gun was raised.

"No," I ordered as the smoking hammer fell. The concussion rocked the boat. The bullet missed. "The savages now know where we are."

"It will be easier for us to find them," said Newport.

Innocence is a noose looking for a tree, I thought to myself. At the bow, fish turmoiled in the clear waters. Fins flashed and fell against the wooden hull. A dull thud dissolved into lethargic scratching as the wake's fishy catch folded upon itself. The air was shattered with frightened geese. Between man and sky a living shadow rose, filling the air with the hysteria of its own echoing fear.

"If there is as much gold in the land as there are birds in the sky we'll all be rich," came a voice.

"Who do you think will be the first to find it?" said an exhausted youth. "Who do you think, Captain Smith?"

"The one who lives the longest," I said to the laughter and cheers of the boat.

"I know, I'll be the first," said the youth. "Gold is for thems that can keep it. It is the dream that miracles in our grasp, is it not? My mother gave me this lucky badge. My father wore it when he sailed against the Armada," he said as he polished it against his cloak.

"We all have one of those," said one of the few laborers of our crew. "What you need for luck is a little needle and hole work. I ain't meaning from your mother." Men will deny with their heads what they believe with their hearts, so the old man polished his own charm while he taunted the youth's.

"Gold is for thems that can keep it. Ask the Spanish drowned," said someone.

"Dreams are dangerous things in the mouths of fools," Captain Newport whispered in my ear, seeking friendship in shared secrets. I smiled in silent agreement. I watched the river turn. It seemed to thicken in its flow like a jellied ghost.

Five herons began long, slow circles of ascent, rising in graceful peace, these feathered clouds of flight. The morning sun rose above the trees. Its tilted rays began to wax the water's surface with heat. The river meandered sharply to the left. We followed its path, low to the earth, prowling like a cat. Beyond the bend the air seemed to fill with perfumed dust, scintillating as it fell, not through deformed and twisted twigs, but through a living light where trees stood so wide, their bark sculptured in gargoyle's threads as if this continent had clawed its own earth and planted giants, spaced so far apart that you could see for miles; and through the fractured light, leaves, in twos and threes, glided and fell, rising sometimes in the soft and gentle skin which was the air. And on the earth a weave of flowers, of red and blue and white and pink, in such complexity and mesh one would think it was a tapestry whose picture was lost in simple dots by the closeness of the eye.

"There is no finer park in all of England," said Newport, now standing. "An Eden...an Eden...."

And through the trees savages came, laughing and singing, their hands clapping, down from the forest to the water's edge, some dancing in circles on the hills, smoke circling upward from their tobacco pipes. A few threw themselves on the ground, scratching wildly the earth, tearing at the ground, softening it, laying mats upon the wounded soil and, around the mats, baskets filled with corn and pumpkin in exotic shapes. On the riverbank they danced in plaintive ecstasy, beckoning us to join them, their hands touching their hearts, reaching outward toward the boat, welcoming us, begging us, imploring us, as if we were lost children, to return home.

The Coming of History 15

"My God…they are full of noble innocence, are they not?" Newport's words seemed a prayer, more to his hopes than to any deity.

"What do you think?" he asked, looking at me.

"The world is a screen," I answered, "and on it in blood is written the names of those who would only touch its surface…. Intent always begins in secrets."

"There is nothing to fear…from thems…that welcome us in such pleasant fits…" said Thomas Mutton as he rose.

And on the hill they danced and chanted, stamping their feet, the dust from the ground rising, mingling with the smoke of their tobacco. As a ghostly steam it rose through the air, dissolving slowly like the earth's breath.

I stumbled forward, tripping over the bramble of lace and ruffles and billowing hems of coats scattered between the seats. Reaching the bow I raised my gun. I had seen too many *ambushados* in the East. I fired. The dancing figures on the hill froze, as if in astonished rest. Heads turned toward the sound which moved in hysterical echoes through the trees. Savage eyes followed. I waited for those eyes to turn toward me. The boat rocked gently. I felt all their eyes. They braced my skin. There was a passing image in my head, an arrow piercing my chest, my mind evaporating into death. It wouldn't happen. Fear wills its own plot. My mind solidified. I raised my gun above my head and lowered it, placing it between my feet. I shouted, "Lay down your weapons," both in words and in gestures, at the crowd gathering at the water's edge. My hand touched my heart. "We mean you no harm." I gestured again with my gun as I spoke the absurdity of sounds which to us were words, but to the savages just throat.

My red hair blazed in crimson prodigals. The sun upon my red beard. My face rimmed in a human flame. The savages' mouths agape. Never had they seen hair such as mine. What priest of fire is this to wizard lightning and thunder from a stick? I had become the rainbow exploding from its silhouette. They stepped back. They stared at me, fingers now in point. With a hesitation, bows, arrows and clubs were laid by the river's edge.

"Turn toward the shore," I spoke words that seemed to triumph on my breath.

"Who is he, a counterfeit noble, to give orders?" someone said. "He is a prisoner, a mutineer."

"He knows his business," said Newport nodding his head nervously, telling the others to obey. The bow moved in its arc, now facing the shore, its sharpened edge cutting across the water's flow. Moving closer, the savages reached outward, beckoning, groping with anxious fingers the empty space. Some jumped into the water, drowning the agony of anticipation with physical pain. In my ears were the garbles of mysterious words; in my sight, the scramble of confused and frantic gestures and the quickening movement of the boat. I began to see from beneath the icy run of the river the cloudy heads of rocks, frozen in their orbit, floating like abandoned moons in the turbulent mud. The bow of the boat rushed to meet them. "We're going to run aground," I cried.

The savages were at the side of the boat, their hands reaching for the gunnels, some trying to touch my beard. The boat swaying, our loosened sail flapped like an empty skirt against the mast. We were almost swamped with flesh. Oars were raised. Some of the crew reaching for their swords and guns, I fired my pistol in the air. The confusion shocked in calm. I touched my heart, then gestured for the savages to keep their distance. They did reluctantly. One savage tried to grab hold of the boat again. I hit his hand with an oar, firmly, not to do damage, just to make a point. He cried, but understood and backed away.

"We should be out in the middle of the channel,…making plans… Savages got changeable natures…. They be curiously friendly to us one moment…and cannibals eating us the next," came a voice from behind me.

"These are not cannibals. They have no skulls around their necks," someone said. Rumor and folktales had now become the science of our fear.

"If I be a cannibal…I wouldn't advertise it around my neck…. Scare away too many meals," the voice continued. There was nervous laughter from the crew.

"These are not cannibals," I said, knowing we humans are always afraid of being eaten by something, whether sea monsters, or giant birds, or our own kind. It is a fantasy birthed of a fearful truth, knowing what we do to each other each day.

"They're naked," said the youth, diverting his eyes from the breasts of the women and young girls. His inexperience spoke the words we had all banished to our thoughts.

Where they had no clothes they scarred themselves with lines and pictorial devilments...a bird, a fish, rendered in a childish understanding, an amusement for simple fiends. The skin of the face they painted in reds and whites and blacks as they did their bodies. In what pain did they live in this human mask? ...In their ears they hung claws of animals...in their hair bits of flattened copper...about their waists animal skins decorated with colored stones and nails of copper. Each was more a fantasy of a being than a living thing.

"But where's the gold?" was the general whisper of the crew.

Captain Newport now stood and addressed the crew. "Treat them"—he pointed to the savages—"fairly and honorably. Measure all responses against the great enterprise which we have now begun. We come not as conquerors but as teachers; not as masters but as partners; not with Spanish greed but with English resolve. We seek no jewels or slaves; we seek only to till the earth as one with those who are our wards and our brothers, and to create such works in such multitudes that all will feast in wealth and ease."

As children with their blocks, so are men in their minds with ideas. To do in a wilderness, among a people whose language we cannot yet speak, what was never done in England, is to project an image of earthly heaven onto a tangle of weeds. And such weeds there were, liveries of herbs and oysters and fruits, baskets filled with pumpkins, piled in all their galaxies to an overflow. And everywhere tobacco, leaves dried flat, browned in age, cured to smell sweet in succulent sting. And sometimes tobacco twisted into chains hung from offering arms. Our crew's eyes wide, white as smoke. "Whatever shall be, we shall not have diseases," said a youth.

A shadow rose on the barge. An old mariner named Jonas Profit turned away from the boy, his face graved in darkness.

The youth asked, "Is not tobacco the miracle herb, it heals wounds as it cures all diseases?" He pulled at the mariner's ragged shirt. "Better to beg replies from stones," said another sailor, "old Jonas sleeps with his mysteries and answers only to his own. He keeps a ghostly company." Old Jonas turned his face toward the river, his ruined leathered cheeks, the wrinkled canyons on their wilds of a gentle poise. He said nothing as he watched the savages bear their baskets of strange fruit. He had a courtly bearing held in silks of a lesser cloth. He was a man of buried meanings. "Beware," he said, finally, "the cure may confection its own disease."

"Old Jonas was an alchemist, it is rumored, an Oxford scholar," said another mariner. "And now a prodigal to all books, but why has our Jonas taken his withered self to the sea all these years?"

Jonas's right hand swept the river's icy gore. He raised his arm, his fingers gloved in a silken wash. Before his tormentor the old mariner stood, his hand still raised, the pearls of liquid falling on the man's forehead. "All transformations come by water. There perfections do perfect the world to destinies. The sea is the womb of fate. The sea is its own herb, it is awash in alchemies. To some it does bequeath its soul in oceans, to some in cups, to you but in these few drops."

OUR BOAT CLOSER TO SHORE, NEWPORT JUMPED OVER THE SIDE into the shallows, telling us not to follow. Keeping the savages at a distance, he waded in the knee-deep flow to the front of the barge, grabbed the bowline. Lifting it over his shoulder with his one arm, he pulled the boat with great exertion, his eyes closed, while some of us rowed, until our boat held to the beach.

In that one small act I saw our only hope, man revealing himself to the world in selfless action. For me such actions live eternal. I would be as a seed, a planting, from which all that is to follow must spring. I must be as an alchemy. My existence a sacrament, my actions a transmutation, my death not quite a death. My life the spiritual body for the history of this new land. And although in years to come, through its veins other bloods will flood, and through its lungs other breaths will slide, and through its eyes, other lights and alien images will fill, the body alive, immortal and perpetual, as a reflection, however distant, of that other life, my life. I would be the unconscious motive of a new continent to transcend one's history, one's strangling memories. To forget of all pain, to be purified in the world, to be an archangel of the flesh, to be no one, to be everyone. And so, as the savages gathered around Newport, I on the bow of that beached craft, took my vow at the final moment before the coming of history—selflessness, balance, humanity.

Newport dropped the rope and walked from the river. The water fled before his passage. The barge swayed. The rope undulated in its watery nest. The day calmed. Now reflecting the sky, the river smoothed, as it flowed through the land like liquid light. The savages, in a half-moon, faced Newport. I jumped from the bow, walked to our admiral's side. Newport turned to me, angry that I had disobeyed.

As our eyes met, the line of savages parted, moving back against itself, forming a corridor through which a stately figure passed, acknowledging with a regal pride the courtesy of his subjects.

Before Newport the chief stood silently, wearing a crown of deerskin dyed red. The left side of his head was decorated with a large plate of copper. On the right, his long hair was pulled back. Around his neck were numerous strands of beads, and on a fine woven copper chain, the head of a fox. The chief pointed to the earth, made a circular motion at his waist with his finger. Then he raised his arm toward the sun and chanted the words of what might have been a prayer, and then he touched his heart.

"This man's hands are as cryptic as his lips. Does he speak to any of your understanding, Smith?" Newport looked over his shoulder at me, his anger slighted into a better question. Newport knew when in London last I had visited Thomas Hariot, who had been at the Roanoke Colony in 1586, on his return completing a dictionary of the Indian language. This I had borrowed and studied, Hariot teaching me some rudimentary phrases. I the only member of the colony to make such an effort. "The language is of a similar tongue to that of Roanoke," I said to Newport.

"Why does Newport always ask Smith? It's indecent. He should ask a noble, a man of social position. Smith's a prisoner. He still hasn't been tried for his mutiny in the islands," said an enraged gentleman.

"There's nothing proven there," said another.

I turned from recrimination to watch for meanings in the alien gestures. "This savage king welcomes us in peace and thanks his gods for our safe passage."

"My name is Captain Christopher Newport," was Newport's response, the first words of the first conversation of our new history.

"What meanings do we bring by our names alone?" I asked. "Our fame here bears a light concourse. It sovereigns only a arting of our lips."

Newport nodded at the bitter truth. "And how do I draw some understanding of the great distance we have come to bear our greetings here?"

"Tell the king we wish to be his friends and we will do him no harm."

Newport hardened to a passing anger. "And how do I potent dumb speech to that advice?"

"Give him gifts and acknowledge his authority. All authority suffers acquiescence gladly." The crew laughed. The savages stiffened. Newport swallowed his anger, almost choking on the calm.

Someone behind hissed, "The insolence of the man."

I reached into a small bag of trading trinkets and gave Newport a string of blue beads. "When you present these, hold them in the flat of both hands like something precious, something that befits a king. Do so with ceremony. Some value comes only by the effort of the pretense. Offer them in fair displays to the earth and to the air, that he may think they are magical."

Newport took the beads with great care, presenting them with the reverence and with the stately demeanor of an ambassador at court. The savages marveled at the gift. The chief raised the beads over his head into the sunlight. The gaudy strings seemed to shiver in his hand. *What a silly gift to bring to such a garden*, I thought.

In the distance, panic flashed on the water. Birds rose, crying in their sharp complaints toward the horizon and its last Edens. The chief placed the beads about his neck. They clashed with the claws and furs at his chest and the scars and painted colors of his skin. He touched the cold blue of the beads. Envious I was of this chief, who could, no doubt, think himself a human moment of the sky.

"Are they not as children playing at a nation?" said the youth. "They cannot believe that all this ceremony and its pomp has any more meaning than passing biscuits above a game of tea."

"A people believe and defend what gives them faith. Remember it is the English who love their tea."

Jonas Profit, who was close, spoke in answer to the young man, "All the world has spirits voiced for different ears. When you have seen the ruin that comes by too much belief, as I have, you will tread lightly with all your certainties. Arrogance births many surprises as it brings its doom. Pray you never know the full truth of what I speak."

The chief gave Newport a string of fresh water pearls, valueless as trade, these twisted but shining eggs. Nothing received for nothing given. A chain of the braided leaf was hung about Newport's neck, as dried tobacco leaves were placed in his hands and at his feet. Baskets of fruits and nuts and oysters were now brought as an offering before us. Newport handed the tobacco to Thomas Wotton, our surgeon, who examined the leaves, sniffed the pungents of those brown flats. He kissed the fragrance against his lips. "It is the medical herb, not the best for smoking, but a good leaf to brew many cures," he said, ecstatic that he might boast his great knowledge of this herb and its curing nectars.

"Nicotiana rustica," whispered Jonas Profit, "tobacco's second herb. This weed in all its variety is but a taunt. Everywhere it haunts me to its endless pleasure."

The old mariner turned his face away, as if the surgeon's words had come in slap, rude and hurtful. The mariner's cheeks blushed red beneath their leather before the words were ever said. "What memories color in their rough silence as they squeeze my blood," he murmured.

"Nicotiana rustica." Thomas Wotton held up the leaf toward the sun. The savages sang and danced approvingly. "All offerings here are in tobacco. It is the divine leaf, the one currency that brings all favors from the gods, even health. All the savages of the Indies, of Florida, the great Aztecs themselves used tobacco as a cure. So it is written in our histories and in our herbals. Even the murderous Spaniards acknowledge this one truth." The surgeon sang his anthem to the leaf, gazing through its fabric into the sun. "Nicotiana rustica is grown in Canada and in Roanoke it was known, in Florida and all this coast, the most common tobacco plant in English gardens, and France and Spain and Portugal. It is the medical leaf. Nicotiana tabacum, the other variety, is the plant of the West Indies and the New World south of Florida. Cortez found it in Mexico, and the French in Brazil. It is the tobacco of the sweeter smoke. Not gardened much in Europe, being delicate and needing warmth; although the Spanish have a strong commerce in it for those who have the wealth to afford its taste. It is said it is the leaf John Hawkins and Francis Drake found at Santa Marta in 1560 and first brought to England. Drake bringing an even greater supply five years later from Panama, and again…Well, it is a well-known story, hardly worth the moment to have it told."

The old mariner walked to the surgeon. "And what do you know of Drake? Are his histories so easy on the page, so forward to the eye? There is an alchemy in his tale that fouls all your nectars, venoms all your cures. Beware your pretty herb. Its practice sits not well its ink."

The savages danced their merry welcome. Tobacco played its smoke in the zephyrs about their heads. What medicine is this that the savages sport its humor so casually? Its cures no terrible physics. All was a dream of pleasure and its use. "I will not listen to an old mariner, no matter how many alchemists he pretends to be," said the surgeon.

"Tobacco is a tale of mariners, and who is so spiced with all its history than we?" said Jonas Profit, continuing, "From Columbus to Hawkins to Drake, this weed rises in dreadful alchemies. All my words come as vapors. They can hold their own truth. Oh that I had been a better scholar with a better quill, dipped in the kiss of a deeper ink. I would have stayed at the university, been the playwright and the poet, but my drama too thin to mold, my actors true. I taught to my depth and so I learned my talents not good enough." The old mariner, his finger held as dagger against Wotton's chest. "And you, dear surgeon, to what dead physics do you pretend? When I practiced to become a physician I read the ancient text. Desire is not the salve of hope, merely its tomb. I became a doctor of woundful cures, tobacco in all its garlands at my bench."

"Then you know the truth of its cures," interrupted the surgeon. The mariner in horror, silently shaking, said nothing, but walked away.

Chapter Two

GUNPOWDER, CORN, AND
THE BLADES OF DIPLOMACY.

HE CHIEF BECKONED US to follow him. Newport chose ten to stay behind and guard the boat. We asked the chief for five hostages to keep against our safe return. The chief agreed. Newport ordered that we give each of the five many small trinkets to assure all that they would be treated kindly.

The others of the crew gathered their weapons and our trading goods, the beads, some small knives and metal hatchets. And then they whispered among themselves, checking their observations against the compass of their limited experience.

"Those devils sport an easy spirit, wanton in its honesty, very welcoming, no educated guile ruins their appetites. There can be pleasures here, many pleasures" said a voice. It was Captain John

Ratcliffe, a man of no history, who invested more money than he had in this enterprise, 50 pounds, mysterious influences casting him to power as a member of the governmental council. He was a spawn of secrets and a troublemaker, perhaps a spy, and the only man I had ever met who spoke each word as if it were rolled in dirt. His face was oiled with sweat, not from work, but from some inner heat.

"I can see a commerce in more than pretty toys." Ratcliffe smiled, showing his rotting teeth. His armor decayed, rusted in neglect. His beard untended, tangled to a thatch.

I turned away, watching the breeze sculpt the surface of the water with its own image.

"Scorned by your own, shall you now adopt these savages? Brief men have short histories, as small voices ever frequent big mouths," Ratcliffe said to me, his words in weighted daggers. He hid his face with his arms as if he were about to be hit. When nothing came, he stepped back into the shadows and I walked away.

We followed the savages up along the hill into the woods. The land rolled under the carpet of the grass like a sleeping sea. The savages sang and clapped their hands and danced, turning from side to side, circling sometimes, always moving forward, always along the path, the chief and his council ahead, intoning nothing, leading the way.

As we walked farther, it was as if my mind moved away from my body, my own ghost raged, angry at the place to which I had come, so alien in its beauty, so indifferent to our presence, so willful in its power. I became a vulnerable thing, disconnected and apart. No earthly, no physical thing should have such perfection as this garden wilderness. Its beauty mocked thought and suffocated speech in its own breath, divided self from soul, enticing with sensuous whispers, thoughts from silent prisons. Only in action would I be safe here. Only in forgetting my captivity in Eastern Europe would I be free; but I was caged, caged on this land, eating of its heresies, dreaming of its treasons.

Around us, trails were well marked. A stream meandered through the trees. Its water, like liquid glass, flowed over its rocky bed, sometimes bubbling in momentary peace, then dividing between polished stones, before being swept forward once again, a single current, chasing, catching, falling coolly over its own chaotic flow. In the canopy of the trees the songs of our guides echoed in the heavy air, its scented breath rising on its own winged pageants, our senses all enthralled. And through the trees that formed a living roof, slanting sunlight fell, the scattered rays playfully chasing butterflies in a harmless hunt.

As we left the forest there was an expanse of meadow and carefully tended farmlands. Savages planted crops on small hand-sculptured mounds, not in furrows, as did we. Several types of plants grew together on a single mound, corn and beans and pumpkin. Around the fringes sometimes grapes, or giant sunflowers, their size so regal we turned away, astounded at their natural splendor.

Near our path, yellow flowers burst in natural bouquets as choirs of bells in their trumpet shapes hung in perfumed sounds above a great fall of leaves. These leaves on bowing necks the downward arch of graceful stems. The crop tended differently than the rest. One young plant cultured on a single mound. The earth now a pedestal to host these blooms. "Such a beautiful leaf. What garden this?" asked a youth.

"Nicotiana rustica. It is tobacco," said the old mariner, Jonas Profit.

"Are we not another Columbus, he having been given tobacco his first day in the New World? He discovering the leaf before he discovered gold."

Before us on a rise was a small village of a dozen huts variously sized, some beehive shaped, some semicircular, all made from saplings bent to form a frame, tied with vine, then covered with reed mats of bark or hide. Surrounding the village was a circular stockade, which wound in upon itself like the shell of a snail. The only entrance was a small passage between the circular fences at the head.

Mats were placed upon the ground. The chief gestured for us all to sit. His council at his back, he sat facing Newport. Baskets of corn and pumpkin and nuts were arranged near the stockade wall. Fires were lit. Still savages sang and danced. There was an elder who must have been a devil priest, for tied around his neck and hanging to his thigh was a garment like a woman's dress, made of animal skins with the fur reversed. It entirely covered one arm and exposed the other, with which he made signs upon the ground, sprinkling corn upon them. Then he wailed and cavorted with the rest, his eyes wild, seeing nothing but his own hysteria, as great rancid clumps of fur fell from under the hem of his dress.

The savages brought a newly slain deer to the fire and began to prepare it as our meal. The chief offered us corn and bread, which seemed to be a corn paste that had been boiled in water. We were entertained and fed, and at the closing of the meal all the food we did not eat was carefully put in baskets and given to us. The chief explained in sign that once food is offered it can never be taken back. We accepted our gifts and offered some trinkets in return, which were refused.

Finally, a tobacco pipe made of clay was brought, the bowl of which was bound with fine copper wire. The tobacco, which the savages wove into ropes, was cut before us and placed in the bowl, then lit with the delicate touch of a single translucent flame. The chief took the pipe, placing the tip in his mouth. Then he inhaled, as if in reverence. He held his breath. Slowly exhaling, he watched the smoke rise into the air, carefully following the dissolving circles of its ascent, seemingly trying to decipher in flight the swirling hieroglyphs of fate.

The chief passed the pipe to Newport, who almost coughed as he drank the smoke. Exhaling, a fine plume left his mouth. Forced upwards, it mixed with the clear air and spiraling smoke of the chief's.

"It tastes bitter," Newport said, handing the pipe to me at the chief's gesture. I took the pipe in two hands, feeling its weight, holding it in delicate balance so its long stem would not crack. I placed the tip in my mouth, inhaling in long, slow, concentrated thought, feeling the smoke warm my chest as it melted into the fiber of my being. I exhaled leisurely, the pleasure in my throat, feeling the coldness and emptiness in me returning. The smoke rose, twisting in itself, riding the turmoil of my breath. I licked my lips, as if to find its last taste.

"Smith, to his low estate, the smoke breaks his lips without a grace. Where did he catch the fashion, from a chimney sweep?" And so a gentleman boasted his perfection with the pipe. Tobacco such a rage in London, it was studied as an art. Gallants and young country blood paid private tutors to learn to hold the savor of the leaf within their lungs, or shape its plumes upon their breath. Frivolities fashioned to vice. Placards in St. Paul's advertised the specialists who knew the mysteries of the leaf. Our gentlemen all well-schooled in their empty affects, each to the other aroused in his grotesque display, but this was not a London street.

"This Smith is too small to have much breath," laughed another gentleman.

"And shall we all pledge to teach this, our savage, the uses of the pipe, as if he ever owned a leaf?" replied Ratcliffe.

I handed the pipe to Ratcliffe, who examined it, caressing its bowl. He seemed to take a certain sensual pleasure at the dead clay in his hands. Before the pipe stem was in his mouth he was drawing a deep breath. Empty wind and the anticipation of taste made him groan. When the pipe was in his mouth he drew only half its smoke, holding it in his lungs, then exhaled in short puffs, reluctant to let the sensation go. Hesitant, the smoke tongued from his mouth in pear-shaped balls, the signal bells of an internal fire, revealing in its hints not only the desire to know a desire, but also to hold it fast. Some gentlemen, even in anticipation, fingered in their pockets the silver of their own tobacco cases.

The pipe was handed to every one among us in turn. Each smoked in the fashion of his spirit and passed it on to the next, until Jonas Profit, who raised the pipe to his eye in salute but would not take a smoke. The pipe then returned to Newport, who smoked it one last time at the chief's urgent nod. The circle completed, the pipe was handed back. The chief laid it across his knees, then softly sang some incantation. He looked at Newport, gestured, speaking. He blew his breath toward heaven, opening his arms, raising them. I moved closer to Newport. I, too, began to make signs, filling the air with a pantomime of images. I had done it before in Hungary and Eastern Europe. However flawed the movement, there emerged from that cacophony of gesture a shared alphabet of meaning and a shared dictionary of thought.

The smoke rises on our spirit. The chief pointed to his chest. *Can you not feel the moist fire, which is your life's breath, and see the smoke cloud, which is your soul?*

The chief said that the smoke of the tobacco is like prayer; not of words, which can lie, but of the spirit, which is only truth.

Newport through me replied that there should only be truth spoken between them, for lies corrupt those who speak them sooner than those who listen. The chief nodded in agreement.

"We have come great distances…beyond the sea, from a great land. We wish to be your friends, " Newport continued, pantomiming the vastness of the distance we had come, as I translated our intent.

The savages understood the idea of distance. They even seemed to have a remarkable intuition about a land beyond sight, over the horizon toward the east. Friendship is an easy thought to gesture, but more difficult to fulfill. In all, the savages told us their names and that of their tribe, the Paspaheghs, and that our host was a *werowance*, as they called their leader. He was only a vassal to a great emperor called Powhatan. This Powhatan lived in a village farther up the river, and would soon join us, as runners had been sent to all the tribes in his vast kingdom to announce our arrival. The name of our host, this king under Powhatan, was Wowinchopunk.

Newport told the savages that he was a subject of a great king, chosen by God himself as ruler of his nation. The savages seemed little impressed with our god, but asked many questions about our guns and our hatchets; they having little metal that I could see, and what little they had was used only for decoration.

Such curiosities we are, even in our accustomed grace. Wowinchopunk asking of my red hair, *What flesh is this that bleeds in fire?*

"A mother's gift," I answered. "She, too, had such hair." Slight thought I gave to the gesture on the words, playing lightly with the intrigue.

Kings come by families, and so by wombs our magic. Was your mother a werowance? The chief looking into my eyes in that gaze that weighs the soul.

"She was but a mother with a mother's mysteries. Nothing more was she given than she could give," I answered.

Wowinchopunk thought, then touched my beard. *Cold, more hidden, the deeper may burn the flame.* He smiled as he spoke, then looked toward the young tobacco plants.

Unique I am among these savages. We come by accidents to be our fate. My hair the course to speed my passage, I thought. Newport touched my arm. "The chief asked me of my family," I whispered, as I slighted the truth, hoping to dull its retribution.

Newport then asked if they had ever seen a yellow metal that we call gold. Wowinchopunk said that he had knowledge of a yellow metal, but he did not know its name. As none was now in the village, he would have some brought to us. It would take some time as it was up river and far away. There was murmuring among the crew. Newport said that we had brought many valuable trinkets and would gladly wait and trade for the metal and for food. Wowinchopunk nodded and asked if we would shoot one of our guns for him. Newport hesitated, looking at me, questioning. "A friendly demonstration of superior power is a friendly way to keep friends," I said.

Newport agreed. I stood, walked to our boxes and bags of trade goods and pulled from one box a flat metal plate, a foot square and about a quarter-inch thick. I hung the metal plate on a tree and motioned to a savage with a bow and a quiver of arrows to stand with me about a hundred feet from the tree. The whole tribe was now standing, watching. I told the savage to let fly his arrow at the plate.

After fitting an arrow onto a leather bowstring, the savage, in a single motion, raised the bow toward his face while slowly drawing the string back. The muscles of his chest tightened. The bow grew taut, as if drawing a vacant breath; the arrow at his cheek; the bow now wide; his muscles in hardened line, sustained and beating in chords of blood. The arrow flew. Hitting the plate, the arrow shattered into a crumble. Splinters flew from its broken shaft. The arrowhead smashed, exploding into dust. The savage screamed at the sight. Humiliated, he fell upon the ground, beating his fists into the grass, tearing at random clumps with his teeth.

The members of our crew leaned forward, the burning tapers mounted on the hammers of their firelock rifles smoked, strings lit at both ends as a precaution. These tapers snapped forward when the trigger was pulled, igniting a small charge of black powder which fired the gun. The smoke of the tapers circled upward, their ends undulating wildly, convulsively, like thrashing tails; the two red eyes of the tapers' slow fire burned, glowing as a resting dragon.

I raised my gun to my shoulder, my cheek at rest upon its wooden pillow. By how many fascinations am I entranced? The red eye of the taper facing me, I watched the glow, as if held by the enchantments of a snake. The savage on the ground I ignored in all his plight. I aimed, breathless against my expectations. The hammer fell backwards toward my cheek. The concussion broke. Now the obscuring smoke, the target lost. The bullet tore through the center of the plate, cleaving it in two. Savages ran like dried leaves before the thunder's gust. Wowinchopunk stood his ground calmly, not showing any emotion. Picking up the two pieces of plate, I gave them to Wowinchopunk. He returned to his mat and asked Newport to see the gunpowder, a small hill of which was poured into his hands. He flattened it, moving it between his fingers, examining carefully the tiny black pellets. *It is a strange seed that brings a strange smoke. If I sow this in the earth what plant will grow?* was signed in his halting gestures.

"These are made, not grown, and only we have the secret," I replied in the language of the pantomime.

Wowinchopunk thought about what he had seen, saying nothing, nodding to himself at some passing inner world. Finally he asked to examine one of our guns. He held the instrument in his hands, checking its weight, sniffing the smoke of the burning taper, holding the weapon to his shoulder, his face now on the barrel. *Not as good as a bow when wet.* The chief smiled. The physiognomies of space smiled as he gestured, gauging the limits of our power.

"I hope he isn't contemplating a little murder in the rain," Newport said.

"We have pistols," I said to Wowinchopunk, pulling a gun from my belt, "which do not use fire, but have a flint to cause a spark." I showed the chief, letting him hold it in his hand, letting him caress his reflection in its polished barrel, allowing him to feel the weight of its power.

I wish to have a trade for this gun, replied Wowinchopunk in rapid mime.

"We have not enough for ourselves, so we cannot trade a gun. But we have many other valuable things." Wowinchopunk's face hardened into aloofness.

I will trade you a bag of tobacco seed for a bag of gunpowder, said Wowinchopunk, his hands a hurricane, eager in their gestures.

Newport was ready to agree, just to be friendly. He would have begun the enterprise on any terms just to begin it. Let the beast loose. Let history, like a flooding river, find its own course. Not I. I knew we were now in the realm of consequences. All our futures would be children of what we did today. In history, no event is an orphan.

"No." I shook my head. "We need ten baskets of corn and the tobacco seed. Only we have this magic powder and only from us can you have it." I decided that without guns, the only thing they could do with the powder was plant it or blow themselves up.

"A little heavy-handed, don't you think, Smith?"

"If we don't show them we're willing to be by strength their friends, they'll always be at our throats. We don't have a lot to trade. We must set the rate of exchange and keep to it."

Wowinchopunk signed in agreement. *I will plant black powder with the tobacco,* he said, his words now all inflated in the dance of flesh. *And in the fall, I shall see what blooms.*

Chapter Three

POWHATAN ARRIVES WITH INVITATIONS.

OR MANY HOURS we stayed and discoursed of the land and of the people and of the beasts that howled in the fields. Many things did Wowinchopunk tell us. Most seemed to us as bragging, empty gestures in the wind. No savage tribe could, with the crudeness of their tools and the simplicity of their understanding, so sculpt a wilderness that it was remade into a garden cornucopia. No savage wisdom could so instruct the earth with gentle ministerings that for one day's work a year, all told, one savage, on one acre of land, could grow enough food for a year.

"Not with those crops all intermixed like that," said our surgeon. "Those plants must murder each other in the root before those savages ever see a bud."

And yet, Wowinchopunk's village, no more than one hundred strong, had in sum no more than one hundred planted acres that I could see.

I sat and listened. Behind me some men laughed, others held their lips sealed, feeling that here war was the echo of offense. Sometimes Wowinchopunk stiffened at the laughter, but mostly he continued answering our questions without guile. His fingers still groped for meaning in the air. We listened with our eyes and tried to understand. *Men hunt and fish, make war and clear the fields. Everything else is a woman's work*, he said, adding that clearing a field was done simply by cutting away the bark around a tree and letting it die. *It will fall when it will to become our firewood, or hollowed to be our canoes.* Women built the small mounds on which they planted, putting the seeds in the holes that they made with a stick.

"If the savages can do half of what they say, no Englishman should think of work. Even to discourse on it is too much an effort," said our Captain Ratcliffe. His thin tongue licked the wind as if to taste the fragrance of its will.

The land seemed to rest. Nothing stirred in the heresy of its bloom.

Only the tops of the trees swayed, as if the warming of the sun had sent a gentle shudder down the earth's spine.

"Sweet posturings are the only dance to bend this back," said John Russell, his wide belt straining to fence the acres of his flesh.

Now there came general excitement at the fringes of the group of savages, a wave of chatter, moving in a growing swell. Heads bobbed, turning in the direction of the noise. A mass of savages stood aside, clearing an aisle of grass. All rose, except Wowinchopunk, who shouted a salute befitting an evil spirit in its heat. Newport kept his seat, as did we all. A tall figure walked toward Wowinchopunk. Around him walked sixty warriors as tall as himself, armed with bows and arrows held in quivers, which were tied on their backs at their waists by the tails of some animals. Many carried long cudgels spiked with sharp stones. This was a personal guard to impress the unwelcome guests of an emperor. And this was Powhatan, who sat, adjusting his figure on his mat to the proper dignity, so even the air would be nervous, reverberating with his pride.

What ancient this, who comes now as a worthy ally or as our ruin? I wondered. He was powerfully built and painted red, bejeweled with shards of copper, the feathers and wings of birds. From his ears hung the heads of rodents. He had the sour look of one awakened from a pleasant sleep by a nasty dream. His cheeks were sunken, as if life had been sucked out of them from the inside, collapsing his skin into the hollows of his mouth. He had a small beard, which hid not his chin. He seemed to be tired of everything but his dignity. Perhaps he had seen too much killing. He wavered slightly as he sat, as he might in his policies—inconsistent friends could be dangerous enemies.

Newport introduced himself and his crew. Powhatan responded with a gentle nod, not enough to crack the patina of his station, but just sufficient to acknowledge another living thing. To me he gave a somewhat different nod. *Your priest?* he asked Newport, looking at my hair.

"No, no," Newport so sweetly formed as he lathered his explanations.

What disaster is our comfort? What grovel is our pride? Newport, having dealt with the English aristocracy, felt quite comfortable with this savage and his charade of birthrights and privileges. He ordered a deluge of gifts to be spread before Powhatan. His desire to impress, if not ingratiate himself, unbalanced his sense of proportion. He might have given away the entire expedition had I not touched his shoulder, whispering, "Enough." Newport pulled away from my hand. Powhatan smiled at all the largess. Wowinchopunk stiffened, feeling slighted and cheated, no doubt, at the thought of his simple gift of a necklace compared with all this bounty.

Newport explained that we came as friends and that we required a little waste land further down the river on which to build a settlement. These few acres were useless to Powhatan, but in consequence of this gift we would be his friends, trade with his people, protect them from their enemies. And so we trivialed the crime to squat the land. The old chief tended his plans with diplomacies as he withheld his answer.

"Of all the enemies who treachery upon this earth," Newport said, "the worst are the Spanish, who sail the seas in great ships, stealing land and enslaving those who welcomed them as friends. No evil too much, even the kidnapping of children, carrying them to foreign lands, forever gone, forever lost." Powhatan looked at Wowinchopunk as I thought to myself what a strange silence it was that intervened. The savages seemed to know each other's words. I wondered at the tale they knew that broke its legends into secret histories.

Finally, Powhatan smiled, as he had found a balance on which to trade that small of land we stole for a greater empire. He said that he had many enemies, and that the tribes along his borders raided constantly, and if we would make war on them, he would be our friend and give us much land.

So subtly the subject changed. I wondered to myself what kind of alliance Newport was making and how many wars we would be obliged to fight to keep this aging savage smiling.

"What you sign in the air may shortly be written in our blood. Be careful of these alliances," I said. Newport nodded in agreement as I continued, "These tribes must compete with one another for our friendship. Be vague."

"We will be friends with all who treat us fairly and cause us no harm." Newport was pleased with his own words. "As Powhatan is now our friend, we are sure his enemies will be our enemies." Newport turned toward me and winked, wanting my approval. *He is ingratiating us into slaughter*, I thought. I looked at the grass and the dark earth beneath. Water spurted to its surface in slender streams, like the tearing fingers of an imprisoned spirit desperate to be free.

Behind Powhatan the devil priest now danced, orbiting a small piece of ground, a rattle shaking in his hand, chanting, appeasing the earth, purifying it with the contortions of his human cries. Powhatan then rose and said to Newport that we must visit him at his village the next day. Newport eagerly agreed as he stood to salute the departing emperor. The two embraced, then Newport asked if he might have guides to the village. Powhatan instructed five savages to join us and show us the way along the river. One of those chosen was Wowinchopunk's brother-in-law, a fellow with shrewd eyes and a wakeful intelligence called Naurins.

We were all standing now, except John Russell, our stoutest companion, who struggled on his mat with the restraints of his own flesh. *Our master John is of goodly disposition*, I mused. *He battles against an easy sloth. He may yet prove a fair use.*

Finally three of our crew pulled him to his feet. He settled onto his legs, his body undulating like a spring. Powhatan pretended not to notice.

Ratcliffe was at my back. I could hear the congested gravel of his breath. He whispered to one of his companions, who wheezed, "Have you noticed all the women have firm breasts? Even on the old they do not hang." Ratcliffe choked momentarily on the anticipation of another breath. "Every gentleman deserves his pleasure, ever we should tongue the hollows and enjoy our appetites. Let fools dance a fete of longings. I shall not lick an empty spice. We are alone and we are the law. That thought the tickle trills upon the spine. As you, I hunger in my animal, frenzied to savor of its beast." Ratcliffe looked toward me whispering again, "We are no longer the nothings nothing of some drooling aristocrat. Power here is power in the mind made flesh." As he smirked, his lips seemed to fathom in their dirt. "And Smith there, for all his beard, give me the whip. I swear small dogs take better to the lash. For all his strut, he looks more hound than savage. His head hardly to my chin. Ever does the splinter have pretensions to the tree." His voice then lost to drown among the noise.

In what shadows are my mirrors? By what fragments my recognitions? I did muse. To the savages red hair, my height a slight upon its crown; a difference, yes, but a difference more a portent than it is strange. Here the savages see a token that may mean a priest. My size and tint, I have some claim upon their notice. It is a joke stricken from a scowl, but yet it may have its use. And Ratcliffe and his company think of me by taunt and hollow, their threats always in an under voice. My monster here is I still have beliefs beyond my flesh, and so I am paused by a blessing in a curse.

Powhatan began his exit. He left with the long cheers of the savages following his figure and those of his legions as they disappeared behind the planted fields, walking toward the low, rolling breasts of the hills and their mysteries.

We gathered ourselves together, giving Wowinchopunk his bag of black powder, taking our tobacco seeds and our ten bushels of corn, which were carried to our boat by these pleasant people as a gesture of friendship. On our leaving, Wowinchopunk gave us one of their woven ropes of dried tobacco, telling us to smoke it so the spirit of our souls might mingle with the breath of this new land. We thanked him with all the sincerity we could gesture and departed.

Chapter Four

DRAKE, IN MYSTERIES, AND OLD FRIENDS RECALLED.

LL THAT DAY along the banks of the river, the savages stood, baskets of fruit and corn and nuts and oysters at their feet, gesturing to trade, an enticing and colorful parade of a land and its people in the frenzy of a harvest. We stopped occasionally, Naurins acting as interpreter. He had a natural intelligence and a gift for understanding our signs. Through him the landscape of our thoughts was made manifest by the boat's ever-increasing cargo of food-filled baskets.

The breeze was now at our backs. We unfurled our sail, letting its ballooning skirt carry us up the river. The bow of the boat dug into the resisting weight of the river. Waves flew backwards over the bulkhead, disintegrating into tongues of water, hissing as they fell back again, dissolving into the receding flow. Four of our guides were at the bow, their long hair flapping, buoyant on the rushing air. Naurins sat with me, teaching with repetitions and signs a few simple words of his language, alien sounds slowly evolving into the image of common things: hair, sky, river, trees. Then numbers and shades of colors, progressing as we were from the hardness of things to the transparency of thought.

Ratcliffe and his companion sat conspiring, their heads close together, like pigs at a trough, breathing their own foul breaths. The others of the crew sat closer to me discussing the day, its savages, their costumes. So easily we forget how exotic man is, even to his own eyes. "These are a good people," said the stout John Russell, his servant adjusting his ruffles as he spoke. "It is an honor for us to defend them against the Spanish. Some day we will be as one nation in union with these that now seem so humble." He raised his fat hand as to deflect an argument that never came. All around murmured the crew, agreeing in their agreements as I watched silently while the sun sat detached on the horizon's edge, drowning its own light as the day slipped into darkness.

WE ANCHORED. THE MOON HAD NOT RISEN. EARTH AND SKY MERGED into the hollows of an overhanging black. Stars burned in the heaven like light through a thinly thatched roof. The boat swayed as invisible surges of the river rolled past us in the liquid dark. The night screamed with the predatory sounds of life hunting life, the earth echoing, as bushes were crushed, twigs cracked, heavy bodies struggled in desperate contortion beyond sight. Their only images were motions in the fleeting silhouettes. No pain. No blood. No bodily form. Just the sketches of movements on the canvas of the land.

On the boat, someone coughed, someone called a woman's name, someone stifled a whimper. I could almost feel the tears on the blanket. I sat at the rudder, apart from the crew in the darkened pillow of my exile, thinking. All sensations were an interruption of my empty thoughts. Images pressed their gossamers to my eyes. I wanted relief. I was drawn to night, my brain crystallized into blackness.

Nineteen days after we sailed from England I was thrown into irons in the Canary Islands because I dared to express my opinion concerning which islands were safest to take on food and water, and which coves offered the best anchorages and the best havens. Landing where these gentlemen had proposed, we would have been at war with the natives, would have found nothing and would have been Spanish prisoners in an hour. They had never been to these islands. I had. So I spoke against their plans, and they accused me of mutiny and treason and wanting to be Virginia's king. Such absurdities slander all thought, cleave words impoverished from their meanings, and these gentlemen do dung their presumptions as they self-appoint their own crowns, these our bugs of consequence. Wingfield kinned most to offense, and called for vengeance, me to be in chains. Now factions warred in calumnies, some to my defense. The compromise, I held in irons a few days then to be released. In my cabin I sat my dark, the only rounds of light a single candle, the ocean beyond glowing eternity in its sphere. I met him then. The old mariner brought me food. I looked at him, his cold gray eyes, his long hair shocking in its purity of white. "For a small of truth they have cast you heretic," he said to me, smiling.

"And what do you know of heresy?" I replied.

"Enough to draw its likeness on a cloud. I followed Drake through all the years of his adventures, through all the theologies of his wars — lived the tale, the memories are upon my flesh."

"You were of Drake and you say Drake a heretic?" My question asked, I bathed the waited answer in my doubt. The old mariner stood his silence as I added, "I know of Drake. I met him when I was a boy," I bragged to puff a bit of air into his face. "He gave me gifts when I with Lord Willoughby's son played upon the deck of Drake's fast ship, I at the wheel, the lord as my crew. We rode the dock, Drake's compass in my hand, his glass to my eye. The crew laughed until the lord and I lifted three great cannonballs and I screamed 'I have the shot. There is the flame. Who dares hide my powder now?'"

"You were that boy?"

"I was, and the Drake I knew was no heretic."

"You and I have also met." The old mariner smiled through a strange seriousness. "Remember of those days and your adventures through the Plymouth streets. A hand to hold both yours and the young Willoughby's. Merchant stores, mysterious bales and barrels, weapons and tools, a candy frolic before a war. I was that hand you held. I placed the bowl and brought the sweets. Willoughby and I some friends from long ago. See my face. Think on those days."

I mustered memories of a swaying ship and a child anxious to be the threat to be the man. "Those days speak to me as through a veil," I said. "There was a Moor. One other who told me of a child never born. He was a wizard, some wanderer who joked and called me 'twice-born son.'"

"You know half the tale, the child's half. To join the parts is not always to know the whole," said the mariner. "The frenzy gapes, and I between the moment and its memory. Come my would-be son. Let me father a greater world, speaking geographies into your youthful liquid ear. Drake so wanted you as child, an orphaned father to have an orphaned son." There was a noise at the door. The mariner lowered his voice. "There are secrets in secrets in Drake's life that bear upon this enterprise. But I am not the yet to tell it now. Soon the tale, and you who once I led by a child's hand, I will lead by a long-dead voice. The puppet is not the plot, though he may play a scene. Drake had greater hopes of you than strings and now more than coins will be your inheritance."

"When I was a child I would have been Drake, his name a coax upon my life, and you knew the man alive in all his adventures."

"Gold is twice gold to the alchemist," Jonas Profit now spoke. "It is a journey of the soul through the rings of metal, from lead to tin, to copper, to silver and to gold. Alchemy is the chemistry of resurrection. The baser metals are an emblem of our world. They are us in our fallen state. All spirits need a guide. Some by cauldron, some by men. I, too, chose Drake."

I looked at the old mariner. What an accumulation is a man, what an apothecary his dreams. "Were you Drake's alchemist?"

The old mariner now rose, cloistered in the wings of his own shadow. "How many histories have I stood upon, this clay now its mortuaries," he whispered in gentle sorrows. He turned his face from the flame, darkness his mask, as he walked to the door he spoke again. "But we shall speak on all this later and raise ghosts in all their hurricanes."

"Shall we not speak a little of Drake?" I asked.

"It is a tale eaten of the sea...later," Jonas Profit answered as he disappeared.

I transfixed in thunder, lightning flashed in chills upon my spine. To know in certainties all the legends. To know the motive is to have the life. I, in all my hopes, had the key in flesh to open more prisons than were ever built in stone. And so I sat upon my barge. At my feet, my gentlemen.

A flight of geese drew with its beating wings a blackened curtain across the stars. Now and again I heard their lonely calls, constricted and far away. With their passing, the clouds took up the shroud. The land was vacant black and of slightly different texture than the sky. Black on black. My breath began to steam in the descending cold, which rolled in a thickening tar across the boat. I took up the rope of tobacco, tore a piece, crushing it in my hands.

"Might I also have a tear of the pudding, so to take the whiff?" said a gentleman. In his hand a silver tobacco case, inside a set of expensive clay pipes, a flint, a steel to make a light, a pick to clean the pipe, a knife to cut the leaf. All this ceremony for a gentleman's fashion now all the expensive rage in London. I had but a vulgar wooden box, cheap clay. Tobacco I gave to the fellow. With a silver tong, he took an ember from our fire, lit his pipe, then mine. We smiled, returning to our place. We toasted each other in the smoke of our democratic vice. I drew the bitter smoke, which defined my lungs with warmth and with the pain of a delicate taste. I watched myself exhale a fume of spiraling white. My soul and the darkness intermixed in a desperate journey through the night.

I WONDERED IF THOSE ON THE COUNCIL — CHRISTOPHER NEWPORT, Edward Maria Wingfield, Captain John Ratcliffe, Captain Bartholomew Gosnold, Captain John Martin and Captain George Kendall — would ever let me take my seat. Gosnold and Martin might, but they were sickly. Newport, perhaps. He respected my judgment, if not the dramas of my ways. But no audacity spurred his hungers and he was weak. The question was Kendall. The others — not unless they were forced. They would probably sooner see me hung. Too much danger, not to the colony, but to their fragile selves. Haunted by the dreams of men they could never be, they saw me as competition. Jealousy and too much reality is a dangerous truth for those who would be giants if they were not dwarfs.

I was appointed, as were the others, by the Virginia Company in London. They did not announce the council members before we sailed, but decided, rather, to write our names on a piece of paper which was sealed in a box only to be opened when we anchored in the Chesapeake; thus avoiding political trouble and intrigues at home, I suspected. They knew Wingfield and Ratcliffe and the like would never accept me as an equal. Especially since Percy, the brother of the Earl of Northumberland, and a real nobleman, had been passed over. A delicate political situation in a wilderness is less trouble than one at court, where one's head is closer to the block. Or mayhap they thought by the time the box was opened I would have either proven myself, or gotten myself hung. Clearly, there was a group in the company in London who thought I was worth the effort. I blew a ring of smoke, an empty circle with a spiraling wheel of breath.

A breeze like the earth's sigh blew the design apart. I thought of Wowinchopunk. How pretty to sculpt with smoke an image of one's own soul. Such is the sport of prodigals for a spring night in the New World. I knew Ratcliffe would approve. How well we deceive when we deceive ourselves, and to those that do, death is an easier truth than truth. Ratcliffe and the rest would never let this be, until one or all of us was either in exile or dead. How slippery is the political balance when greased by the work of fools!

Chapter Five

I MEET HER IN THE MORNING. A PRINCESS.
AN EMPEROR. A RECONCILIATION BY DEATH.

IT WAS MIDDAY when we reached Powhatan's village, which was seated on a hill overlooking a small inlet of the river. We rowed ashore, climbed the hill. Looking back, the face of the river was still, as though its currents only ran deep near its roots, leaving the surface a camouflage of reflections of earth and sky and passing human things.

The village was well proportioned, surrounded by a circular stockade spiraling inward for half a turn to form a gate. Against the inner wall many houses. The longest of the buildings, Powhatan's castle, stood in a central green, at each of whose corners was posted a well-armed sentry, hardened and alert, as if his being had been compressed to stone by the weight of his responsibilities.

We were met by Powhatan, who guided us to a pleasant meadow before his capitol. There, mats were laid on the earth. We sat, Powhatan facing us. Naurins sat between Newport and the savages, ready to sculpt from the vagueness of gesture the precision of thought. The kindly chief Wowinchopunk sat behind Powhattan and to his right. Directly behind Powhatan was a fat woman, Oppossuno, who we learned later was queen of the Appomattocs, part of Powhatan's empire. She was naked to the waist, her breasts almost lost in the rolls of flesh that fell from her chest. She wore many copper necklaces and flat plates of beaten copper in her hair. In a semicircle behind her were many stately women of her court who were silent, yet attentive, ready to be solicitous to her whims.

Behind Powhatan and to his left was another chief, taller than the other men. His eyes were nervous, so dark they seemed to eat the light. He sat rigidly, as if his blood were ice. A man of many secrets, I thought. As he moved, he moved in legends,

To every pig the world is a wallow. Ratcliffe whispered and called him a fool. No fool ever conspired with the elements of his birth to create such a regal presence. This was power and cunning and the imagination to wield it. Compared with him, Powhatan was a toy. His name was Opechancanough, half brother and second in command to Powhatan. He watched Newport, studying him, as if weighing his soul with a glance. Then he looked at me. I stared into his eyes. It was as if looking into the mechanisms of the dark. He nodded to me. I nodded back.

Next to Powhatan sat a holy man, one of their devil priests, the animal skin shaped like a skirt falling from his neck. The devil priest stood and began to dance, stamping on the ground as if he were trying to awaken the earth, a prayer played in pantomime, as if the spirits were so near at hand. A column of insects played through the trees on a geyser of light, which seemed to rise from the land, rather than fall from the sky. A pipe of tobacco was passed. Opechancanough inhaled deeply, letting the smoke drift from his mouth, at first a smudge of white, then an ever-growing mist, finally a cloud and a whirlwind of ash. He smiled at his own show, satisfied with his soul, which he gauged to be intact.

The devil priest rolled on the ground as if in a fit, his arms and legs in a grotesque tangle, his face contorted. He rose, biting at the air, screaming a song of pain. He chanted homage to some devil god. "Okee…Okee…," he repeated, whirling in place, his hair flying as he raged, his eyes blank. He stopped and pounded his feet upon the sod as if he would have the earth awaken, echoing, "Okee…Okee," falling upon the ground, his hand stretched outwards, prostrating himself before the empty air, before some devil idol, I supposed, in his imagination.

"Okee?" Newport repeated, questioning Powhatan.

Powhatan nodded, explaining that Okee was their god of evil, he who must be appeased with rituals and sacrifices. He was in constant hunger to be indulged, a player of mischief, a bringer of pain to all, even to those who were good. What edged this Okee to make such an uncertain world even the savages did not know, and so they offered up their tobacco as a gift. There was another god who brought happiness and bounty to everyone, even those who were evil. This god was never worshipped. *How sweet the genius of his nature*, I thought. As with men, he was ignored.

Seizing his moment, Newport said with an air of triumph, "Our God is only love."

Opechancanough responded, his words dividing the heavens on their tongue. *As the earth has many seasons, so it is unwise to be only one thing.*

"A clever riddler, this devil," whispered Newport in my ear.

"These are not riddles. These are words, words like pillars on which nations are built, that bring a people to its causes," I replied, Ratcliffe and the crew hearing.

"Savages have their many in its seasons, and yet," so spoke a cheerful Ratcliffe, attempting to lead the crew by the leash around his own neck, "a single spice may rule a stew. Many are the forms of the natural world, yet in man's mind all things are only thoughts. All things that are have a use; all things are but a convenience. The mind reduces the forest to a single log for kindling, the arbor to a single grape for plucking and we ourselves to puppet a gesture as the mind itself prompts. You see, friend Smith," Ratcliffe paused, his face burning red, "we become our appetites." Several of the men laughed, shouting, "Hail to appetites!"

The savages stiffened, looking at one another. Opechancanough's eyes narrowed. I was glad he could not understand Ratcliffe's words. Newport said to Opechancanough in sign, *My men salute your wisdom.* Opechancanough relaxed into the shadows around him as I said to Ratcliffe, "I am sure your skin is well decorated with the lacerations of your pleasures."

Ratcliffe smiled as Newport discussed with Powhatan the size of the chief's empire, which encompassed most of the Chesapeake Bay, extending to the falls in the river. It seemed a kingdom large enough to be a country. All the tribes there owed allegiance to Powhatan, laying tribute before him. Beyond the falls in the river lived Powhatan's greatest enemies, the Monacans, who raided his people each year at the time of the harvest, stealing women and children.

Newport said that one day he would deliver the chief of the

Monacans to Powhatan. He strangled the air as a gesture of friendship and alliance. Powhatan said that if we attacked the Monacans now, he would muster five hundred warriors for us to lead. Newport said the time was not yet right, but as a symbol of our good intentions, when he returned from across the sea, he would bring Powhatan seven muskets as a gift.

Powhatan was pleased. He explained to us the way savages made war, which was to hide behind trees and rocks, and fire their arrows. When an enemy was brought down with wounds, they would run out and bash in his head with their wooden swords and stone-tipped cudgels. To the savages, war was the action of the tribe, rarely were there individual moments of heroism, and those who performed them became the chiefs. How strange, here among savages in a wilderness, courage brought with it its own equal portions of power and privilege.

To the savages the position of chief was not hereditary. Their leaders came by election. Their rule was not absolute, but constrained by a balance of power and moderated by custom. I looked at my civilized crew of royal pets, as they pondered the rewards of groveling. To the vacuous, the nonentity is king. Not one of them had any skill other than his happy chance to be born to the proper family. Expectation was the privilege of their station, and their privileges would be handed down, perpetuated without regard to merit or talent. I thought of my own invisible shackles, those I would wear because I dared to give advice. At that moment I would have gladly torn off my English garb and taken my chances with these forest wolves.

Newport was now holding a piece of flattened copper in his hand. He bent it between his fingers. "They have no ability to refine this metal," he said. "It's pure...just a pretty rock they found and hammered with a stone." We told them our copper was better because we knew how to mix it with other metals to make it stronger. "We know how to heat it in great fires, so it will melt and ooze and flow like burning water," said Newport. Powhatan was impressed. Jonas Profit scowled. Opechancanough sat motionless, almost bored.

Behind the chiefs, beyond where the other savages stood, hanging from the low branches of trees by strong ropes, were flattened wooden boards, covered with soft fur. Tied to these were infants, facing forward, immobile, tended by their mothers, who swung them in the breeze, playing with them and watching with loving expectation their every gurgle, their every smile. All the young seemed to be a happy lot, well fed, fearless, inquisitive and sunny sweet in their childhood joys.

The older boys at the edge of their manhood watched the proceedings with a careful indifference, well learned from their elders. The older girls stood together giggling, whispering behind their hands into each other's ears. They stood in their girlish ways, self-possessed. They didn't shrink or seem differential to the young braves who sometimes walked past. One of the young girls didn't cuddle with the rest. She was standing alone, apart, her firm breasts bare, her long hair shining darkly as nights in collision, her eyes a blackness beyond depth, innocent and regal in her nakedness. She watched, standing, a colony of one, like a lighthouse beacon signaling enigmatically, *Come to me and beware.* Our eyes met. She didn't glance aside. My lips moved. I forgot Newport and Powhatan involved in their gestures of state. My gestures were of private thoughts and imagined breaths, short and urgent. She still stood, calling me, pulling me away from my moment of history, from my thought of my great enterprise.

Strangling in the airlessness of my own conflicting dreams, I suddenly realized someone was screaming, "Smith...Smith...they're thieves." I turned, the scene moving in a watery blur. The youth, Thomas Mutton, and three of our crew were struggling up the hill, wrestling with three savages as they advanced. Near the top the whole mass collapsed into a fit of squirming limbs, distorted faces and twisting backs. Everyone rushed forward, Englishmen and savages trying to separate the flailing pile. Arms and legs and bodies were pulled apart like two halves of a reluctant muffin. Dust was brushed from faces and mouths. The simultaneous shouting in many languages was quieted. Then the stories began, Naurins doing the translating.

"This could be war," whispered Newport in my ear.

"Men will be boys and savages will go a-savaging," I said to Newport, as I thought to myself, *The arrow at our heart is the pin on which the compass needle turns. How we hold the spin of this will determine the path our enterprise takes.* As Newport walked closer to Powhatan, I counted the opposition. Opechancanough watched me. I considered placing my hand on the polished wooden grip of my pistol, just for the effect, but I decided against it as an unnecessary provocation. Opechancanough continued to stare, gauging my intent. Was this the moment, the seed from which all our history would bloom? There were no facts to yield a decision, so I decided to fall upon the current of the moment. I walked into the middle of the forest of gestures and its shouting.

Newport, always the impulsive, and always wishing to please the savages, berated his men, ignoring simple justice and failing to ascertain the truth. He hoped, no doubt, to prove his friendship with Powhatan by taking the savages' side without question. "Maybe this Eden has a snake not of our own bringing," I whispered. I was ignored. Each time young Thomas, no more than a child, tried to explain what had happened, Newport's rage choked the words in his fearful throat, squeezing his voice into a high-pitched wheeze. Opechancanough stood scowling, as if he had just tasted something bitter. All Newport was proving to these people was his own weakness.

Ratcliffe stood at Newport's side. He started to slap the child. "Silly...maggot...I'll wash your face in your own blood," he said, each blow harder, more mechanical than the last. Ratcliffe smiled. He was enjoying it, feeling safe, protected by Newport's authority, a coward denying his cowardliness in mindless brutality. Thomas raised his arms, trying to protect himself, but resistance made Ratcliffe furious. Now with both hands he inflicted the monotonously spaced slaps that fell in sharp cracks across the boy's face. Ratcliffe closed his fists. Anger now my inspiration, I took an indulgence to myself. They who rule me, rule by half, in this wilderness of violence, I presumed. I blocked Ratcliffe's hands with my own. He turned toward me and I put my fist across his face. He vomited wind like a squeezed bladder. He staggered in pain. As he rose he drew a knife from the scabbard hanging at his belt, hiding it in the motions of his sleeve. The old mariner lunged, something in his hand, a vial—a lace of liquid splashed into Ratcliffe's face. Ratcliffe's mouth in screams, his eyes tearing anguish. His knuckles buried in his brow, rubbing as if he would tear away his own eyes to cleanse them of their pain. "That wizard and his red beard cat!" he raged. Two of his group went for their swords. I was faster. I brought my pistol down on the wrist of one. He cried and slowly knelt, as if buckling under a heavy weight until he was my height. I pushed the barrel of my gun under the eye of the second. Holding his throat, I said, "Do you wish to see through your ears?" I pulled back the hammer just to demonstrate the concept. The sword dropped slowly from his hand, serenely as a leaf .

"Enough?" I said. The man nodded. I released his throat, keeping my pistol in my hand, as I carefully retrieved the sword. Both I slipped into my belt. Ratcliffe still in screams. "Take the water and wash his eyes," said the old mariner. "Be intrepid to the play. Craft a magic to the scene. Opechancanough is watching." I did as the mariner told. Ratcliffe revived. Others helped him and his companion to their feet. I went over and dusted them off slightly. "Smile, Ratcliffe! We can't let these savages think we ride a divided horse." Ratcliffe's sullen face grinned in humiliation. "Good! Now embrace me as if we were each pleased with the other....Your life may depend on it." Ratcliffe grabbed my shoulders.

"As a child of Drake, you will be of many births," whispered the old mariner. "Your orphaned father would be well pleased with your ardor, but not your wisdom. It is by luck I had a little brew of pepper to spice his eyes and you a little water to set a magic cloth and whet the curiosity of our new friends."

Newport stood, openmouthed, silently. I told him to follow me, which he did, like a ghost on a spirit leash. Even uncertain, my juggler's boldness is the motion. To what am I the heir, that I am its birth? Newport stood by my side, breathing memories of himself back into his soul. Finally, his color returned. I asked the young boy what had happened. Wiping his bloody nose with his hand, he explained, through his whimpers, that he had found the savages stealing trade goods from our boat. When he and the others had tried to retrieve the trinkets there was a fight.

Through Naurins, I told Powhatan that his people had been stealing from us. *In our country theft is a crime,* I said, and here it seemed an unfriendly act. Powhatan swore his friendship again in pleading gestures, which I acknowledged with pledges of my own. I returned to the three savages and held out my fist, opening it for our stolen items. They ignored my hand.

"Forget the goods. Shall we endanger the progress of this great enterprise over the theft of a few trinkets?" asked Russell, supporting himself and his gout on the shoulders of his servant.

Powhatan stepped forward and spoke quietly to the savages. Two of the savages handed me small trinkets. Others brought from the village a hatchet, a knife and two bags of shot, and other toys and trade goods we had not noticed were gone.

"Marvelous thieves, these woodsmen devils," said someone.

"They're savages. They steal existence from their Okee, their hostile god. Why should they not steal from us?" came the voice of Thomas Wotton, our surgeon.

The crowns of the trees bent in the wind like inquisitive heads. Birds screamed indignantly at their own echoes. Powhatan continued to stare at the one unrepentant savage, whose muscles seemed to tighten, pausing, as they molded themselves into a thought of flight. Finally the savage bolted, running toward the open fields. Powhatan waited, counting the seconds, giving the savage a lead, as if it were a sport. Then Powhatan was after him, his long legs eating the distance in strides twice the length of his fleeing prey. I had never seen a man, an aged man at that, move so fast. At the crest of a small hill the two figures merged. There was a yell, a thud and rising dust. Human forms struggled briefly in the rolling clouds. Then Powhatan stood and by the hair pulled the twisting body along the ground. The savage fought his return more than his defeat. Powhatan dropped his human sack at our feet, which lay moaning, trying to clutch the blanket of the earth to himself. But the earth did not move or give its solace. Powhatan pointed to the whimpering heap. In his devilish tongue, he spoke words that hissed in venom. Six warriors raising their wooden swords surrounded the man and beat him as he lay, until his body swelled and turned the color of a darkened grape. When they finished, he was no longer of human form, but a jellied bag, a boneless fish. He groaned motionlessly. No one tended him.

A satisfied Powhatan turned to Newport and said in gestures, *We will be friends.* The rest of the tribe swayed, quietly chanting. They had seen this all before.

Speaking with exaggerated signs, Newport said, *In our country we hang our thieves; but here, since we will be friends, I will, this once, be magnanimous.* Newport then gave back to each of the savages the items he had stolen, keeping only the two bags of shot.

"This is not wise," I said to Newport, but I could not stop him.

"I will not have war over a few trinkets," he said. "Our kindness and moral certainty will be an example to convert the savages to our cause." Lost in the thicket he crowned himself with pretty thorns.

"Powhatan almost killed a man for our good opinion. Now, by rewarding the others, you are embarrassing his authority, not to mention showing these savages that we will treat their offenses casually."

Newport looked away from me in anger, and so again my wisdom was rewarded with a curse.

"A few bought savages will make easy allies," said Ratcliffe. "A little bribe always lubricates a friendly discourse. For, Smith, the trouble here is that no one will be his friend, even for a price." Some of Ratcliffe's simples laughed. Opechancanough touched the head of his cudgel, then let his hand slip off as he saw me watching. Then he suggested that Newport spend the night as a guest in his village. "I wouldn't do this," I said. "You could hang on his mercies. Tell Opechancanough that there is not enough time this visit. Tell him that you wish to explore, that you desire to see the falls of the river."

As Naurins translated, at the mention of the falls, Powhatan said that it would be unwise for us to travel beyond them, as he could not give us protection, the land being very wild. It was the territory of his sworn enemies, the Monacans, a vicious and bloody people. There would be great danger for us in that country. Powhatan asked again for an alliance with us against the Monacans. Newport evaded the issue. Now Powhatan insisted that Newport spend the night.

I dawdled the moment. "Newport is as our father," I said. "Where he sleeps, we, his children, must also sleep. If Newport rests in a village, we must rest there as well." Powhatan and Opechancanough looked at each other as I continued. "We wish to see the falls, as we were told of their great beauty, and we want to know the boundaries of our friend Powhatan's kingdom, to see for ourselves where we may safely go."

Newport then said, "I cannot leave all my children, but if you would take one of my sons and show him more of your ways, I would gladly leave him with you for a while."

Powhatan answered in words as Naurins gestured, *Our village is small, but we would gladly have a son of Newport as a guest. As for the falls, if you insist on seeing them, I will meet you there at sunrise to protect you from my enemies. Our guides will show you the way along the river.* Newport and Powhatan embraced. Thomas Mutton choked a whimper in the gurgle of his throat, he to stay with Powhatan. "Nervous child, bravely now," Newport said, "This is a great honor. You must learn the savages' language. No harm here for you, you are the honored guest of Powhatan."

Mutton is an orphan of no account, I thought. *Newport plays his hand with a hollow chip.* I doubted Powhatan would waste a murder on this child.

.   .   .   .   .

THE ORDER OF THIS CONGRESS AT AN END, WE ROSE AND TURNED toward our boat. The whole tribe began to follow us. The young savage girl who had stood alone stepped forward, almost leading the rest. She walked around the beaten man, who still lay on the ground. She seemed displeased by the impediment. As she passed by me, I signed to Naurins to ask her what she thought of the battered man she so casually ignored.

It is our law, she replied, looking at me with a mixture of curiosity and studied contempt.

"Who is she?" I questioned Naurins.

"Pocahontas, the favorite daughter of Powhatan," was his answer. She walked now along the crest of the hill above the river, as I descended toward our boat. Our paths divided. Each time I glanced up, she was watching me. She from her fearsome height, I in longing, my reflection on the water. She neither embarrassed by her own stare, nor frightened by mine, self-contained in her power, she beckoned to those shatters of myself, her thoughts in whispers of her flesh, sighing, *Come unto me and be made whole.*

I would have gone to her, but what chains we carry forged in our will, the fiery remnants of thought, which bind not only our limbs, but our breath and tongue in the irons of imaginary steel. Death by a thousand ghosts. Fear, not of a physical death, but of a spiritual one, held me back; a spiritual humiliation of self, ever haunted by discoveries never made, visions never seen, ambitions never quenched, oaths to ourselves betrayed. Feathers in my chest flapped, as the heart which is a hawk beat its wings and flew at the prey which is the mind. The girl walked on.

Ratcliffe said, looking up the hill at the young girl, "Not here three days and already a conquest."

"That's Powhatan's daughter," I said.

"A savage princess. The aristocracy have always found me entertaining."

"Remember, captives here are tortured to death as entertainments for their women."

Ratcliffe whispered enticements as he almost laughed, "Oh, Smith, that girl, that savage innocent, of what freedoms does she know?" He looked at me as if awakening from some heat, his foul breath ballooning through his words. He said, "And whose lips will not part for the indulging tongue?"

Chapter Six

HE NEXT DAY a rainbow glowed, a deluge rising in the morning's painted sunlight. From the crags above us, a shower of mist fell, the earth bleeding water. I almost touched a solitary moment of its endless passing with my hand. Our boat rode in its ascending smoke, the convulsing clouds of its evaporating rains.

The boat held to its anchor, as the breeze from the cataracts swept our decks in a wilderness of spray, soaking the crew, our baggage, our clothes. We had sailed to the falls, as far as we could go. At one end was the sea; at the other, these moving cliffs of water. Our world now encompassed, first by the will of nature, second by the will of Powhatan.

"We will make for shore," said Newport. "We'll go no farther here."

The bow of the boat swung to the grassy beach. The crown of the falls seemed to shudder and bend toward our shoulders, perfuming our thoughts, beckoning us to the land beyond sight with whispers of mystery and promise.

We disembarked, walked upon the beach. Newport sent Ratcliffe to climb the falls to briefly survey the territory that so enticed us. On reaching the summit, he called back, "It is a desperate land where demons herd rocks and the trees grow in riots, strangling the earth in their roots…."

"Fearful, isn't he?" said Newport.

"He likes to exaggerate difficulty. It makes his limited accomplishments seem all the greater," I replied.

Soon Powhatan arrived with sixty warriors. We walked to the river's edge and again Powhatan asked us to join him in a war against the Monacans. Newport avoided the issue, but assured the emperor of our friendship. Powhatan listened silently as Naurins read our signs. Naurins and Powhatan spoke among themselves for a while. Their words were never translated.

Newport invited Powhatan and his braves to join us for a meal. Powhatan agreed. We prepared a side of pork roasted over a great fire. The meat brought with us to festival our sail. A few savages went off to hunt deer and collect fish and ducks for the banquet. Sitting upon the ground with Powhatan, we smoked tobacco. The old chief spoke again of our spirits rising from the burning ash. We passed the pipe as the body of the earth slept before us, its hills rolling and blistering like the folds of the drying tobacco leaf.

Smiling in his secret wisdoms, the old mariner glanced at Wotton, our surgeon, as he gestured to Powhatan, "And what remedies are held within your tobacco? What does it cure?"

Powhatan answered in simple mime, *Tobacco is only a messenger. Its value is that it is given to us. The bearer of prayers to the sun. It is a winged voice, but its medicines are not known to me. It is an appeaser of the gods, but its cures are none.*

The mariner looked at the surgeon and said, "And now do you chance that all your alchemies may be false and all your learned books do sport a wanton tale? Did they not say that the Indians use the leaf as a cure?"

"These savages have never discovered the medical nature of the divine herb," the surgeon replied in anger. "Not every truth is known to all apostles. Spare me the venoms of your proof. There are miracles in this leaf that exceed all the misuses of the pipe."

Some of our crew playfully tried to catch threads of smoke in their cupped hands. At first it was a child's game. Clouds of smoke, ballooning as they drifted, set free from open hands. Smoke rose through the stardust of its own gray, polluted light, spiraling upward, as eyes followed its swirling flight. Some tried to catch the smoke again, reprison it in their hands, repowder its half-apparent face with more breaths, as if the smoke really were the body of their fading spirit, which only a desperate remedy could renew. Some of the crew laughed at the silly sculptures of smoke; others, half believing, hoping that belief was a halfway marker to the truth.

After the meal, Newport took a hammer and a crude wooden cross from the boat, walked to a shoulder of ground, set the cross, adjusted the hammer in his hand and pounded the cross into the soil. The hill seemed to heave in agony, the grass to shudder.

"It is a wondrous thing to bear the eternal to a savage wilderness," said a voice.

"The only eternal I know is the hand before my face," said another.

The savages rushed forward, holding their bows and cudgels in their hands. Menacing words echoed around the falls. Our crew, now standing, caressed their swords. A few held their pistol grips. Newport came running back. "It is a sign of our friendship," he said. "The crossed arms are the eternal union of the love of Powhatan and Newport."

Naurins's cryptic smile expressed a knowledge he would never totally reveal. He spoke to the other savages. The savages calmed.

Powhatan sat again, motioning to his warriors to do the same, which they did, looking at the cross, grumbling.

Newport continued to explain himself. He ordered the crew to stand and salute Powhatan with three rousing cheers, which greatly pleased the old emperor and his cohorts.

The conversation having begun again, Newport asked Powhatan if he had ever heard of our colony at Roanoke, whose colonists had vanished in the wilderness some twenty years before. Powhatan held his breath on the sinews of the words he would have spoken. Then said that he had never heard of such a place, but perhaps great ships like our own had come and taken them away. Newport said that that was not likely. Powhatan began to speak, then stopped again, as Newport continued—*Our king grieves for his lost children and will never sleep in peace until they are found.*

Children lose themselves in many ways, Powhatan gestured, adding, *I will make inquires of this place as a sign of our friendship.*

The air and its pleasant breath played with the ruffles at our necks. The perfume of its touch spoke of a love beyond body and a burning ache beyond pain. In its warming quilt, the sunlight fell upon the land, which slept the sleep of vigilance. For hours the savages sat in communal silence. Suddenly Powhatan rose and said that he did not feel well. *Your rich foods are a fire in my gut.... They poison in their sweetness.* Newport suggested that he stay and our doctor would tend him. The old chief said no, that our medicine, like our foods, could carry hidden poisons. As he spoke, he addressed the wooden cross, staring through Newport toward the stake.

Newport awkwardly embraced Powhatan, who seemed uncomfortable with our captain's closeness. Birds sculptured lonely circles around the setting sun. The air freshened in the oncoming night. Newport bid the old chief farewell, restating that on his return he would bring as a present seven firelocks.

Powhatan brightened momentarily. Then, remembering his stomach, he walked toward the woods with disintegrating dignity. As he passed Naurins, he told him to stay and guide us back to Jamestown. Our crew gave Powhatan three more cheers, and the old chief was gone, disappearing into the cover of the forest with his men. As quickly as it had begun it was over, with no fanfare to guide our passage.

We broke camp, loading our gear into the boat. "I hope this accident will not be the murder of our enterprise. I pray Powhatan doesn't think we tried to poison him," I said to Newport, who laughed at the suggestion, as insects buzzed in the tall grass, indifferent to our noise.

The anchor weighed, the currents of the river moved in their relentless waves, pushing against the hull. At first we gently drifted, the boat sometimes pivoting in the pleasant confusion of its course. Then the river, in a surge of power, rotated the boat fully in its rush. Newport tried to control it. No sail, no oar could stay the river's pressure and its will. We were expelled by water from the grotto beneath the falls. The cross on the bank was lost behind the waving grass. The air no longer warmed us. The light faded into darkness. The sky was clear. There were sounds of thunder as a faint glow held to the horizon in the east, as if a second sun were being born.

PART TWO

Shadows on the Water

THE ALCHEMIES OF THE RIVER

What is this season in its brief beginning?
My blood no longer flows in ice. My flesh fills my eyes.
Shadows swim through me again. I taste of life.
My waters as their tethered heaven.

Chapter Seven

DRAKE. A BOY. A MEETING. FROM DESPERATE
PASTURES, I AM RETURNED THE PILGRIM.

 STAND ON THE DECK, the wind forced into my face by
our forward progress. The river flows backward against
its own current in the illusion of our rush. Two shadows
stain the water's surface, rising on the foam of the bow's
thrust, then falling into the broader pit of the river's rolling landscape.
Ratcliffe is at my side. His mouth moves. I could not hear him. His
words, caught in the wind's voice, seemed only a lipped pantomime.
I wonder at the two of us: Ratcliffe wanting only his pleasure, I
wanting only to find an immortality in a union with this savage land.
Neither willing to fate his desires to others' hands. Each indifferent
to all the rules but his own. Each born but to betray, a traitor in his
fashion. I look at the silhouettes on the river's flow. I can't tell the two
apart. I wonder at the changing shapes of our now-projected forms,
as I wondered in what wars would I bring my innocence upon the
innocent, and to what flower would I be the seed?

We sailed. The river rose in heaves in wide enticing flats. I looked
through its rolling reflection of the sun, our spreading wake beneath
its surface. The oozy colors in their shapes drew me forth. How
many rivers have I seen? The slip of currents under how many keels?
I watched the river's flow as I conversed with my memories. Are we
not all of water born? How many baptisms make a birth? My head
lain upon the flood before a drop ever fell in church, and I made
certain in my name. In 1580 I was born, the same year Francis Drake
returned to England from his circumnavigation of the world, and so
by memories we are made before we even know their weight. I am
held in the arms of shadows as I succored on the birth of fates. How
circumscribed we are by circumstance.

My father was but a yeoman, owning some acres and a house.
His lands were near the estate of Lord Willoughby de Eresby in the
town of Willoughby by Alford in the county of Lincolnshire. Lord

Willoughby, fond of my father, leased him lands of his own estate, and so by work we prospered to be if not gentlemen, not peasants either.

In 1586, Drake was in Plymouth preparing a great fleet to sail against the Spanish Main. Lord Willoughby, who had some interest in the plot, asked my father if I could accompany him to be some companion to his son. And so I did my venture and sought my consequence. Vast the feeling to the vastness felt. Six years old, by power small. All my dominions were a pin. And yet I took the gate and had the road to Plymouth, I and Willoughby riding in the baggage train. It was children among the bundles, a romp of youth, we the brethren of the wagon town, our lord ever watchful at our side. His carriage our emperor's throne, there our meals to sweet sulk our play, the road in ruts bounced our heads to the rattle of our bones.

Plymouth then was the sanctuary of our fleets, masts, the gargoyle colors of their hulls, water wanton in their stink, docks crowded with goods. We walked a gauntlet of such bustle, by paths we passed the plenty to feed our war. Young Willoughby and I had our games, mock battles with the phantoms of our enemy, Spain. We played our soldiers well, had our victories, routed armies, their ships all drowned.

Now to adult arms and their giant wars. We to visit our English fleet. I, at six, no taller than a cannon in its mount, to stand on the admiral's ship, I walked the dock, my hands in Lord Willoughby's, the young lord also being led. What ships to loom their bastion, rising in their painted hulls; what pretties these to flower in their cannonades; and all my youthful dreams did sing the songs of far aways. The ship before us in its greens and reds, a blue face and on its eyes hung anchors on their chains. We walked a swaying plank and had the deck. Before us three men stood. One dressed in embroidered silks, splendor sewn on the palettes of its threads, and at his side a silver sword and a golden hilt. The other a moor dressed in breast armor, his cloth fine but not so fine. The last seemed a rumple in a cobweb cloak, more a mystery than a man, as if some dust had been vapored by some magic to have a life. And Willoughby was greeted by the men, who spent a moment to play a tickle and indulge the younger guests. "All the world's at war, and these our infants have come to pipe the fight. Good wars make children men," said the moor, looking into my face. How strange his eyes, pleasant grinned a stare upon that smirk. I pretended shy and wanted him to go away. I clung to Lord Willoughby.

"This one may be a squeak too short to play Diego as a lion."

"I will not be small. I am not the one who stoops to have his say. Height is but an easy step." I walked over to a cannon's mount. I stood upon its wooden carriage. "I am less short when I stand upon an iron neck. I have now the height to look you in the eye," I said, folding my arms about my chest. The men all laughed.

"This pup has more tongue than teeth, my Drake, this boy we keep." The moor grabbed me in his hands and danced me in the air around the deck. "Some day, my son, we shall make our war and I shall call you Cimarrone," he laughed. I fought the frolic, not knowing what all the words did mean. One of the men took me from Diego's grasp, lifting me high to ease me to the deck.

"I am Sir Francis Drake." The man with the dark eyes bowed as he spoke. His expressions came in sunshines open to the world. His beard a closer trim than most. His skin still smooth, but for a single scar on his right cheek. "I am honored to have such valor stand upon my cannon. And this, my friend Diego, whose dance you have won. He is a Cimarrone." Again that word. "And Jonas here, his head all filled with pranks. He can upon a moment trick a coin from a young man's ear. Such my crew. I hope you do approve."

I bowed. Lord Willoughby nodded to the pleasantries on every face. I rose. "An ear may hold a coin," I said, "but it is the fingers that pay the debt. I have seen the game. It is an infant's sport."

HOW MANY HOURS DID WE FLUFF TO DAYS, LORD WILLOUGHBY attending to the freights of war, we to spend the clock in Drake's cabin? Presents there for young Willoughby and myself. All those treasures to a child's eyes: trinkets of polished wood, or elfin boxes, or a porcelain horse frozen in a gallop, or a knight dressed in iron mail with sword and lance, a plume of feather to breeze atop his helmet. What miniatures to dainty in a child's hand. So like ourselves, we loved them for their size. My father could not afford this wealth. Drake, in his generosity, gave his gifts. My world now his cabin floor.

Each day when the men had their talks, we were taken to Plymouth or to play the deck, Diego or Jonas to watch or lead us for a time. And so we strolled the quay, our hands in Jonas's hands, our adventure to bribe our silence for an adult hour. And so we went to pluck an afternoon by wandering the wonder of those streets, searching for a treasure to be purchased by a copper coin. Jonas led us through the shops. Our dessert not bread, we sought a sweeter meat. Jonas to his own delights, in shops he paid the keeps for strange jars, bottles, stones and powders.

"Let us to the ship, and I shall entertain the deck and show some magic to delight your eyes." Jonas happy in his mood. "I almost had a child once," he said. "I am a game of ghosts. I shall play the father if you shall play the son."

On the ship again we sat the deck. Jonas with clean water in a cup, passing his hand above the rim, the water burned, flames in bright colors leapt the cup. The crew joined and watched. "I have never seen Jonas play at tints, or fashion fire for a smile," said someone. Diego passed then paused to share the fun, one foot upon a cannon mount. Jonas with a sweep of his hand pulled a white dove from his hat. The bird then released to fly to our mast, then away. Bright silks in tied ribbons now exploded in celebrations from his hand. Diego laughed. "Jonas spends the air. All his treasures are a trick."

Jonas smiled at the taunt and turned to me. "Well young Smith, are there enough mysteries here to entertain your afternoon?"

"I know there is a sport that fools the eye. Could you wonder us a second gift and spend the secrets in my ear, so I could be the father and play the game at home?"

"What son we have chosen," said Diego to Jonas, "the one who would be the sovereign of his own birth."

The next day I sat on the floor of Drake's cabin, young Willoughby at my side, gifts at our feet, the wide planked deck strove in the landscapes of our games. Our toys our vassals; our scripts the drama of a thumb. So long ago I was that child. I remember it all in shards. Time is as fleeting as its memories, in the mind its sight dimming past its noon. Drake and the lord were at a table, their words not to our understanding, shuffling feet, a map unrolled. What was this play, its freight upon a page? Willoughby and I stood in our curiosity and squeezed between the swords to see what could be seen. Under a gesture of a hand, a map in colored profusions lay its paper prodigals across the wood.

An angry voice pulled violence on its tongue. "Get the children to the deck. This ship is not a nursery, this map no swaddling." One of Drake's gentle hands upon my head, his other pointing to the world. He shushed the voice.

"I have searched the horizons around the world, drank the waters of distant continents and grieved the grief of stories never told. So many in Mexico, in Panama, in places south and west. North, in places without a name. So much I have seen, their lines upon this map are but a rumor of a sketch. Some day I shall tell you more than children's talk, but now Diego, who loves you as his own, will take you to the deck and teach the adventures of this ship. He might, if asked, fire a signal cannon, or show you how to sculpt in wood."

And so the day was spent with Diego as our guide. The cannon fired, shrieked and laughed its smoke as it drifted to its far away. Diego sculpted us a beast with fangs and claws. "A lion with a wooden roar," he smiled as he handed us the prize. We searched the ship, played the wheel, our hands pulling on its heavy ropes, Diego telling of his home in Panama, of its jungles, of his friends, of the Spanish, of secrets he could not speak. "All that you see, this fleet is a venture brought of Panama." He pointed at my nose. "And you, my child, will live by its jungles in the London streets. You, as Drake, were born where paths collide."

Then Drake walked on deck, two oranges in his hand. "A treat for your day." I had never seen this fruit before, so rare and expensive were they in the shops. Drake gave one to me and one to young Willoughby, smiled and left. Diego showed me how to peel the skin. "I wish I were a son of Drake," I said.

Diego looked me in the face. "Dangerous words, dangerous words, to deny your father to be another man's son. It is a house well bloodied by the heads of fools."

That night the Willoughbys dined with a local lord, I left abandoned to the fort. Drake adopted me as his evening child, I to his castle to meet the young woman who was his wife. She chose me as her own. Diego and Jonas talked of Panama and of the voyage round the world. After dinner I walked through the house. "This marble is our world," I said, spinning a wooden globe. "Far larger on every side than the shadow of my hand," twisting it hard in the candlelight.

"Far larger," said Drake, showing me the museum that was the artifacts of his life: the tools, the stones, the collections he had gathered and the drawings he had made. One was a sketch of a body lying on a table. "I should not show this," Drake said, taking it from my hand. "It is my brother's elegy."

I slept that night, dreaming in a castle. At dawn the Willoughbys came for me. Drake gave the lord two letters: one for my father praising me, and one to be used on my behalf at Willoughby's discretion. A small bag of coins for my education. "Return when you will and be our son," he said. And so I left, my life now turning upon a memory.

To my small world I returned again, I not so subscribed by chains of rank. Drake's letter well pleased the gossips of the town. The bag of coins was used to buy me books and have me to a school. I released from the toils in the fields. A week after Plymouth, my father had me pledge my allegiance to Lord Willoughby. "It is the first step to rise, invest with privilege," my father said. The lord, in reflections of Drake and of my pledge, pledged his own. "The boy is born of something wild. He will come to fame if he has the luck." So said the lord, who in his kindness was never false in his trust of me or in his aid. He was ever the mercy that one hopes is at the heart of power. All my life I used this connection well.

I was a child in my summer furies when Drake destroyed the Armada off the distant coast of France in 1588. That battle was all the talk. I was being formed by gleanings of a history I could not see. Could I be Drake if he, like I, were but eight years old? I now made orphan by a memory. In 1593 from school I ran toward rumors of Drake about to sail again to sea. My father caught me on the road to Plymouth, not so far from home. All weeds on my landscapes were myself. "You are not yet the man to be upon his ship," my father said. I who would be more was but a boy. For two years I sat my school, my dreams of adventure the libraries in my mind. "Drake will not remember you." My father raged good sense at my ear. In 1595 I was untied from youth to waste a year in London as an apprentice to a merchant, an appointment had through Lord Willoughby's influence. Not for me; all numbers are but ticks in empty air. What knight has armor made of sums?

London boiled in its rumors and its fashions. Everywhere tobacco was the rage, either in pleasure, its pipes in smoky recreations, or for the wonder of its cures. The leaf was sold only in apothecaries, or sometimes goldsmith shops. It was usually adulterated with shavings of wood or burnt sugar or straw or other herbs or dung or poisons. Gentlemen sought only the purest leaf from the few honest vendors. Physicians wrote tracts to recipe how to best brew the herb: whether in salves or lotions, powders to purge, oils to drink, snuffed through the nostrils as was the favorite physic of the French, or smoked pure and hand mixed from the Spanish tobacco of the Indies smuggled to England and priced in silver weights. And what pleasures pleasure this, England in our Protestant crusades, still warring Spain to free the precincts of the Dutch.

My father died in 1596. My mother soon remarried. I left my trade. "I the shadow, and Drake my calling. Where is my venture that I am its knight?" I cried. Through Willoughby's intercessions and kind resolves, I was made soldier to Captain Joseph Duxbury in Holland and the Low Countries. What Spain is this that sits upon our Dutch? Philip II, having received from his father, the Holy Roman Emperor Charles V, upon his abdication in 1556, the mercuries of a divided world. Philip to have his Spain, his Naples, the Netherlands and the New World in all its Indies. Charles's brother to have the German states, Austria, Hungary and Bohemia. All this to save the Hapsburgs from the genealogies of a civil war.

What the inheritor inherits is but the intent, the substance may be a far different due. Philip, with all his wealth, was always in debt, near bankrupt again. The route of gold and silver of the New World flowed through Spain, then north, sailing in galleys to Philip's bankers in Antwerp. Fearing the influence of the Protestants in the Netherlands, his world assaulted by an idea, his credit lines — on which the puppet of his empire danced — swung in the air of a Lutheran wind. Philip, in errors and misspent theologies, brought his war in all his bigotries. By his certainties Philip had birthed murder, tolerance cast to cannonades. Each idea in its renunciation, by what hell their salvations? For thirty-five years in assassination and through truce the battles raged. Now it was my time to serve. All that would be of earth are families by blood. I of no name came of no rank, but I knew somewhere in all this wreck there would be a hint of fame for me. And so I sought my cause to be another Drake. Crusaders we are who gallop on our dreams. The landscape is but slaughter to someone else.

To keep our health, we never bathed, as was the custom, to preserve the natural moistures of our skin. We washed our bloody wounds with urine or white wine, afterwards the cut wiped clean with a linen cloth. Two green tobacco leaves well supped with their own juice, or with distilled juice alone, or the dry powder of the leaf mixed with other herbs in confections of turpentine and brimstone were set as a curing scab upon the skin. Such plasters the only shield against the rotting of the flesh. In consequence, some of us were kept from death, we thought.

To free ourselves from the exhaustion of war, we smoked, I learning then of the medicines in the art. So stings the folds of quenching warmth, the smoke into my lungs. The blood bears away its drug in excited alchemies. The heart beating in fists more powerful than before. Thirst and hunger assuaged. "By what lunacies does tobacco make its cures?" I asked. "To what madness am I the slave?" My pulse raced through my veins in wild measures. We marched, eating nothing but the tobacco smoke, chewing on the green leaf or its dried powder, soldiers measuring their health in the volumes of their spit as some physicians suggested. Around the campfires, heatless in the cold, our physicians sat decanting on the medicine of tobacco in all its thrones, discoursing on the great authorities and their books: a century of printed works, chained libraries in claims and counter-claims and where the source to seed the ideas into a hundred years of bloom, but all did document the one idea that death and disease were not the only demons of this earth. There was also tobacco, crowned in all its miracles.

Liébault's work, *L'Agriculture et Maison Rustique*, offered in Paris in 1570, held more fascination than the rest. On those pages were first told the story of Jean Nicot, Liébault claiming he heard it from Nicot himself. In the year 1556 or thereabout, sometime before Nicot arrived in Lisbon as the French ambassador, a Flemish sailor brought from Florida the seeds or plants of tobacco to that city, the herb then being only a New World curiosity. Most of the ship's crew chewed the leaf, or smoked it rolled about itself in tubes called cigars, which was the custom in the West Indies, the savages there not using the pipe. In Lisbon, a small plant and some seeds were given to the keeper of the royal gardens, Damiao de Goes, who loved the beauty of the leaf and grew it as a decorative herb in all the municipal prospects and for the king himself.

Nicot arrived in Lisbon in 1558 and was given a bag of seeds, perhaps from de Goes. The story not quite clear and ever does history sing its secrets in its song, but it is known that Nicot planted the tobacco in his garden where it bloomed waiting for its moment. A relative of Nicot's page, having suffered with an ulcer on his face, did, by a plaster of the crushed tobacco leaf and its green juices, cleanse the open sore. The wound healed, the lesion gone without a scar. Nicot excited at the news. A few days later his cook almost severing his finger with a knife, was cured without infection by the same plant. Nicot now so experimented with tobacco it became known as the *ambassador's herb*.

In 1560, the queen mother, Catherine de Medici, and her son the king in Paris received from Nicot some plants and seed. In his reports, Nicot discussed the medical uses of the leaf in plasters and in its pure oils, or in confections, but he sent only snuff, few knowing of the sneezing remedy until then, the queen mother using the gift to cure her headaches. Snuff becoming then a fashion at court, its cures were soon forgotten in a habit of empty consequence, the queen mother herself using almost three ounces of tobacco a day. But tobacco's reputation now flamed throughout Europe as a medical panacea.

"And do you know why Nicot sent snuff to his king and the queen mother?" I was asked by my army surgeon all those years ago in Holland. I shook my head. The surgeon smiled the smile of learned meanings. "Nicot had read the murderer's book," he said, "Gonzalo Fernández de Oviedo y Valdés, that Spaniard who was governor of the city of Santo Domingo upon the island of Hispaniola. He the apostle of butchery. He the apocalypse. By his law whole peoples disappeared, worked to death in the gold mines or in the fields. They transported from their distant islands. Whole archipelagoes depopulated."

In 1535, Oviedo had published his book to explain to the Spanish king the greatness of his service to the crown. Upon a digression he told of the Indians' use of a brown powder called *cohoba*, which was inhaled through a y-shaped hollow straw, the two branches placed into the nostrils, the single foot into the cohoba. The forked stick the Indians called *taboca*. Oviedo thought the ground powder was the leaf; but it was not. It was the crushed seeds of a sacred tree that in its smoke made men walk stupefied in trances. In his arrogance, so confused, Oviedo named the brown powder tobacco, not knowing that that was the Indian name for the y-shaped straw. And so by mistakes we have the naming of the leaf. As the errors dwell the murder's lips, it is our history that is flavored by their kiss. Believing the savages used tobacco only medically in a snuff, Nicot sent that to his king and the queen mother. To honor Nicot, the leaf was renamed *Nicotiane*, though that held only briefly, even at court. But a name rarely squanders all its meanings. We may see it yet again in a different form.

And so through these discussions I marched in my youthful wars. Books are heralds that museum our fragile histories. Our reputations linked forever, even in their lies. Our shadows bloom their lost in words, and he who would rise must bear some witness of himself. One day I swore I would write a book, as I pondered in what history would be my name.

I RETURNED TO ENGLAND IN 1599. LORD WILLOUGHBY HAD GRANTED his two sons three years of travel, two servants, two horses and the sum of sixty pounds. So much and so little. My father's lands and all he owned worth seventy-seven pounds at his death. Such is the gulf and the cast of rank. Now so disciplined in war, I was to accompany Peregrine to Paris and to his brother's side, and then to attend them as guide and servant for the remainder of their stay, Lord Willoughby much impressed by my manhood. I was given some money for my pocket, and so we made our way to London.

This new London was a different England than I had known, those of some estate brewing in their current fashions. They held me small and simple in my country quaint. Dandies in their silks walked in airs of license to swank a better opinion from their own. And so they pranced in their empty affects each to the other, while gentlemen boasted their perfections with the pipe, they well schooled in the tobacco art by private tutors called professors. These professors more professional dupes, hanging their placards in the fashionable lanes, advertising their skills in sculpting a better breath to forge a wiser ring or puff a better fist of smoke. Tobacco not elite enough for these gentlemen, they founded their separate clubs in their carved halls, and fashioned their public vice into a private art. Laws were passed to help them in their spite. Gentlemen could sit on the stage and smoke their leaf during performances of plays, even Shakespeare's. What heretic smoke this is that hoists its own beauties.

My first pipe was a carved corncob smoked through a straw. Tobacco was expensive, so little grown in England, and none of any quality. The leaf was now sold by any vendor who could procure a cargo. It was often adulterated as before. And so another pleasure made poison in its secret brew. The best leaf came by illegal trade from the West Indies, smuggled from Spain through Flanders to England, though Spain and England still at war. But what are lethal politics matched against the pleasures of a vice?

Physicians and herbalists made tracts to tell by recipe how best to brew the leaf. This herb in all its alchemies now called a panacea, nothing contracted it could not cure. And now in our picture the world divides, physicians accusing smokers of wasting the gifts of the precious leaf. Through all the debate I wondered in a question I never asked. My father had said not until 1570 did he, himself, hear the name tobacco mentioned in all England and then it only sang with the name of Drake. If this leaf with its medicine were known to the savages who gave it to Columbus in 1492, why were its cures left to be undiscovered and unknown for so long? Why was all of Europe given up to death, while lying on its garden path great cures awaited?

After London we made our way across the Channel, had our meeting and began our tour. For six weeks I was greeted in the castles of Willoughby's friends and introduced at Court by cavaliers who would be knights and who bowed their chivalries to any guest who could tell a welcomed tale. And everywhere tobacco used in a snuff, the Court a choir of noble sneezes, or the perfume of the pipe, or the few eloquents who had taken up the Spanish fashion and smoked cigars or paper-wrapped the leaf in tubes now called cigarettes, the palm leaf wrapper of the Indians totally forgotten.

"All fashions decline to a tiresome etiquette, then in boredom they die their death." So the French gentleman spoke, holding a silver snuffbox under his reddened nose. I watched him pose to the admirations of himself in the reflections of the mirror across the room, and so we flirt ourselves in the feebles of our wisdom. "Are we not all entranced with the tobacco leaf, so refreshed by the novelty of its intoxication? But the best is we are the savage's smoking twin," he laughed, lisping into a rude cough. "Elegance always courts a savage consequence."

"The best consequences all have a slightly savage taste," said another Frenchman, interrupting, his long stare in its concentration, his nose most eloquent in its lift. The intrusion unwelcome, but not quite ignored, the conversation continued on the edge of a double knife. The second Frenchman, caressing the innuendoes in his voice, smiled across the threat of interruptions and said, "At its birth, an attitude slightly to our ruin always wantons to a fascination."

The first Frenchman, embarrassed in his rouge, flamed indignations as he faulted to his subject, stammering, "Reborn, we are children to the Indians. Each nation took up the leaf as saw it used in the New

World. The Spanish preferring what the savages used in the West Indies, the cigar, the cigarette. The French the pipe Cartier had seen at Montreal in the land of Arcadia, or snuff Nicot had learned about in books from the Spaniards who had been there. Or the English the pipe learned mostly here in France when you fought with the Huguenots. Even your Raleigh taking up tobacco on our soil, not from the savages in the New World, as was the legend. But history moves its ghosts on many paths before we know its truths. Your colony at Roanoke, before it was lost, seeing again the pipe. And so all Europe is a child to parents never seen." Then the gentleman turned away to have his snuff and wine, and sorrows.

ALL THIS SPLENDOR AND ADVENTURE, BUT IN TRUTH THE Willoughbys were needing funds, and with three years still to tour. A small purse was given to me and with much sorrow I set out for England and for home.

But dreams have protocols on whose slide the sleeper bears his life as a living sacrifice. More waters were now to claim a portion of my fate. My ship from Holland all fouled in storms, the ship washed in wreck onto a rocky beach. The English coast we had made, but not as we presumed. By luck my compass still had the point, I not far from Berwick where Lord Willoughby sat as governor. There I was given aid and had the chance to make some presentations to fellows of the Scottish court.

They being all of honest Scottish fold, treated me as well as kin. But I could see a yeoman has not the pockets of a courtier, nor the gilt about his frame to entice his plain manners into flatteries. Only the false can make the false seem true. And so I departed, returning home the most traveled youth in town, besides the Willoughbys.

I now to settle down, it thought, expected to marry into a wilderness of sense. How many daughters did I meet? How fair their eyes, at my fortunes they turned to yield, to have my father's lands. How sweet their shadows tasted on my anxious lips, and all those gentle concerns, and they the luxury under the feather of my touch. Lovers freight their love in dreams. I to be flattered, knowing the offerings of their skirts. Busts so laced in the bounties of their flesh called me forth to lay my cheek onto the softness of their flow. But I would not squire myself to suffocate as breath to breath I tore my life with heat—in that gentle that follows to a sleep.

Soon I roused myself from flatteries and all embrace, and with a horse and a servant to be my man, some books of science and of war, I lived upon open pasture near a wood on Lord Willoughby's estate. Permission I had to hunt and ride and have the use of his library and all his books. My own land was but five acres, not large enough. By what famines am I quenched? I needed seclusion on which to practice as I dreamed my knighthood into flower. I read of ways to voice messages by codes and signal lights, of bombs and fires stormed from iron tubes, a war by mechanisms, all slaughter now by alchemy. All this I learned as I followed my own path to be a knight. I taught myself to ride a horse in battle. Lord Willoughby so impressed, he asked his cousin, the Earl of Lincoln, to have his riding master instruct me further in the art. What we are, we are by accidents and turns. We are the shards of happenstance.

The earl sought to introduce me to some of his friends. His rider was a sometime assassin and always Greek. I stayed a time at Tattershall, the earl's estate, and learned of horses and of history and of the butcheries of the Turks. Theodore Paleologue told me of the slaughter. "Why do Christians fight Christians in the lowlands of the Dutch when the heathen Turk wanders murdering in the east?" he asked.

A knight needs dragons of the flesh. And I the cause that strove to have a cause. Paleologue, always seeking converts to his hate. And I who sought fame now sought a war. In those days when chivalry withered on the bitter vine, I alone thought myself an almost knight. Oh why is youth the last to know that which he in his idealism would defend, sleeps not in a passing dream but in its death?

Chapter Eight

TWICE BETRAYED. THE EASTERN WARS. THREE
HEADS. AND I HAVE TASTED OF MY DEATH.

HE AUTUMN of 1600, I tired of comfort and the Willoughby estate, and put all that I had in a trunk and a few small bags, and sailed from Dover to find adventure in the eastern wars. As ever, I would ride my consequence to be a Drake. On that ship I met with four gallant gentlemen who made brag of their quality and befriended me. At the next French port they told me they would guard my trunk and my possessions, as I put all my goods into their boat, bidding me to follow in an hour. "All is safe. We will wait." All my clothes and money they stole away, such are the pirates who pretend a noble title. In such a rage I did cry against the captain of that ship, who must have known their sort well. Passengers came to my aid and would have murdered the captain for allowing me to be so abused. They gave me as they could hospitality in clothes and coins.

But charity is in truth a pauper's word for fair. I walked to the town where the men were said to live. Not finding them, I swore into a rage of many fits. The local lords, hearing of my plight, a stranger used so badly by their own, they all came by rescue and gave me all the lodging and repair they could. But chance ever walks near on many crossing paths. By a great stand of trees I found by a summer luck one of the cheats. There by sword in a padded war, by thrust and parry, I spanked the man, his worlds so small in great humiliations. Soon, hearing of the noise, some farmers came and subdued the fun. The man confessed, saying he too was cheated by the other three. And so I left him to his wounds. His hurt was not deep enough, but still I had some justice to stir the pot.

First, I wandered south and west. All directions seemed but the flight to hope. In Dinan I learned of Count Amaury Gouyon and his Chateau of Plouer, a few miles down the River Rance. The count I knew. His father, a Protestant, had fought with Sir John Norris in the religious wars. Norris being related to the Earl of Lincoln by marriage, I had met the count not three months last at Tattershall.

Such inheritors we are of all our circumstance. The count welcomed me as a lost friend. Delights and entertainments I was shown the chateau, with its great inner halls, its statues, its fine wood, its marble stairs. My eyes moved upon its philosophies, swept by such luxuries I had never known. The air about was spiced with a succulent blend of herbs. The count had one of the great physic gardens of France. There he grew his exotic plants and herbs. All that bloom for science. The count, an herbalist, spoke as he walked the paths around the plants, all those blooms in luscious depths of many hues. Two species of tobacco he had. "Histories are upon this leaf," he said. "This, the Nicotiana rustica, grown from the first seeds Nicot sent to France. The other, Nicotiana tabacum, is not so common in my country. The Aztecs grew this plant by cultivations on marvelous fields in Mexico and the Indians of Yucatan doing much the same. This was the only tobacco that the Indians of New Spain grew as a crop. The Nicotiana rustica grew wild in the West Indies. Its taste not to the Spanish liking, their preference being for the Aztec leaf. The Spanish imported Nicotiana tabacum seed to the West Indies in 1535. Now it is the only tobacco there."

I looked at the count, knowing most of the leaf in Europe had grown in private gardens such as his. Only a little to be had in England and some in Portugal farmed for commerce. Sixteen ounces of fine West Indian leaf priced at 4 pounds 10 shillings in London. Green gold, this leaf, in all its intoxicating luxuries. "The Spanish learned how to grow and prepare the leaf from the savages they slaughtered in the New World. What crimes were practiced to bear this leaf to us? What curse marked the plant? What cries for justice echo in its smoke? What lethal vengeance may in secret foul its medicines and turn its cures to venoms in our throats!"

When the count had finished his speech we walked again upon the countryside wide with haunted prospects. Ruins, hollowed in their toppled and scattered stones, called to us from the foreigns of an ancient time.

WHEN I WAS TO BEGIN MY JOURNEY AGAIN, I WAS GIVEN SUCH CLOTHES and money and means of war, pistols and swords and a shield, that I was an iron knight. South now I walked the road to Bordeaux then

Bayonne, to the beaches of the Mediterranean, at dusk the waters to my right. The landscape's blue stained with golden shadows of the sun. At Marseilles, I took passage on a boat to Italy. That boat a wreck, we went but fifty miles to Toulon, where we docked in fear of sinking. Another boat. This time a storm forced us into the shelter of a small island just off the coast near Cannes. There were many discontents aboard that night, many of the passengers pilgrims bound for Rome, and I, an English Protestant, subject to our sovereign queen. Diverse remarks and empty stares I had, rage and hate, until a mob grabbed me and all my trunks and threw me into the sea.

By grace of God and lightning, I walked the shallows and wallowed upon the undertow, and dragged my trunks to the island. There, in my discouragement, I found some peace among the cows and goats and other domestic animals of the field. In the morning, the storm still not past, another ship made shelter in the cove. I sat, drenched on the beach, contemplating my discomfort, water running down my back. Seeing me in my abandon and distress, the captain, whose name was La Roche, brought me to his ship. His home was St.-Malo, not far from Chateau Plouer, and he, by chance, a good friend of Count Amaury. La Roche offered me passage on his ship, which now cut its wake east to trade in Egypt.

Few Englishmen had seen what I was then to see. We sailed east and south to Corsica and Sardinia, to Cape Bon on the African coast, then far to sea to avoid the pirates. Seven hundred miles to Cape Ras-et-Tin, then to fabled Alexandria and the Nile delta, where our goods were sold. So many ships plumed in all their sails. What white clothes in wraps and smells in perfumes from the air. It was a world dreamed in mysteries, so strange its touch was as a bite.

We sailed to Aleppo, the city where silks held the breezes as its flags. The harbor waters thick with warmth and strange debris. La Roche wanting to know what ships were at the docks. I asked where would we anchor and fill our hold with ivory. La Roche smiled and said I was young and soon would be rich. We sailed then north to Greece, La Roche always watching toward the sea. Passing the Strait of Otranto toward Italy, we came upon a large merchant ship, the *Argosy*, just sailed from Venice. Captain La Roche brought all sails, hailing by voice and sign flags that he wished to speak with them. The *Argosy* sailing from his voice, we in chase. Our horizons now in rolling decks of wait. We, the smaller and speedier ship, our men standing atop our railing, watching the slower vessel. A cannon from the *Argosy* spit its lethal spark. One of our men blown to wreck, his body torn in geysered rags of flung bone and blood. "Rage heat, come vengeance," screamed La Roche, as he brought a broadside upon the *Argosy* in cascades of boiling smoke and iron sparked in flames. The *Argosy* rolled. Her rigging torn in falls of rope, she now sought escape and chased to the open sea. Our ship raced to keep the *Argosy* under siege. Another broadside, her waterline struck. She luffed her sails, then stood to her own defense. Fires glanced as our cannons spoke their reddened lightning through the burning ash. The *Argosy* shuddered as she was torn to derelict. Sinking now, she surrendered to La Roche. We boarded her to stop the leaks and chain our prisoners. All this ruin and such wealth we found: silks and velvets, tobacco, hordes of gold and silver coins. For a whole day we rifled through the spoils and brought it to our ship.

La Roche, so fair in his new fortune, gave me five hundred coins of gold and silver, and a jewel-encrusted silver box. I now with smiles in my new found wealth set aside the Turks and decided to educate myself as would befit a gentleman. I never saw La Roche again, nor heard his name. He to the wilderness of his sea, I to Italy to adventure in the spring of Tuscany. Was ever a country made so luscious in its bloom? It seemed ever an eternal rest. In Siena by chance I met again Willoughby's sons, who were recovering from wounds in a duel. I showed my silver box. We spoke our tales as friends, my coins giving some equal station to my jests.

From Siena, I then to Rome to visit my education on its histories. All those marbles there that stood the earth as some ancient guest, speaking languages to overwhelm the eye. All senses faltered. I cast down my flesh and held my bones as a lesser twin against the polished stone. "Was all this but the toys of giants? Were all miracles to them but a whim?" I thought.

In Rome I thought again of the wars against the Turks. I went as an Englishman to visit the most powerful Englishman in Rome and sought Father Robert Parsons, an English Jesuit, asking him for aid to join the eastern wars. The rector of the Catholic English College heard my tale and gave his letters of introduction and his advice. I, the Protestant, thrown into the sea by the Catholic pilgrims, now given aid by that Catholic clergyman, a blacksmith's son, who rose much by crudeness and some by wit to be secretary of the exiled Dr. William

Allen, the English cardinal. They both to urge Philip II to send his Armada against our queen in 1588. Dust now his company, a squalid man almost forgot, age has not worn his intrigues well.

Parsons and I shared a pipe, smoking then new in Rome. "An English habit well exported and well received," he said. Parsons added as he forced a smile from his lips, "Of course, smoking is not so new in Italy as is told. The Spanish mercenaries, when that country ruled Naples, brought the herb. The herb disreputable then, tobacco mostly used to ease the pain of syphilis and gonorrhea."

FROM ROME I SAILED DOWN THE TIBER. I WANDERED NORTH TO Siena again, the Willoughby brothers gone to travel in places I did not know. Then to Florence, the city of Da Vinci and the Renaissance, where men hatched titans from their morning eggs—next to Venice, where the light at dusk and the light at dawn are all weighed and balanced in a cup, and shadows sing their lines in harmonies and piazzas, their adjourning streets curved to bridges above the envy of the drinkless waves, such a motion above such a depth. So like the waters of my youth, blind to blind, I determined not to see the mirror in its face.

From Venice I sailed by long routes about the Adriatic. Trieste not two hundred miles to the east then blockaded by the Venetian fleet to hold the Christian pirates from raiding on the Turks. Venice calling itself a neutral in the eastern wars, trading with the Turks, that commerce being most profitable. And so the Italians did war upon their own. The sun is a coin and on its orbits hang our politics.

I followed the chains of their alliances east and west. Landing at an open port on the eastern shore, I bought a horse, riding the mountain passes north toward Austria, toward Vienna, that city always under threat of the Ottoman Turks, they battling along the Austrian border. Who would spite the dare? Too close this destiny. Emperor Rudolf II having moved his capital to Prague for safety, surrounded by his scientists, his alchemists, his painters, his Protestant nobles, his philosophers and his Rabbis (the Pope considering Rudolf a heretic). He then the most tolerant Catholic monarch in all Europe. Why not to war for such as he?

In Vienna, with my letter from Father Parsons, I gained an audience with Lord Eibiswald, who was then raising an army to march east. He queried me as to experience and knowledge. I told him of my history with the Dutch, and of my readings, and how I was acquainted with all means of signals and secret codes. Eibiswald listened and took notes, impressed, I thought. I told him of explosives and new alchemies of war. "You will have your use," he said, and sent me to his chief of artillery, Baron Khissl, who was most practical in all matters of religion; and who, knowing I was Protestant, sent me to the Lutheran regiment forming in Vienna under the command of Count Modrusch.

East now to war we marched. Landscapes turned to devastations. The land where we wandered was a skull. How bleached this wreck and ruin. All earth was bone, all pastures were hollows as the sockets of an eye. This Hungary was a world no more. What humans we saw had eaten dogs. Forests now were heads on stakes. Young girls blown to hags on winds of pillage. Children so starved they ate the bodies of the dead. Adults fought to cannibal on scraps. It was a world where men had come to be cruder than the beasts. No torture was pain enough to satisfy the lust to inflict more pain. Nothing urged that was not ripped by lunacy into hate. No lust confined, no madness mad enough that was not turned to a wisdom of a wanton sort. No foul so foul it did not smile and pretend some good. It was a place where men dreamed murder in their turns, and I the morsel left to lounge the tongue and wipe the fangs of another's tooth.

By the summer of 1601, Eibiswald first marched to liberate the Hungarian town of Nagykanizsa, only to find himself surrounded and under siege by Turks in the town of Limbach. The Turkish forces were divided by a mud stew of foulness we called a river. Baron Khissl and Count Modrusch above the town in the hills with reinforcements and supplies but no strength to lift the siege. *Why not prompt the fate,* I thought. *What of me is there to lose?* Caution is a welcomed but never honored guest. Meeting with Khissl, I spoke of my knowledge of signal torches and of my discussion with Eibiswald about them. "If I could gain a hill, I could with luck signal Eibiswald for some joint attack upon the Turks, so allowing our reinforcements and supplies to gain the town." Khissl listened and agreed. The signals made, Eibiswald responded, displaying three lit torches from the walls. "On Thursday night I shall charge on the east. At the alarm, attack," was the message I sent.

Khissl, hearing of my success, now brooded. His forces, he thought, were not strong enough. "A diversion we must have to hold our hand upon the lock and twist the key," he said. So on that Thursday night I had runners carry on their shoulders boards hanging with burning strings of tow as to appear as the lit tapers of three thousand firelocks. An army of illusion through the dark, as pastures in points of glow marched to our aid. Cries! The rush of alarms now tore the world. The Turks sortied to attack the fields of sparks. As they marched across the river, Khissl and Eibiswald struck them from behind. Floods in fear, the water's panic at their necks, the Turks escaped to have their death by drowning. The river drank them to its own. A third of the Turkish army lost that night. Limbach reinforced. The Turks withdrew to find a safer battle in that war. I was rewarded, made captain of a troop of two hundred and fifty horsed cavalry. Khissl himself so honored me. Now I had my rank and some little fame, but fame is a hunger that is never solely quenched by fame.

A YEAR OF WAR PASSED IN LIGHTNING BEFORE MY EYES. SO MUCH war, my mind became a church, its images tinted glass, stained, to be recalled on each reflection of remembered light. Such spirits grounded in their perpetual shrieks, each lance forever in its charge, each sword caught eternal in my counterstrokes. My horse dying in its always death as it fell, flinging me to the ground. So many riders, their horses dead. How slips the memory to robe the hurt, as always victory the elusive in our cries.

All war is a shift. No mud is firm, the earth never holding to its root. The soldier steps, his heel is but on air. Only the dead are certain of their circumstance. Modrusch and our company pledged to fight with General Basta, who was sent by Rudolph II to quell the war started by Zsigmond Bathory, once king of Transylvania. Zsigmond had abdicated this throne twice: once in 1597, wanting to trade his crown to become a cardinal after marrying the sister of the queen of Poland. The marriage, never consummated, was annulled, Zsigmond being judged impotent by reasons of witchcraft by a Vatican commission. Four months later, without his cardinal hat and scarlet, Zsigmond changed his mind, returned, claimed his throne and was welcomed by his people. In 1599 he abdicated again, this time reducing Transylvania to brutal invasions and civil wars.

. . . . . .

AND SO THAT SPRING, THE EARTH OVERSPREAD WITH GREEN, Modrusch with squared battalions marched eight thousand troops onto the Plain of Regal and up to the walls of Alba Iulia, the ancient royal capital of Hungary, those high walls against the turmoil flat of a brigand's waste. And so we sat as the wolf before his cage, and dug our trenches and laid our siege.

What siege is war, our trenches dug, mounds of earth phalanxed against a weave of wood in barricades. Twenty-six cannons were marshaled in our redoubts. Walls of mud faced walls of stone, and on the city's parapets the courtly ladies stood. They gazed upon the deadly works, enticing with their gestures some practice of courtly sports, a game of lances and of ax, a knightly duel, a diversion before we diverted ourselves to war. And to joust the boredom of that place, a Turkish Bashi, a captain of their rank, issued a challenge to any Christian of the same rank to battle unto death. The prize was the trophy, to the victor went the vanquished's head. A duel on horseback, each to be fully armed, in neutral ground, no interference from either camp. When the head was taken it was done. A gentlemanly match to rule a gentlemanly death. And fame to perch the shoulders of the one who in his hand held high the head.

So many of our rank were eager to have the field and contest their souls in a lethal game that lots were drawn, and I would have the fate to bear the luck to be the one.

The next day the world was eyes and trumpet calls. A sky of banners and ladies graced the city's walls. The armies had an hour's truce. I on my horse in my armored soul, with a squire to tend my lance. He led my horse. I swayed upon the rolls of cheering companies. I was to myself first among the first to ride into this gallant joust. Fame, in its instant contentment, would have me fear no death.

At the opening of the city gate came he who comes to battle me. A janissary walked before him, bearing his lance, the ramparts all festooned in cheers, and ladies begging a glance to insure that each was his only one. Such armors he had were polished to weighty mirrors. Eagle feathers, all compact and framed in silver and garnished with gold and precious jewels, decorated his shoulders. *And so to his death he comes so displayed to die,* I thought.

A brief salute, a nod, a grin behind the visor reflected flat against the metal dark. Our horses turned. We faced each other, our lances in our hands. More calls, more trumpets. Even memory forfeits and holds the moment in its breath. Our horses now beat thunder through our souls. We charged. But his lance was too low, his horse too dull in its vacant strength. I rode my lance high. My horse galloped in its strategies, my charge and my intent never clear. I spread deception on the dust. I came wide and closed for the kill. Theodore Paleologue would have thrilled to see his instruction so well displayed. My lance struck through the visor of the Turk. His face, pained in ruin, exploded like a bloody grape, his head broke into a shattered skull. Into a ready death he fell. His helmet mine, I cut off his head.

What trumpets now in blood, the choirs I heard. I displayed the head. Through ranks and companies all progressed to scream my name. I offered my trophy to my general, who kindly accepted it.

As the dead, fame ever has a friend. Not an hour had passed when I received a new challenge from another Turk. Two heads for one, my head and that of his friend for his own in another duel. Twice is twice, its twin in better reputation. Why not have the sinews to make a double of the bet? And so it was upon the morrow we had our festival. What heralds these trumpets to my ears. I am called to wrath. I am bound in fame. My challenger and I saluted our appreciations for this chance to die. His horse charged, our lances broke upon each other's shields. Seeing a pistol in his hand, I reached for mine. His shot marked my breastplate but did not penetrate. My sights, my pistol now engaged to fire. The shot. His armor holed in the left breast, blood washing the polished iron. His arms went limp, his horse reared. He fell and was so broken in his fall. I took his head, and, as a grant of pride, I returned his body and his rich apparel to the city gates. Thus another of my gestures gave its coins to fame.

What gallant boredom can be a war. We were getting fat. I went to Modrusch, asking for permission to issue my own challenge to the Turk. "Two heads now cry in custom to beg a third. Two is a lonely number. Why not play for the sacred three?" I asked. Modrusch, whose father was killed by Turks, nodded his consent before my persuasions half were spent. All we persuade are but consequences of the past.

My challenge was issued and accepted that very day. *On that morrow, what three heads of oblivion shall I carry on my lance?* I mused.

The next day, captains bore the severed heads on pikes. The trumpets, our lances mulled their forests in the air, the lines of cavalry, the field a flat where I would soon speak in my destinies to its dust. My challenger rode from the gate. Banners waved in open flutter, their colors all the perfumed that noon. Cheers in streamers through the air. Heralds calling drums to call for trumpets, and there he sat his horse. No lance, but a pistol, a shield, a battle-ax and a sword. His armor painted red, his helmet horned with lightning shafts in gold. On his shield, a simple flame upon a field of black. "And what hell has risen to gain itself this day?" asked Anas Todkill, my always friend and another Englishman of the company who acted as my squire.

What face is armor that its head did nod salutes? We passed in eyeless gaze to take our place. No lances, each with the weapons as was agreed, my pistol in my hand. At the signal, our horses bolted into gallop. The sights down our pistols were our deadly shafts, the joust was done in sparks and ball and the discharge of powder. He fired. Powder cracked in flaming smoke. No one was hurt on either side. Now battle-axes and their piercing spikes held in hand and urged upon the strength of arms to weight their strikes in hammer blows. My armor belled darkness in my head at each jolt and shock upon my helmet and my shield. We each became the anvil to quench the other's sharp and heavy ax, and so by stroke and counterblow we warred ruin in each other's face; until by a mighty blow all passion slipped my mind and I began to faint. My battle-ax fell from my grasp, the earth called to receive my fall. My leg loosened on the saddle. A great cheer came from the city walls, as if it were a fit of breath from a foreign lung. The horses now entwined in dance, the Turk in lethal swing, his ax above his head. But my horse, by dash and turn, laid such dexterity in that broken race, I had the time, my mind to grasp the moment. I drew my sword, my falchion to my hand, its curved blade now warred my resurrection above the clouds of dust. Our horses closed in their twists and counterturns. We rode our hopes. Sword and shield and battle-ax all contested above the hooves that sped the beasts. No advantage had. We struck strategies from our fists, and in a turn of luck, I wedged my sword under the armor of his back, and thrust with many stabs until the blade broke through his chest. He fell from his horse, but regained his feet and stood until he sunk to his knees. This was not a man but a pawn that bled. I enjoyed my victory, I hacked his neck to meat and cut off his head.

Such rewards and fame I had! A guard of six thousand to bear me to my general's tent. Three horses before me, each rider having on the point of his lance a single head. I received a horse with fine apparel, a gold-bejeweled scimitar and a gold and silver belt worth three hundred ducats. Modrusch granted me the rank of major, a rank I would never use again, as I had his words but lacked the written commission to seal my proof.

Single combat is but a pastime to a war. Our cannons mounted on the nearby hills now broke by cannonades in fixed lightning on the city walls. For fifteen days in such stormed avalanche our shot blasted stones to ruins and to dust. Two breaches in the walls. We filled the plains with banners and stormed our trumpet calls in the impending heat. Regiments gathered in their squares and across the fields. In blackening turmoil the cannon smoke held night upon the noon. What relents but nothing in the throb of drums, lances and pikes all swung in their quizzical heads and shafts, pointing in predatory forest toward the slopes upon whose crests were the ruins of the city walls. Our army marched in blackened squares, patched movement across the flats. Muskets tore lines in flash, their murder hidden in the smoke. Ranks fell in rank, hardly speaking a sound to mark their death. The slopes now rushed, stones and logs and bags of powder rained their lethal weight upon our troops trying to make the walls. Such crushed men shattered flat, their armor torn to cavern on their chests. The stones, the debris, the battle soon seemed lost. Modrusch and our three companies were held in reserve. Our time was now. A grand gesture is but a bait to death. And so we marched our conclusions to the fray. Swords and musket fire all confused. Moments all held lethal in the rage. And when is the whisper more the whirlwind than the storm. We turned the moment now to us. So small we were, so large our deeds. The Turks fleeing in panic from the walls now made haste to the castle and their last defense. The city we plundered as we would. Such booty is not often found in such a wreck. The women well discoursed by sword to any pleasure that was sought. But my company was in disgust, held itself aloof.

Zsigmond now arrived to celebrate the victory with a mass and give such honors and rewards as were due his loyal subjects. I had my audience with the king. Our generals all stood as I approached. Zsigmond took me in his arms, granting me a coat-of-arms, three Turkish heads framed in a field of vines. He called me "gentleman," which was a rise in rank, and gave me a portrait of myself in a golden frame and a pension of three hundred ducats a year for life.

Within weeks Zsigmond abdicated for the last time and fled to Vienna. Rudolph II now gained all the lands that were Transylvania. Modrusch joined with Basta, as he was a Catholic, thus less offensive than the Turk. And so we pursued our war, as our war now hunted us.

EACH DAY ITS FLOWER BLOOMED IN BLOOD. THERE CAME REPORTS of Turks and Tartars and Cossacks marching in the east. More lands despoiled. All the east was in revolt. Basta ordered Modrusch to march. Our path was along the cataracts of the river Olt. Through a narrow gorge our marshaled squares and armed companies spread their moving quilt. On each side great slopes, gray rocky crests and boulder falls. Above our heads we saw a likeness of a great battlement, a red anvil of stone among the broken cliffs. Red Tower Pass was a slot between the mountains, and in the rolls of thunder in our steps it was a sluice to our other destiny.

Once through the pass we encamped. Reports of more troubles to the borders further east. Small companies of Tartars were plundering Walachia near its frontier with Moldavia. All this and nothing much confirmed. But war is a youthful sport, as we play the dagger we renounce the costs. Modrusch and our eleven thousand ordered to march and plain that havoc to a pin. Not long we followed the ceaseless pastures east, where roads were few, only tracks of balding earth furrowed by the wheels of heavy carts. Alone we were. The wilderness had become a rolling flat of grass and wheat and hills. There was nothing there but the sky to grave the empty land. News arrived that the Tartars on the borders were not so few, but forty thousand swift horsemen in their hordes. There was no time. Safety was a hundred miles west at Red Tower Pass. Modrusch was in full retreat. Ambushado was in the air. How the world seemed to conspire in its emptiness, and we the spot where all arrows pointed. We forced our legs to abandon pain. No rest, we marched with little food. We found our panic and strength in fear. All the hills were now dressed in the dark cloaks of horsemen in a double gallop. Around us they circled as they gathered to be a lethal wall. The air grew thick with stratagems and yells. Still our squares forced themselves forward. Battles were now confused with our retreat. We made a woods, but there was no sanctuary there. Wars now raged in the hollows of the forest floors. We were surrounded, but still we marched to make the western edge, as lines of mounted

Tartars galloped on the hills and sang praises to their god for our coming slaughter.

That night I met with Modrusch to speak and plan conspiracies against what seemed our coming fate. "If we have fear, let us share it with our foes. Let terror be our blade. Let science be our ghost, its cut is always cleaner than the ax." I made our chance with powder, rags, all turned with brimstone and turpentine, confectioned in the clay cylindrical casts called trunks we used for explosives. Three hundred so prepared, then tied to the heads of lances and given to three hundred of our horsemen at the edge of the wood. The stars glowed as ice in their indifference overhead. Our horses marshaled to courage in their beast. The fuses on our lances lit. Great fusillades of sparks now geysered in the night. Our horsemen cried as a ghostly serpent wails, one voice on many a rush of breath.

The horses charged. The Tartars, all confused in fright, saw the dagger lines of fire now bracing at their hearts. Down the slopes, across the flats our feet raced upon the blackness underfoot. The Tartars were as waves of shadows parted in the dark. The screams of their horror echoed in the hills, and we passed through their lines, not one of our army lost.

Nine miles to Red Tower Pass. Dawn and five miles still to march. Anticipation weighed upon our backs. Impatience tore upon our flesh, our march seemed slower for all its speed.

From the east the sun now cast a withered light. The thirty thousand of the horde rode thunder at our backs.

Black the mantle of the earth as we turned to scream our pebbles at that sea. Our rear guard was soon engaged. At the head of the pass we made our stand, dug our trenches, set cannons in a forest of sharpened stakes. A wall of these hasty lances would be our last defense. Then we stood before the works in our marshaled squares as the Tartars set madness to frenzy in a final storm.

What is this shade that swiftly comes our way? Muskets braced and readied in our hands. In forty thousand falling hooves the shallow gloom overcast the hills and raced in its urgent rush upon our lines, trumpets calling to herald the thunder on the earth. Drums broke their shivered snares and throbbed pleas to our waiting cannons. What pageant is war? What festival brings these armored gargoyles to my door? So polished to reflect, their helmets beaked in iron menace. Lions, hawks and claws veined the sinews sculptured on the arm of war. Why ride horses? On your back are iron wings. On your shoulders an iron hawk. Upon your helmet stands a bloody claw, dripping in an iron blood.

Now our cannons broke their waiting whirlwind into storm. Our salvos grinned the lethal sport. Ranks of Tartars' horses dying as they tumbled in their fall. Tartars were thrown or flung into death. All that was was ripped to blood, armor cut with holes of many musket balls. No death was one, but Tartars died in choirs. Their horses agonied wide-eyed, appalled, screamed to beast their language in their pain.

So much slaughter, but so many more to die. Where died one, a hundred came to fill the gap. "Where is my land that it comes to me to ply its murder at my feet?" cried Modrusch, heated in the violence indifferent to all death, his horse bolting lightning in its hooves.

When armies clash, in that moment of collision there comes a sigh, like a throttled joy. Released, we hold the slaughter beneath our fingertips, and what we do, we do as if by another hand. Our iron stinks with the heat of war, and blood displays no courtesy to its wound. And I, the seeker, sought such depths. Chivalry my plume. I myself my only knight. Age bequeaths to me regrets. I am born of circumstance. My haunt lethal to my mind, the ghost of me who might have been. How many years have I sat and offered feeble memories to my politics?

The Tartars retreated, but forced us to retire behind our tangle of sharpened wooden stakes. Plumes in scars of war upon their helmets, the horsemen gathered for a second charge. Anxious horses bore angry heads, shaking in nervous flourishes. How many thousands now lay upon the earth? All this rubble that once was flesh, had life, and spoke in some whispers for a hope.

What sparks the sound that lightnings in the trumpet call? Is it the howl that begs the air for life? What sport is weighted in its scream? What swarms those flags? Now all in gallop, their displays are raced above the wide stampede. Hooves plunder silence on their thousand falls. The Tartars now rode to trample us beneath their regiments. The breeze now filled to the cataracts of their battle cries. We fixed our eyes down our musket barrels to aim upon the urgent mass. Now line on line so swift they urge their horses blind to sweep us under hoof.

We knelt in our battalions between the phalanxes of our sharpened stakes, a withered forest to impale them on their own attack.

How come you now, to me, to bring upon yourself your death?

Our cannons flashed their salvos wide to break corridors upon them in their wreck. How many in their thousand torn so vacant they became the air, destroyed to blank, a nothing was more a human thing. We retreated a few yards to better reveal the stakes. Now the air cauldroned upon the heat. They so close, the earth descended into a single scream. Stakes impaled horses on their shafts, horsemen were thrown to be impaled as well. Frenzied in their pain, horses bolted, chained to agonies, the stakes plunging in their throats. Necks were ripped to naked blood, stomachs gored, exploded in the thrusts, entrails loosed from bodies fell upon the earth and were trampled under hooves.

The front ranks of the Tartars writhing on the broken stakes. We now raced to murder them in their agonies. The second ranks of the Tartars soon among the stakes. Thrusts poised in counter strokes. Thousands more we battled in the blood. Murder was overwhelmed by death. More and more impaled, but more Tartars rode to have our lines, all of the stakes now blunted with those they crucified. Tartars hung in bloody vines, arms cut, heads defaced, limp, the weight moistened in their torn sacks. Everywhere the world a rage, and still the hawk with the head of man ate its fill of carrion and nested in the slaughter.

So many Tartars dead, so lay the rubble of their attack.

We gathered our voices into fists and cried our victory. But victory is not a gesture or a word. All this war so far was but a faint, a level cup of broth, the taste that comes before the bloody meat. The horde in its thirty thousand now attacked. Our stakes blunted to broken ruins, the world swept us in its hand. The hills pressed its butchery to our face. We formed our closed ranks, squared to meet our slaughter in its teeth. Slowly we marshaled our retreat up Red Tower Pass. The Tartars rode plunder upon the earth. The earth torn to gallop on the salvoes of their hooves.

Chapter Nine

FATE EVER IN ITS FALSE ESCAPES. LOVE AND SLAVERY.
THE RUSSIAN STEPPES. A WESTWARD TREK.
ADVENTURE AS THE COMPASS GHOSTLY GLIDES.

OW SOON the whirlwind tears itself to dark. Each cry its lamp, the beam to guide the wings of what eternal night. My own blood has made me wet. I swim on a hard mud. My agony is my lullaby. I am bedded in a mangle of the dead. The lifeless fingers of my enemy imprison me. I am sick with new wounds. Modrusch has gone, escaped with eleven hundred. I am a Protestant crucified to the Catholic plan. That trap, I feel its teeth upon my side. Basta sent us to find our death, and so we are a strange success. I laugh, but cannot gain my knees. Shadows etch their columns in the dark. They move as wingless birds, their claws honed as knives. Torches with flames, clear as jewels, a crystal fire iced only to illuminate itself, wander among the screams. Somewhere a throat is cut, a cry drowns in its own blood. Pillagers who plunder from the dead now walk the battlefield. Above me they stand as faceless hawks, their heads robed in shadows. I am now the plunder to be despoiled for a coin. The knife upon my throat, my armor glows in the firelight with my own blood. I hear words that barter fates I do not understand. I am not to die. I am lifted to my feet and borne away.

It was my fine armor. I was thought to be a noble, worth more as a ransom than as a corpse. Such is the husk, the illusion that would be the man. My captors tend me in my chains. Tobacco is placed upon my wounds. Even the Turks now have the herb. I had come my ambition round, and now ate of my circumstances in loaves of dust. I am ransomed by an accident to what fate? For a month we travel south, behind my wagon file the chained survivors of our army. The wagon smells of the dead, the wooden planks all rot. Around the campfires in the night the captive women are all passed to serve. Most have forgotten how to cry. Such is the academy of the Moslem Turk.

When I am healed, I am chained and marched with all the gathered wreck of what once we were. We shuffle now in derelict, an army burdened, its ranks lost to memory. The Turk would have us become the beast on which to litter his own heathen scraps. Everywhere the Moslems' eyes do wait. It is said we are to be sold into slavery in a market town.

What grins there were. I stood the block. My flesh had become the bag on which rested the coins. My wounds were displayed, considered to assay my worth. I wrestled with another slave to show my strength. I would have killed him if I could. Anger was now the humiliation to bind my hate. Men smoked as they judged me, as they would a beast, tobacco crawled its breath around the open air. I was bought by a Turk named Bashaw Bogall, a small man of nervous fat, a man who almost choked as he paid his silver coins. He was sending me as a present to his mistress and his love, but I was not born to be sold to chains.

Walking with me in my shadows, Bogall sent a message ahead saying to his lady that I was a Bohemian noble he had taken in a fierce battle, and that I was now hers to do with as she wished. So men often purchase with their coins, lives they in fiction do display.

I was chained by the neck to be chained in a square, twenty by twenty men forced to march imprisoned in this patch across five hundred miles to the great city of Constantinople. Where men squatted in the empires of their robes, their tobacco smoked in great water pipes. The herb now grown in the gardens of the East, almost replacing hemp among the Turks, even in great Constantinople itself. There we were delivered to our masters, I to the fragrance of the young Charatza. How soft her touch, so tender it seemed to gather all its sense in warm reports from beneath my flesh. First I saw her white in the mirrors of her silks, eyes that called their mysteries into mine. Glance my love with silence upon my glance and I am drawn to the wisdoms in a sigh. So pearled her smooth skin. So curious she was. She spoke a little Italian. She was a Greek not yet of age, fifteen perhaps. I spoke my history in her caress. Charatza asked her friend who spoke a little English, or French, or Dutch, to hear my tale, so she could compare my story to itself in its many tellings. "I am an Englishman, wounded in battle and sold as slave. I am an adventure that has come ill turned," I said. Charatza, in her compassion, pitied me. I the tide to be swept upon what flood?

We, in our secret ministries, did speak of love. I thought of marriage.

From all slaveries I would be unchained, only to be joyously a slave again. The house seemed a wall of whispers now. What fear was this that wounded us? Charatza now fearful that her mother soon would become suspicious and sell me to some brutal master, conspiracies are always the passion of a plan. Charatza telling her mother that she had no need of a slave. I was to be sent to her brother to learn to be a Turk, and come to be as he, a governor of a military district or fief they call a timar. My future not set against my past. I carried a letter from Charatza to her brother, informing him of our purpose. With love the hope upon the signet, perhaps I would return one day to claim my only as my own.

I NOW TRAVELED UNGUARDED NORTHEAST THROUGH BULGARIA FROM Varna, sailing on the Black Sea, into the Sea of Azov, up the River Don, past two towns, their stones the color of dry bones. For six days we sailed, passing under the cannons of five castles. I was well treated. On the seventh day, we disembarked, then traveled overland for two days, arriving at the castle of Charatza's brother. That castle was more a fist placed as warning upon the land. Tymor Bashaw received me in his court, taking his sister's letter from my hand. Then he read it. Grim his flesh turned in its rage, his understandings too much, his disposition robed now in cruelty. I was seized, stripped to naked skin, beaten, my hair all shaved off, given wool as clothes and a thong of leather as a belt. Around my neck an iron corset was riveted. Then I was chained and given to slaves to be their slave. Humiliations were inflicted to wreck me in my soul. "Mine is not the couch to rest your foul," said Tymor, raging his tortures upon me. Beatings, food that starved us in its filth, entrails of horses or of sheep, boiled in a gruel of spoilt grain, this we ate; while in the table of the Turkish court, Tymor Bashaw ate chickpeas, pilau of rice, beef or mutton or horsemeat kabobs, and lounged, drinking coffee with his meals, smoking tobacco from a water pipe.

I was the lowest of the low. In the pens a hundred galley slaves lived as beasts. Other Moors, other Turks and Christians, captives we the refuse who still had worth. Charatza, such comes of love in a court of fiends. In the night, we whispered of escape. The oldest slaves knew we were surrounded by the endless steppes, beyond which the Tartars rode in their hordes, eating tears of horsemeat they carried half cooked underneath their saddles. The heat of the racing animal is the stove that brought the boil to their feast.

The time for harvest now approached. I was sent to a great field a league from Tymor's castle. There, with a wooden bat, I worked threshing and beating the grain from its husk. Tymor found me one day alone in a barn, he in the rage of some lunacies, in his anger all enthralled, he set his glance to me in his fists, kicking me and beating me. He seized with a fury that fed upon itself. Fearing I would lose my senses and my life, I protected myself the best I could. But I am not a wealth of stone. In a rage countered to his rage, I broke my wooden bat upon his head. Lost in the wilds of those lethal strokes, I the mechanism that had jumped the confines of its spring, and in repeated hammerfalls the bat cracked blood from his skull. My anger not spent even in his death, I flailed the corpse, as if to extinguish in exhaustion for all my life any memory of him. What is the price of what we forget?

I killed the brother of my love. I exiled my love with hate and so for the ever of my life I sought to fill that hollow with an emptiness that has a weight. But what we do betray, its surrogate is always chambered by the disease. I should have tongued the pain and found her again in the softness of her flesh, for thought cannot free us, following it alone always brings a rudeness to reason, wherein all wisdom is undone.

Fear now the callous shadow at my back, I dragged the corpse to a solitary corner of the barn and stripped him of the garments that had some use. Clothed in his clothes, I exchanged our estates. I hid the body under a pile of straw, stuffed a knapsack with corn to be my food and closed the barn door to have its secret, and now I had my chance of escape. Outside, I mounted Tymor's horse, put urgent spurs upon its flanks and galloped at clipped thunder across the steppes.

For three days my adventure was but an aimless wander. Alone, no direction called me home, I was lost. My map was an imagined guess. If I was captured by the Turks, they would know by the iron collar about my neck that I was an escaped slave, or, if they had heard the news, Tymor's murderer. I knew there would be gruesome punishments.

On the third day, I found a dusty track, no more than a scrape following to the horizon's edge. I rode upon its graying blush to markers where the road divided. Three signs were etched on a stone plate: a sun for China, a crescent for the lands of the Turk and a cross for Christian lands, whether Poland or Muscovy I could not know. I took that sign as home and rode that track for sixteen days until I came to a wooden fort all palisaded in huge logs, a Muscovite outpost, its name I never knew. Years later I tried to find it on many maps, but my salvation was, and ever will be, a nameless place of memory.

Through its gates I rode, almost collapsing into the governor's arms. I was fed and told my tale. Those lands were always under siege. The Turk was ever on the frontier. But for chance and the scald of luck, any one of them could be as me. Such is the precarious string that binds us to our happiness. All this they knew, and so I was given aid and courtesy, my needs supplied. After the iron collar and chain were struck from my neck, we smoked a pipe to salute our sympathies to each other's fate. Tobacco now traded on the steppes, carried by caravans from the West. I breathed my lips upon the pipe, the fumes through my throat again, remembering within that taste there rides in warmth a plaintive appetite. The governor's wife nursed me back to health. She was not beautiful, but kindness has its own radiant face. Her real name I never knew, or perhaps I am a forgetful knight of an inconstant soul.

I joined a caravan on its trek north toward Moscow. The governor put in my hand letters of protection and his own separate document testifying as how I did come to him in chains.

At Dankov, I rode toward Poland and the west. Everywhere I was well treated. How my horse's hooves now sang in their impatient joy at the thought of our homeward race. Yet human happiness is but a passing mist, for all the noons of all the world are chanced with calamity. Within months of my departure from the steppes, those who aided me found themselves consumed in a violent war. Such disasters to the good, I never knew of their fate. Oh, their memory comes to me in the faces of their loss. Maybe not knowing is a cure. But I was made wild in all my doubts. Did Charatza plan to have her brother treat me with such cruelty? I cannot see the cause. Was it but a Turkish trick to see my worth? An adoption through a second pain of birth, a passage to buy a better circumstance. And did she know I was the one who brought him death? How fell those imagined tears upon her cheeks, and what passions were there in her thoughts for me? I had seen enough of grief. Why must all ambition be paid in blood? I swore all my name would come in sovereigns of another coin.

· · · · ·

I TRAVELED SOUTH AVOIDING POLAND AND SILESIA, WHERE THERE was then a general murder of all Protestants. Now I came north again. I rode toward Prague, hoping to find Zsigmond and have my promised three-hundred-ducat stipend and a written commission to prove I was now a major with the right to bear three Turks' heads as heralds upon my shield.

In Prague I heard that Modrusch and Zsigmond were in Leipzig. I found Modrusch without much delay. He was pleased that I had survived. I told the horrors of my tale. He said only one other Englishman had escaped the massacre, Anas Todkill, my friend and sometimes squire, and he had since returned to England. "We are the few who are the memories of that place," said Modrusch. I asked him about my commission and of Zsigmond's promise of a stipend. Modrusch smiled and said, "Even kings are only as great as their loyalties." Then he took his leave.

Two days later I was brought before Zsigmond, who rose from his bejeweled chair upon seeing me and placed his arms on my shoulder. "I have heard how you have suffered in my cause," he said. "I have written your commission as you have wished and here is a small purse of coins to redress your losses." The commission finely penned in Latin called me "gentleman," and confirmed me as a captain of two hundred fifty horsed cavalry, authorizing my shield to bear three Turkish heads, relieving me of further service and asking that all lords of all the lands through which I might travel grant me aid and protection. The purse, which was in truth a small chest, contained fifteen hundred gold ducats worth six hundred pounds. In that one gesture I became both a captain and quite rich, tenfold my father's worth.

"Madness is only half a lunacy. Zsigmond is more loyal to me than to all his estates," I thought. Joy by joy, my pleasure then unbounded. Zsigmond nodded to Modrusch with a smile. "Do all kings take such pleasure in their grants?" I wondered. It was justice and my due. "Zsigmond has his own code: fidelity to those who serve," said Modrusch as we walked from the chamber.

Modrusch and I made our pledges of farewell. He to his, I to have a tour of a few fair cities thereabout. I had a purse and time. My ambition was no longer sought in war. I wandered down the Elbe to Wittenberg, where began the Reformation. I walked upon the cobbled streets of its university. "How much to know, and all this learning is but the toys of gentlemen," so I thought. My joy diminished before my own eyes, my hand still the hand of a lesser king.

From Wittenberg, I traveled south to Ulm, then to Augsburg and finally to Munich. Everywhere men smoked, claiming they had learned the use of tobacco from the English pipes of English travelers. Students and burghers sitting in the taverns and the inns intoxicated with the herb, smoking over their steins of beer. From Munich, north again to Frankfurt, where I wandered through the stalls of its great book fair, observing printers displaying libraries in their wares. A world circumscribed by the cut of words. What minds caught bright to illuminate in ink, such black upon the white upon the sculpture of a page. And so do we all sleep in words that our memory is a voice. A book not yet a river in my blood, but one day I swore I would confess myself to pain and be that quill to the heralds of my ink. From Frankfurt, I traveled to Mainz, where Gutenberg had, one hundred and fifty years before, molded letters into lead type, waxed all their faces well in a darkened flush, held them tight in gathered words and pressed them to a page, and so was the first to print a book.

By ship I sailed south upon the Rhine. The river flowing in the channels between the cliffs. Only was the water smooth, its abyss running beneath the overhangs of rock. I came by ship visiting Speyer and then south again and west by horse to Strasbourg and the Lorraine. In France again after three years, I heard of the death of Elizabeth two years before, in 1602. Do all our lives come to this, a spot of gossip on a Paris street? Now those thoroughfares all conversed with whispers of a peace between England and Spain. Secret negotiations were then at hand.

I traveled west to Nântes on the coast of Brittany. And with peace rumored as a hope, I sailed the storms across the Bay of Biscay to Bilbao to see the feudal sights of a violent Spain. There the land was but a turmoil underfoot. The Inquisition still had its stakes and fires. A country had torn out its heart to cleanse its soul. Nothing thought that was not already known. Superstition was their science, dust the marble of their Parthenon. With negotiations in Paris, the Spanish government did not want to give the English crown a cause, and so with Catholic Zsigmond's pass, I felt quite safe, and so wandered at some leisure east and west, but always south. A heretic may have a pleasant pilgrimage, even when under threat. I saw the Escorial and admired a few monasteries. But I knew, as Drake had known, peace with them was but a feint of war. No peace could come until either we or they would be the ruin of the other.

At Gibraltar, its docks piled with tobacco from the Americas, its bales carried from the ships by Indian slaves—the polite miseries of the secret crimes of Spain. Columbus in his first return from the New World brought tobacco, gold and ten savages to be sold as slaves. And so the deadly trinity was linked in chains of future histories: tobacco, gold and slaves. In Gibraltar I gained a ship and sailed for Tangier to witness the robes of those exotic streets. But Tangier was but a hollow seeded by a legend long since past. Low buildings, white their shadows on the white, their walls all bleached to the stones of sameness in the heat. Then to Safi, the greatest port in all Morocco, and changed ships, finding a French captain named Merham, who invited three others and myself to try our luck at sea. A lesser corsair is but a lesser Drake. Why not an adventure against the Spanish fleet? That night a chance storm gave us the excuse to slip our cable and spoon before the contentious winds, westward three hundred miles out to sea. Sailing among the Canary Islands, I learned of that place where not three years hence I would be imprisoned by Edward Maria Wingfield for advising caution. But that was 1607. In 1604, Captain Merham and our crew still hoped that good luck might birth from accidents, and we might find a treasure lurking on the horizon under a hint of sail.

Soon we captured a bark loaded with fine wine, then learned five Spanish men-of-war were in those waters. Merham being now in fear, we sailed east hoping to make Safi again. But this time chance was not our luck. Two Spanish ships, fast upon our wake, overtaking us. We pretended parley, hauled down our topsails. They danced their sails, as if to come aboard. Too close, Merham was almost caught by his own trap. We sprang full our sails, held close the wind and tried our escape, but we had not the speed. The Spanish ships were overtaking us. The war now set. The battle joined in darkness. Boarders swung on ropes through the forests of our masts. Our muskets lancing lightning through the gloom. By the morning twenty-seven of our crew were dead, a hundred on the Spanish ships, we guessed. We were leaking and on fire. We saved the ship, limped to port, a hundred forty-eight cannonball holes in our sides.

I was exhausted from adventure and longed for the comfort of familiar things. I had my rank and some wealth. I had done what could be done, kissed luck upon the cheek. Now being my own

Drake, I made for Lincolnshire and home. Twenty-four years and half my life was spent, and what the gain? Six hundred pounds. My slaveries, my histories not yet a book, and where from here did my life have tracks? Uncertain the whirlwind on its uncertain tack.

Chapter Ten

THE GREAT AWAKENING. LONDON AND ITS SHAKESPEARE. THE NEW WORLD BECKONS THE ENGLISH NATION.

EMORIES IN THEIR IMPASSIONED SLEEP haunt our wakefulness. All this by counterpoint, by their affinities they are linked, and we are but possessions of the past. How different was my return to England in December of 1604. Anonymous was the charter of my life. So much done, so much gained for so little fame. No cheers, no waiting expectations. Ambition's ever growing hunger was my legacy and pain. But I had a purse and London lured me with its prospects and its pleasures. Why not play my rank a time and see the city as a gentleman? I took some rooms and walked the thoroughfares. How damp the dirty chimney smoke. Carriages crawled their way in filth, crowded streets, the food was mostly spoiled. Sometimes garbage smelled sweeter than my meat. Rot is not a spice. Everywhere there was disease and death. Skin on the faces of the poor ulcerated and peeled and sickened into boils and wounds. The gentry used powder to cake their blemishes into a false health. London made its fashions to hide its plagues. Whigs and powder and silk bespoke a desperate remedy and tobacco was every-where and still the cure. It was a vice no alchemy could support.

A few physicians questioned the overuse of the herb. In 1602 a pamphlet published, *A Work for Chimney-Sweepers*, the first to attack tobacco, claiming it caused sooty brains, sterility, damaged the lungs. But the prop was smoke and London smoked, some gallants carrying silver porringers in which to hold the saliva they spit during the day's smoking of the leaf, the correct weight a measure of the smoker's art. What world is this that men weigh their defecations as if it were gold?

Tobacco now sold in special shops called tobacconists. I ventured into one, the leaves in jars on shelves, leaves hanging from the ceiling like dragon wings; the tobacconist at his table, tearing pages from a book. A pile of rough torn pages next to a pile of unread tomes, each volume awaiting the hands of its executioner. The tobacconists buying unsalable tracts, using the pages as tapers to light their customers' pipes, or to wrap the tobacco, which was dried over candles. What cure is this that murders books? And I, who had sworn one day to write my history, would all my immortality pass away as smoke? What fiend this pleasure? Even I had questions of the leaf. Everywhere in learned circles physicians debated the value of the herb. Books battled in the stalls to be the first to sell their opinions. The tobacco wars were now fought on pages, their landscapes drawn in ink.

Even the theatres were no sanctuaries. Dandies and gallants and their girls taking their pleasures in the better seats, forced the monitors to allow their chairs on the stage and there to smoke. All truth to vanity is cruel. Ben Jonson at the Globe made his own satiric war upon the smoky recreations of the fops and their professors of the artful pipe in his play *Every Man in his Humour*. I myself saw it performed. I sat in my balcony, no groundling I. William Shakespeare himself was in the play that night, the greatest of the great fretting in the scenes of a lesser great. And Shakespeare born of language, enthralled of visions. God dwells magic in his metaphors.

All imagination needs a stage, some plot to dance on canvas the gestures of its dreams. All our theatres open to the sky, rounded in their walls, these citadels. All things of man are edifices. On three sides of the stage, flung wide in circling arcs, galleries rose tier upon tier above the waiting stage, blanked but for shadows, where soon men would act war, their ambitions waged on other men, their echoes playing commerce with the street. Below the stage groundlings walked in their grotesque conversations, amused, bought wine and oranges; pickpockets working strategies to gain an unsuspecting purse; women of the street playing infatuations with country squires. And in the galleries, diversions in their portly privilege dusted with extra coin. And so do men affirm their pleasures as they pretend to live.

The play now begun. The audience with some efforts quieted. Occasionally, some shriek or argument, some conversation over said intruding into a scene, as actors unfolded Jonson's comedy. Slowly does the drama take its urgent hold and we are fisted blindly along its flight. On stage, two profane city sophisticates discuss the claims of tobacconists, comparing their specialties and their exotic arts. "This Cavalier Shift has the pretense by nose to instruct at such affordable rates to all gentlemen of newly inherited wealth the most novel pleasures of the leaf." Carlo Buffone stood pontificating to the gestures of his wrists as he spoke. "And we are supposed to inhale our tobacco smoke at lunch, chased with four glasses of canary wine, then travel hard by carriage to Uxbridge and there, only at our own discretion, exhale said smoke." With great concentration Carlo Buffone held back his laugh. "Such pleasure could last a week, me thinks, if we could but breathe through our ears."

As he watched a gallant, his snout in the air, pipe in hand, Cavalier Swift with an iron rod stretched his nostrils to allow the easier flow of smoke. "Pleasant fools make such sweet disaster. I swear he could teach a dog to smoke and bark and fair cook a pie, if its reward was a pipe." Buffone played by Shakespeare, his subtle deeds, his depths speaking in humanities through Jonson's lines. Vision is the soul that sculpts rough genius into majesties. The play progresses to the pursuit of love, tobacco now the lover's leaf. The weed all perfumes her gown, her ruby lips blushed savage. What man would want such a woman so seduced by fashion?

In the end all women won, all villains staked on their proper punishments, all vanities overthrown. Only the weed survives, not quite undone. But all this was a counter-vice. Jonson was well addicted to his pipe, the play written to gain some favor at court. King James hating the weed, physically repelled by its odor. He called it "the stench." Never convinced it was a cure, he saw the contradictions in all the competing claims, and was first of monarchs to rant against the leaf. "How can this tobacco aid the agitated man to sleep, yet at the same moment refreshen the brain and awaken our understandings, heal the gout, as it soothes our melancholy? Its vapors to the lungs, yet the skin is healed. Its ointments to our skin, yet the stomach refines its digestion, quickens as it slows. How can this leaf in its many remedies so work against itself? It can't. This is the herb of ruin; a sin, a lust that intrigues our wisdom in the passion of a dry drunk. It is the leaf of savages, those slaves of Spain. This is a foreign novelty. This plant bears a devil's fruit in its smoky apple. So much of our nation's wealth squandered on the leaf, some gentry paying 400 pounds a year on their appetite."

Not days after my visit to the Globe, a pamphlet entitled *A Counterblaste to Tobacco* was published, anonymously in London. It was an open secret at court the king himself had penned the tract. Throughout Europe and even to the East, monarchs taking license from our king's example, sought to ban the leaf. In Turkey, the punishment for smoking was soon to be death by beheading. In other states hanging, the pipe thrust through the tobacconist's nose. In others, the nose and ear cut off. In the name of war against the leaf, monarchs made war against their own.

Only in England, blessed England, where morals rise just enough to kiss the stitchings of the purse, we practical our sins to a more human world, and so our blessings bless us with a wink. King James now sought to prevent the trade by raising the tax on tobacco from two pence a pound to 6 shillings 10 pence, an increase of four thousand percent. "If the trade is not ended, at least the crown will be rich," was the argument at court. The tax increased without consent of Parliament, which angered the commons and the lords. The king publishing his decree, written in such slanders as it pandered a soothing nod upon the better sort, "It is a corrupting drug on which the rowdy squander their few coins, wasting their labors in a disregard of their children's welfare. Our gentlemen, being more temperate by nature, use the herb only moderately as a physic to preserve their health." The streets where gentlemen walk their vanities in wanton smoke satirized the king's own words. So does a king compromise his throne by speaking words no one believes. Sixteen thousand pounds of tobacco imported into England that year; perhaps an equal weight smuggled from Holland or Flanders to avoid the tax. Tobacco more popular than before. The king's blast coming as a puff. Now governors ordered the few tobacco farms in England suppressed, which caused a small rebellion, that riot quelled with compromise. Those farmers always impoverished from the poor quality of their leaf.

The king in his rage now took the thing he hated to himself and made the tobacco trade a royal monopoly. Only those who held a royal patent, bought from the king himself, could import or sell the leaf. His world was the leaf, his court was smoke. James believed tobacco was first introduced into England in 1584 when two captains, sent by Sir Walter Raleigh to explore the east coast of America from Spanish Florida to Virginia, returned to London with two savages and their pipes and a small store of the leaf. The captains, Philip Amadas and Arthur Barlowe, Raleigh ordered to find a pleasing location to found a colony, which they did. That place becoming known as Roanoke, its colony lost since 1586. The king hating Raleigh, jealous of his talents, fearing his intrigues and that his imagination might rouse the country into a new war with Spain. The king raised in the Scottish court by Sir Walter's enemies, all things Raleigh did he despise. But there were a few who knew the truth that Raleigh was not the father to the leaf. And so do our histories ever come dressed in the cloak of gossip and its rumors.

AFTER SOME WEEKS, I LEARNED LORD WILLOUGHBY'S SONS HAD returned from Europe and were then in London and so with anticipation I called upon those whom I had not seen in four years. Robert and Peregrine received me in their loyalty. Robert was to be married soon, and that week made by the king a knight of the Bath. He was to leave in March on an embassy to oversee the signing of the peace treaty between England and Spain. Uneasy drinks the ink into that uneasy page. For half the world was bound as Spanish slaves, and still the king would have his foolish peace.

With them was a young man of long face and eyes heavy with imagined tears, a sorrow in expression hiding the deeper sorrow within.

"John Smith, George Sandys." Peregrine waved his hands as if blessing the introduction. We bowed our courtesies. Sandys, consumed by thought, moved upon a muffled flourish. There was something of a wounded child in his pout.

"Oh, come now!" Peregrine mocked clever, intoxicated by his own good feelings. "Our friend Sandys is overcoming a marriage. It was a fair purpose that angeled discontents."

"None of it my purpose, none my pleasure, marketed for a pasture." Sandys words little humored by Peregrine's sweet barbs.

"Several good tracts and farms, many a field for sports and wifely courtesies. She was a pretty beast, I am told, perhaps a bit forward in her country flavors, and definitely not to the taste of an Oxford scholar, but still we can't all be judged by the depth of our manners." Peregrine stared into the air, savoring his own smile.

"I was contracted; my line in birth ruled over better wisdom," venomed Sandys. "I was sold for the income of hay and oats."

"And she as well. Both of your affections spent as coin, a bribe against tomorrow," Peregrine replied. George Sandys was the last of seven sons of the Archbishop of York, and would perforce inherit little, most of those lands bequeathed to his eldest brother. The archbishop contracted with a wealthy Yorkshire landowner, John Norton, for the hand of his youngest daughter, Elizabeth. She with her landed dowries for his youngest son and he with some small adjoining lands for her, mutuals by contract if they both approved. With little in prospect, little was their choice. Elizabeth becoming the archbishop's ward. George to finish his studies at Oxford, then the Middle Temple and the law. John Norton, being a Catholic and under continuous suspicion, his family having sided against the queen in the Catholic revolt, was pleased.

But presume no success when parent plays more parent than is wise. Elizabeth cast a meanness from a frugal purse, Sandys more indulged to sweet a constant pleasure for a harmless rate. Too different in their ways, it was a match that flinted sparks and fires. The marriage only married them to a farce.

"I was manacled to dirt. My bondage in chains of blood." George Sandys' words now his in violence. Such anger is the heat that icy boils thoughts to frigid continents.

"It was a father's loving error," said Peregrine, flipping humor at the nose of Sandys' rage.

"My father's presumptions sold me as goods, no better than a slave. My brother Edwin to have the inheritance, no encumbrance there to skirt his contents.

"Your father sold you to be a master of prospects, and she in her beauty, her arms, fair prisons, wherein their warmth, hunger cannibals on its own delights." Sandys little pleased or moved to smile. As always, Peregrine amused. "Smith here," he said, "his father sold him to a chair, shaded by a scowl, to be the lord of paper and guardian of sums."

"I was far worse than chained. In the east, I was sold as slave to the Turks, yet I escaped." All in surprise, all eyes to me and Sandys, his interest wetted on his stare.

I told of my adventures, my wars and my slaveries and my newfound wealth. With all I told, I told of discontents. "Where from here do my tracks portent?"

"Fair conclusions do not come by war," said Peregrine, "but still you have a rank and a better purse and have proved yourself against all circumstance. What more would you will?"

George Sandys arose as he spoke. "You have taken your freedoms to yourself. Adventured in distant lands. Would I have had such pulse to forfeit all ties, slant all to me, myself, my only, and quaint my English will against foreign prospects? You are courage, Smith, and I am thought. And yet I may still be some shadow to the man."

"And I in that odyssey, what have my battles, my adventures proved?" I said.

"The world is a goat. It browses among the scrapes. You and I, Smith, should live the proof that proves by exceptions. Why not some fame for you, and some orphan liberties for me? Why not unbirth ourselves, take the umbilical in our teeth, gnaw by freedoms through our own flesh? I would be you, Smith. You and I, our equal prospects always less. My brother profiles to a different twin. They had all the lands. None for me, I of the lesser kin. My prospects swindled to a shrew."

"Now Sandys, it may not please your rage, but you are a scholar, a lawyer soon, an author of some pleasant verse," said Peregrine. "Your future is not all that mean, and there is your brother Edwin, unless you aspire to be a brother only to yourself, a genealogy to a dot."

Sandys quieted for a moment. "Any kin, Smith?"

"None," I answered. "Unlike you, I was betrothed to air. My shrew was circumstance, hollow was my birth. My strides in pigmy boots. What cause is mine? Where are my expeditions that I might array my shields? I am the turmoil. All kingdoms are not suffice. I am larger than the air. I have seen the continents. I seek new worlds."

"As for me, I am staled with life, I need reflections. Perhaps travel is the drug. Smith, would you recommend the alchemies of your eastern brew?"

"I have seen the east. What Jerusalems there are may be for you," I said.

Robert Willoughby smiled as he stared at me. "While you adventured east, there were adventures to the west. There all directions join. That is where great service and great enterprise can be had." I was then told of such events and such histories as I never did suspect. In 1602 Bartholomew Gosnold, a cousin to the Willoughbys, had sailed a small bark from Falmouth harbor heading west toward America with thirty-two aboard her. That bark plied the waters north along that foreign coast, exploring a great cape Gosnold named Cape Cod. There he found those lands in such a bloom of forests, a sea so ripe in fisheries that abundance was not the word to fill the truth of all its plenty. Gosnold had returned home to pledge himself to found an English colony in the New World.

"I will eclipse Raleigh's failing star and found a better Roanoke," said Gosnold. And so we would dream ourselves a second life and be Drake's vision and free the world. We to commerce now for allies among the chained and in the New World build an English Eden for the freed. The next year Gosnold's second in command, Bartholomew Gilbert, sailed as prelude to Virginia to seek Raleigh's lost colony, finding nothing, only to be killed by savages in some dispute.

All England was then alive with thoughts of Virginia. Peregrine told his tale, and I knew then that place would be my second birth. What songs we sing sing only of ourselves.

DRAKE HAD SAILED TO ROANOKE IN 1586, THE YEAR WE MET. THE world spins its clues by circles. My line now drawn. By hint my path is marked. Some fathers can be the exhaustion of the child, but I shall be the better son and claim an adopted destiny. I will be the completion of Drake's great plan.

George Sandys pursed in thought, his silence now to words. "My brother, Sir Edwin, has long desired a Virginia enterprise, an English colony in the New World. You could be some forward to that plan. I shall give you letters of introduction. Make his acquaintance and that of Thomas Smythe, our Willoughbys' cousin, who, with others, holds Raleigh's Virginia grants."

"Good ho!" said Peregrine. "And letters from us as well, but speak first to Gosnold. Therein is the tread, plead to the blood. All coincidence here is but a family. Gosnold's mother-in-law is stepsister to Smythe's own mother. And so we are a kettle of the same stew."

I looked to Sandys as I asked "Why not a journey to the west and join our Virginia plans?"

"That direction I now bequeath to you. It is my gift. I to the east, when my circumstance allows....I am familied enough."

With letters of introduction, I sought out Bartholomew Gosnold. "We are all some shadows of a lesser Drake," Gosnold said upon our first meeting. "He is always the frontlet before my eyes. That vision he lived in Panama may yet be our salvation." How much Gosnold was the silver to a better gold. So much like Drake, and yet so different. The explorer had become the colonist. The inherited dream, the equal, on the balance slide. Does all we inherit come from decay? In 1599 Gosnold abandoned his destiny in the clergy and sailed instead as a privateer in the West Indies to fight the Spanish. Such is the sweet heresy that history sings. His family was disappointed, but his fortune was made. Gosnold spread a map before me on a table. "North are the French in Canada. South, the Spanish. Between is Virginia, a cut along a fifteen-hundred-mile coast from French Arcadia to Florida. Peace will bring a teacup war. All will be in strategies. Here will be our Eden and our second England."

I looked upon the map. I saw my face, my profile on the land. My life in sketch in lines of colored ink. I pledged my six-hundred pounds, my every wealth. Some pledging fortunes more, others less. My brain gone beast in all this hope, my joys unbounded. What more famous adventure could there be? Gosnold told me of the riches of the north coast near Canada, and of Roanoke. Raleigh's patent on the Virginia land had been sold to a group including that Willoughby relative, Thomas Smythe, who was then in Muscovy on a matter of trade, but would be returning soon. Smythe was then the greatest merchant in all England, and we had hope of his influence with the king. Another Willoughby relative, Master Edward Maria Wingfield, was interested in the enterprise and made his pledge of support and of money. And so from three, such great things were earthed. I would be my own fame, create myself in Drake. I sought out those who had served me in the east, finding Anas Todkill and some of the surviving few, hiring others with my meager wealth, all those coins gained from Zsigmond. But many of those who pledged deserted before we had our final company.

Edward Maria Wingfield was not a happy circumstance. When first we met, he gauged my estate and weighed my worth on the titles which I had, which were but one: captain. My words hung as if unheard before his ears. He seemed to stare through me when he looked my way. So high was he in his own regard, he never saw the earth, or acknowledged the ground that tripped his every step.

Thomas Smythe returned from Muscovy in the spring of 1605 and persuaded some of his great merchants to invest in the enterprise. George Sandys gave some wealth, and his brother, Edwin. But the king would not grant a charter, fearing perhaps another war with Spain. So we sat curtailed, pillowed in the luxury of our dream; but many a salvation comes by indirection to lay its chance at our feet. In the summer of 1605, Captain George Waymouth returned to England from Virginia with five native Indians he had kidnapped along that coast. Two were sent by carriage to London to be interviewed by the lord chief justice of England, Sir John Popham, regarding the legalities of their presence in England. The law was still the law, and savages or not, kidnapping was still a crime. England was not Spain, where Indians could be legally stolen from their lands and sold as slaves.

All proclaimed in his pompous ceremonies, Lord Chief Justice Sir John Popham sat, scarlet cloth robed his flesh, ponderous he moved, so slow in the mountains of his fat. His mind by trickle came to thought, a sigh, a whim, a grant, and soon the savages walked through the presumptions of the room and stood, their faces painted red, half-naked in their buckskins, moccasins upon their feet. Costumes of strange artifice, each a hint of a multitude of worlds the lord chief justice could scarcely know. John Popham stared at the savages, reminded of a plan by gentlemen merchants and the like to settle Virginia, letters he had seen and requests and an enterprise in formulation, needing his influence with the king. "I am affectionately bent toward the plantation of Virginia," he announced. "I foresee a land where our idle vagabonds, our poor artisans, our population without work, and with little prospects of such, our cashiered captains and soldiers may find a useful employment and adventure...without threat to the state, our law or the king." As for the Indians, it was ordered that they be returned to their lands as a sign of peace, as soon as an education and other benefits could be given them.

John Popham, portly in his kindness, slow in the snail of his reason, but with power to have our enterprise happen, now ventured to be our angel. Thomas Smythe and Edwin Sandys and their merchants persuaded the lord chief justice to a better wisdom. The Virginia Plantation was no longer to be a poorhouse for our derelicts and surplus soldiers, but a joint stock company with shares and investors, and a chance in some distant future to have a profit. This was not an enterprise that sought gold, but rather to farm and trade. We were to be emissaries of a nation seeking allies and to show the whole world our moral worth.

On April the tenth, 1606, the king put his signature to the charter of incorporation, the Virginia Company now had the words to have its birth, we began our final preparations. Thomas Smythe's Muscovy Company was then the financial backer of the voyage to discover the northwest passage to China by way of the North Pole. The captain of that ship was to be a well-respected mariner and mapmaker, Henry Hudson. Through Smythe, I was given letters of introduction to him. Hudson received me grudgingly, and as Smythe requested, gave me instructions in mapmaking and surveying. Hudson was not an easy man, having some of that brutality that comes of strength gone havoc without a soul. His respect was ever hostile, even knowing of my exploits against the Turks, but it was respect. "I am to survey and map the Chesapeake Bay," I said, pushing my worth against his face, "and to draw conclusions of it being the eastern entrance of the northwest passage. I shall inform both Smythe and yourself of this or any waterway which may be so." Hudson saw my use and set his angers to a leash.

I met many worthies in those few months. Richard Hakluyt, the great geographer and chronicler of English voyages and explorations, said to me, "We are a destiny that has not yet recognized itself. We are manifest in the tales that should be ever told. My pen is the tongue for those voices that would have a book." Hakluyt, not always dreaming his dreams in ink, indebted himself to help Smythe purchase Raleigh's Virginia patents, even to writing later some of the government instructions to the Jamestown colonists. Through Hakluyt I met Thomas Hariot, that learned mathematician who served Raleigh, and who lived in Roanoke from 1585 through 1586. There he made a dictionary of the Indian language, making translations of common phrases into English. I received from Hariot's own hands a manuscript copy of his book, it never being published. My travels in Europe had taught me the importance of serving well another's tongue. Hariot and I visited two of Waymouth's kidnapped native Indians still in London in July of 1606. In my interview with them I practiced of their language and learned a little of their ways, the only member of our company to be so interested in those we wished to have as allies.

THREE SHIPS WERE DOCKED IN LONDON AT BLACKWALL, NOT FAR from the manor house where lived both Sir Sebastian Cabot and Sir Walter Raleigh, within sight of the East India docks where Sir Thomas Smythe held influence upon all English trade. So the seed never abandons the flower until it is ripe. Our victuals were loaded on our ship. At the same time, the king received as homage two crocodiles delivered from the West Indies by a privateer and a man well acquainted with those American coasts, Captain Christopher Newport. Newport having served the crown at sea for many years, even sailing with Drake against the Spanish in 1588. It was rumored he had courage and determination, making many voyages to the West Indies, losing an arm in battle there in 1590. Newport was no Drake, but he was the most experienced Englishman in those waters. The king, his crocodile well chained, appointed him our admiral and while at sea, the company's commander. Gosnold was second in command, too young for more authority than to serve. That all of this was his idea had little morrow against the power of the dawn.

The other captains and gentlemen of our company were mostly relations of Lord Willoughby or Sir Thomas Smythe. More lords than laborers, more gentlemen and their servants, each practiced well the privilege of his estate. The ships now filled, all captained and crewed and well supplied. Newport with seventy-one on the *Susan Constant*, Gosnold with fifty-two on the *Godspeed* and Ratcliffe with twenty-one on the *Discovery* waited for the proper tide.

Around me a history all concealed, its moment walked my watch, and what I saw was but a movement about my face. On Newport's ship sat a locked chest wherein were the seven names of those appointed to the governing council, including that of our president. My name was one, placed there by the influence of Lord Willoughby and Bartholomew Gosnold. All names were then unknown, the chest only to be opened upon our reaching the Chesapeake. On December nineteenth 1606, three ships took their sails to their masts and set their keels to break upon the widening waters.

Chapter Eleven

A WAR NOT WAR. DEATH NOT DEATH.
A TRIAL BY RUMOR AND A FORT.

 ND SO, on the Jamestown beach, we just returned from the falls and our first meeting with Powhatan, the president of the council, Edward Maria Wingfield, stood before us, dressed in reds and pinks. The badges and medals and ribbons of his station and his titles hung from his chest like caught fish. He wore an iron helmet, which resembled a capsized ship, its pointed ends both front and back like bows, its central metal spine a keel. Wingfield held the others back with a gesture of his arms, reminding them of the dignities of his station and that he must be the first to speak to Captain Newport. Only Lord Percy would he let through to stand by his side, knowing that by birth and politics, the brother of Northumberland was not of trivial flesh.

"They came in heaving clouds of paint and feathers. Gales of arrows they shot. We were unarmed, our guns...," a voice whimpered, as if expressing embarrassment to stern parents. Wingfield silenced the voice with a look. Others started to speak.

"We'll have none of that. I am in command. Privilege will speak only to privilege," said Wingfield, adjusting the tilt of his head and the placement of his hand on his sword. Properly composed, he waited now, satisfied in his control, assured of his station.

It was a nervous group of men who swallowed hard on their mortality and waited as the hull of our boat scraped the gravel of the shore. The shore seemed to groan in annoyance, the small faces of the rocks withdrawing into the soft mud, like the heads of frightened turtles.

"Where's Newport?" asked Wingfield, his gaunt cheeks blushed in a displeasing yellow, his thin head and nervous eyes looking about, not noticing the man standing in front of him.

"Before you," said Captain Todkill, cutting away the ceremony to the obvious.

"Ah, Captain Newport," Wingfield said, as he nodded at the figure in front of him, seeing only his own embarrassment.

Wingfield cleared his throat, as if the truth were a heavy burden for his pipes. "Two hundred savages came at us this morning. Our men engaged in desperate sorties with painted devils. Our guns were all packed away. Our ruin was at hand. It was only after a canon shot from one of the ships blasted a tree, killing several of those fiends, did they retreat."

Across the clearing that was to be our town, bodies, convulsed in grotesque contortions of pain, lay on bloodstained sheets. Wotton knelt now by one, from whose shoulder a bouquet of five arrows rose. He snapped the shafts and then with his knife, cut away the flesh to free the darts, sewing the wound with a rough thread, covering it then with a plaster of tobacco and wine and sulfur.

"Seventeen of us are hurt and one killed. Them savages smashed in his head, he being just a boy," said a laborer, scowling back at Wingfield, who turned to silence him.

"In our account, let us not forget the injuries to six gentlemen," said Wingfield, "who, by the refinement of their bearings, suffer most grievously at the slightest wound."

As the wind filtered through the transparency of his words, some gentlemen's heads wobbled in vacant nods, as if on strings. They had agreed with all this before. There was no content to their gesture, only motion. The laborers murmured among themselves in idle rebellion, unhappy to be so discounted, but strangely reassured that they stood so closely to the human manifestation of nature's order and its power. The land and sea stretched their own presumptions across our sight. In the echo of space we were alone. I could feel the unity of our little band begin to disintegrate into nuggets of individual fear, each man holding to that essential idea, that part of his identity that made him feel unique and whole and safe.

Captain Newport began his address, but I was forced by potent needs to interrupt, as I thought to myself, *Why not take the hour that is lent? Entombed in the perceptions I would rather be. Cradle me. I am a changeling, swaddling through the suffocations of a second birth. I speak in echoes.* My lips pursed in borrowed lexicons.

Now to the crew I spoke, "Toward the success of this great enterprise which we have now begun, I believe we have but one recourse: to forget who we are. All assumptions, all births, all titles, are monuments to the moment which is passed. We must now strive, in this vastness, to be for each other, that we might be for the ages. Here we must become no one, that we might become one. Here our community will be our history. Here our nobility must rise above its birth. We must become but one hand with one purpose, one mind with one thought," I said, trying to create with my one soul the character of the whole.

"Hear, hear," said one of our crew. The other members of the council stared at the ground, building walls of mud with the toes of their boots.

"To be no one is to be nothing!" screamed Ratcliffe. There was a hollow murmur among the crew. It seemed far away, as if sounds were being uttered beneath the ground.

Wingfield interrupted, looking at me in restrained contempt. "Your thoughts are well said in their surface flash, but at their heart there is a treason. Our station at birth is another aspect of God's natural order, as is the king. To forget our class is to dismember that order in treasonable disobedience, an unnatural mutiny against both God and king. For it is that order and its natural light which give our lives their essential meaning, their essential purpose, their divine luminescence. There is no true movement without their pull and no true meaning without their reflection."

"There are no thrones in this wilderness that aren't first built in men's minds. Is not my own God in me?" I replied. My words were like the wind, showing no effect on Wingfield but the distant ruffle of his shirt.

"The question here," said Captain Archer, an almost lawyer who presumed his law, having studied at Grey's Inn, but never succeeding to the bar, "is do we have the authority to build a fort? By our own charter, the king must approve all our laws. Isn't any presumption of that authority a treasonable thought? Can we alone take any action without his consent?" As Archer spoke, his eyes watching Gosnold. Denied the lawyer, he assumed the law. It became the scaffolding of his flesh, the only bone of his imagination.

"We were sent to these shores to found a colony," said Bartholomew Gosnold, his blond hair protruding beneath his helmet, his armor of polished black and gold, always trying to be the lawyer trained to a better law. "Are we not a continent unto ourselves? I believe building a fort is within the limits of our authority, if we choose to read that authority with good sense in the broadest terms." Gosnold had been the only one among us who could sway Archer beyond his limits, having been his friend at Cambridge and his captain when they sailed to the north coast of America in 1602.

But Archer would eat his own.

"Do we have the right to make assumption of that king?" he said, on the verge of taking a tantrum to plead his case. As Archer spoke, I imagined several arrows falling at his feet, which I assumed he would kick away as if they were a casual annoyance.

There was a scream from one of the wounded, his pain his only consciousness. He drifted into darkness, anguish still railing in his eyes, as his eyes turned inwards, disappearing into his skull.

Captain Archer was interrupted in his soliloquy by Wingfield, who said, "There is a more important question and that is, simply stated, will the building of a fort seem to these savages a provocative act?"

"I would think that the attack on us this morning would be provocation enough," said Captain Todkill. "Look about you. Our blood now fills the river beyond this field."

"We are the English and a civilized nation. We must rise above the mere appearance of war," said our stout John Russell, his servants huddled behind him, rubbing their hands like nervous vermin at their feed.

Wingfield's voice rose in chastising thunder. "I might remind our company," he stormed, "that we are under strict orders from the king himself not to injure or abuse or offend the savages. I believe a fort would be seen by them as a grave offense. Heavy is the weight of this our mandate and heavier still will be the retribution for those who cannot be its champion."

As each man would cast the nation of the whole from his own limits, I now spoke, setting aside the diplomacies of silence. "Could an ocean ignore a storm? Could a dry leaf ignore a gale as easily as we ignore the ramifications of this attack? Dead things are more alive to the possibilities of their circumstance than we who think and count them rude."

Captain Archer stepped in front of me. Ever the pudding of a man dressed in his own shadow, he appeared as the everyone no one would notice. Plain in profile, his resemplances without character, a torn cloth beneath a dented armor. "I believe it is inappropriate for

Captain Smith, still under the accusation of treason, to speak on these most important matters."

I brushed aside Archer's suggestion. Blind to myself, I craved the blindness. Anger would not be my epitaph, as I said, "What have our lives become if we do not build a fort to defend ourselves but good sense orphaned to a word? But there are other words, words that birth a thought, which, given the sinew and muscle of action, become the flesh of reputation, and when recounted by others, become our history — the spirit of all our purpose. We must seize that purpose. We must live those words. We must build the fort, for ourselves, for good sense, for our enterprise." There were cheers. Hats were thrown in the air. The council stood silent. "I would follow if others would lead, as I would now lead if others would follow."

"Lead us and we will follow," was the cry. Wingfield tried to quiet the crew. I spoke again. I could not let my future moments lie in shallows and forgotten graves with a council buffoon. I pressed my argument until I felt the sword of my intent hit the bone of their stupidity. "Thoughts may war, but here, beneath the talk, there is a desperate reality. We cannot last a week without a fort."

"The fort must be built," said Captain Newport. "When my three ships return to England, you will have no defensible place, no place to retreat in time of attack. You will be alone, without hope of rescue."

Wingfield began to protest that the power of the council was being usurped. "General opinion sits on no throne when it speaks to matters of the state. Only the council can decide if it has the authority to build a fort, and if it does, whether such action serves well both God's purpose and the king's commission."

"The king in London has his advisors, as he has his Parliament," spoke Reverend Robert Hunt, a friend of Hakluyt, appointed chaplain of the expedition in his stead. Hakluyt then fifty-six, Hunt twenty years his junior. "Why should the council here not listen to those whose lives are most directly affected by its decision?"

"Here," said Ratcliffe, addressing the whole company, "we are under siege, not only by the savages, but by the very immensity and loneliness of the land. It is as if the land, this great hollow nothing, could call from our skins ourselves, evaporate our minds into the wind. All of us are endangered." Ratcliffe held his hands close to his chest. "Without the discipline of English resolve and English custom we would simply dissolve from ourselves into the land and become one of her demons, the very savages which we now face. Would any among us now rip the English clothes from his back and dance naked in the wood with these fiends? Would we betray our souls for a song? Not now. But the wilderness is a subtle seductress. She perfumes the mind with forbidden thoughts. We must protect ourselves. We must be more English than any Englishman has ever been before. Distill the essence of ourselves into our government. Only by holding to the last codicils of our law, the last decrees of our divine council, can we form an iron identity that no pagan wilderness can plunder." Even as Ratcliffe spoke, his body trembled, his voice wavered, his teeth chattered, as if the meaning of his words hid other meanings desperate to be heard. Ratcliffe held his arms across his shaking chest, squeezed them tightly, holding his body together, fearing, I suppose, that even as he spoke his body might explode into a geyser of hysterical sparks.

I watched Ratcliffe, wondering what his words denied that his actions would affirm. "All power to our council and our king," he screamed. Others echoed his salute. One of Ratcliffe's band yelled, "Ratcliffe will save our souls, as he will save our lives. Ratcliffe should be the president." Our company disintegrated into a cacophony of words and fragmented phrases, gradually quieting to a steady buzz, as if a tribe of bees were tearing apart their hive.

Wingfield fumbled with the decorations on his chest, lifted the ribbon of one hanging metal, kissed the gold color of its coin. The certainty in himself renewed, he spoke. "I was chosen to be on the council by the king. My name was placed in a sealed box, opened a few days ago, as you know. That commission I do regard as sacred."

"Then why do you deny Smith his seat?" Todkill yelled, his powerful shoulders, his armor dressed for war. "Wasn't he chosen also?"

"Captain Smith still stands accused of treason. Until that charge is resolved, he will not take his seat." Wingfield started to walk away.

"When will those charges be resolved?" Todkill asked, his young face already scarred by service in the East.

"In England. By trial," said Wingfield.

"No. I want to be judged here in the face of my accusers." I addressed the company. "Are those who seek my destruction so cowardly that they must hide behind an ocean, shielded by distance, to make their slanders? Let them stand before me, here, that all may see my innocence."

"Justice for Smith. Justice for Smith...now!" came the chant. A press of faces, both glum and determined, blocked Wingfield's path. "What about the fort?" cried a voice.

"The gentlemen of the council will consider in due course," said Wingfield. "We are not common rabble and will not be coerced by those who are."

But frustration is the noose to those who wildly speak. Still no path opened for Wingfield. He tried to push away bodies as if they were a tangle of tall grass. Their flesh would not yield, as Wingfield screamed, "In a wilderness, I am the government by law, by birth, by privilege. I was elected by the chosen council. I will be obeyed." As he screamed, Wingfield's eyes protruded from his head, sweating lunacies as they drank the light.

An angry groan moved through the crew. A beast in the mind had been awakened that now was on the scent. Captain Newport tried to calm the men. "I know these words of the president speak more to his determination than to any sense. As to the fort, I am appointed to absolute command while this company is at sea. Since no town has been built, I assume we are still at sea, in spirit if not in fact. Therefore, I order the construction of a fort...at once."

"Mutiny is the beast which is now upon our flock," raged Wingfield. "This is mutiny and treason."

"It is a wise captain who knows the haul of his own sails. The wind is only born to enthrall the wise," said the old mariner with his leathered skin, his eyes alive with the inner fire of some cold and icy light.

Captain Newport gently raised his hand to quiet the speaker. "Jonas," was the only word Newport spoke.

Wingfield turned to stare in hate upon the old mariner. He could have had the man flogged, his back so cut he could never stand again. It would bring a measure of appeasement to Wingfield to inflict some wounds. If Wingfield thought the man weak and easy without cost he could have had his violence upon him. Such is the cowardice of power. The battle hardened mariners now moved to close about the old man, as if they were a cloak, their hands upon their swords.

Newport spoke. "Old Jonas adventured with Drake some thirty years and knows many a haunted tale of the sea, and even of this coast." Wingfield did not consider of a merry tale, but saw no easy practice of his will to have the old man punished.

"I have been to this coast twice before and know it to be ever protective of its lost," said the old mariner. "This place births mysteries, its flower ripens secrets in its seeds."

Wingfield ignored the old mariner's words, considering on the will of the company and the matter of the fort. "I am not so casual to all this as some may think." Wingfield pulled a cape over his shoulder, straightening its creases, tightening its fit, armoring his body against the world with the cut of his pink cloth. "I will not be that fracture that drains his life into this land," he raged, as rounded cannonballs of clouds slaughtered the light as they passed across the sun. His hand smoothed the ribbons of his shirt. Feeling his own touch emboldened Wingfield, allowing him to yield in protest. "I know who I am and what I am about. Build your fort!"

"And Captain Smith?" questioned Reverend Hunt.

"His trial will be within the week. Captain Gabriel Archer will be the prosecutor." A path now cleared. Wingfield walked through it toward the ships, which rocked on their foundations like hollow toys.

Chapter Twelve

I AM PLAYED A TRIAL. GENTLEMEN WILL STARVE US YET.
A POISONED CUP. A TAVERN. DRAKE BEGINS TO DRINK.

USK HAD COME to ease the day. Around the fire our company sat. The old mariner stared into the flames, remembering other heat and other light. "I was with Drake in Panama in 1572," he said, his face glowing more brilliantly in the excited sparks of a momentary flare. At the edge of the fire's stain the night surged in a darkened surf. The molten light hung upon us, as the weathered sailor then told the tale I only knew in parts.

And oh my years do drift their passions into gray and I think back on that long ago as I write the mariner's tale. Man is the only creature who can draw an image of himself or who has the need. My written history the ear that holds the mariner's voice. I am his last quill. His last resurrection. Memory is the man. Remembrance is his food. I eat of the darkness spoken on many tongues. So many years ago, the memory dims. I hear his shadow creak. My two eyes are locked in stares to see again the many passing things. The mind between. We are specters of the middle gate. And so the pencil draws its dreams in sketch, and so the tale is told. And who the teller is is half the tale. Memory is the singer of the demon tune. And so half by half I give it whole. Man bears himself, his truth the lesser silence. And who is there to speak our elegies? Our fading works, the landscape despairs each its season. It is our blood that is our ink that holds the hours of our epitaph. We are the departed—I am the future of his life.

I see the arms of the mariner outstretched above the portals of the fire. I am of him and his remains. I grasp his thoughts. By what seditions do we sleep away our wakefulness? The moment turns as I tell his tale. I am the mariner now. I am his voice. His words through me. By what contrivance do our desperations make each other whole?

"We were a band of seventy-three, with us Drake's two brothers, John and Joseph, all to face an empire—two ships, and a cargo of three pinnaces carried in portions on our decks, and the scent of Spanish gold in the air like a whiff of saintly dust. We were going to capture the Spanish treasure town of Nombre de Dios. Seventy-three of us, with a few firelocks, some pikes, swords, a trumpet and a drum. It took a man like Drake, who could dream with his eyes awake, to scheme this into a man's soul so he would follow him even beyond the hills of madness.

"Drake's plan was in its glory simplicity with a knife edge of daring. The Spanish had brought their gold and silver and jewels up the Pacific coast of South America to Panama, a sewer of gold flowing up the coast and across the isthmus to Nombre de Dios, to fill the cisterns of the Spanish king. And there it was stored in the king's treasure house, until the flota could sail it to Spain. And we, just orphans of the sea, a-wishing to take a drink, we could seize the king's golden draft while it was still in the bottle.

"Drake anchored us off the coast at night. A mist rose from the warm ocean, like the lathered breath of some maddened beast. It was July twelfth, 1572. The crew waited and slept and argued among themselves. The tension held the ship in its chains, until even our own lungs worked against their invisible ringlets of iron. We were imprisoned by our own design. The moon moved behind a curtain of cloud, diffusing its light into quilts of ghostly fire. 'Upon our fates,' said Drake. The pinnace's sails were raised, the water again was sliced. We moved upon the breeze.

"We passed a sleeping ship, two broken masts, a mutilated corpse that in the shadow rose from the sea in a soundless scream. An exhausted voice hailed us in Spanish. We responded in the same. There was a distant greeting and a sigh. On the shore we divided into four groups. Twelve stayed to guard the pinnace. Drake, his brother John and John Oxenham took sixteen each, forty-eight men to seize a town. Behind the clouds the moon whispered in its light. We grasped our brief farewells, cloaked ourselves in darkness and marched into the night. I was with Drake, who was to hold the center, the others to guard our flanks. I walked beneath our banners of stitched rags. Our legion was few. The hope of surprise and our resolve bolds courage into ghostly multitudes. Archangels, let our terror be your wings. As angel clouds they came in their mists to hide the progress of our march. A musket blast, the signal for our attack. Our drums advanced as the heralding trumpets blared and we displayed our banners to snap upon the cuts of wind. Drake proudly marched, no sneak nor shadow thief was he. From three directions our marshaled lines converged. Alarms, the town in fear. Nervous light now lit to enthrall the dark. Bells rang. Sounds fled before us on the cobblestones, as if a shadow raced in scrambled terror. Spanish voices, cries, carts overturned, wood breaking, barrels and crates thrown into the street. In the dark a barricade was being built in the center of the town.

"The *alcalde*, the provincial governor, a sword in his hand, stood behind a barricade, dressed in his nightshirt, surrounded by other nightshirts with muskets in their arms. At the end of the street a Spanish volley. The line flashed and danced in it necklace. Their shot falling short struck sparks upon the cobblestones. Drake, yards in front in the face of the lethal hail, was wounded in the leg, but did not cry out nor ever said a word. Our own volleys scratched flashes now in wire light. Our shot and arrows fell around the Spanish works. John Oxenham and John Drake soon arrived to thrust on the Spanish flanks. Our three prongs now rose and charged as a living trident on the Spanish ranks. Screams fevered in the air, arms raised in panic to blows that never came. The Spanish fled. Two prisoners we had, who, so eager in their fears, led us to the governor's mansion.

"There it stood on a deserted street, its gray stone walls the color of bleached bones rising against the flicker of the trembling flames of our torches. We faced the mansion as it faced us, its shuttered windows, its fastened doors, like a severed head, dreaming of the sweet smell of its own death. The doors we forced, and on the floor of the great hall was a pyramid of silver bars, twenty feet across, thirty feet in length and seventy feet high. How would we carry it all to our ship? It was as if the earth had vomited wealth, and we forty-eight, with spoons and broken bowls, were there but to take a lick. Drake sneered at silver. He wanted gold. Out into the night again, in search of the king's treasure house. 'To the docks,' ordered Drake. Through the narrow streets we walked, Drake, hiding his limp, the bloody boot, unnoticed. Halfway down an open way the sky opened in deluge, the rain all but drowned the very air. Our clothes were wet, our gunpowder drenched, our crossbow arrows spent. Our weapons useless, except for our swords and pikes. Drake stood under the eaves of a house thinking, blood now from under his pant leg oozed, coloring the rain in the gutter's wash.

"His brother approached and asked about his injury. The pant leg was cut away, the torn flesh revealed. I bandaged it with cloth, the cloth blossoming with a corsage of blood. For half an hour we stood feeling each our breathes slide its heat upon our throats. We waited, muttering among ourselves, fearing the Spanish would regroup and attack. Our torches flickered. Each shadow in the street became a prophecy, each creek in an alley an oracle. We waited, holding to the sight of our companions for reassurance, as if we each were a splinter of the sacred cross.

"'Too much is against us,' Drake said. 'Another time it will be ours.' We moved slowly toward the pinnace, Drake supporting himself on his brother's shoulder, hopping slowly on his one good leg, heavily, like a doll in a child's fist. Through the street we went, the darkness holding to the corners of the houses and the alleys. A man, crawling like a vine of silence, moved behind us. With the grace and guiltlessness of breeze he ran forward and took Drake's other shoulder and lifted him. 'We should go fast now.' The man wore the rags of a slave. 'My name is Diego…I go with you.' He did not speak in pleading, but spoke as if suggesting a good idea. He was a black. 'We kill Spanish?' Diego smiled and waited for Drake to consider. 'You come with us,' Drake spoke, his voice hushed with exhaustion.

"We sailed to Bastimentos Island some leagues to the west and disembarked. Diego showed us how to make shelter from palm leaves. Drake was tended. We cursed our lost fortune.

"The following day the *alcalde* of Nombre de Dios sent a visitor under a white flag. He came unarmed, dressed in purple silks, with a blue lace collar and lace sleeves. At the sight of his elegance we tried to hide the tears in our own clothes, hatred to him who made us hate ourselves. We conducted the Spaniard to Drake with all the pomp that our imaginations could pretend. Drake was under a tree, his leg bandaged. The ambassador inquired after his injury, and asked if he would desire a Spanish doctor.

"Drake said, " 'No, I am well tended.'

"The ambassador wanted to know if he was the same Drake who had raided the coast before. Drake said with understated gestures, 'I am as ever and for all times.' The two sat for some time and conversed of war and peace, and whether Drake could be bribed to sail away. He could not. Finally the ambassador stood to take his leave. Drake ordered that he be given so many presents that his arms were overloaded. The Spaniard left, bowing, leaving a trail of lost trinkets in his wake. Only Diego was not amused.

"It was a strange war, " said the mariner, his fingers white and bloodless, as if crusted with salt, "to oil our thievery with presents. But Drake had his reputation and his humors, and he was going to live them until their meanings were a choke around the Spanish neck."

AT JAMESTOWN THE FIRE CLOTHED THE EARTH. RATCLIFFE AND HIS group sat apart. Ratcliffe spoke in whispers, his tongue buttering his teeth, as his companion smiled, beguiled by the sweet ministerings of Ratcliffe's soulless thoughts.

The mariner arranged himself on the ground, sipped from a battered cup a small portion of the day's allotment of aqua vitae. He relaxed into the ecstasy of his swallow as one of our companions rose and walked to the edge of the fire, where a few cedar logs stood upright in a ditch—the beginnings of a fort begun that day. As the man moved, he loosened his pants and his codpiece, disappearing behind the logs to do some natural business.

The breeze from the bay smelled of the great distance to home, spiced with salt and rot of dying fish. A lone sea bird called in the blackness like a lost spirit seeking its own soul. The old mariner put down his cup and moved closer to the fire again. "Where was I," he said, "when the sweet elixir called my tongue?" Then he chortled softly. There was a thud and a scream from behind the cedar logs, and the sound of an angry brew bubbling in the throat. Our companion stumbled forward, his pants around his ankles. He held his neck. He turned toward the fire, his eyes widened in surprise and fear, an arrow through his neck. Blood spurted through his fingers as his legs pushed against the bounds of his own pants. He fell forward onto the ground.

The tapers of our firelocks lit, we ran forward, some to the man, who now lay drowning in his own blood, others to the stockade poles. As Thomas Wotton cut the arrowhead, the figure convulsed on the ground, like the tantrum of a petulant child longing for the comfort of a favorite toy, which somehow had forever slipped beyond his grasp.

At the poles we peered into the night, which welcomed us with a soft breeze, short and hesitant. It touched our faces with a lover's touch—ghostly, almost, far away, silent, this earthly simulation of an amorous wisp.

The figure now lay still. Someone pulled up his pants. Another covered his face and his body with a blanket. The earth was dark and still. No savage celebrated his death.

"Anything?" said Wingfield, at my side. I shook my head and watched for a departing spirit.

THE SUN ROSE AGAIN ON THE FAITHLESS EARTH TO WHICH WE committed to the shallow of a small hill the purse of life, our comrade's body. We stood in silent testimony. Reverend Hunt spoke the tired words which, even inflamed with an ardent voice, seemed dull. The shadows of the land shrank back till noon, then grew again with the setting of the sun, as if the night first grew upon the land before its contagions spread into the sky.

The mariner sat by the fire again. "The land of this new world breathes elixirs," he said. "It can intoxicate a man until his own ghost wouldn't recognize the corpse. I've seen it happen. Wandering among all the new marvels of the earth, you come to think you are its spirit. We are succumbed by landscapes. I've seen it happen." He repeated, "I've seen it happen."

Ratcliffe walked his watch beyond the light, the red glow of his gun's taper moving through the darkness like the eye of a predatory cat. Wingfield had abandoned the company of men for the moment, lounging with empty titles, and the invisible wounds to his pride. John Martin, a member of our council, turned over stones, carrying specimens to the fire, examining them for the faintest sparkle of gold. He seemed as something rodent, ever sniffing at his cheese. All that is the man was nurtured to the child. Martin's father Lord Mayor of London, Master of the Queen's Mint and goldsmith. The coin of our parents' love, no matter what the pain, makes puppets of us in our emulations. Martin's sickly son now suckled to the same disease, gathered his own stones, so delighted he was to be the contagion of his father's love. John looked at me and smiled, pretending with an involuntary gesture that nothing had occurred that day. Archer slept upon the ground. It was early evening. Someone was describing the best way to cook and spice the flesh of a dog.

I lay back in my exhaustion, watched the mariner and thought about the day, its images seen again on the columns of smoke which rose and convulsed in the wind like a chained bird.

Some of us had worked all morning felling a few trees, trimming away the branches, cutting twenty-foot poles, each pole sharpened to a point at one end. These we dragged or pulled by ropes or carried on thick branches between two men, six men to a pole, who set the poles upright in a ditch six feet deep, which when completed would be one hundred yards long. Three ditches would form a triangle; at each corner a semicircular trench, a half-moon bulwark where we would place our cannons. We sweated in the heat, drank the briny water of the bay, spitting out lumps of slime and bits of filth. Some gentlemen sat, discussing our work. Their servants stood behind them adjusting their clothes or lounged on the earth and yawned, scratching their noses absentmindedly, like overfed cats. Some set up pins and bowled in the low grass. They did not work. The mariners and the yeomen worked, Newport and I with them, organizing, dividing the tasks, setting sentries, which the gentlemen were willing to do, as it did not have the stigma of common labor. Wingfield sat at a table with Lord Percy and a few of the other nobles and watched and complained about my command and our progress.

"Smith takes his authority from the air, then he puffs it in our face," complained Archer, who was not a member of the council, but longed for power he could never wisely wield. "He's using this bluff of his to undermine the legitimate power of the council. If he's trying to escape his trial, he's only adding more evidence of his guilt."

As I heard Archer, I placed the ax I wielded on my shoulder. Around me twnety men toiled, while sixty took their pleasure on a boat, or near the beach. I watched the sky, which seemed distant in my thoughts, and then I watched the earth. On one side of us, to our right, was a marsh of tall grasses, which, in their endless battalions, waved in the breeze, waiting like a predatory thing. To our left there was a good stand of trees, from which now could be heard the agony of work and occasionally the roar of falling timber.

"All my hesitations I must overcome," I thought. "Blind resolves, my actions now. How much of the sovereign am I in the kingdom of the fool? I the wiggle that worms their mind. My own doubts not fully spent." But I had had enough. There was danger, but danger was all around. Why not an action to taunt a fear? I walked toward Wingfield, passing men struggling to set poles against one another in our stockade wall.

"He hasn't even begun to discuss the building of our houses." As Martin spoke, he eyed Wingfield, inviting him to join the discussion. "We should really be exploring and searching for gold."

Wingfield looked past the conversation to his fingernails. "I'm appointing myself justice of the peace," he said, not seeing me approach. "I will now wear the medal of that office...of course."

"I need more men if we are to have a fort." I stood looking down at Wingfield, who looked at nothing. Archer and Martin cleared their throats and acted bored.

"That's none of your concern," said Archer, moving behind Martin. "In terms of law, and I your appointed prosecutor, you should be in chains."

I turned toward Wingfield to speak such pleas as to defend this enterprise from his sins. "There were no chains when I gambled all my wealth on this, our hope. Did not Gosnold and I in search of better prospects bring you to our counsel? Were not we, by our passion and our coins, then equals in this venture? I who survived the Turk...you the Spanish...Gosnold his ventures to the north. Can we not spurn our vanities for the greater good and cast ourselves in equal portions, as I was chosen for the council same as you, raised men for the Company, same as you, spent coin. Where is our difference that it cannot be set aside?"

"It is not our purpose here," said Wingfield, looking toward Lord Percy for assent, "to tear about the fabric of nature's law, not to mention English law and custom, as a service to your ends. If you cannot convince others to work, make do with what you have. I have deeper purposes to ponder." Wingfield dismissed me with a wave of his hand, adding, "All adventures are but luck. Your coins are rude. If you had all the wealth of all the continents and its kings, equals we would never be."

"I do not consider this evasion an answer. When the savages come, would you hide behind your vapors? "

"In every syllable Smith spits there is mutiny," said Archer.

"If those forest savages do not work, but leave most of the burden to their women, except for war and hunting, why should English gentlemen? Did we not bring our own English derelicts to toil in our slots?" said Ratcliffe, sitting next to Wingfield, insinuating his fondness. Ratcliffe always the dog that jumps the beg at power's scraps. Archer laughed.

"Why don't you explain your policy to our companions?" I said to Ratcliffe, asserting for him a panorama of the world with a sweep of my arm.

"This is more of an annunciation of a privately held inclination," he replied, "than a public policy. I'm sure you understand."

"And you, Captain Wingfield? Will you detail your policy concerning gentlemen and work to our own?"

"I have little desire to explain myself to any common butt, whether it is by ones or in marshaled herds. May I remind you, Captain Smith, by English law, no gentleman has to work. All labor is saved in charity for the poor who must by some means feed their own. A gentleman by sanction of king and Parliament lives from his inheritance, or by the toil of others. Why should I now sully or demean my station with explained regrets over a policy which is known by all?"

What Wingfield said was in itself true. So little work was there in England, so many unemployed, that gentlemen, by law, did not have to work, to save the employment that there was for others. But this was not England. "Here all custom is a noose," I said, looking at Wingfield, not knowing that it was also a buffer to spare us from what had been spawned, as I added, "Who in this company is to do its labor? What is your plan? State it before the crew. State it now, this very moment, so none can say he did not know your mind."

"Smith should have his trial first. All this arguing and posturing is a ruse," said Martin.

"No, Captain Wingfield should state his policy," said Reverend Hunt. "It seems fair."

"If I am mutiny, as it is supposed, I will take my judgment from a jury here," I said. "My only condition is that Wingfield states his policy, which, peeled to the nut, is, gentlemen do not have to work."

"Agreed," said Captain Wingfield as he rose, summoning with voice and gesture the crew, whose heads rose and turned toward the beckoning figure. Steps following sight, the crew laid down their tools, the gentlemen their toys. Some rose from the earth, the ground, the dust. The etched designs of wrinkled cloth swept clean by punishing hands, the closing circle of men from disorder and separate trial and games, to attention and anticipated stares.

"I am here to be judged," I said, "for conspiracies that never were; for mutinies whose only treason was they sought to reconcile command to the possibility of disaster, if certain of their policies be pursued; and for being concerned with the safety of this enterprise rather than the reputation of its captains. That is my crime, if it be a crime. Of that I am accused." I looked at Reverend Hunt and added, "But before any judgment is asked of you, and before any sentence is apportioned, Captain Wingfield, our president, will speak about his policy concerning work."

Wingfield stepped forward into the light, a figure who seemed as shallow in the flesh as his shadow on the ground. "I do not and will not require any man to do what is not in his nature. Mine is the policy of the three harmonies: harmony in nature, harmony in government and harmony in ourselves. We do require only what reconciles us in complete accord to God, to nature and to our conscience. Thus all of us are a part of a great natural symmetry, each a lens through which that great spiritual light is purified and compressed into a great godly heat, a simple divine spark, if you will, we call a soul. No soul here shall drown itself in flood on some alien river. Each shall do what is God's proportion: commoners to work, gentlemen to give counsel. No gentleman is to work except as a volunteer. And no commoner is to give counsel, except when asked, including Captain Smith…whose trial shall now begin."

The crew growled. Heads turned toward each other, eyes eyeing eyes. Mouths spit words into mouths spitting words. Breaths intertwined, coolly circling each other in transparent currents of rage. The whole company struggled in its phantoms. Wingfield raised his arms.

"We are here…We are here." His words lost in a surge of competing wills. "We are here," Wingfield yelled. Reverend Hunt raised his hands, shaking his head, gesturing for calm. Men obliged Hunt. There was a brooding murmur of an uneasy peace.

"We are here to create an outpost in a new and hostile world on English terms," Wingfield continued, but I interrupted, pushing all for my moment now.

"Either we shall all work, or none shall eat. We are a small company, one hundred and seven, too small our number to carry any as leisured guests. But to believe this, in Wingfield's world, is to be accused a traitor."

"Hail to Smith, the noble commoner," called a voice.

"Judge Smith innocent and set him free," called another.

"There will be no need for Smith's trial today," stormed Wingfield. "He has strangled in his own words. He is guilty of mutiny."

"There is no mutiny when it contradicts such folly," yelled the faithful Todkill. "Wingfield bathes in oceans dunged in folly and we're supposed to love the smell."

The company laughed. "Maybe he thinks we should harvest it for our victuals," came a voice. "We can call it gentlemanly sweetmeats," came another. The whole company roared in gleeful thunder, the joyous noise so thick it seemed to quilt the earth. Archer and Martin stood by Wingfield's side in sheepish silence. Ratcliffe laughed with the crew, as if he had always been my friend, encouraging Wingfield's torment. I watched our pet dog, ears turned back against its head, drag its slouching frame beyond the unfinished stockade. It looked back one last time, its sorrowful eyes announcing some lost innocence in a confession of watery glances.

THE CROWS IN THE TREES SWAYED IN THE BLACKENED WIND THAT night. The fires blew low momentarily, then rushed skyward again. The trial required little time. Archer read the accusation, which was broadly worded, and the evidence, which consisted mostly of my advice about streams and game and the Spanish in the Canary Islands. Martin and Archer elaborated some tales concerning my refusing to speak to them respectfully during the voyage. The whole crew as my jury, I was adjudged innocent by acclamation and awarded three hundred shillings for being slandered, which Wingfield was forced to pay. No small sum, and all the treasure Wingfield had upon his person,

I believed. I gave the money to the whole company for their general use. It was a gesture that might bring some future peace, I thought. It came to nothing. Archer gave an address asking those who respected him to reconsider the verdict and saying that his finely wrought and beautifully phrased indictment had been misquoted and slandered; and he desired compensation also. No one listened. He argued that my acquittal was not a true acquittal but only a suggestion that acquittal might be possible under certain absurd circumstances. The whole company laughed. Archer argued that the long-held English legal principles had been disregarded, such as the reputation of those bringing the charges, and that this boded ill for the moral character of the whole enterprise. This little speech won him few friends and many cat calls. He retreated into silence, saying, "We should forget the whole nasty business and begin immediately with Captain John Martin a search for gold," which did bring a small round of cheers.

In the end, Wingfield, Ratcliffe and Martin still refused to seat me on the council, which enraged the company. Martin now joined with the obvious powers, hoping to gain some advantage for himself and his young son. Newport and Gosnold were for me, as well as that relative of George Sandys, Captain Kendall. He was thought to be a spy, having been employed by the Secretary of State, Sir Robert Cecil, the Earl of Salisbury, for some years. The earl and the king, fearful of a war, wanted secret reports on the colony. All this a whisper, but whispers coin believers in their mint. Reverend Hunt and Captain Newport stood apart and discussed the situation, which I was sure they would try to bring to right. I knew my victories here would be in slights, my successes on the wings of dust.

DURING THE AFTERNOON SAVAGES HAD HOWLED IN THE TALL GRASS for a time and shot two hundred arrows at us, but as they were afraid to approach within the range of our firelocks, their arrows fell without causing any hurt, except to one dog, which they killed with forty arrows, putting arrow after arrow into the dead carcass, as if it were the only object that gave their anger any release. Finally, they dragged it off, probably to eat it, someone said.

Wingfield favored his nobles with some tobacco from our canteen, which was our common store, those supplies to be shared in equal portion by all the company, but so does rank reward itself. When we protested, Wingfield displayed his medal and sneered.

"Why should we be neglected because we work?" spoke a young innocent of the company. "It be long known that the savages can live for many days by only smoking tobacco. The herb has remedies that quench hunger and relieve thirst. Ask the mariner."

"Once I bribed a hope from half a truth," nodded Jonas Profit. "That was an alchemy well worth a book, but now I have cast my cures aside. My studies dust in libraries. I wish I could forget. Tobacco is the devil's mount. Its history rides a two-headed horse, the tail courses white and black in flung smoke. The horse's eyes are fiery coals, it snorts in a laughter, crying madness. All this I know. I have lived its work. Tobacco is my haunting. It lives upon me as a ghost. This leaf blooms diseases in its cures."

The company listened to the mariner, some asking him to tell his tale. Martin interrupted, his greed thriving in his voice, as he asked, "Plow your tobacco under foot, alchemist. Can you turn base metal into gold?"

"That is the common belief. In truth, alchemy transforms nothing but to itself. It is the art of appearances." The mariner stared in wizards into Martin's eyes, his shadow cast in menace across the earth. "Alchemist's gold is not gold at all, but only wears a deception that appears as gold. It is a costume that hides a counterfeit." Martin's avarice now appalled, the mariner smiled, then he continued. "Alchemy commerced first in Egypt by jewelers who wished to create inexpensive trinkets that would appear as precious gold and silver. Their confections alloyed metals with each other, a pretty science, a novelty to pleasure and grace the neck, the arm, the ankle in a harmless trade. The recipes kept in secret, known only to the learned few, their art so refined, so many fooled, those who had the recipes believed they made real gold. So do cloistered wisdoms ever delude themselves. No contradiction to counter and complain another truth. His own joke the joker played upon himself. That is how it is believed that the alchemist makes real gold, but he does not."

"Half a gold is better gold than none," laughed Martin. "Even a false silver may have some commerce." The company joined Martin in his jest.

The mariner held his finger to his lips. There was silence. "All that we see in nature, all metals, all liquids, all vapors are made of one primary material. Alchemists called it *prima materia*. There are four elements: earth, air, fire and water. By adding or removing the essence of these elements, the essence of earth, the essence of fire, the essence of air, so the *prima materia* is changed to a specific substance, whether lead or gold or wine or smoke. The world is a bounty of illusions and behind it all there is a one. That is what alchemists believe. But some wanted more, more than just to bring some counterfeit to some coin. They wanted remedies. They wanted to transcend the material world, lead it to the spiritual ideal. They believed in their own confections. They studied the juices of plants. The alchemist became our physician, gold became our flesh. We published great encyclopaedias of plants that listed their uses and their cures. In these herbals, in slights of truth, is the story of tobacco." The old mariner looked about and said, "Tobacco is the alchemist's weed."

"So tell us that history, old man," called a voice. "You once told your soul in theatres. You wrote plays. Is that not your boast?"

"I am not the law, I carry only its judgment. I was not sufficient for my plan. I failed. Great writing must move with the same depth that it informs. Seek the hieroglyphs of the kiss. That is all I've learned, but that time is past, perhaps for a better tale," he said.

"Tell us that better tale, old Jonas. And how did you acquaint yourself with Drake?" sneered Ratcliffe, the liar ever believing all is a lie. "Tell us of your first meeting, please! I beg, or has our bag of bones so tubbed falsehood round his skin, another word would burst the stitches."

"I am come of wilderness into this, my dereliction, my paradise. What you call in me is a tale of many meanings," his hand upon his leather belt near his knife, the old mariner approached Ratcliffe as he spoke. "Your mind is thin of magic, but I shall plate this camp with such wonderments that even the hollow of a grain of sand shall count you flea." Ratcliffe's face blushed to the red of a heated iron. His thoughts flew to violence, but seeing my hand to my pistol, he brooded into a silent rage. The old mariner returned to the telling of his tale as we listened.

"We live our secrets in the world. We act our dramas to ourselves for all to see, if they have the sight. My wife and unborn child dead. What cures, my alchemies had failed the lethal test. So sure the certain scholar, my pain now the pay of arrogance, my world an emptiness. I fled Oxford to find some death. My coward would not dare the act itself. Where I wandered, who could say, my roads in darkness, my directions plain, my compass pointed grief by grief. Until by month my life slipped past and I in Plymouth at a tavern drinking my last coin. My cloak in tatters, in hanging threads, in stains of hanging dirt, I raised my arms. 'See the fire in the hearth, I shall tint with magic its flames to blue,' I announced to the room. 'But alchemy does not sport its magic free. Some drink to my hand, a cheap price for a wizard.' There was laughter and a tankard of ale. Some powder from my pocket I threw upon the fire. The flames to cobalt in their icy heat. The crowd in gasps and murmurs. Another drink placed in my hand, I swelled the room, turning in my filthy cloak. 'Another color for yet another drink—perhaps a green, a red.' And so I spent the evening making rainbows for my pay.

"Until a young worthy rose from his chair, a gold coin blazing in his raised hand. 'Wizard, this gold coin for alchemies, not childish tricks. I chance this wealth your toys are no deeper than your game. Play me your best magic in all their fascinations and I will give thee this, if the sport has some genius in its ride.'

"'And if I fail?' I asked.

"'You will not be so drunk as might. I suspect a grim loss to you,' he joked.

"The laughter and that jolly mood. The room with contagion to my mind. 'Why not an amusement to a better thrill? I care not for life. A wager: three gold coins against this, my right hand I hold above my head.'

"'Shall we have it as a piece, or the whole wizard in the pledge?' a voice called in laughter.

"'By piece, by part, by cloak, by man. Whatever is sufficient to feed the bet,' I said.

"'I want no injuries, wizard, just a play of wits,' replied the young man.

"'And I seek wine in barrels.'

"'I'll have the bet.' Another stood from his chair, his cruel liveries about him. It was Morton, captain and sometime thief, his sword in his hand. 'I'll have the bet,' he repeated, 'but be warned, I might take the head before I take the hand.' Morton roared in his drunken mirth. The room swallowed on its chuckles as it giggled into silence. All knew Morton meant his words. 'I have but two coins,' said Morton, swallowing his amusements. 'Who will join me to take a finger from this pie?'

"Entertainments thinning to a grim conclusion. 'I have the coins.

The bet was first to me. I accept the rate,' said the young man, offering me a chair. 'Now, wizard, what sorceries shall be your jest?'

"'I shall undo all my alchemies as trick. It is believed opposites cannot be merged. The four elements of earth, air, fire and water are separate unto themselves. But alchemy has distilled its alcohol, which is a liquid, water and yet it burns. I shall unmake the loaf and turn red wine clear, the spirit wine into water. Let that magic be my brew.'

"'It is worthy of the bet,' he nodded. The three coins, jeweled in their golden suns, spread upon the table. A cup of wine was brought. I looked into the reflections of its violet blood, smelled the charities of its perfume. My hand passing above the cup, sweet salts of lead held secret between my finger and my palm. The powder into the wine, the color clearing. I showed the cup to the young man. He looked into the diamonds of its clarity.

"'Drake, the bet is water. Better taste the brew. Your coins are won or lost upon a drink,' said the older man, some companion, I guessed.

"The young man took the cup. I grasped his wrist. 'I would not let that liquid touch your lips,' my voice edged droll in its authority.

"'I fear no wizardry.' He smiled his bravery in his easy youth.

"'Then fear this, the water now is poisoned.' The more the warning the better for its bite. I looked into his eyes. 'Judge the truth and do not drink.'

"'Then who has won?' was the cry across the tavern.

"'None,' I said. 'We have done our charities and amused each other. The sport is done. Keep your coins and I shall keep what parts I have.'

"'But if I drink the brew, call it water before I die, the coins are yours.'

"'I will not have all my treasures come by taint. Already I have murdered gold. Take my hand if you wish. I will not have your death on any coin.'

"The young man sat forward in his chair, whispering to me. 'What transformations come by sorrow? You have more soul than most. Why not better prospects?'

"'I seek no prospects.'

"'My name is of no account, but it is Drake, Francis to those who care. I am to have my first command, a small ship of a large fleet to trade upon the Spanish in South America. John Hawkins here, its admiral and my cousin. If you seek some death, why not the sea? It is great with obliging mortuaries, and if you live, there may be some wealth, wines by their barrels.'

"'Why not the sea?' I asked to myself. 'Its pastures rest on oceans. No herbs, no alchemies, all to forget, perhaps some death. Why not the sea?'

"'Out there, even a failed wizard may find his place,' Drake whispered, looking into my eyes, his nervous fingers tracing mysterious signs upon the table. 'Bind your life to salt and sea. Is not the philosopher's stone some part water? Out there, I am blessed. I will be your guide.' "

At Jamestown the old mariner looked at the company enraptured at his feet. "Does history have a philosopher's stone?" he asked. "This man, who would be an idea, who would be of water, would be my guide. To the alchemist all souls need a guide, and I in anguish.

"'The sea in its sorceries can elixir more in the mind than ever scalded in your wizard's glass,' said Drake. 'Come, sail upon a new magic. We need men we can trust.'

"We all change through what we know," said the old mariner, rising to his feet. "Why not alchemy of a different sort? Why not the sea? Why not the sea?" When he had stood, his face now in shadow, he turned and silently walked away.

Chapter Thirteen

AFRICA. SOUTH AMERICA. THE COMMERCE OF
BLOOD. AN EXECUTION BY FIRE.

HE NEXT NIGHT the skin of the old mariner seemed dark and leathery, as if it were the tanned hide of some exhumed mummy. He sucked his lips, which were encrusted with knots of flesh, barnacled, no doubt, by the same seawaters which swept his ships. He sat, an artifact of an unwritten book. I remember him. Time and distance but a flat upon my brain. The mariner's face less clear, his sentences break upon a phrase, my words to reintoxicate his tale. The mariner's life sings through me. So much lost. The mariner has become my words. He rises to his second death. I bleed another life. What fault this fiction is that it's true. And all our worlds are marshaled in their hidden clocks, ticking destinies in their secret hours. Now let us unwind the spring and eat the ghost of echoes in their passing things. The mariner sits at the Jamestown fire, his vision once again upon his Panama. I hear a voice. It is the line beneath my quill.

"We sat on that island for three days with Drake," he said, "waiting for a noose to rise from the sea and hang us from a Spanish tree…but no noose rose and the sea ran calm, as if the sea itself held her watery breath."

"Tell us of the history of your tobacco," someone cried. The mariner ignored the words as he continued.

"Diego sat with Drake, tending him, caring with the gentleness of a black angel. A Negro who would cut a Spanish throat just to watch the blood spurt, yet he had that healing woman's hand.

"It was Diego who changed Drake's life. Drake didn't see it happen, Diego and the tree and the vision. I am one of the few still alive who was there.

"We grumbled on Bastimentos for three days, Diego and Drake alone, in a deadly council. Diego told Drake of Panama, of its secret armies, its history and its jungle. Drake listened and he learned as he slipped down a well of another truth. The weather turned sour. The seas rolled heavy under pallid sweeps of spray. Lightning sutured the sky and thunder cracked its domes. The rains came in baptismal floods.

"On the third day, Drake told his brother John to go with Diego and find a group of escaped African slaves called Cimarrones, who fought, raided and harassed the Spanish near a town some leagues west and south called Veragua. They controlled that land in such strategies that even the Spanish would not enter it. The Cimarrones were of a fiery humor. They once sent messages to the Spanish saying that any soldiers who invaded their territory would have their heads severed and mounted on stakes to mark their roads.

"Drake now to his strategies. We were only a few and the Cimarrones were about three thousand. An alliance between us would draw a knife across the Spanish throat in Panama, and out would pour gold for us all. While the corsairs were holding their hopes at sea, waiting and hunting for Spanish ships, we'd have the gold in Panama before it ever saw the coast.

"We sailed at noon in our three pinnaces. The sea had spent its anger and ground itself into the gray of a potter's dust, sea and sky had fused into a single hue. We turned southward, searching for the horizon or a sail. Diego and John Drake we put ashore on a rocky beach where the land seemed to ooze mist into the sea. As the pinnace rowed to the land, our oar strokes left footprints in the surf. We waved from our decks. 'Godspeed. We will be at our camp on Pheasant Bay. Find the Cimarrones,' Drake cried. Diego waved back. 'It is done before its doing. A Spanish head on every tree.' His two arms opened wide, as if to embrace a jungle already hung with his deadly appointments."

As the old mariner spoke, his eyes reflected the living dance of the flames. *He lives his past as if it were before his eyes*, I said to myself. *What is this present but a longing swept in dreams?*

Suddenly I added aloud, "We are all a wanderer and a ghost, a soul searching for a spot of earth to haunt."

Profit looked toward me. "The one divides into its similarities, and we the likeness. What strange philosophies we mask in our resemblance, each in his own wisdoms."

A voice interrupted him to break the seal of our friendship. "Alchemist, tell us all in your physician considered truth your story of tobacco. Hoist us a learned hour with your wit. Sport us tales of your adventures, so well abused in your venoms." So spoke a gentleman as he strutted, his pipe newly filled with the Indian weed, another gift to privilege Wingfield had taken from our common store. The gentleman and his cronies saluted us in their pleasures. "Reward for the estate that rank persuades," he said. The mariner turned, watching the campfire, ignoring in that moment that anyone might be alive.

"We sailed southeast now," the mariner continued, "Drake needing supplies, our food and ammunition becoming a memory in our hold. A lesser man than Drake would have put ashore, conserved his victuals and waited for what might be, lying down in his mind before the death rattle were in his bones, but not old Drake. He had done that once at San Juan de Ulúa in Mexico four years before and he'd never do it again. It pinched his soul so hard that to his dying day he would still feel the pain."

"Drake is Drake. Leave him to his armadas. Tell us of Raleigh and how he seduced the court and invented pleasures that gave us all the weed," sneered the gentleman, half drunk on his privilege.

The old mariner looked up, surprised to see anyone around him.

"Should I tell you the tales of the weed?" he said. Then he shrieked and laughed with the madness of one possessed. "Cast down your Raleigh. All history is a lie. Drake is the story of tobacco, and you pray to hear it, eh!" Those around the fire gestured for the mariner to continue. "It be strange, all and all," raged the mariner, "tell a tale going backwards as it were, not coming forward…but you'd be wise to listen, for though Drake came to these shores where we now sit but twice, his spirit still wanders the breeze in its whispers and in its longings. The smell of him is still in this earth."

The old mariner sat back for a moment, straightening his spine, listening to the air. He heard nothing, I suppose, for if he did he gave no sign of it. Finally, he began to speak. "All mysteries are omens of tales men fear to tell. Even from the very beginning it be true. So it is we build our legends in our lies."

I was then to have the tale of Drake in full, a man whose life I knew only by bits, rumors, and here and there a poem, so little did he tell by his own words. And I, his ink to scribe his final page. What prodigal is a child's love? I to adopt a father by his histories? But how else could I, by myself, be set? We are cast by our own thoughts, by our own image we are made. And yet my blanks are not my home. Drake not just a memory in a quest. The search is not always what is sought, the treasure not always of a coin. I am in birth, to what am I born? A child who ever seeks his father may forever lose himself.

"Columbus in the New World but a few hours," said Jonas Profit, "when a savage in a canoe offered the admiral some dry leaves. Those leaves, when burned, had a sweet and wholesome scent much like incense. History did not then have a name for that leaf, but names are soon made for men to play their schemes upon their toys. That savage offered friendship with the leaf, as was their custom. The Spanish had no use for peace or the weed, they wanted only gold and women and slaves.

"Some days later Columbus sent two of his company ashore with an Indian guide. On a dusty road, no more than a jungle track, they saw a group of savages, men and women, walking toward them, the men carrying lighted sticks and tapers in one hand and in the other a leaf rolled into a funnel. Some of these tubes were one to two feet in length. Into the mouth that broadened into a horn, the savages pushed a quantity of the crushed tobacco, which they would constantly light and relight with the burning taper. To those Spanish it was as if the savages did drink smoke. Spain had witnessed its first cigar.

"Luis de Torres, one of those Spaniards, was a scholar and a linguist of great facility, a learned Jew, perhaps the last of his people to have an important position at the Spanish court. He was to be ambassador to the lands of the Khan of Cathay. In truth, his people under threat, he sought for them a sanctuary, a new Jerusalem rising in the West in a new world. But it was not to be. Before Torres returned to court, Ferdinand and Isabella had ordained the expulsion of all Jews from Spain, a thousand years of history now a ghost. The next year, all the Muslims. A million people forced to flee, a disaster in the market towns of Spain. A population gone. An economy ruined. Poverty now brought itself in greed. Universities soon but hollows, no science produced, no new inventions used, all progress crucified. The Inquisition had brought punishment upon its own. Spain became the country of the tomb. Torres now unwelcomed at home, around him dangers. He fled to the New World, settling finally in Cuba, where he was discovered by the Inquisition and burned at the stake.

"The second Spaniard's fate was no less cruel," said the mariner, as his hands grasped at some burning embers floating in the wind. "Rodrigo de Jerez of Ayamonte acquired the tobacco habit, as did most of Columbus's crew. It was said he was the first to publicly smoke the leaf in Spain. In his native town of Ayamonte, the neighbors, seeing him drinking smoke, thought he was possessed of demons. They called a local priest, his boyhood friend, who arrested him, sending him to the Inquisition to be tried. Tortured, no explanation wise enough when suspicion is the law, de Jerez to rot in prison for fifteen years, only to be released into a Spain quite content, enjoying its own smoking habit, the same pursuit for which de Jerez was imprisoned by the Inquisition. Such is justice when its license is by ignorance and by whim."

The mariner sighed, "When Columbus sailed for Spain again, aboard his ships was the new trinity of the new age: gold and tobacco and dozens of savages to be sold as slaves. Within decades, ten thousand slaves in Andalusia alone. In other regions of Spain, thousands more. In the West Indies whole populations sent to work the gold mines of Hispaniola. Ships so filled with men and women and children it is said one could navigate between the islands by sailing only by the floating paths of corpses riding the currents. A hundred thousand Indians shipped from the Yucatan to Hispaniola to work and to starve, exhausted in the mines. Death was a bargain. Indians worth less than the food to feed them. They died by the Spanish cruelty, while their masters had their pleasures and smoked the weed or snuffed it or chewed it with white powder of crushed seashells. That use being discovered by Amerigo Vespucci on the island of Margarita off the coast of South America in 1499. The Indians offering Vespucci the leaf to slake his thirst, there being little fresh water on the island. And so the rumor came in all its false witness that the savages lived on the weed for days to relieve their hunger and quench their thirst.

"And so do rumors begin to spread their imagined truths, woven in the spiders of their entangled web. Tobacco now mentioned as a remedy, on such slight hopes do men brew their cure, but the story not ending there. So tobacco was spread by mariners along the coast of Spain and France and of all Europe, though smoking a curiosity mostly seen about the docks. In the West Indies tobacco was farmed as a novel pleasure to enthrall some idle recreations, the lazy Spaniards seeing little value in the crop. Most of the Indians of the islands dead, the numbers of the slaughtered never to be known. The weed was grown by black slaves newly arrived from Africa, they to replace in their agonies the agonies of the lost. African blacks cost more, the Spaniards investing real wealth in their flesh. Their treatment better, more survived. Such is Spanish kindness. For twenty-five years tobacco held its casual use, the weed left for others to exploit, until 1560 and Portugal and Jean Nicot and a world awakening to the rumors of great cures. What new day is this that dreams to a different light?" The old mariner smiled ironies in his wisdom.

"In these early days when Drake followed John Hawkins, it be an easy but desperate living in the sea for those that dared. The Spanish government held monopoly on all trade in the Americas. Special licenses were needed, which could be bought only in Spain. But for those who had the courage and the blessed lack of scruples, it were possible to steal goods or slaves on the high seas or in Africa, sail to South America, bribe a Spanish governor and trade 'til your ship burst with gold.

"John Hawkins had invented this trade, made many trips and done so well he brought his cousin, young Drake, into the business as a family favor. The problem was the Spanish government knew of the illegal trade, and in a fit of royal displeasure, several local officials were hung, as a humane reminder to the rest that some laws were meant to be obeyed occasionally. Needless to say, this newly found Spanish enlightenment closed down the trade for good, or at least until the corpses cooled. Into this new moral sea sailed Hawkins and Drake and I in 1568, all fresh with excitement and disgust from a little piracy off the coast of Portugal and a little slaving on the coast of Africa. Drake never having the stomach for that trade, his humanities always deeper than his greed. Hawkins only to his accounts and his merchandise. I was then a man angered in the grief that I could not die. Anger was a lethal noose, but only for the soul. I who had studied to be an alchemist to cure the sick, compassion to be my inspired eyes, to see disease, search out the cause. And I believed as did my fellow alchemists that when God created a disease, for that disease he also made a cure. Our calling was to seek that remedy in the world, cast potions and confections as God has done. God in me as I in God, this world as my saber, I wield it about my head with a double will. And so I studied nature and its metals and its herbs, and the new leaf they called tobacco, the cure of all cures. So simple is the power we offend. This practice brought to what? And still God hides, and still to Hawkins on this voyage no prospects seemed too bright, and no profits seemed so easy, only a few dead and a few wounded.

"Hawkins' fleet of six ships now crossed the Atlantic, sailing for the little town of Rio de la Hacha, on the bowl of South America along the coast of Colombia, a hundred miles north and east of Cartagena. And so things return to their beginnings to begin again. The governor of Rio de la Hacha had indulged in spasms of corruption so corrupt Hawkins thought him a friend. But in truth, there had been trouble two years before when one of Hawkins' commanders, a Captain Lovell, had been denied a license to trade in the town, and the venture had gone sour. In the end, Lovell abandoned sixty black slaves on a beach for the Spanish to find, rather than face the expense of bringing them home.

"Drake had been a purser on that voyage, and Hawkins knew that his young cousin had a little tingle of vengeance in his liver. Now Drake commanded an advance party of two ships, which sailed all bright in fair breeze into Rio de la Hacha. Drake being to the Spanish, even then, the devil's grandson, he pushed those ships into the harbor, their sails and banners to the wind all plumed and taut. The Spanish about lost their eyeballs with the shock.

"Now, the town's governor, Castellanos, then being still newly converted to the ways of the righteous, and having his victory of Lovell to live up to, not to mention a little guilty roll to his swagger over all the trading he had done in the past, was afraid, he was, that the town be better at remembering than forgetting. So he ordered three cannons fired, the noise being more important than the direction. Them balls splashed around harmlessly like hollow fists, Drake answering with a cannonade of his own, putting five cannonballs through the governor's own house. There came a general exchange of firelocks, cannons, pistols, tongues of fire from the cannons almost lost in the smoke, which swept in drifts over the town and ships like a rolling beast. Our ship crossed before the face of the town, not firing now, showing the colors of our determination. We were there for trade, after all, not war. The guns of the town were silent. Some of the buildings burned, the roofs pushed outward, beams protruding through the smoke and the hints of fire. Figures ran hysterically through the streets, their shadows following like demons on the walls of the stucco buildings.

"Drake sailed out of the harbor, anchored and blockaded it, waiting for Hawkins and the rest of the fleet. When Hawkins arrived, he was in a fury. He saw most laws as inconvenient and those who obeyed them more inconvenient than most. He held Castellanos's conversion as a momentary religious spasm, which a large portion of profit would cure, but Hawkins was now low on supplies of fresh water and food. The slaves in the hold were costing him a fortune to feed. He had six ships bouncing aimlessly in the surf. The men were grumbling and Hawkins had backers who expected a profit. One of them is said to have been the queen herself.

"Hawkins was a desperate man, but in his desperation he was patient. He wrote to Castellanos saying he only wanted a license to trade, adding that his ships had been blown off course, and all he needed was a little commerce so he could reprovision. These were lies, but Hawkins hoped they would give the governor an excuse to take the most self-evidently reasonable course, which for Hawkins was the most profitable. Castellanos, fearing he had more to lose than a few coins, said no.

"To Hawkins, such determination in the face of profit was insanity. He himself was always reasonable in his vices, unlike the French corsairs; but, like Drake, he was a strange mixture. It was a many-spiced blood that flowed in both men. Hawkins would have his trade and his profit, even if it brought the whole Spanish empire to his throat. Passions are wisdoms of the beast. Hawkins did not understand that he was about to commit an act of war. To him it was merely shrewd practice in a business he had pioneered.

"Early the next day the sea rolled softly, as if it were still half in slumber. Cowering in its watery breath, two hundred well-armed men slipped over the sides of our ships down ropes to waiting boats, pikes and crossbows and firelocks on their backs. The oarsmen ready, the boats rocked gently in the impatient heat. Hawkins had decided to seize Rio de la Hacha and force Castellanos to grant him a trading license. We are all servants to the pleasures that allow us to forget. To Hawkins, a signed piece of paper would legalize all that came before, and commit to armistice all memories of the destruction and the killing, all the ruins, and so again would sweetly surge the ambrosias of our trade.

"The boats cast off. We rowed, the fleet diminishing in distance as the land rose before us with opening arms. We landed and marched toward the town; ahead of us, festooned in their gallant rags walked our trumpeters and drummers, scattering noise. Down the main street we went, past shuttered windows and stuccoed walls brooding white; our shadows, like deformed needles, thrusting at their plastered silence. In the town center Castellanos and his militia knelt behind barricades of barrels and scraps of wood, waiting. 'Come sweet death,' I prayed, 'let me kiss your breathless lips.' The Spaniards rose, motley in their rags of war. They volleyed in their broken ranks, a lazy cloud of smoke rising behind their disappearing thunder.

"'I am not dead,' I cursed. One of our company, his face torn away, fell to his knees screaming, coughing blood in the bugle of his throat. His agony was ignored as a hail of arrows in their threads wove the air. We fell back, more in surprise than fear of hurt, releasing our own vengeance in shots and crossbow darts, which fell about the barrels like the clatter of iron teeth. Spanish figures rose in wounds and terrors, arms flung wide, falling backwards. Others ran in panic. They were gone, we let them go—the Spanish, their Indian militia and some blacks, trusted slaves, holding weapons. The town was ours.

"But what conquest did we have? An empty city. The entire population had fled into the hills, hiding in secret places all their jewels, their gold, their treasure. All the wealth that we would have. There in the town we sat, defeated in our victory, watching the breached doors of houses sway in silent mockeries. Words turned rancid in our throats. Still scheming his salvation, Hawkins had a plan. He wrote a friendly note to Castellanos saying it was a shame events had come to this unhappy pass. But he, Hawkins, bore no ill will and still desired a license to trade. Castellanos answered from the hills by burning all the crops in the fields. We could gather no food. Hawkins paced the streets of his empty town, kicking dust at dust in his fury, smoke from the fields rising like a fiery beacon at his back. But Hawkins was a resourceful man. Since the Spanish did not want his slaves or his cloth, he would trade them for their own town. He wrote another letter to the governor saying unless he received forty-five hundred ducats, Rio de la Hacha would be burned to the ground.

"With torches in hand, running through the streets, our eyes bright with expectation, like children at hideous play. Twenty buildings were set afire, including the governor's own, smoke from the fields and the buildings rising in wind-swept columns, merging far away in the float of distance, two intents now in a powerful unity. 'If you fire all the buildings in the Indies, my answer will be the same,' wrote Castellanos, 'now and forever *no*.'

"It be a hard biscuit in old Hawkins' mouth, eh Smith?" The eyes of the mariner reflected the light of our raging campfire. The dancing embers in its smoke raced upward to journey with the night, joining with that sweet breath of the wind that in my imagination I saw as the fleeing smoke of Rio de la Hacha. The old mariner's arms lay on his bent knees. His hands were limp. He stared ahead. "So we sat," he said. "For Hawkins there could be no real war. The Queen would only accept an incident in the pursuit of profit, not a general conflict. For the Spanish there could be no real peace. To barter with us would mean the governor's head.

"As the night bears its own shadow, so an enigma bears its own solution. He came sweetly, carrying his own death, as he came with a gift to buy his own resurrection. He was a black African, a slave, one of the Spanish irregular militia which the Spaniards added now and again to the numbers of their local forces. He came in ragged protocol to offer a proposition. 'Take me to my freedom beyond the Spanish and I shall take you to where is hid the town's treasure.'

"Hawkins pulled at his own collar to hold himself up, as his knee almost bent in gratitude. There were no agreements or pledges more solemnly sworn, or more honor encrusted in any words than those that were spoken there. The black led us to atop a small hill near the town. There were one hundred in our party, all well armed. As we approached the crest, there came a howl from a distant rise, as if the earth, expecting an injury, had already felt imagined pain. On the other hill, the townspeople gathered, crying, cursing the air with voices and waving fists. Someone fired a shot, which we ignored. The black man, our informer, jumped and laughed and waved his hands, making such faces that once he even dared to show the Spanish the air of his behind. Then he fell to whimpering, telling us of his suffering and of the Spanish brutalities: children with their hands cut off for stealing, women torn apart by wild dogs as a sport, their infants in their arms. He was a soul made mad with memories.

"Near a rock at the hill's crest our shovels tore upon the earth, our bodies sweating avarice. Within an hour we had gathered all the gold and jewels and silver, plates and pearls and cups. We marched to the town, singing, giving praise to the bounty of God's plunder. It was a king's ransom, maybe twenty thousand ducats, I would guess. In the town again, we burned the cathedral in the honor of God's love and his wisdom for making us Protestants. Then we ate, the black cooking our scraps of meat in the cathedral embers. Then we slept."

"Black or Indian, it makes a fine alliance to put at the Spanish throat," came a voice from the campfire at Jamestown. "That's why we're here to forge steel from flesh." The company cheered, then quieted again, listening to the mariner.

"It is a strange flood of ice that ran through Hawkins's heart. What spice it was, the vinegar of his blood. You would think we'd pack our ships and sail away, but not Hawkins. Gold would not suffice. He needed cloaks to cover all his crimes. He knew the queen could not afford a war with Spain. He knew the Spanish would demand the return of all their treasure, and the queen, in all her grumblings and all her delays, would sweetly return it to them, packed in rages and cradled in her curses. Hawkins wrote again to Castellanos, demanding either a license to trade, or he would keep the treasure. It was a clever humanity that brought a stranger vice. Castellanos had no choice. He had to negotiate. There, in an open field, the two sat, a crude wooden table between them, exchanging pleasantries and gifts, as if loyalty and memory were just conceits altered to fairer currents when a moment's need arose.

"What admiration there was in those courtly twins, Hawkins and Castellanos. The day was fine. The wine was good. They smiled. They danced the dance of commerce, as birds playfully slaughtered worms at their feet. Drake, not important enough to have his say, was on his tiny ship. Hawkins traded his goods for forty-five hundred ducats and some dozen barrels of tobacco, that being of the good smoking leaf, Nicotiana tabacum, not well known then in England. Hawkins accepting this first supply, believing it would have its value, there being no real store of tobacco in Plymouth or London or on the eastern coast, but for the few private weights owned by mariners. Castellanos had most of his town's treasure, plus one hundred and ten slaves, some cloth and spices as evidence for our conscience and for the crown that what was received was for trade not for ransom. The two stood, shook hands and gestured their satisfaction with a hug. Castellanos offered Hawkins another glass of wine to salute their friendship. Two tobacco leaves were rolled into funnels, then stuffed with more crushed leaf. One was handed to Hawkins. The cigar was lit. These cornucopias protruding like trumpets from their mouths, they enjoyed the taste on each blossom of smoke, smiling to each other through the elixir of the weed. What remedy is this that brings its secrets in practical cures? War avoided, profit to all in brotherly commerce.

"How full Hawkins was with himself, to be so hollow. He was filled with that determined worm of joy which, as the sea slug, invades all things, even the rotten cargoes, with the shadow of itself. As we turned to lift the treasure to our carts, Hawkins ordered that the black be given to Castellanos as a prize. There is a scream in silence the earth does make that pierces the ears of men, into their very souls. The black in silent thunder stood and from his bones his flesh did slide. He came at Hawkins, cursing with savage oaths. The Spanish seized him, bore him in his rage away. Castellanos patted Hawkins on his back. Someone in our party would have helped the black, but instead we spit at the earth as if it were more guilty than ourselves. How many times must we fail before we know we fail? And so in our hesitations we do offend, weeping in our dry tears the legends of the lost.

"We rowed to our ships and brought back the cloth and the slaves as was our pledge. Chained together on a beach, surrounded by bales of cloth and barrels of spices, we left them. They seemed confused and unsteady. Through the throat of the street we could see the town square. There the Spanish had dug a stake in the earth, piled cords of wood around to the height of a man's chest. They tied the black to it. He struggled as if he would have fled from his own flesh. The Spanish threw oil on the wood and lit the pyre. It is strange to think that he who has an immortal soul would have such fragile meat, to see him, a black man, melt.

"We left the harbor heading north. When we were beyond the sight of land, the smoke from the pyre, a whirlwind shard, floated like a plaintive wisp, a beacon column, calling softly to errant ships sailing on the drum rolls of the sea."

Chapter Fourteen

'WINGOPHOW' AND WAR. THE CURSE OF SAN JUAN
DE ULÚA. THE GODS IN WILLFUL LONGINGS.

IN JAMESTOWN, we awoke to mists in their exhausted light, wandering aimlessly through our camp. In the trees birds screamed hysterically, flapped their wings and waited. Others huddled in the riggings of the ships, dark and round, like predatory fruit. Some of the cook fires were being nursed with damp wood and curses. Their smoke drifted upward, mixing with the mist. Ghostly forms around me rose now, half-dressed, ragged shapes, as if the earth were vomiting forth its dead. The dew on their faces, clothes drenched, they staggered in their forgetful sleep.

At the black iron cook pots, men ladled worms from the boiled oats. More water was poured into the pot and pieces of salt pork were cut from large clubs of flesh. In the half-light, it appeared that men did cleave their own flesh to spice their stew.

Wingfield had ordered that gentlemen would take their meals first and sit with gentlemen. Others could eat later, all taking but one bowl of food; although it was said that gentlemen, if they held back from work a time, could take a second dip. While food was bad those first few days, those with money or goods to trade could purchase extra victuals from the sailors on Newport's ships. This kept some of the gentlemen half-content. But I wondered to myself how would it be when the ships departed. We had been at sea six months instead of the expected three. A good portion of our supplies now consumed, our corn being planted late in the year, we sat with our futures to our backs, while we faced I knew not what.

I sat among our common men as we picked the remaining worms from our boiled oats, deciding with a smile and a laugh, what was pork and what was worm. The mist began to burn away, the departing sigh of clouds revealing in its flight the sun's warm coin. Martin staggered by, still examining rocks for traces of gold. His son, fifteen years old, at his side seemed drawn and sickly. Wingfield was demanding that all at our tables stand when he stood or just happened to walk by. The discussion was how close Wingfield would have to pass for a standing to be appropriate. The general consensus was about ten feet. Someone suggested a mile. Wingfield would have had the man flogged, but Bartholomew Gosnold objected. Standing behind Wingfield, Archer urged the punishment in whispers, knowing if those in power fell, he would be sure to rise. The effect on our enterprise he did not care. Ambition is the cannibal that swallows the whole before it eats a piece. Ratcliffe smirked as Gosnold and Wingfield fought. Captain George Kendall stood watching, his advice not sought. Finally Captain Newport and Reverend Hunt interceded and the man was spared, his punishment being a bucket of cold water poured down his sleeve.

Near the shore a sailor fished from a small boat, which rocked on the quiet rolls of surf. Our life, in desperation, had returned to its indolent struggle, believing we sat only on another English countryside. Only Newport's sailors worked, cutting trees and hauling logs for our fort or fishing for our food. Our few farmers mostly argued who should plow and who should plant, not wanting to leave their English ways behind, where their jobs were specialties and no farmer did them all.

I had stood and watched this decaying wreck a week or more. No houses built, most men still slept on the bare earth. Anger in me surged. I would mold the colony to the shape of my own hand, I swore. I called to those men near me to pick up their tools and follow. Fools need examples if they are to labor to the full, while others are fed by history's cup, what I, myself, could not forget. Perhaps in action I could find my solace, like Drake.

Twenty men took up their labors, myself at their side. We felled a great tree from whose wounded trunk gushed a liquid with the smack of fine vinegar about it. We barreled many cups, which we set in a common store for all to use.

At midday two savages approached and made signs of peace, which we acknowledged with our own. Wingfield advanced to show his authority, I by his side as interpreter, and so we would have made some parley with them, until one of our number fired a shot which scared the wretches so they fled and hid behind some stumps, screaming "wingophow," which is their word for peace.

With some patience, and a few little gifts, I convinced the savages that we were indeed their friends. They rose slowly from behind their stumps and said that they had come from our friend, the chief of the Paspaheghs, to offer some advice: cut down the tall grass around our camp, so none could approach without being seen.

We gestured thanks to the savages for their advice, and they left happy with our gifts. That day some few cut the grass as the savages had advised, while the rest who would, labored at the stockade wall. Archer complained to me that I wasted time on cutting grass and building walls, while no one had yet set up his tent. And he and other gentlemen whose servants were left at home were forced to sleep on unprotected ground, or on the ships, or under trees.

I said to Archer, "You are a captain of our company, and would be of the council if you could. Gather a work party for yourself and set up all the tents you desire." I thought the conversation had ended. I turned my back and left Archer muttering in the dust, "I am not here to dung at manual tasks that are beneath my station."

Not turning around, I replied, "Since what day have you been beyond giving an order?"

"The men only follow you because of your mutinies," he screamed.

I left him, his feet still flat. We toiled in the heat that day, drinking water that smelled of fish and tasted of rotting things, our store of wine and beer and aqua vitae being low. Wingfield decided to have a well dug, a wise project it seemed to all. But then it languished, no one appointed to oversee it done, or man its labor. And so we drank the stale water of the bay or the dwindling shipboard kegs. It was Newport a few days later who set his sailors to dig our well, he then ready to leave for home and fearing for the health of his sailors on that long voyage. The well, when dug, was only a few feet deep. So high did the water run within the ground that it soon tasted as did the bay. Nothing accomplished there, I fear, but a waste of time, and the idea that Jamestown was a bad place to build a fort.

As evening began to drill its darkness through the sky, and the heat still hung in curtains on the antique light, Ratcliffe and a companion left the camp unseen, in their hands a few gifts, the gasps of their restrained laughs choking in their throats. I saw them leave, I let them go. Ratcliffe's licentious needs were stronger than his cowardice, and stronger than my restraints. Besides, if any among us was capable of learning, Ratcliffe would be a purposeful lesson. I sat quietly by the men, eating barley soup, spiced with the usual worms and bay water. The screams came shortly as we talked. Ratcliffe ran in first, his eyes the width of moons.

"Two savages attacked us," he gasped. Behind him his companion stumbled, six arrows in his back and three in his chest. He fell forward and the arrows pushed deeper into his chest. The shafts splintered. He rolled and screamed and gurgled in his faint. Our surgeon attended him. He was not dead. They carried him toward the ships.

"What were you doing beyond the sentries in this heat?" I asked.

"Exploring for berries and for a few delicacies to warm the porridge of the crew," Ratcliffe said. The men mumbled, looking at their soup.

"Be careful how your fingers scent," I said. "There are berries here that will gnaw your arm."

We sat around the fire, listening to the wounded man's cries, as if the moon's egg had hatched a very peculiar bird, and mused that night on a land where trees bled vinegar and gestures of peace brought war. For three days he screamed and screamed as if he were calling for his own lost death, which found him at last, unconscious, on the fifth day.

"But here, at least, we eat," said a youth whose clothes already lay on him like rags. "In the north country where I come from, jobs are so scarce that some did hunt and steal in packs and eat the bark of trees. In bunches on the gallows they were hung, as you would think the earth had grown a new tree with strange fruit that dangled in the shape of men."

"And when Newport and his ships are gone? What are we then but souls who carry their own graves slippin' on their backs," said one, sucking on the bones of an eight-foot sturgeon one of Newport's sailors had caught from a small boat, the fish rising on the sailor's line from between the thighs of the waves, as a thing born to death.

"We will still have one sea worthy boat," said Archer, watching the pinnace roll on the invisible tide. "We could make for England in that."

"Not all of us," said a gentleman sitting at his feet, the sweat on his face reflecting the firelight.

"Enough to bring help," said Archer, smiling as a man counting his opportunities.

"A six months' trip to England and back, with luck. And if you returned, what would you find? A Roanoke? A whisper in the trees? A ghost so cold it couldn't even raise a shade?" said the man.

"It's a bad thing to quit," said the old mariner, "even if you have your own good reasons. The smell of it never leaves thee. It makes a restless dark where you lay your head. I saw it with Drake after San Juan de Ulúa. Every man is a binding of a curse and a vision. For Drake the curse came at San Juan de Ulúa. The vision came later." The old mariner poked the flaming logs of those fires of long ago. I can see him, hypnotized by their undulating light, as I speak now my memories for him.

"After Rio de la Hacha and the burning of the black, the winds never tasted right. Hawkins sailed north to the town of Santa Marta, where we feigned an attack on the town to supply its governor with an excuse to trade with us. We left having sold one hundred and ten slaves for a good profit and a few barrels of tobacco. Then we sailed north again into the Gulf of Mexico.

"Hawkins, who was now well pleased with himself, decided for home. But the sea can be a fickle host. Hawkins's plan had been to sail the passage between Cuba and Florida and then to England. I sailed with Hawkins on the *Jesus*. She was the largest of the fleet, an ancient hulk, carrying twenty-six cannons. Drake commanded the tiny *Judith*. Three weeks out the sky turned into a brooding plate. Swelling waves clawed our ship's hull, their white foam heads, blown by the surge of the storm's breath, hammering at the wooden planks. Our ships swayed and rolled, plunging into the water's canyons, only to rise like helpless tubs on the accelerating fury of the storm's exploding crest. Mountainous waves, their water smashed to smoke. Ships lost sight of ships. Clothes were stripped from our backs. We tied ourselves to restraining ropes and groped along the decks, blind with stinging rain. We gestured in the half dark, our eyes crying visions of strange beasts, men drowning in the air. Night and day merged in a seamless howl. Men's lips moved, speaking silence, their words blown dumb. We lost ten at night. The last, his shoulders bobbing above the receding waves, was held rough, as in a lover's grasp, his mouth round in soundless screams, his tightened fist waving as he disappeared.

"For eight days the storm chased us northwest, tearing our sails and battering our leaking hulls. The others of our fleet, seeing the call of our sails, gathered to us like frightened chicks. One ship was lost, the *William and John*. She eventually made England alone. But on the ninth day the sun rose, the sea calmed into a shimmering peace. Below decks soaked timbers began to buckle. We cut away part of the upper deck and threw it overboard to relieve the strain. We were desperate with fear, cheering as we tore the ship apart. We had become cannibals, greedily consuming our own flesh. On the tenth day, our ship still in danger, we found ourselves near the coast of Mexico in waters no Englishman had ever seen. Our sails torn, our hulls creaking in distress, we had no choice but to make for the nearest port and make repair for the long journey home.

"At midday we hailed a Spanish ship going south, which we detained. From the captain we learned that the only usable port for one hundred miles was San Juan de Ulúa, the gold and silver treasure port for the inland city of Vera Cruz and anchorage for the Spanish treasure fleet. The flota, Hawkins was told, was due there in two weeks. Hawkins had no choice. He would make for San Juan de Ulúa and hope he could complete repairs before the flota arrived."

The old mariner looked up from the fire, his eyes flowing, as if purging heat. "Some will say it was a desperate and foolish gamble old Hawkins took." He smiled. "The only breeze to blow us home funneled through that town, and that's where we had to go.

"San Juan de Ulúa wasn't even a town. It was a dusty tongue of a road, protruding into the sea, protected by a finger of land and an earthwork fort with a battery of cannon on a small island. At the foot of the road were a chapel and a few exhausted huts for the laborers. At the door to one sat an Indian girl on a low stool. There was a chain around her neck, attached to a spike in the ground nearby. I was aloft in the rigging watching with a spyglass. A Spaniard came by, threw some coins into a bowl. Even at my great distance I could see the girl rise as if with a great weight, then they both disappeared into the hut.

"Eight small ships were scattered around the harbor. None was large enough to be part of the flota and none was armed. They all slept, their noses buried in the gentle waves, their crews ashore, their denuded masts riding above the tiny swells like leafless trees. The town seemed to sleep an exaggerated dream of sleep.

"Our ships in a line, Hawkins sailed our fleet into the harbor. It was September fifteenth, 1568. We had been away from home almost a year. The Spanish waved handkerchiefs, guessing we were the first units of the flota to arrive. Some of us leaned over our damaged hull, others knelt by loaded cannons behind our gun ports, praying for boundless luck. Half in the harbor, a small boat rowed from the shore. Two Spanish dignitaries, a few soldiers as honor guard and the unarmed oarsmen approached us. We lowered our ladders. The distance between the two boats closed. I wondered how long it would be before the Spanish noticed the bleached English Standard flying from our masthead. It should have been struck. Our own mistake had nailed the Spanish to a joke. I watched our faded flag struggle to unfurl itself in the exhausted wind, studied the reckless advance of the Spanish craft and smiled as I hummed a sea dirge in my head. No man, however wise, can see the surprise mapped on the tip of his own nose, I thought.

"There was a cry from the Spanish boat, hands pointing at our flag, oars frantically beating against the motion of their own race. Hawkins rose, looking over the gun ports of the ship, six men with firelocks at his side. He gestured to the Spanish to come aboard and be his guests. The Spanish conversed with each other. A gun port of our ship opened and a cannon pushed forward. A sailor stood with a lit taper. Hawkins gestured again. The Spanish nodded their consent as if it had been their idea all along.

"The two Spanish of rank who came aboard were Martin de Marcana, deputy governor of Vera Cruz, and Francisco de Bustamante, its treasurer, coming to greet the flota and Don Martin Enriquez, the viceroy of Mexico, one of the two most powerful men in all the Americas.

"Hawkins played the drama sweet and acted as if the news were not of much concern to him. Our little profiteering adventure had come fair winds to an act of war. Hawkins decided he would seize the town and its fort, but he told the Spaniards only the better half, which was that he had been blown off course by a storm and only wished to refit his ships, then leave. He would pay for all the provisions he took and all would be well treated.

"The Spanish did not seem well convinced or well disposed to have English visitors, but surrounded by one hundred and fifty well-armed men, they had little opportunity to protest, especially after Hawkins mentioned they were to remain on his ship as a guarantee of their good faith.

"Our ships anchored along the roadstead, our bows and their rigging overhanging the road as cows feeding at a trough. We went ashore, took control of the fort and greeted the surprised Spanish soldiers by disarming them. Barricades and cannons we set up at the head of the road. Parties of our armed men faced west into the hardpan of the land, and batteries of our cannon faced east, toward the cruelty of the sea. Then some began to repair our ships, while others, having nothing else to do, reclaimed their steady feet upon the constant unmoving earth. We caroused with our reluctant Spanish hosts, sitting on dirty chairs in the shade of faded rags, drinking wine and spirits. We got on well with the Spanish then, they having no recourse. Several Spanish drunks even swaggered with our fellows, arm in arm, stumbling down the road, bottles in their hands, their songs uncorked, their feet unsteady, wobbling, seeking the path to visit the Indian girl. A few playfully fought with each other over who would go first, bowing in mock courtesy for their companions to have the opening honors. I was in the mast repairing some sails. I could taste the wind and feel the smell on my flesh. Apart, I watched the Indian girl, who looked no doubt on us as the same old plague speaking a different tongue. It sickened me to see our lads take up with such ease Spanish cruelty. I could do nothing. I just sat and watched the silent convulsions of the clouds move in heralding flows against the distant armies of the air.

"On the second day the watches in our mast cried, 'Thirteen ships bearing Spanish sails....' The mouth of the waters opened to the horizon's tongue. It was the advance guard of the flota. Within an hour we could see clearly two Spanish warships and eleven armed merchant men moving swiftly in their predatory grace toward San Juan de Ulúa. Already Hawkins had ordered shields and iron-covered barricades erected amidship of most of his docked fleet. Men with crossbows and firelocks watched seaward, swinging gently in the rigging, their figures drifting dark against the wind, like sweet berries of some exotic vine. On the island, the fort was reinforced with new cannon. Hawkins wandered in his cabin, thinking, emerging to gauge the confusion in its desperate landscape. For Hawkins, his fingers were in a dam of flames and he knew it. He had the military force to keep the flota from entering the harbor, but to do so would be an act against the peace so heinous that Queen Elizabeth would be obliged under Spanish threat to exact some punishment. Hawkins decided on another desperate wager with the fates. He would strike a bargain with the Spanish flota and Don Martin Enriquez for the time to complete our repairs. Hawkins would let the Spanish enter the harbor.

"A boat was immediately dispatched, our small craft disappearing into the oncoming fleet. The flota trimmed its sails. It anchored and sat waddling in its own surf, like a seabird in its digestion and its rest. I am told that Don Martin Enriquez was not a gleeful prince when he was quietly informed that his return to his own harbor would be delayed, and there would be a price. But he had few choices. Storms come suddenly in that gulf, so his whole fleet, without safe harbor, would be at risk. True, he was embarrassed, but to prolong negotiation was to prolong his shame. It took another day to seal the agreement with the Judas kiss. Then, with resisting winds, the flota struggled and tacked and found its way through the bay, docking at our side, their main ship next to the *Jesus*.

"It was another merry night, after the flota set its anchor and ropes alongside our own; Lutherans, as they called us, and Papists trading drinks of spirits and tales of the sea. The night was mild and I walked the road, a bottle in hand, looking up at the Spanish ships, which on closer sight seemed less asleep than I had thought. I listed not my thoughts upon the cause, which was a mistake, the Spanish being but bred to lie. And I was walking that night on drink-reluctant feet. I swayed in the direction of somewhere down the road — and so we all deceive ourselves into practical crime. We love ourselves too much to act the judge unless it serves some better need. I walked toward the chapel and the gray, windowless huts, ghost pavilions whispering secret protocols from their dark chambers.

"I passed our barricades, our sentries. 'There be a lot going over to the other side tonight,' said a figure resting against a cannon. I belched a reply as I climbed over the pile of barrels and logs that served as our fort line. A full moon hung in a mist, its light dim, illuminating only silhouettes, as half-exhausted flares. I to relieve my pain, I blamed my wife for her own death. She not the fault, it was I in all my alchemies. And why not debauchery? Why not beast upon the voices in ourselves? Are we not an alchemy of sorts? Is not lust a brew? All memory is a deception to explain a passion, and so we taint that piece that reminds us best. And if that piece we find be hate? And so I train the tatters as I seek the passions of the whole, my loneliness grieving again the aging of my youth. My lost love in its darkening ardor. I found the hut. Around its door men lay like discarded boards, some half-drowned in their own vomit. By the door the small stool stood overturned. Coins fell from the overflowing bowl. The Indian girl crawled from the door, eating insects from the ground, naked now. She didn't look up. By the hut was a mound of human dung. The place smelled as if it were a corral of beasts. The girl looked up. I pushed her back. The blackness complied, and so in weakness we seek our cures. By how many mistakes do we in wanton necessities war in murder against our souls?

"In the morning when I awoke the hut was filled with sleeping men, English and Spanish, in pleasant rest. I stirred. The Indian girl was again sitting on her stool. The small bowl at her feet was empty now. I wondered who had taken the coins. She gazed into the distance as if her sight were her only landscape. The smell of the place made me sick. Under its weight I could only crawl. I shuddered, wondering what perversity of need had brought me to be a Spaniard. I dragged myself across the hut. Outside there was that spike driven into the ground. The chain was fastened to it. I played with the last link, fascinated, like an idiot consumed with the magnetism of his own dirt. I rose to my knees and pulled the chain, clenching my teeth, expecting the pain of struggle, but the spike moved easily upwards, free from the earth. It dangled in my hand like a caught fish. I walked toward the girl and put the spike into her hands. She looked up at me without expression.

"'You are free...go!' I gestured to the distance. The girl didn't move. 'Vamonos.' She turned away again and looked back into her own stare. I pulled her to her feet and shook her until I thought her eyes would fly from her head. She sat again on her stool, as if in defiance. I slapped her in fury. 'Don't hit her. She'll give you what you want.' The voice was exhausted and Spanish. I ignored it in my shame. If I could free her, I could free myself. I raised my hand again.

The girl stood, took the spike and chain from her lap and walked to the door of her hut. I gestured to the distance. She smiled and knelt, putting the spike back into the earth. Then she rose, turned and disappeared into the hut.

"'What you want?' said the Spaniard, resting his head on his hand as he lay on his side in the dust. 'You want buy for your own? We have many.' I looked at the dirt in his beard and the stains on his pants. Sweat had left dark runs of color on his shirt. 'We have some better, if you wish.' My own guilt made me a deadly saint and thus have we ever served the will of our own grim conversions. The toe of my boot seemed to move of its own toward the man's mouth. He rolled out of the way, screaming as he rolled, 'Lutheran, why do you do that? You crazy? You want to start a war?' I wondered if his murder would bring me release. The man sat, the dust rising about him. He patted the ground. 'You sit…here…no kick.' He questioned with a glance, pleading, I made helpless in my own confusion. 'No kick?' I didn't move. 'Sit.' A group of unarmed Spanish soldiers marched near the barricades, their officer looking our way. The thought of his murder set aside, I sat by the man.

"'Nothing in these Americas is straight in its own head. The Indians are not like us. That is why God has given Spain the New World to own, the savages, the slaves. Their kings are dead, their emperors lost, their cities ruins. Every savage there, all that is of their life and labor a vassal to a Spanish lord. Their flesh springs no soul. Even you, Lutheran'—he pointed at my chest—'even you are less a beast than they. And till the Madonna sings in Seville they'll never change. You will see, their spirit demons treachery. This I know.' He spoke, pointing toward the sky, as if he were the air's personal messenger. 'This I tell you. Ten years ago two Spanish ships, while making voyage along a coast in the distant north came upon a large bay, which we call Bahia de Santa Maria. Your name for the waters I do not know.'"

At Jamestown all faces turned toward Captain Newport, who was known to have a knowledge of Spanish maps. "Where is Bahia de Santa Maria?" asked a voice.

"Where we are. Its waters lie at our feet. It is the Chesapeake Bay," answered Newport, gesturing toward the blackness.

"The Spanish have been upon these lands?" asked the voice.

"It is known," replied Gosnold.

The old mariner wet his lips, waiting for silence so he could begin again his tale. "Attend my words." The mariner leaned forward toward the company. The mariner smiled, knowing the urgent ear leads a better listener. He told the Spaniard's story straight, his voice a little staged to play the drama neat.

"'The captain of those ships, one Pedro Menéndez de Avilés, anchored and began to trade with the local Indians, who, as was their custom, paddled to the ships in their canoes to greet the strangers. Among those savages was a great prince accompanied by his two sons. One savage so impressed Menéndez with his regal intelligence and his fine royal bearing that the captain asked if he might take the child over the trail of waters to show our king, Menéndez swearing to return the child the next year. Sorrow was on the face of the great prince. He threw tobacco into the bay to read the mood and mercies of the waters, Menéndez still pleading his cause. Finally the savage with all his hesitations did agree.

"'The child was brought to Spain. King Philip so impressed, he ordered the child to be given a princely allowance and fine clothes, the child to be educated by Dominican friars in Seville, to be taught Spanish and converted to Christianity.

"'For five years the child learned our ways, read our books, became in all things a surface of Spain and Christianity. It is said he understood diplomacy as well as warfare, and could have become one of Philip's advisors. He was as intelligent as any Dominican, and, they said, as crafty. After some years, he asked Menéndez and the king if he could return to his people to convert them to our Christian church. The king was well pleased. So was Menéndez. It was agreed. The boy was sent to Mexico under the protection of the governor, Don Luis de Velasco, who adopted the boy and gave him his own name, Don Luis. So you see, Lutheran,' the Spaniard smiled at me, 'how the son of a petty savage chief becomes in Spain a Don Luis. And soon you shall see why your misery over our chained pretty one is misplaced.' I watched the man shake dirt from his beard, roll it in his finger, then let it fall to become indistinguishable from the other filth of that place.

"'With much Menéndez's influence, an expedition was organized,' the Spaniard continued. 'Two Jesuits went along, a Father Quiros and a Father Segura, just to keep God's earthly eye upon Don Luis and to make help for him in the conversion of his people. They sailed, and by their unlucky star, they found Bahia de Santa Maria.

"'Don Luis was received as one who had descended from heaven. Times were hard among his people. There was little food, which, in kindness, the Indians shared as best they could. Don Luis's younger brother now was king. He offered Don Luis, who was the eldest and first in line, the throne. Don Luis refused, giving a great oration to his people, renouncing all earthly things, asking only to show them the glories of heaven and the truth of his new faith. This pleased Father Segura and Father Quiros greatly. But I am told,' the Spaniard said, 'the savages of that land bind their souls to the devil with evil brews and must forfeit all goods and titles in order to claim the right to rule. Don Luis's words carried shadows in each carefully considered phrase. I think he was abdicating with one hand what he was claiming with the other.

"'He was made prince to his brother's king and moved back to his people with the Jesuits' permission. Once with his people, Don Luis began to wear his native clothes. He took many wives, as was the custom of those savage kings. Father Quiros and Father Segura were horrified at his transformation. He was called before a religious court and flogged and forced to endure cold saltwater poured over his wounds. In defiance and humiliation, before all assembled, he renounced his Christianity and fled into the woods.

"'Father Segura, feeling he had bungled the enterprise badly, and knowing the anger of the court and King Philip, tried to make peace with Don Luis. A meeting was arranged in a small grotto in the woods. All went well until Don Luis rose and, at his signal, the priests were seized. Their skulls were flattened with blows of large clubs, their bodies humiliated with dismemberment and their remains burned in a great fire and buried. Then the Indians attacked our small settlement, killing all except a small boy who hid in the woods.

"'When our government in Florida learned of the disaster, a fleet was sent to give vengeance for such a betrayal. It is said that Don Luis was captured and hung along with fifteen of his chiefs.' The Spaniard looked off into the sky. 'Who's to say we ever captured Don Luis? We Spanish are too optimistic about the beneficial effects of our slaughters. We like good and simple news, ordain easy justice with all our villains. Too many complications confuse our opinions and bring angers to our priests. I believe Don Luis is yet alive. Among the common militia we are not so good at details, especially when blood is on the nose. I was there. We killed who we caught. Who's to say their names? All blood is blood. How you say?' He looked at me and shrugged his shoulders. I rose and smiled down at him and then, with one sure kick of my boot, I caved in his cheek. He rolled against the earth, his hand holding back the gush of blood and chips of teeth, screams suffocating behind his hands. I looked about. No one had seen. I walked away. When I turned back, the Indian girl was kneeling above the Spaniard's chest. She spread his hands from about his face gently, in a soothing touch. In her fingers something flashed. The Spaniard's neck exposed, she placed a shining thing against his throat and leaned her weight into its hilt. Beneath her, the body raged momentarily, as if in violence, then exhausting its surprise it slipped into quiet, then to death. The Indian girl stood and walked to another sleeping form, took the knife from its belt. Turning its face upward, she slit its throat, then stabbed its chest. The figure crawled to its knees, stumbled forward, holding its neck and the shaft in its chest. Then it collapsed without a sound. The girl returned to her stool and sat, watching eddies of dust in the small whirlwinds of heat. She didn't seem concerned that anyone had witnessed what she had done. Maybe the Spanish pretended she didn't exist until they wanted her. Maybe she didn't care. I wondered how long she had held her silent war, as I hoped the Spanish would think all the dead were just another drunken brawl.

"By a hut, two figures slept. I kicked one of the figures on the ground. It groaned. Whether it was Spanish or English, I could not tell. I was confused with anger. The soul is the compass that points ever to itself. I walked off, cursing and swearing I'd return and free the Indian girl, bring her to the refuge of an English ship and then to England. And so we pay our conscience in vain promises for its forgiveness. How subtle is God's vengeance upon the world that his true wars are fought in shadows and in fusillades of pins. I felt better that they called me Lutheran, even though I was pure English and my mother half a Catholic."

The campfire in front of us danced in blades of flames. Captain Wingfield leaned toward the exploding sparks of incinerated bugs. "Will he make himself known?" Wingfield's arms swept in an arc of darkness.

The mariner, his white eyes cast in hues of fire, said, "If he's still alive...."

"Who do you think it could be...Smith?" asked Reverend Hunt.

"Yes, let us ask the advice of one traitor to find another," answered Ratcliffe. I leapt to my feet.

"We'll have none of that!" Bartholomew Gosnold's figure loomed above the fire, his arms outstretched. He seemed to glow, as behind his frame the curtain darkness curled.

"Powhatan or Opechancanough or someone we have not met as yet," I said. "But who is to say if the story is even true?"

"This land," the old mariner patted the earth, "eats its orphans for its meat, and makes elixirs with their blood. There is more than one lost child here. There is also Roanoke, our lost colony and its souls, and there were others."

"Others?" cried Archer.

"Others! This land gathers its lost into its whirlwinds," the mariner nodded. "But we will have to hear about San Juan de Ulúa, where Drake got his curse, and so lead to Panama where he found his calling…before we can know how rounded is this world that all its mysteries come to this one point." He tapped the earth with his finger, then he continued his tale.

"Walking back on the roadstead I could see groups of sailors standing and talking. Others walked, examining each other's ships, their strolls avoiding the stationary bands of conversing figures as a wash of shallow does round a rocky coast. The ships of the two fleets were docked in cohorts; the English anchored next to the Spanish. Between them floated a mastless Spanish hulk, a blackened memory of a ship, a blasted coffin, so crumpled in its death, it had become its own grave. Aboard the Spanish hulk sailors were cutting holes in the railing of her top deck, suspiciously like gun ports, I thought, and only on the side facing our own English ships, the closest of which was the *Minion*. Next to her the *Jesus*, and so on further down the line, until Drake's *Judith*, the last of our ships.

"On the shore Spanish sailors arranged pulleys. They turned their backs when I walked by, hiding their occupation, fooling no one as they played with both the lines of the Spanish hulk and those of our own *Minion*.

"I boarded the *Jesus* and found Hawkins on the upper deck, his spyglass at his eye, observing the island fort behind the Spanish ships. Drake and all of his other captains stood at his side.

"'The wind smells of Spanish betrayal,' I said. 'They're tampering with the *Minion*'s lines.'

"Hawkins nodded in that way that said he already knew. 'As a gentleman, Don Enriquez still assures our safety, but I have for a second time sent Barrett as an ambassador.' Sending his second-in-command showed the seriousness of the issue. Hawkins looked across the deck of the *Minion* toward the Spanish flagship, as he addressed his council. 'Barrett has not returned and we must assume our friend is in prison or dead. We must now ready our ships for the worst.' Then he ordered me to pick a dozen of our best to pass among our crew on the shore, and without arousing the freckle on a Spanish tail, and have ours back to their ships. Armed sentries were set in the masts of the *Jesus* and the other ships. Weapons were quietly passed to the crew.

"I was on shore whispering Hawkins's orders in English ears, slowly making my way toward our barricade, deciding which Spaniard I would kill at the feet of the Indian girl, ruminating on her expression of release as she understood at last she was free, watching in my mind the dust-consumed blood and shattered oyster of a Spanish brain.

"I could see the barricade up ahead. As I passed the *Minion*, I noticed the bow lines at an angle strangely rigid. Spaniards on the shore were laboring at pulleys, slowly hauling the *Minion* closer to the Spanish hulk. The distance between the vessels closed. I thought, 'They're going to try to board her.'

"A Spanish officer was in the rigging on Don Enriquez's flagship, waving a white handkerchief. Someone from the *Minion* fired an arrow in his direction. A trumpet sounded. Over the roadside our world of conversation dissolved into a roar of men in panic. Waves of Spanish soldiers ran from between their ships. Unarmed Spanish sailors grabbed shovels and pieces of wood and battered in the skulls of our sentries at the barricade. My last sight of them was the heads of shovels falling in their deadly arcs. I bolted then. Through the gaps between the ships I could see boats filled with Spanish soldiers rowing toward our ship. Soon our stern cannons opened fire, some of the pinnaces in their desperate attack exploding in sprays of broken wood and pieces of men. Soldiers boiled from the belly of the hulk, climbing into its rigging, the Spanish pulling frantically at the lines, drawing the *Minion* closer. Sailors on the *Minion* threw launches over the side, trying to keep the two ships apart.

The road was filled with massacre, the armed and the unarmed distracted in the frenzy of slaughtering. I slipped through and made for the closest English ship, which was the *Minion*. I jumped, grabbing the dangling lines of her bowsprit, and pulled myself into the safety of their tangle. I crawled forward and reached the main deck as the Spanish mustered for a boarding along the side of the hulk. The swivel guns of the *Jesus* fired across our decks and blasted the Spanish ranks, the *Jesus* herself much taller than the *Minion*, her swivel guns mounted on her railing. Each blast peppered the deck of the hulk with goodly portions of English nails, chain links and pistol balls, clearing a butcher's path of red where once only Spanish sailors stood.

"Behind me on the road the jaws of the Spanish trap closed around the dwindling groups of our still fighting men, as though a beast that would soon consume what it was about to kill. On the *Minion*'s decks, waves of Spaniards rushed over our side, the guns of the *Jesus* blasting, the Spanish dead falling forward as pieces of their heads blew back. We met the Spanish in their teeth, our pikes skewering them like ripe plums. Our swords sang the song of their smoking blood. But they were everywhere. The weight of the Spanish attack drove us back almost to midship. Then, on the railing of the *Jesus*, Hawkins appeared, a sword in one hand, a silver tankard of ale in the other. 'For England and Saint George. Save the *Minion*!' he cried. A Spanish bullet tore through the silver chalice. It bled ale. Before its spill was through, Hawkins defiantly drank the rest. 'Their bullets make good salt for our beer.' With laughter and violent thoughts of revenge, the crew of the *Jesus* flooded to our rescue over our sides — the bright steel of England wielded by English men for an English God."

At the fires of Jamestown men rose in a simple voice and cheered, as if their souls too had fought that day at San Juan de Ulúa. It was a story we all knew. We supped upon the sailor's words as if they were our own mother's milk. "A Spanish treachery against one is a treachery against all," cried a voice. The darkness consumed his identity but not the chorus of the cheers.

The mariner continued. "Above the *Minion*, Spanish and English arrows wove themselves in flights, while below, a Spaniard looked surprised, his eyes turned upwards and agape at the arrow that had pierced his forehead. Slowly he deflated to collapse, falling sideways like a discarded button on a pin. Our decks were now carpeted in the desperate struggle. I found an unspent pistol and discharged it into a

Spaniard rushing with a pike. Near me an English sword cut across a Spanish face. The Spaniard smiled in blood as if he had grown another mouth. His jaw fell loose. A water barrel wielded from behind smashed his skull. In that sea of shapes all domestic and pleasurable things became tools of war. We would have killed with spoons. So there we parried, Spanish and English, our two hatreds boiling each other's blood until the Spanish beast had had enough, and, as if all their minds were one, they retreated, flowing backward over the *Minion*'s side, like a spent wave, to the blackened hulk.

"Now, from the island fort, cannon smoke billowed in rolling thunder. On the *Minion* a few wounded souls staggered a cheer, supporting themselves on bloodied swords. Then, on their feet, they raised themselves like heavy weights. 'Our boys are in it now.' Their words cut dumb as the first Spanish volleys tore the works of the *Jesus* aft in a spray of splintered wood. 'My God! The Spanish have the fort!' Across the bay above the fort's brooding earthen walls snapped in arrogant flutter the Spanish flag. Next to it, as if in honor guard, were fifteen pikes on top of which were skewered the heads of fifteen English souls. 'They be devils to taunt us so,' told a nameless English voice, half in tears. These words no sooner said than hull to hull, the cannonade in smoking volleys erupted in a cinder flash. The Spanish ships opened fire, as did in successive instants each English ship join, its guns alight. Thunder answered thunder. Clouds in rolling cloaks boiled soot on our sweating flesh. Spent flakes in hot dust stuck burning to our skin. At our bow, men with axes cut ropes, pounding the decks, which reverberated with their blows. They labored in their sweat like demons at a hellish drum. At the stern we strained on ropes, dragging at our rear anchor, working, trying to pull the *Minion* and her smoking cannons free. The Spanish threw grappling hooks across our decks to hold us to their trap. With our swords and axes we hacked those ropes. Our swivel guns raked their deck. Slowly...slowly...with heaving force, our breaths squeezed thin, the *Minion* began to move, the *Jesus* too, in desperate trace.

"All along the English fleet ships moved astern. Crews hauled on aft anchor chains as sails fell free, limp, unfurled from spars, which soon the wind caught full in a billowing snap. The Spanish cannons tore at those tiny ships. Out of range of the Spanish guns, only Drake's command, the unarmed *Judith*, slipped the slaughter unharmed and sailed to the harbor's mouth. There in obedience she rested, anchored to her elegies. There was little she could do but watch like a grieving child, bearing witness to the murder of her kin.

"The cannons of the *Jesus* and the *Minion*, now in deadly colloquy, tore hole after hole in the water line of Don Enriquez's ship. Sprays of surf blew above her decks. The hull, soon riddled with our shot, bled air as it drank the sea. Around her the battle rose, as wallowing at her dock, she settled, sinking like an exhausted sun. Our guns now cleared, they chorused war against the next ship in the Spanish fleet."

Chapter Fifteen

THE EGG IS CRACKED. THE BATTLE ENDS. AS FATES
DIVIDE, DRAKE CHOOSES HIS ALCHEMY AND HIS SWORD.

HE OLD MARINER stared across the Jamestown fire. His hands searched above the flames for a heat felt long ago, trying to rekindle in his icy flesh the sensation of a dream long thought lost. "The Spanish had but two real fighting ships, Don Enriquez's flagship, which we had just sunk, and the next ship, the *Capitana*, in the line. All the others were armed merchantmen, with few real guns. If we could sink the *Capitana* and silence the shore battery, we might, with lots of English luck, not only escape the Spanish trap, but take the whole treasure fleet." The mariner nodded to himself, as if in one gesture he brushed away the past.

"With a little luck"—he bit his lip—"just a little . . ." The mariner seemed to fight the inevitability of his tale. His vision choked his throat with contradictory breaths. He gasped for air. "I never saw the Indian girl again." He spoke in labored calls. "She, like so many, disappeared in smoke." Half drowning in the meaning of his words, the mariner struggled, as if to find a way to change their lean, to carve from the sinews of his breath a new vision of the past. But for him, as for us who knew the tale, it was more powerful in its relentless truth than any dream of triumph. Then, with a blessed sigh, the old mariner surrendered to its pain and took up again the narrative of his youth.

"While the *Minion*, with full broadside, tore the *Capitana* into a derelict, the Spanish hulk swung herself into the *Minion*'s deserted berth and came to rest against the *Jesus*, holding her in place. The brocade of whirling smoke obscured the ship, as from the newly cut gun ports of the hulk, chain shot and ball pounded the mast of the *Jesus*. The *Minion* answered. The gun crew labored at their charges, their skin sweating heat, firing at the *Capitana*. In that instant when quiet turns surprise into a shudder in itself, the *Capitana* exploded, the whole craft evaporating in an upward rush. What geysers flashed in crimson meteors and fumed in bleeding smoke? What cinders these that bloom in the shapes of men? We are by flames a silhouette. The answer in the human of its counterpoint. This was alchemy by war. And so in justice the sea did drink its second salt.

"The *Jesus* still struggled, caught in a web of agonies. Crews from our other ships swam to the *Jesus* to join the desperate wrestle to bring her from her berth. She was a gallant ship floating on her watery cross, her foremast gone, her mainmast blasted. Still, her crew fought to bring her out, as if one last defiant act could circumvent her death. Axes cut twisted ropes, broken spars were thrown overboard, men, the muscles of their arms combed with cords of now fatiguing flesh, pulled against the weights of the anchor lines. Slowly, painfully, suffocations upon their lung entombing breaths, they brought the *Jesus* free. Free into what? The lethal winds of the Spanish cannonade.

"The *Jesus* heaved as the Spanish cannons found their range. With each concussion, shattered planks flew back. Her last sails fell. The *Jesus* shuddered in the sea, as a great beast scalded in her own blood.

"'We are by wreck, so blessed in our saintliness. The tale is now told,' said Hawkins as he signaled the *Minion* to move some distance around the *Jesus* to be sheltered by her from the Spanish fire. Then he signaled Drake's *Judith* to come alongside and retrieve its surviving kin.

"The obedient *Judith* raised her sail, her bow lowered in the slow forward thrust. The sea around her rose in plumed meteors, as the Spanish cannonballs fell short. On she came, that defiant speck, like a puppy in an avalanche. She came along our side, dropped her sails and held her place. We pulled her tight in an embrace of ropes. Men in orderly retreat now filled her decks, while our guns spit comets through the billowing smoke. The Spanish answered with a crushing rain of shot. The decks of the *Jesus* were a wreck of twisted ropes and broken wood and bits of human friends. Our gunners slipped in their own blood. Still, the *Judith* sat at our side. Our wounded and our retreat brought onto her deck. The tiny vessel stayed indifferent to the lethal hail until her decks were filled. Then Drake cast off and sailed again beyond the range of the Spanish guns.

"Now the *Minion* came to the side of the *Jesus* through the hurricane of smoke. The air boiled, spits of gunfire wandering in the gray turmoil and lightning flashes, our lungs burning with the mists of war. We pulled the *Jesus* to our side, loading her treasure upon our own, men carrying the gold and silver and pearls from Rio de la Hacha and Santa Marta. All in orderly withdrawal we were, until through the whirling clouds of smoke sailed a burning ghost. There, bearing down on us, was a blazing ship, her masts alight, her hull cloaked in flames.

"Men whose nerves were already shredded with the sight of death and exhausted with hours of battle revolted against their English birth and rose in panic. The crew grabbed axes and swung them above their heads, letting them fall, severing the ropes that held the *Minion* to the *Jesus*. With each thud of the axes the ropes loosened. The *Minion* and the *Jesus* began to part. Weakened ropes snapped. The sea took the *Minion* again in her ceaseless roll. 'The *Minion*...the *Minion*...,' chorused voices on the *Jesus*. Heads turned. Eyes widened, mouths devoured air. Legs moved in the hysterical pull toward the side of the *Jesus*. Gun crews left loaded cannons unfired, swords and pistols, shields clattered on the deck. Men fell over falling men, all in a rush to gain the *Minion*. Over the sides of the ship sailors jumped, rising in the air, then descending to the *Minion*'s decks, like rapids in a river of men. Chests of gold and jewels were thrown onto the departing ship. Through the swirl of its own smoke, the Spanish fireship, bore upon us. Like a glacier of flames, it floated a course as relentless as its heat.

"On the decks of the *Jesus* the wounded, with pleading fists, grasped at the air, hoping that God above would thicken the breeze's breath into a helpful pull. The last ropes cut, the two ships moved apart. Men jumped the widening chasm. Some held treasures in their arms. Some were so weighted they missed their mark and fell into the sea. When they surfaced, their faces were filled with anger at their lost wealth. They tore at the sea with fists and hands held like palsied claws. Many dove under the waves again, trying to retrieve from the sea what the fates had snatched away.

"Hawkins swung with a rope across the chasm, landing on the

Minion's deck. He saw his son on the *Jesus* holding in his arms a gold-encrusted crystal plate. Afraid to jump and break his trove, he stared at the sea and the departing ship. 'Jump,' called Hawkins. 'We'll pluck you from the sea.' But the boy, fearing the loss of his precious plate, could not move. There he stood, stamping his feet and crying in his terror. The distance between the two ships increased. Sailors swam after the departing *Minion*. Some in rowboats took up the chase. Hawkins still screamed to his son to jump, long after he was lost from view. A child, orphaned with his treasure to a Spanish fate.

"The *Minion* sailed toward the *Judith* and together they limped beyond the harbor's mouth. The Spanish did not pursue us. The day had exhausted even their treachery. The sun bled its failing light into the western sky. Against a quiet beach the fire ship burned itself harmlessly to sleep. Outside San Juan de Ulúa we anchored, Drake and the *Judith* not far off. There we waited, the two forsaken children of the storm, touching each other, embracing in distant glances, while in that Mexican roadside the Spanish call a town, our friends and kin and comrades were borne into the darkness of the eternal night. So desolate in our sorrows were we that no just anger, no sworn revenge could fill our cup. We were in a precarious perch as well, as we prepared for the long voyage home.

"We tended the wounded the best we could, fixed torn sails, refitted leaking planks, but we had little food and water. The *Minion* cradled two hundred men instead of her usual hundred. She rode low at the water line and waddled in the sea. Men filled the decks and passageways below, crowding each other into small corners. Though the sea rolled unchained in its doom, we drank each other's breath and breathed the elixir of each other's sweat.

"That night many died. Only the dream of morning kept us in hope. The night, through its tattered mantle of cloud, let glow a few stars, which, in their signal and promise of light, faded into black behind invisible puffs of dark. The sun rose that day on a deserted sea. The *Judith* had disappeared. 'Drake has abandoned us,' screamed Hawkins. His voice coughed disbelieving words, as his hands sought an imagined throat. He had ceased to think in words, but rose in violence to the religions of revenge. 'What cousins this betrayal? There must be Spanish blood in that demon's veins,' he said, swallowing his visions as he spit back words. 'There has not been a treachery like this since Gethsemane.'

"Young Drake had turned his first small command into a disaster. Hawkins swore blood. Why Drake left it is difficult to know — a momentary cowardice, perhaps. The *Judith* was in no better condition than ourselves. Drake had never sailed the Atlantic. Maybe he just wanted to get it done. Whatever the story, Drake's reputation, if the *Minion* saw England again, would be forever tarnished. And Drake knew this. He held this blazing truth to his breast for the four months it took him to sail home. The human soul is a wondrous phoenix, it frolics in its own ashes before its rise. For four months Drake had eaten of himself. I not there to witness his transformation, hearing only later. The wizard exiled from his magic, I paced my derelict brewed to the philosophies of a different pain. And what alchemies to be my thoughts, and where my absolutions, my philosopher's stone?

"The sea rolled its beckoning waves. We followed north. At a small island we called Sacrifice a hundred of our comrades were put ashore, there to face, with little but a few weapons and some meat, the long and uncertain way home. In truth, their prospects were no better than our own. All had chosen to leave the *Minion*, and we had no means to disagree. They thought that chances were better on the land than with us. As we set our sails that day, whispering in waves of prayer, little did we know that only three would we ever see again. Many were murdered by savages, or burned at the stake by the Spanish, or died in the miseries of the long trail.

"That morning when we sailed again, the sea bled sorrows. Hawkins kicked the planks of his deck.

"'Never again will I leave a human soul,' he said, while miles and many days ahead, Drake on the tiny *Judith* would look into the morning air, above the shrouds of his own dead. Drake had always been a Protestant man, like his father before him, but fear of censure at home and sorrow for his dead kin changed him; for that day the sky above him cracked and he sipped his communion with the sea. He raised his hand to the godly waters and spoke down the cataclysm of his breath to a new faith. 'Oh sea, which is now our father's tattered cloak, take up our cause, oh take up our cause. I am now and forever your servant and you my God.'

"Drake fingered his father's Bible as he spoke. What deadly pledges are earnestly made with all the passions of the divided heart, what frenzies now to seal the breech? All consequences birthed on the furies of the twin, the two-headed dragon of the double neck. As

Drake spoke, the twin mouths of the worm ate at his soul, the pain in forked visions speaking phantoms and gods in all their revelations.

"Drake's words now spread upon the warm west wind, whose silence was but a wait that turned from hush to cyclone when the Spanish Philip sent his Armada against our God, our land, our goodly Queen Bess.

"When Drake arrived at Plymouth, gone was the chicken down, and where his feet had scratched the earth, now an avenging eagle stood. The Spanish had ruined his career, stolen his goods and murdered his kin. To Drake the Spanish were now his personal war. Religion, profit and revenge joined into hardened steel in men like Drake. And so it was in Panama, then three long years away, that the first whisper of the sea's answer came; there with the black Cimarrones and their sacred tree, through the jungle clearings. Words that whispered vision and visions that in their whisper sounded thunder."

"THE SPANISH STRANGLED GEORGE RIBLEY AND BURNED HIS BODY AT the stake," rang a voice like a memory from the darkness.

Above Jamestown the moon reappeared from behind a small front of clouds, its light reflecting the faces around the fire, featureless orbs that bobbed and spoke to other featureless orbs, who spoke and bobbed and repeated names and stories of those whose agonies had pushed England toward war and the Armada toward the English coast. "Robert Barrett they burned alive in Seville," said another. "Michael Morgan of Cardiff lived the rest of his life as a slave in a Spanish galley, after being mutilated with two hundred lashes." The company recounted names of friends, of relatives, of legends, whose sufferings after San Juan de Ulúa forced Queen Elizabeth to seize as compensation a Spanish treasure fleet.

All that was, that is, hungers. Its momentums course to where, to what resolve? The moments thread the coming weave, the needle mindless of the many patterns in a single stitch. History we are, its marriage to a ghost, its wine the invisibility that intoxicates. I am flesh, I cannot stand to the hallows of an ancient name.

Am I my father's twin? I thought on the tale the mariner told. My eastern wars and slaveries, are they the taunt, the trail to plead my life in parallels! I to be a second Drake. I am the shadow that his profile bleeds! Our desperations are by war: my battle at Red Tower Pass, his at San Juan de Ulúa; my Russian trek, his voyage home. And so we by slants do shave the brother line. When does similar become the same? My orphan birthed to be a shelter of his life, and I by ear to be his kin. And his doubt and mine, is that the chalice to seize a better faith? And do I dare against all known discretions, seizing other heavens from the whirlwinds on a pin?

"Hawkins and Drake arrived at Plymouth in January of 1569 within four days of each other." The mariner continued. "It was a great feat of seamanship for Drake to have made England at all, and Hawkins knew it, their kinsmen blood being thicker than any accusation. Both had starved and suffered on the voyage to Plymouth. In truth, there was little either could have done for the other's miseries, even had Drake stayed at Hawkins's side. And so they made within a year an uneasy peace.

"But a new Drake, distilled by grief for his slaughtered friends and kin, now rose in his magic to be an alchemist. Only the pure in their inspiration can see the power and mysteries in the material world. Drake, his Bible and his sea. Where two reasons war there is God in the turmoil. God is in the search, not in the answer. Where God is not, there God is. I had seen it all before in my alchemies, my teachings not lost. And so by its wisdom I am born again, the fragments of myself seeking that last completion to forge myself reborn. Was Drake now the adept? I knew I would follow him forever to guide and see the answers that he found."

"Drake had experience of the West India Sea, something few Englishmen could boast. Even with reputation tarnished he was of value to the queen, who did realize a small profit from the expedition —most of the treasure being transferred from the *Jesus* to the *Minion* and most of the tobacco received as trade at Rio de la Hacha still aboard the *Judith*. And in one expedition both varieties of the American leaf were first imported into England in large enough supplies to create the need to commerce in the weed. The news of Nicot's experiment now upon the lips in London and the physicians of the court. But I knew of it years before it had the common tongue." The mariner's eyes stared, as if he looked through the very earth. "Beware the cures angels bring in their powdered kiss."

Ratcliffe rose and said, "It is an old story I've heard since a child....It grows more transparent with each telling." Men moved from Ratcliffe's side. The mariner stared and said, "Nothing is so old that ghosts cannot recall to life. There are, in these trees, mysteries of haunted things that once I knew in Panama. No earth is so new it does not clothe some secret." Then he was silent, listening to the lonesome song of some forgotten beast howling through the wind.

AT NOON OF THE NEXT DAY THE SUN ROSE INTO A FIST. SOME SHADOWS toiled in the fields or erected poles for the growing fort. Most rested, or stood their ground, or bowled, or talked, or walked aimlessly, as if they were at a park at home. Thomas Wotton knelt as if in prayer at a few small hills of dirt, planting tobacco seed. The moistened reddish clay in his hands, its color the dark blood of wine, he pawed the ground.

"What boons in its secret remedies," Wotton said, taking the bag of seeds which Wingfield had deposited in his charge. "This tiny seed"—Wotton opened the bag and held a dot between his fingers —"to think we...we...*I* could be the first to fathom all the mysteries of this thin brown leaf." Wotton pointed to the small mound of earth, imagining, I suspect, the twisted ropes of tobacco the Indians had given us. I nodded to him as he looked up toward me, seeing visions of discovery where others could see only matted earth. Wotton's brow sweated in the heat, his eyes seemed exhausted in their sorrows. Only the hands that touched the mounds of tobacco seemed young. "My wife and children died....I, a doctor, could do nothing." The words seemed to speak themselves. "This tobacco is the seed to remedies..." The shadow of his head nodded on the earth. "But why this leaf, and where the heart, where the knowledge to spell the recipes and claw the secrets of a lipless thing? I could have it first and be the hero in the telling." His words shivered as he spoke, as if the icy words of a desperation had overwhelmed his tongue.

I put my hand upon his shoulder and squeezed his flesh. Wotton continued his labor and I departed. Turning back to watch this gentle man till the earth with his grieving ghosts, I walked toward the bay, where the great arteries of its converging rivers flowed from the heart of this unknown land, like veins of a great tobacco leaf. On the waters now was a single sail, far off. Captain Newport had returned from a day exploring. The wind was fresh from the south. The water rolled and swelled in its white knuckles bearing Newport's skiff toward the beach. His sail boasting full in the wind's breath, its silhouette growing larger as the distance waned. Toward the camp, by Newport's three ships, boxes, crates and barrels—our only provisions for six months

—stood unattended on the shore. *Our stores of food are low,* I thought, *but...* I could not give the compliment. Newport's sailors had eaten well from our exhausted victuals. His ships had stayed too long at our dock; our starvation was now their cargo.

Chapter Sixteen

VERYTHING THAT IS, is a fragment. So much passing, so much lost. All memories are voiced in shards. I think of him that night in Jamestown, as I plume his tale upon my words and have him speak again.

"For a year after the battle of San Juan de Ulúa Drake lived in disgrace. England and Spain snarled at each other across our holy channel, each digging its claws into the beach where lay the last sands of peace, each scratch leading through its darkening slits to war. Elizabeth seized a Spanish treasure fleet docked in Plymouth as restitution for the Spanish betrayal. That fleet carried the pay for Philip's army fighting the Protestants in the Netherlands. Now God and nation and all profits warred in their holy swords. Some of the money, it was said, was sent by old Bess to finance the Protestant cause. That Elizabeth, always a crafty one, having an enemy pay the wages of a friend.

"The Spanish, in reprisal, began to confiscate the goods of English merchants in Spain and Portugal, imprisoning our countrymen, and giving them as heretics to the Inquisition to be tortured and executed. Reprisals are just another name for war. The politics of men is like a witch's cauldron—it feeds its boil on its own internal heat. The flames around its base are but a prop. And so Drake, with the small proceeds of the Hawkins expedition, waited, watching his personal war become the beginning of our nation's struggle." The eyes of the old mariner widened. "I can see even now Drake, as he tapped his few gold coins, their click like the seeds of a distant drum, beating the thoughts of a golden vengeance.

"Now like all great men, Drake was a flesh of balances: his gods warring in their passions through his soul, the god of his father, the god of the sea. His vengeance contesting with his humanity, his greed with his generosity, each turning in its predatory orbit, eyeing its opposite kin for the right to speak the all of his master's breath. But more than the struggle, it was his calm — his seemingly endless calm, while his very elements warred —which was, in all its reflection, like the sea: gentle in the one part the other storm, while beneath its surface fiends strove with fiends for each other's life.

"Drake waited one year. Then, in the early months of 1570, with a small horde of gold, and with a few investors, he bought two ships, the *Swan* and the *Dragon*, desperations crafted in wood and brass, mast and plank. For Drake, this might be his hope's last confident breath. I to bear the witness of his search, I in his crew, Drake sailed from Plymouth. Whether any noted his going, except with good riddance, it is hard to know. He sailed for the Spanish main and Panama, and was the first Englishman to sail those waters round. There he explored the coast in the spring of 1570, sheepishly at first, taking a few Spanish prizes, as a child might, splashing in a pleasant tub; then returning to Plymouth with a small profit and the beginnings of a reputation, for nothing brings a reputation faster than the prospects of a profit. Drake had gained greatly in knowledge, that vapor men discount until it hardens into cash. In June of 1571, Drake now understood better than any Englishman, even Hawkins, the Spanish West Indies and its defenses, and its gold convoys and its flota.

"Six months later, Drake sailed again from Plymouth. This time he only brought the *Swan*, the smallest of his ships. He needed a vessel with a shallow draft. He had learned on his last visit to the West Indies that the Spanish gold route across Panama did not go straight to Nombre de Dios, but wound along jungle roads, guarded by ill-armed soldiers, clothed mostly in the conceits of Spanish incompetence. First it went to Venta Cruces, a small village on the Chagres River. From there the weightier bouillon was shipped down the Chagres by barge to Nombre de Dios to await the flota and its final transport to Spain. The other treasure was shipped overland by mule. Half the treasures of the world flowed through the sleepy, dusty little village of Venta Cruces. A river of gold and silver to spice the venom of the Spanish Philip.

"Drake's plan was to sail up the Chagres River and take Philip's treasure before it ever reached the sea. He meant to cut the throat of the Spanish empire while its sleeping head lay on its pillow. And only Drake knew the path—or so he thought. Now, no Englishman had ever sailed that river, and no Englishman but Drake would have dared such an attack.

"The *Swan* was a small ship and we were only a crew of forty. Daring and surprise were our only allies. We bore them as signs upon our bow, a silver bird holding a golden lance. Around our necks we each wore a white feather. We assembled every dawn to kiss the Bible and every dusk to toast the sea. Drake would stand at the rail of the ship at night, watching soft, tropical waves tongue our passage, distance dissolving into the hiss of whispering foams. How many nights did I walk the deck as Drake stared silently, listening to the sea, as he watched the setting sun turn the watery field of gold to blood red? Slowly, color evaporated into blackness. At dawn Drake was still at his watch, as that shock of strange green flame exploded across the sky, as if the light's first breath were a spark of flint, and then, at the hint of the sun, the sea turned red again, this drama but two ends of a great communion, separated by a sermon in the dark.

"Hundreds of miles away the coast of Panama was already in alarm. A Frenchman named Nicholas de Isle had learned of the Spanish treasure route from an escaped black slave, Pedro Mandinga, whom de Isle had taken to France a year or so before, to confirm by his presence his narrative of Spanish gold to wealthy investors. After raising the moneys needed for the expedition, de Isle returned with Mandinga to Panama, sailing a few miles up the Chagres River and attacking a few barges. He gained nothing, but alerted the small Spanish fleet of decaying ships that guarded the Panamanian coast. When Mandinga tired of his prospects—being not quite a slave and not quite free—he deserted by swimming to shore. De Isle lost his nerve, reconsidered his enterprise and sailed for safer waters, the Spanish reluctantly searching the coast for his ship, hoping that their bluff would be as painful as a bite, the empire could return to its usual sloth and pursuit of pleasure.

"Out of the sea before us rose the spiny coast of Panama, its hollows black, its peaks green and misty, like the back of some huge reptile wallowing at its rest. We anchored some leagues from the mouth of the Chagres River. Drake had a bucket of water drawn up from the sea. Each man he had kneel before him. In one hand Drake held the Bible, the other hand he dipped into the warm water of the bucket. Then, with his wet thumb, he planted the watery imprint of the sea on the forehead, between the eyes and on the wrists of each sailor. 'Be ever faithful.... Be ever faithful,' Drake repeated as he touched each sailor's forehead. 'What the Spanish have taken the sea shall resurrect in us.' The crew murmured. The ocean ran the sun in light. Drake held his Bible, which seemed to balance him as he stepped sideways. Drake was never as he seemed. He held his beliefs in counterweights. 'He is no Catholic, so how crazy can he be?' whispered one of the crew, as Drake bent to anoint. He raised above his head the book, counterbalancing in desperate symmetry his profusion of beliefs. When every man had been so touched, he spread his arms to the sea and spoke. 'In battle now we are consecrated, O Sea. Your blood is the frontlet between our eyes. Your blood pulses on the blood of our veins. Our life is your life, eternal, as it is transient. Guard us that our cause is innocent. Forgive us that we will sin. Hold us that our stay in your embrace is brief. Bring us vision that we may not live in blindness. Bring us blindness that we may see. We are both the light and the shadow. Give us the courage to accept the touch of each upon our lips.'

"With that, Drake took his knife and cut his thumb, thrusting the bleeding hand into the bucket. There he stayed a moment, looking at his kneeling crew. Then he walked to the railing of the ship and threw the bloody water over the side.

"'And what inspired madness is this prayer?' I cried. 'And what alchemist stone shall arise from the sea, its divinities upon my eyes, and turn all this water into gold?'

"'Water into gold,' called the crew.

"Drake ignored us, his passions pushing madness into wisdoms of a saint. 'The sea and I are now one,' he said. 'That which I have given up in blood now may be repaid in earthly treasure if, but only if, we prove worthy in our compassion. We are now held to a higher standard, not of this earth, but of the sea. We will not be cruel. We will not slaughter or abuse those who have surrendered. We will release those as we can, unharmed. We are here only to find compensation for that which was stolen from us at San Juan de Ulúa, and to teach the Spanish Philip all power does not come from armies, it comes from strength in mercy.

"Drake looked at the crew and in final thunder said, 'The Spanish will fight less when they have less to fear. Let the Spanish and the French corsairs who raid the coast have their mutual slaughters. Our example will eat into their souls, knowing that what we English are, they could never be.'

"So saying, Drake bid the crew to rise. 'The trust every man now holds is sacred,' he continued. 'I expect each of you to do his duty, unto death.' When Drake had finished his speech he turned, letting his Plymouth friend, the ever-obedient John Oxenham, play the power and give the orders to seek the mouth of the Chagres River. John Oxenham, that beard without a point, a round of softness, a weak mouth, a confident shadow with a nervous eye. That man who dreamed beyond his worth. Drake ever the pander of lesser men. 'Let them rise,' he would say. 'Let them rise to their own doom,'" smiled Jonas. "It was to Oxenham Drake gave command.

"The wind in its tropical breath was as if we had sailed into the mouth of a dog. We passed southwest along the Panamanian coast. It was February twenty-second of 1571. Panama lay in its mountain crags to our right, behind white lines of beaches and dense growth of tropical trees and climbing vines. Colorful birds glided through the vegetable falls, calling in witless screams to the lost spirits of that place. Mists rose from the earth, as if the land itself were secreting a hidden fire. Monkeys played on each other's backs, running to the edge of the sea, until the harmless rush of surf drove them back.

"The currents at the mouth of the Chagres ran in brown suds, as if the water itself were rusting in its own bed. The prow of the *Swan* came about, pointing inland. The jungle enclosed us in its sweep as we followed the flowing clay of this river south. Along the shore, huts and stone settlements once built by men collapsed into their ruined soliloquies. Further inland, standing above the jungle's crown, —walls and pinnacles and solemn sculptured faces stood brooding in eternal gloom.

"The wind held its friendly point. The river was not swift, but lounged in its float like an aging snake. Venta Cruces was a dirty little town congealed from mud. Low huts, inns and a church lined the main street. At the end of a long wharf stood a warehouse, its doors and windows closed against the heat.

"As we rushed ashore, behind us there was the blare of a trumpet. We ran with the sound of our advance. We seized the warehouse and the wharf. The Spanish did not honor us with an attack. They crouched instead behind barricades and boxes along the street. We laughed as we battered in the doors of the warehouse. Their porticos gone, the windows smashed, these eyeless ruins stared at us in their dusty gloom. We threw boxes and bales through the windows to our mates. Cloth in bolts lay half out-of-doors in exhausted clumps. We found no silver, but there were silks and spices and precious goods, all the infatuations to make the Spanish drool. We seized it all, parading it down the wharf, bouncing it on our shoulders in playful glory.

"It took two days to load the *Swan*. The heat of the day we wore in sweat. The nights we worked under torchlight. Then we left, following the muddy river, in its meandering and its wandering through the jungle and its green. The river to a broadening after one final twist. There the sea and the sky opened to the horizon's throat. Drake knelt at the bow enunciating unheard things. We headed west, the sea flashing smiles in brilliant foam. She ran with us. For a month we crisscrossed her playful back, taking prize after prize, thirteen now in all. We kept two ships to transport our goods and jewels, enough to fill the stomach of a host of hungry fleets. Everywhere we looked, rich ships in graceful sail brought sacrifices to our altar. It was as if the sea had given into our hands her spoils. It was wealth beyond avarice. Every morning Drake gave service to his gods.

"A man with ordinary disposition would have taken his treasure and sailed for home, but not Drake, not without his gold. So after a month of raiding on the sea he turned the *Swan* back toward the Chagres River and Venta Cruces.

"'The Spanish are already in alarm. They'll be expecting us,' cried the crew. But Drake, held by his unwavering vision, said, 'Boldness is our iron. It is the one dart the Spanish cannot deflect.'

"And so the *Swan* alone went back up the Chagres. We found no gold. The treasure fleet had somehow eluded us. Drake just smiled and nodded at the news. He had done enough this trip. Drake knew that the Spanish transported their gold across Panama in January and February of each year, but somehow he had miscalculated. He needed more exact intelligence. He needed allies to swell his army, he needed spies who knew the Spanish.

"We sailed to the sea again. It was late June of 1571. In a hidden bay we set our anchor and unloaded food and goods for our return the next year. Drake would have his Spanish gold; his vengeance was not yet done. He called that place Pheasant Bay, in honor of the birds. Their hordes above us boiling as an ocean in the sky.

"Drake, without brutality or slaves or a fleet, had made more profit in a single voyage than Hawkins had made in his three. He had moved patriotism closer to prophecy and profits closer to war, and always there were his gods; but in all Drake's heavenly vision there was a woman's form, and it was she who came to him in fire. Oh how I knew a woman's body was like a cloak, it could clothe all things with the image of itself. And so the truth of her was a powerful fiction. Mary Newton, a simple country girl. For Drake, the sea and she were confused as one. Water, tumbling smooth and gently, warm in its liquid kiss, the taste of the sea on the passions of her breath. Drake had known her for several years." The old mariner looked into the cup of his own hands, his flesh defining the darkness that held its secret histories. "It was she who began to heal the wounds of the accusation of cowardice after San Juan de Ulúa.

"'There is no beauty in the skin that is not in the touch. What wondrous medicine is one caress,' Drake would say. The raptures of that woman could turn Drake's vision from the sea to flesh and from flesh into the rolling mounds of the sea. What alchemies there are in the chastities of a kiss. It is said Drake married the girl after his return from Mexico, he being but a starved and slandered waste, but it isn't true. Drake himself said to me, 'I married that girl earlier than anyone knew.' And so the subject lay at rest all these years and I myself feel betrayed in telling you. There is a kind of spirit in the mind that dies of its own telling. All haunts have secret ways, not only to bring fears and terrors, but the will to bind the songs of rivers and sing the souls of oceans.

"When Drake returned from Panama he was rich. He bought a fine home, and announced his marriage to Mary Newton. Drake wanted a son, to see the energy and image of himself carried forth in other flesh. But the sea Drake worshipped granted only to the limits of its self-interest. What he got was an ally. Mary Newton was, as Drake, a distant cousin of John Hawkins. Their blood by half in commons twice, that marriage, and Drake's own success in Panama, helped the two men to make accommodations. In truth, Hawkins never forgot his suspicions of Drake, and Drake never left Hawkins without a vested profit, ever knowing that John Hawkins respected profits more than histories.

"The two men in solemn discontents bore their uneasy partnership, the law of profit the wine to rest the nervous beasts of both their memories. Hawkins lent Drake his seventy-ton ship *Pasco*. Drake had the *Swan*. Together they invested in a year's supply of food and gathered a company of seventy-three men and a fleet of three pinnaces, which were brought to Panama in sections aboard the two larger ships. Hawkins was to remain in Plymouth, warmed by the firesides of his fortunes, while Drake and his two brothers and I on the *Pasco* and the *Swan* sailed on the twenty-fourth of May, 1572."

The old mariner paused, wet his lips. He looked at the sky and its powdering of stars. The land seemed to rise slightly in a gentle heave into the ghostly haze, as if the earth were offering its breast unto the night. The mariner stretched his back, adjusting his flesh to his bones. "We began again where we had begun," he said. "The circle has closed upon itself. To an alchemist the symbol of rejuvenation is the dragon biting his own tail. We stand upon the mouth. The circle he, the tail now bit. Drake, the dragon, El Drako as the Spanish would soon call him, rising from his own pain. His leg bandaged from the wounds at Nombre de Dios, where he, and his two brothers, and I failed to have the Spanish gold. It was August of 1572. Drake was now a man in passage.

"He sat in a pinnace watching the sea waves curl their folding fists around the air, grasping nothing. He could feel their power. Droplets of water fell on his lips. He could only wait, finding solace in his dreams, while his brother John and the escaped slave, Diego, searched the jungle for the Cimarrones. Drake followed the only option he had. He ordered the pinnaces back to Pheasant Bay to rejoin the rest of his fleet, make some repairs, and hope for John and Diego's return.

"Drake tasted salt on his tongue, the wafer of the sea incarnate. It startled his mind. The water shuddered about him; it broke in waves, like beckoning fingers urging Drake onwards. The sea spray flew, blown backwards by the wind, like a woman's hair. In desperation, Drake's only course was audacity. 'Action be the sinews of my fate,' he screamed, standing on his injured leg. The crew thought him fevered. 'We'll attack Cartagena. The Spanish will never expect it. The richest city on the Spanish main.' The crew looked at him in disbelief. 'Madness is only a fever to the weak,' Drake said, smiling as he spoke. 'We must dare beyond all reason or we are lost.'

"At Pheasant Bay, Drake took command of the *Pasco*, and John Oxenham, in the absence of John Drake, commanded the *Swan*. Together they sailed for Cartagena, with the three pinnaces following behind in playful obedience. Drake knew that the defenses of Cartagena were too strong for a direct assault.

"'By sea, we shall come upon them out of the night,' he said to Oxenham, who had rowed to the *Pasco*. The lights in Drake's cabin swayed, as if nodding their consent.

"Cartagena, in its way, was an easy run. The city has two harbors, an inner perch behind a long point of land, a small entrance protected by a stone fort, and an outer bay where most ships anchor, sleeping as they rock on their chains. We arrived near noon, but loitered from the harbor's mouth until night. We did not have a fleet to force the inner harbor, so Drake's plan was to seize the ships in the outer bay, beyond the range of the Spanish cannons, then tow them by the bow out to sea and plunder them at our will. Half the ships in the Indies should be bobbing their noses in that harbor for us to choose. And all our crew with a golden itch and only a dream of Spanish ducats to give it a scratch.

"We sailed under a full moon into the harbor that night, to find the watery landscape of the bay sticking its empty tongue toward the open sea. Not a Spanish ship to be seen, only the bay, its surf rolling in desperate race, trying to inundate the last reflections of the moon. Behind the harbor jaw, like a silhouette of broken teeth, a range of mountains rose. Few lights. Few sounds.

"'No ships to fuel an appetite,' spoke Drake, half-surprised. The crew murmured forebodings. 'The sea will not betray us. Who it will reward, it will first make low.'

"Our ships in silent watch glided through the bay. 'There, a flicker of light…a mast.' Off our bow, half lost but for its own shadows, a ship. Our fleet now crawled and lowly slid its bellies against the water's gentle wash; closer, ever closer on the Spanish ship. The wind groomed our sails in kindly furls until our ship touched the Spanish hull. Our parties on her deck. Our swords cut vapors. The ship was ours, abandoned except for a lone man who had stayed behind while others watched a duel. The holds were empty, the cabin bare, her cargoes memories. Oxenham struck the mast with his sword. Drake hid his disappointment with a laugh and addressed the Spanish sailor. 'I am Francis Drake of whom you may have heard. I abuse none who give me what I seek, and what I seek now is information. Where are all the ships?'

"The Spanish sailor tilted his head in amusement. 'The whole coast knows of your return, Señor Drake. One fox is too many for any chicken coop. The ships are gone, or near the shadows of the fort.'

"'All?' asked Drake. 'Surely not all.' His eyes underlined with kindness the meaning of his words.

"'There is one large ship up the bay, behind a spit of land. She can be yours, Señor, and am I now free?'

"Drake bowed, and saluted the Spaniard with his sword. 'We shall lock you in the hold for our safety and be off. God speed.' And then we left.

"Drake divided his crew among the three pinnaces, leaving the two larger ships to wait. We sailed up the bay, the shadows of the coast passing behind us until the land fell backward, revealing a small inlet and a ship. Silently, in an ever-widening arc, the pinnaces turned toward the Spanish vessel. We each had our task. Oxenham's boat slid against her bow, Drake was at midship, the other at her stern. There was no alarm aboard the ship. There was no watch. There was only her hull and its darkening planks sulking in the lazy swells, the white foam hissing against her, then dissolving again into depthless black of the wash.

"We threw ropes over her side, until her hull seemed littered with dragging vines. Then we climbed up the ropes onto her decks. Some of us carried swords in our teeth, others crossbows on our backs. The first on the decks were met with shouts as the Spanish crew roused from sleep stumbled toward the war. Bells on the ship were sounded. Firelocks flashed meteors through the night. There were screams and battle cries, and things falling with a thud. Men, in desperate embrace, struggled, holding knives in the air. A Spaniard staggered against a mast, clutching a gash, holding back with his own hands the lips of his own flesh, and its blood. Beyond the flashing light of torches, the night was filled with shadows striving in the dark.

"The Spanish captain rushed on deck, agape, swallowing hard his own breath, as the air in his throat turned to stone. Drake, who was behind, gently put a pistol to his head and called for his surrender and that of the crew. The captain nodded meekly and ordered his men to cease their struggle. Soon the sound of riot lifted and we locked the crew below deck, and then, with the three pinnaces as a tow, we pulled the ship from her anchorage toward the sea.

"Now Cartagena was all aglow. From the distant fort torches could be seen moving across her battlements. Through Cartagena's streets came the roar of men in heated run. Drums rattled in distant nervous pulse. Cannon sparks flew across the darkened water, but we were out of range. Drake signaled the *Pasco* and the *Swan* to join our escape. Their sails lifted. The breeze caught them full, as along the shore firelocks in impatient line discharged helpless flashes into the consuming night. Their shot fell into the sea, and we sailed on. We sacked the ship. We took its riches and many barrels of tobacco, then turned her loose, her captain still in his nightshirt, bowing thank-yous for his life.

"For two days we sailed north, Drake leading us behind a small trail of land that was a pleasant island. There, he called Thomas Moone to his cabin. Moone, a great barrel of a man, was the *Swan's* carpenter, and a man who would follow Drake beyond the good sense of his own well-being. Drake needed such men, for Drake would dare what few men would dream. That place where disaster and daring almost touch, through that sliver, Drake would force his desperate enterprise.

"Drake later told me he asked Moone to do something no captain should ever ask. 'We have come to the place of our first trial,' Drake began. 'What the sea gives to us'—Drake's hand swept the air—'is not given from love but from respect, from tethering our soul with hers. The sea does not bind its soul with ordinary men. Those who live their lives braced in easy prospects would rather feast upon their own, or chain their flesh to flaming irons, than lie down with darkness, and travel into the sea's eye, into its horizon, its ever-opening blossom, without thought of coast, nor land, nor limit. We live in the hysteria of possibility. To accomplish all and make our prayers manifest on this earth, we must at times take actions that seem to have danced beyond the reason of ordinary men.' Drake relaxed into the moment, as he watched Thomas Moone digest the thought. 'We are too few to properly man all our ships. The pinnaces must be kept ready. Their shallow drafts are perfect for this coastline. The *Pasco* is the best armed. Therefore, we must sacrifice the *Swan*.'

"'The *Swan?*' cried Moone. 'The crew and I love that little ship.'

"'I know,' said Drake. 'That's why I want you to scuttle her secretly. Let her settle quietly at her anchor, so none is lost and none is hurt.'

"'But the *Swan*.' Moone's eyes bore tears.

"'The *Swan* is a child of the sea. Let her settle one last time into the milk of her mother's breast. Let the sea hold her awash forever in her arms.'

"Moone stood silently for some time, looking at Drake. Finally he nodded. 'If it must be done, it's best it be done by my hand.' Then he left. That night, holding a candle, he crawled into the well of the *Swan*. The ship shivered nervously in the sea. The shadows of the cargo swayed on the walls. The light from the single candle flowed over the mounds of goods like a velvet lake. The planks of the *Swan* blistered and popped and screamed in splintered fury, as Moone drilled three holes near her keel. Water foamed through the wounds. Then he placed boxes and bales over the run, so the water would not rush too quickly and be observed.

"The next morning, while the sun rolled across the heavens like a loosened wheel, Drake rowed to the *Swan*, muttering, I suppose. There was in Drake a belief that only in desperation would his God's will be made manifest. And only through a constant testing of his fate could he be assured of the divine favor that he knew was his alone. All gods demand some coin in blood. If his demanded the *Swan*, so be it. The *Swan* had already begun to settle into her own death. None saw it but Drake. The closer he came, the higher seemed the grave of the waters about her sides.

"Near the *Swan* Drake called to Oxenham, whose figure appeared at the railing of the ship. The clouds in distant race which framed his shoulders were the shape of trumpeting cherubim, heralding an unseen fate that Oxenham could never guess. But that fate was a long way off in Peru. 'Would you like a little fishing today?' called Drake.

"'I would, indeed, like that,' answered Oxenham. 'I need some time to get some gear.' Drake replied, saying that he would wait. Then he added, 'The *Swan* seems a little low in her bath today,' not showing much concern. Oxenham's head jerked back in shock. Looking over the side, he called to his steward to run below decks.

"'We are awash,' screamed the steward, his words repeating through the bowels of the *Swan* in a many-voiced echo of the crew.

"'We're sinking!' Oxenham cried to Drake. 'We'll save her. By this arm I'll save her.' Oxenham raised his fists above his head. The waves, in an indifferent pantomime, slipped past the ship.

"'Do you require assistance?' called Drake. The foam of the sea hissed its tender reassurance as it fell against the wooden sides. The cold arms of the water gently held the sinking form, as she slowly, almost imperceptibly, began to settle into her last repose.

"'No!' called Oxenham, organizing his sense of authority in his own mind.

"All day the crew nursed the *Swan*. At dusk they abandoned hope. The water had risen in the *Swan* to a lower deck. Her planks creaked as she rolled in the swells. 'She's sighing into death,' I said, watching her settle. The *Pasco* was brought alongside. Cannons and powder and swords and firelocks were brought to her, as well as whatever fresh water there was, and food. Finally the crew transferred their few possessions.

"Low waves began to flow through the *Swan*'s gun ports. The *Swan* began to swamp. Bubbles rose between her planks. 'It's time to go,' said Drake. He held Oxenham's shoulder in his grasp, steadying him, urging him with the support of his hand.

"Oxenham fell to his knees. 'Kill me if you think the cause of this was some treason.'

"'You beg too much from death, Oxenham, my friend, you are a little too anxious to die. Let us not urge it—it may find us soon enough.'

"Oxenham then stood and followed Drake. We soaked the upper deck of the *Swan* with oil. In the fading sunlight she glistened red. Then we set her alight, so none could salvage her.

"We began to row back to our remaining ship, the smoke and smell of the *Swan*'s cremation in our lungs, Drake and Thomas Moone filled with their secrets, I the only other knowing. They looked at each other in the locked stares of those who speak treaties in each glance. Moone smiled. 'There is no loss, no wound,' he said, 'that stealing Spanish gold will not salve.' Some around him nodded. Others looked at Oxenham, who seemed pale and thin, as if some ghost did haunt his skin. Drake stood and spoke to us. He called across the surf to the other boats. 'The cause,' he said, 'our great enterprise, is more to us than any loss of any ship. We must fix that in our hearts. As to the *Swan*, Oxenham is not at fault. He served both the *Swan* and its company well. For that, I give him command of my *Pasco*. I shall take in its stead one of the pinnaces as my command. For he who is true to our endeavors should not be held in the tally because of God's will.' So Drake, in his desperate act, showed again his kindness.

"Upon returning to the *Pasco*, he transferred his goods to one of the pinnaces, as was his word. Then we sailed. Behind us the *Swan* raged in its own flames, like a wounded demon bleeding its fire into the night. As we passed beyond her illumination, sailing toward our hidden camp at Pheasant Bay, Drake watched the night quench in its darkness the distant light, repeating to himself the simple words, 'The cause…the cause…the cause.'

"At Pheasant Bay Drake ordered that the anvil and the iron and the coal which we had brought from England be unloaded, and a forge be set up to repair the ironwork of the ships. We worked in shifts for fifteen days, one day at labor, the next day at ease. We played quoits, or bowled, or shot arrows into the butts of empty kegs, or walked and lounged alone on the beach. All the while Drake would only work, trying to forget in activity the long wait for his brother John's return.

"On the fifteenth day, the sand about our camp was cut deep with the hills and valleys of our paths. Birds obscenely waddled. Some hopped and fluttered on their wings as if being kicked by some unseen foot. Drake was momentarily at rest, staring into the sea. Suddenly, in a rush, the wind was filled with riot, as a rising boiling flock of birds fled south.

"Drake turned to see five men push the jungle's growth into a bulge, then cut their way through the last remaining barriers of vines. It was as if the forest were giving birth to men. Diego waved to Drake. With him were three unknown blacks and John. The company along the beach broke into a run, surrounding the five with cheers and hugs and extended hands. Drake kissed his brother, grasping his shoulders. 'I was worrying,' he said, then he pulled Diego to his side as he called for the company to salute Diego with a cheer. The cheer given, Diego introduced Drake to the three blacks.

"'You are already known to the Cimarrones, Drake. They have a great knowledge of your adventures and many spies in places helpful to you.' Diego stepped aside, 'Pedro Mandinga, we are with Francis Drake.' Diego led Drake a little closer to the short black who carried two crossed pistols in a faded belt and a long sword. He was the best armed of the three, and seemed to be their leader. Even Diego gave him deference and respect. Pedro Mandinga smiled. His hair was braided and fell in long flowing knots, as if serpents grew in coils from the sides of his head. It was a curious dress, wonderfully considered to scare the Spanish, who were, by their own admission, always clawed by their superstitions.

"Drake took Pedro's hand, asking whether he spoke English. Mandinga answered Drake in a reasonable French, which tilted Drake's head in a smile of surprise. Drake laughed, as did we all.

"'I can see this jungle hatches mysteries in its thickets as well as eggs. How came you by your French?' Drake expansive in his joy and almost courtly in his charm.

"'The French corsairs, who killed the Spaniard who owned me for the simple pleasure of seeing him die,' said Mandinga. He was a man who had suffered too much cruelty in his life. 'They told me it is usual for the Spanish to die screaming at their hands. I thought I would make war with the French against the Spanish slavers, but the French, like the Spanish, only want the dirt that glows, the rock of the sun which you call gold.' Mandinga was silent then, waiting to judge the depth of Drake's reply.

"'I am a sailor,' said Drake. 'The thunder that rises from the waves rushes in echoes through my limbs. I am like a brother to the sea. The Spanish are enemies to my own blood and to my people. They burned my friends, living, at the stake…betrayed us…killed us…. I want now only vengeance for what they did at San Juan de Ulúa,' said Drake. 'I want their gold. It is the secret of the Spanish power. Take it from them—they weaken.' Drake finished his speech. Mandinga nodded.

"'When I was a boy, I lived in a place far away where my father spoke to spirits in the earth. Spirits—spirits that ran with the animals, that sat on his shoulders, even dwelled in the words of his name. Here you speak only to the spirit of the gold. All the other spirits of the land, of the animals, of your own name, wander lonely and forgotten. It is a strange desolation you visit upon your gods.' Mandinga looked at Drake, who nodded to him as if he were his own reflected image in black.

" 'Their gold is the Spanish strength. I want that power. To steal it is to feed upon their hearts. I am, as you know, a great warrior. What greater coup than to kill an enemy with his own strength?'

" 'I have no interest in their gold. I am hunted. To whom shall I sell; from whom shall I buy? Before there can be value, there must be trust. But I know your name, Drake. You make war on the Spanish so we are joined….' "

AT JAMESTOWN, CAPTAIN MARTIN SHOOK HIS HEAD WITH VIOLENCE, as if trying to cast from his brain some hateful thought. "The black put no value on gold?" he said, speaking his words in explosive breaths, as if expelling a hateful thing onto the ground, where he could examine and crush it at his will.

The mariner looked at Martin. "The only coin the Cimarrones valued was hatred of the Spanish. It was the mint of their fidelity. It was the only ducat in the commerce that one could hold, or horde, or spend against tomorrow. It became the rate on which they exchanged their love."

Martin stood, still strangling in his words. "I cannot believe men, even blacks, could cast aside for other wealth the lord of all value —our gold." Then he walked away, muttering to himself.

"If you had heard the stories of Spanish cruelties we have heard, you would not have much affection for a rock either," called the old mariner, who cursed Martin beneath his breath.

"There were, by my count, three thousand Cimaronne men, women and children, blacks and Indians, all runaway Spanish slaves. What they needed, they stole. Who trespassed upon them, they killed. They had their law, their families, their weapons and their spies. They already knew of Drake's attack on Cartagena. The jungle fed them. Gold they saw as a Spanish poison and they ignored it.

"All this Mandinga told Drake on their first meeting—and something more. In his slavery at Nombre de Dios, Mandinga's Spanish master had been the very man in charge of the treasure shipment across Panama. Mandinga had accompanied him many times on these expeditions. He knew the treasure routes, he knew the method of transport, and he knew the number of guards and their weapons. All this he told. Then he offered as an alliance his men, his food, his help…everything we needed, just for the pleasure of having allies at last, and watching the Spanish die. Drake touched Mandinga's shoulder and said, 'We will harm only those who oppose us. All others we do not abuse. Let strength be our superiority. Let the weak slaughter the weak. We are far better men than they. I am English. I curse the Spanish and other pirates.'

"At those words Mandinga smiled. 'Brother to the sea. There is a saying among my people: To be a king, you must know how to carry two gods in each hand. You are still a child with one parent, and yet you do not know it. One day I shall bring you to the mother of the sea, the greatest of all waters, so you may kiss the other kin that gave you life. We will fight as you wish. You are very brave and very foolish, and to have lived so long, you must be beloved of the gods.' Mandinga paused. 'There are in you reflections of a world that once I knew.' With that, Pedro Mandinga stood. 'Meet me in a week at a place between Isla de Pinos and Cape San Blas. Diego knows it well. Until then.' Mandinga and the two men with him turned and disappeared through the vines.

"'Mandinga will make good war, like Drake…but now we should start,' said Diego. A bird with a face of brilliant feathers screamed in a tree, sharpening its beak against the bark on which he stood.

"'We will make war, and soon,' answered Drake. Then he ordered John Oxenham to make the *Pasco* ready to sail. Diego and Drake's younger brother, Joseph, were to go with him. Drake gave command of a pinnace to his elder brother, John, who was to stay behind and finish the repairs to the boats. John was not pleased, he being a little headstrong in his way, and a little jealous of his brother's authority. 'I've served you well. Why must I be left to wait?' he said. 'I invested my wealth in this voyage, just as you.' There was in John an anger that always boiled a little beneath his skin.

"'I need you here. I have given you command of half our company. I must have a fresh reserve at Pheasant Bay, a reserve I can trust.' So saying, Drake took his leave. 'Two weeks at most, I swear.' He walked away with a wave of farewell.

"'Brother to the sea. He believes it,' John Drake said, I standing by his side.

"'Your brother's a fine sailor…maybe the best that ever was,' I said.

"'He's mad,' was John's only reply.

"I laughed and said, 'Madness is not madness when it brings a profit.' I winked at John, who laughed with me as I followed my captain to the *Pasco*, not knowing what wisdoms I had betrayed."

Chapter Seventeen

GODS DIE THEIR DEATH, AND NEW RESOLVES. AND MY
BROTHER, MY OWN KNIFE MUST TRANSGRESS UPON THEE.

ONAS, HIS WHITE HAIR GOLDEN in the firelight, by reflections the image of a saint, a friend to me. But my suspicions overwhelm. There are secrets that hold a wisdom he will not speak. And how to me is it addressed, and can his hell birth heavens as a sport?

"We sailed along the coast of Panama, taking six Spanish ships, all loaded with food and other provisions. Our *Pasco* now filled to the upper decks with spoils, we turned to the Gulf of Uraba, where we built four secret storehouses, two on a small island and two on the mainland, as preserves against ill luck. Diego oversaw the construction, he being wise in the ways of the jungle woods and knowing the places to find the best stones. Diego's hard work and his knowledge increased our crew's admiration each passing hour. We felt well tended in his presence. What Drake knew of the sea, Diego knew of the land.

"After three days, we headed the *Pasco* toward our meeting with Mandinga. One evening Oxenham gave Joseph Drake the wheel, which pleased the elder Drake, Joseph being just fifteen. Drake stood behind the boy, watching his steady hand hold upon the wheel. The old *Pasco*'s bow cut into the night. There was no sea nor sky, but only the opening mouth of widening blackness. Our ship seemed to be sailing toward the flickering coin of many stars. Francis put his hand on Joseph's shoulder. 'You are more son to me than brother,' he said, and that would be like Drake, he without issue, always adopting in his own head the children of other fathers for the son he never had. His seed was ever in his mind, as the sea was ever in his blood."

I thought of the mariner's words. A chill of pain hollowed me to a blank. Was I but one of an adopted choir? One child more to spend his love upon an indifferent father's indifferent gaze. Am I orphaned to a ghost? Is hell a purge where families drink each other's blood?

Shall I over beast my rage, exhaust the circuits in my flesh? Love the frantic demon that will curse me to a peace? No, I will be the better son, over love my love and shell my winters to an early spring.

"At dawn we passed Cape San Blas. Above the entrance to a small nameless river there rose a pillar of smoke from a signal fire. Pure white it rose, twisting within itself like a liquid salt. The smoke lifted in the air to a flattened head. It could go no further, as if the sky itself had denied it passage. Then the cloud broadened, falling back to earth, a smoking thunderhead of turmoiled white. We sailed toward the source. In a little cove we anchored. On the beach danced a small group of Cimarrones, their heads covered with masks carved from wood and painted, radiating hair of glued straw. Three figures left the dance and walked to the edge of the sea, beckoning us to join them. Each had a bow and was naked, except for the skirt of grass about his middle. Behind them the heart of the drum beat and throbbed its pulse into the air. Drake raised his arms above his head. He stood on the railing of the ship. 'Oxenham, take ten others and follow me in a longboat.' Then he dove into the sea, screaming, his words lost in the thunder of the splash as he disappeared beneath the waves. Rising quickly, surprising the surface of the incoming surf.

"We lowered the longboats and rowed after our captain, who now sat on the sand as the Cimarrones danced in two lines, before a single figure in a mask of horns, singing, as he carried on his back a grotesque idol without arms or legs.

"We landed on a sandy beach. On the dunes that formed a natural semicircle behind the dancers, their clothes were hung in rags over scaffolds of crude wooden crosses. We seemed to walk the ground of crucified ghosts. Their headless shirts, their torn sleeves lay in the phantoms of their ambiguous gestures. Beneath the shirts the pants fell to the sand in a faded rush of cloth. It was as if the dance were fenced in a thicket of ragged horrors, guardian spirits of Cimarrones protecting Cimarrones.

"We walked cautiously to our captain, respectful of the dance before us, then sat by Drake, Diego with us, and watched the movements of the dancers. Words cried out from behind their masks. The Cimarrones stamped their feet and were still. Then they began again. To the Cimarrones all devotions had neither beginning nor end. 'What is, is always passing.' A story is a circle. It can be entered at any pause.

"'We are the witness to what dance?' asked Oxenham.

"'We are summoning new gods as we bury old ones,' said Diego.

"'God doesn't die,' replied Oxenham.

"Diego answered in silence, watching instead the dancers in their heat divine the air with the movements of their limbs. 'To the Cimarrones the gods live both a birth and a death,' replied Diego, after a time. The Cimarrones danced in a rage all night, the flames of their fires biting the darkness with momentary tongues of light. At dawn they removed their masks, dug holes and buried them. Then they walked away and slept.

"Later the next day Mandinga came to see Drake. Sitting by Drake's side, Mandinga said, 'Our old gods were feeble in this land. Sickly they were, without a flesh to carry their spirit. Without the animals or birds that we knew, where can our gods be? In what cave or tree or rock can the hyena god dwell when there are no hyenas?' Mandinga looked at Drake. 'Now they are no longer. They live only in this house.' He pointed to his head. 'The mind is a faithless servant, it tends its own needs first. We must see again with our heart what the head will deny. Our gods have always died when new ones are in birth. Power ever in its changes blooms. Behind the one the many. Behind the many the one. So it is now. We will have our war, Drake. Me, a man in want, a man of faith in a strange land, whose gods I do not know, whose spirits speak to me in a language I cannot understand, and you, Drake, brother to the sea, a man marooned on a beach.' Mandinga laughed.

"'I am not marooned,' said Drake, smiling. 'I am merely resting.'

"'You are marooned,' replied Mandinga, pulling from Drake's pocket his Bible. 'This is the Spanish holy book. I have seen it many times. Brother to the sea, the Spanish would burn you at the stake if you called yourself that and they catch you. No, as you are always in motion, Drake, so are you marooned. Between this book and the sea.' Mandinga shook the book in his hands as he spoke, 'My people have a saying: everything and its own. So, can you chose, my Drake, between this—your book—and your mother, the sea? Can you?'

"The sea darkened in its wash beyond its horizon on rising waves where no spires of Jerusalem could be seen. Drake said a simple 'No.'

"'Good,' said Mandinga. 'My people love stories with only middles, with all choices well considered, always becoming something, not yet finished, as you, Drake, not yet finished. Make your choice if you dare. You will die. Your choice will drown you in torment.' Mandinga laughed.

"'I am not in torment.' Drake watched the sea. 'I am as my word.'

"'Pain is the double vise. It hides itself with itself, one pain to hide an agony. So like you, my Drake, you are twice. All living things choose their own spirit...as guide. You have chosen two, each living in jealousy of the other. It is a daring choice. Even the gods live with it uneasily. If you survive its necessities, there will be no place you shall stand with more power than the place where you receive your death. There the energies shall find release. But yours cannot be the common way. You shall have no tombs but the words of men. You shall have no grave but the heaving waters of your mother's breast. This I can see. We are both the same, both wanderers in exile.'

"With that, Mandinga stood, his arms raised in benediction. 'The ashes of my old gods lie scattered on an alien coast. I have murdered that which gave me comfort that my people might be reborn. It has been ever so with us. Even the gods can be consumed. Let the gods themselves fear, for we who receive their lives hold their deaths.' The knob of the sun rolled in the heavens, its needles of heat pricking beads of sweat onto Drake's face. 'I am naked. A whirlwind chains my soul. Let the powers of my dead gods inform my flesh that this, my hand, may hold the wine of a new earth.' Pedro Mandinga cried out, opening his arms to the firmament as if ordering the sky to crack.

"Looking at Mandinga, Oxenham whispered to me, 'And so he digs the pit to his own hell.'

"'On what mortuaries have we not built our own philosophies?' I answered, thinking how a lesser man would crawl from painful memories toward the exile of a blessed forgetfulness.

"Drake looked toward the sea, whose sun-reflected waters sparkled in such delusions it almost seemed as if the sea's wetness had been sucked dry and in its stead, a diamond desert rolled on waves of sand. Drake shook his head to clear his sight.

"Mandinga still held the Bible. 'Your gods, Drake, carry great eternities in their limbs.'

"As if raging in its chains, the sea rolled against the land. 'That book you hold,' said Drake, 'is not Spanish. It is an *English* Bible. We English say it is a book born of God. The Spanish, in their cowardice, despise it and burn at the stake any who would carry it. They call them Lutherans those that do.

"'This is your god's book?' asked Mandinga.

"Drake said, 'This is my father's Bible that the Spanish hate.'

"'You have a curious family, brother to the sea,' Mandinga laughed. 'My people need new gods. Make us Lutherans of the land that we may share all the Spanish hate.'

"'And will our Drake let this black deny his sea?' said Oxenham in jest. Mandinga, a man of many strategies, knowing more English than we supposed, turned toward Oxenham and spoke. 'My people, through the lives of countless chiefs, were of the land; its rivers our blood; its mud our flesh. There is a saying among my people, To each man his own mysteries. I leave the sea to Drake and so should you, Oxenham. It is a foolish man who reuses another's sacrifice.'

"'And will you also become a Lutheran?' Diego asked Mandinga.

"'No,' Mandinga replied. 'I shall long for the gods we have killed. It is my last gift to my people. I shall stand their watch. The gods are most dangerous after they are buried.' With that, he turned and walked toward his men, Diego following. 'We will take my people's conversion at our village,' Mandinga called back.

"Oxenham looked at Drake in surprise and said, 'They're becoming Protestants. It's a shrewd alliance our captain has made.'

"Drake returned the glance with pity mixed with scorn. 'I saw my father kill a church so that he could speak directly to his God without the interference of a priest. I am truly my father's son. I too must taste the words of my own God in my own way. We are all born into God to struggle in his revelations. No one has won here, no one has lost. A people need more than a hate to make them a nation. Mandinga knows this. Respect him. Such wisdom is rare.'

"Oxenham, feeling Drake's scorn, spoke to his captain in anger. 'How can you, of all men, convert these people? You who have created his own church.'

"We all waited for the thunder of Drake's rage, but he spoke in deference, questioning more himself than Oxenham. 'As my father created a church in defiance of his father before him, I am my father's son.' Drake nodded as he spoke. 'To what church have I not been a heretic? To what god have I not been a saint?'

"'Where only the mad see a purpose, that is where wisdom may dwell,' said Mandinga the next day, as he crushed Drake in a farewell embrace. Then the Cimarrones struggled into the jungle and disappeared. As we rowed toward the *Pasco* a low line of squalls darkened the horizon's edge. We stood in sunlight as we climbed the *Pasco*'s ratlines to her decks, hauling our longboats aboard. We sang to the profits ahead and to the conversion of the Cimarrones, which was to us all only the first glimpse of God's wondrous bounty. No souls, even as golden as those of the Cimarrones, could be spent on earthly things, but surely in heaven they would have a coin to purchase fair reputation with our God.

"To us the *Pasco* seemed to fly in the sea, oiling her slippery trail through the waters with joyous prospects. Drake was quiet the whole trip back to Pheasant Bay, brooding in secret council with himself. Mandinga had told him the Spanish gold didn't cross the isthmus during the rainy season, which gave us about five weeks' wait. Further, Mandinga's spies would inform him of the start of the pilgrimage of the treasure toward the Jerusalem of our theft. The Cimarrones would follow its progress through the jungle, keeping us informed.

"We sailed into Pheasant Bay. The crew on shore gathered at the water's edge. Drake waved to the distant figures, giving them signs of a journey done with fine accomplishment. The men on the beach did not wave back, but stood solemnly as if their very presence did shame the ground.

"'I'll go first and plumb the tide of this agony,' Drake said, half concerned, half in happy jest.

"He rode to shore. There, on the beach, men held their souls tight to their stiffened frames. 'Well, what's amiss?' said Drake, on the land again.

"No one spoke until Thomas Moone raised his bitten lips and said, "Sir, your brother is killed. He was slaughtered pursuing a Spanish ship.'

"'How?' was Drake's only word. It sounded from his lips as a petal falls.

"'Four days back a Spanish ship passed along the coast, so close to the bay we thought she was a gift from God himself, an easy pick for us. But John was not eager, saying that only one of the pinnaces was fit to sail. We had few weapons, but still we pleaded with John to take up the chase, saying, 'It is an easy grip to take this prize. Can we afford to let it pass?' Finally John relented, sailing in a headlong race to catch the Spanish ship. The truth was we were poorly armed. John stood at the bow, a broken sword in one hand, in the other a pillow for a shield. Joseph Bax was by his side holding a small harpoon. It was a brave but silly sight…to cast a comedy for your brother's death. Nearing the ship, the Spanish fired a single volley that took Bax in the head, your brother in the side. John lingered for a day. He died in whispers, speaking of his wife, leaving her all his worldly profits and his portions from this voyage, asking that you would see it done. It was a waste,' said Moone, his sorrow choking his throat.

"'There is no waste,' said Drake. 'Even death cannot kill our cause.'

"Far out to sea where heretic clouds raced against the sky, a whirlwind darkened into hurricane. But pressed by the sun, it exhausted itself into a breath, then into a gentle sigh. Drake was shown to his brother's grave, where he crumpled to his knees, praying. He stayed all night holding himself in a ball, as a pilgrim might, in terror of losing any other portion of his soul. In the morning we found him sleeping against the earth. We let the dreamer lie upon the mounds of eternal sleep.

"For the next weeks, we spent our sorrows in simple tasks, the comfort of known routine that gives the world the illusion of predictability. It was a poor harbor of sand into which we set our rest, but what choice had we than to wait for Mandinga's message that the gold was on the move? A week after his brother's death Drake announced the plan for another attack on Cartagena. By battle and disease our crew had been reduced to sixty. But Drake would not inter his sorrows until he got his treasure. He would bleed our braveries into the sea and pan success in their wash, even if it meant the death of us all. The crew just wanted gold. They were simple men, loyal to that instrument which quenched their needs. They would follow Drake, for he held the image of the golden torch. Gold, to them, was not a purpose or an end, it was a necessity that brought them food. The Spanish filled gold with the eternal darkness within themselves. To Drake the gold confirmed the light. It was the frozen torch of his God's gentle love. Drake against the Spanish, his country against theirs, trial by mutual combat…an ancient concept in modern dress. On that Drake bent his knee, offering his being as sacrifice. 'I am the sea,' he would whisper when he brooded too long. 'I know its face. It is my face. I know its moods. They are mine. I have become its revelation.' He would look to the heavens and grasp his Bible, feeling the substance of his book, the material that gave pain. He was like a captain tied to the wheel of his own ship, his hands resisting the contrary pulls of wind and surf, holding to the funnel of the gale, the center course, while all the powers swung, contested in their wayward spirit.

"A day before we left for Cartagena men began to die. They fevered for a time, tossing agonies in their heads, their skin drying to a weathered parchment, yellow flesh around their eyes. Then they threw from their mouths black vomit. It was as if the river of hell had found fissures in the souls of men, pouring its fiendish bile into the world in steam and hiss. Some of their stomachs were so swollen up, you would think the devil's head was in their gut.

"The crew begged me to brew some herbs. They knew of my alchemies and would I plead again from fate a tenuous bargain. Could I slander hope with desperate cure? Could I take that faith again? They offered me tobacco to make my medicines. What ghost is this leaf that wings about my life in hauntings? My remedies had been proven venom. All my books printed a fool's wisdom. All arrogance is the weapon of our self-murder."

At Jamestown eyes did question in each glance, *What admission this that lays its hand upon the dark?*

"There are histories we speak only in the caverns of ourselves," the mariner said. "But now, the moments tricked, the story wills the teller what to tell. I am by my own kiss confessed. My only love I killed. In childbirth I gave her syrups to ease her pain. I the wizard scholar knew all the ancient tomes. Dust lay like gold on my secret texts. To those receipts I added the most modern leaf, I boiled the brew with tobacco. She drank from the heated cup. What poison is this upon my hands? It is the truth that flows in daggers through my blood. Both dead! And I had not a drop to speed my peace. And so I abandoned death to death, cast down my chemistries and fled to the deserts of the sea. And now it comes again, and all my magics have me a coward to our cause. I knew I could not help. 'Let us drug ourselves with rumors,' I thought. 'They are less dangerous than my cures.'

"In three days ten were dead and twenty more lay ill. We tended all, accusing each other of filling our drinking buckets in the bad waters of the swamp. It was not so. Accusations became pauses between deaths. Five more died in a day. In our minds the air bred annihilation. Two more dead and three more sick. We became caged in fear. There was no wind that did not have fingers at our throats. The sand absorbed the black sickness, then the bodies. Drake tended all. His brother Joseph, now down with fever, lay in one of the small huts. He lay on a bed of palm leaves, his face streaked with the runs of sweat. His teeth chattered, his eyes sunk into his head. He clutched the end of his blanket to his chest. The muscles of his fingers bulged. The blanket trembled. Joseph no longer controlled his own grip. His life was drowning in his body. With his last strength he tried to tether it to a cloth. He vomited blackness again. Drake held his brother's head in his arms, caressing the familiar hair, watching his brother's life drift away, watching him become a stranger.

"Outside, the night blew darkness in our faces. Around the campfire numbed voices flowered on drying breaths. 'How many dead today?'

"'Three more.' The words came exhausted as from far away. 'Twenty in all?' It was weakly asked, the answer already known. In the shadow a head nodded, then it coughed.

"'It was the brackish waters, or maybe a barrel went bad,' said Thomas Moone, wondering what part was his responsibility.

"'The water is sweet....I tasted it myself.' Oxenham looked at the fire, contemplating the changing faces of the heat. Mosquitoes flew in circles above the flames, swarming in the light of a counterfeit day.

"'It's these mosquitoes,' someone said, slapping a distraction on his arm.

"'Them mosquitoes can't cause the fever,' said a knowing voice. 'It's all this jungle rot.'

"'There is no hand that can touch the cause of this.' Two eyes stared, hissing words and reflecting fire. 'It is God's judgment upon us for our captain who worships pagan things. In this, our Eden, Drake has picked from a serpent tree an ocean for his apple. Now we are all cursed and wander in our deaths to die...for his sins. There is no gold that can stop this life we ooze.'

"His brother dead, Drake walked from the hut, Diego at his side. Whether he heard the man or not I never knew, but our company was near to panic, and men, even good men, so close to madness, find salvation in a word, or the voices in the rustling of a branch.

"Drake wandered to the fire at first, as someone drunk with thought; then he came straight on and said, 'My brother...my brother, as so many of us have, has passed into death. We must, for our own sakes, find the cause of this affliction. This cause is in this world, not in God. Here it is manifest. Here we will seek it out. I propose to open one of the victims with my knife and whatever surgeon tools we have'—Drake held his own dagger—'and search out in its very roots, the parent to the cause.'

"'Mutilate the dead?' someone cried. Flames waxed horror-struck faces into crimson masks. Lips whispered into ears. Jaws hung from open mouths, perplexed in disbelief. In the grotto of light, Drake raised both his hands above the fire. In his covenant he seemed to gesture to his crew to be at ease. 'All that can be held by the hand can be understood...even the cause of this disease,' Drake said, in his most desperate act. Brace the crew, fight the terror with a terror greater than their own. The earth itself seemed to hold back its breath, its breezes convulsed in whirlwinds far off. Scratches of clouds in lines obscured the moon, as if a hellish paw had clawed the night, trying to enter in violence the world of men.

"'To pillage even one of those bodies—never!' screamed a sailor, rising to his feet. 'It is to pervert their memory into a bloody ruin. I will have none of it.'

"'You don't have to watch,' said Drake. 'How else am I to save this expedition?'

"'You have become a savage...no better than a pagan,' said the man, stepping back from the fire, his hand shaking before him.

"Drake was so calm, the actor acting the part he did not choose to play. 'If I must plunge my arms into the alchemy of life, let it be with those we once called comrade. The cause of this plague is knowable. It is the last act of faith we can give our dead.'

"'It may be the last chance to get hold of the Spanish gold,' said a sailor who spoke from his knees, praying almost to the golden glow of the burning logs. Now, it is said that a man seeking gold will abide almost any horror, but Drake would not have his men follow him solely for lust for wealth. He wanted more. He wanted what his father wanted before him—loyalty, until it spent the soul. Converts, as Drake saw it.

"'This plan of yours unbalances me,' said Oxenham. 'We tether ruin on our tongue. The men are near revolt.' Drake ignored him and said to the company, 'I had two brothers before this enterprise began and now I have none. Who has given more than I? Who would wish to preserve their memories more than I? But the affliction is upon us.

In days it has taken twenty. Twenty more lie sick. If we don't find the cause, we may all die.'

"'The cause is in God,' cried a voice.

"'The cause is in the flesh,' Drake answered. 'It will be revealed if we have the courage to explore with device and instrument and hope the caverns of our dead. Living or dead, we are all mysteries of God. To discover anything is to discover him. Revelation is knowledge. Its proof we will have in the success of our enterprise.'

"The crew were silent, mostly. There were murmurs. They grew louder. The walls of anger rose again. 'It is the conception of a beast. These were our neighbors, friends since birth. To mock them now....'

"'Who are we to waste a death?' said Drake. 'All that we call friend is but a set of vacant walls. To show our respect we must accept the horror. We must step into their extinction and explore in their remains. There is no other way but to wait for our own death and with it the failure of our enterprise.'

"'Only the bravest of the brave, my people call the wizard fool, would search in the dead for the shadows of their spirits,' said Diego, still at Drake's side.

"The men were silent for a moment, digesting Diego's words. They looked back at the captain.

"'You are no doctor, Drake. If you wish to defile a body, do one of your own,' cried a sailor standing in the dark. The rest of the crew nodded their heads. 'Consume the body of your brother Joseph in your search.'

"'If this will bring the crew some peace,' said Drake, 'it is the proper thing to do. It is done.' He turned, calling to Oxenham to bring the surgical tools. Then he walked back to his brother's tent. Diego and I followed. He carried Joseph outside to a crude wooden table, a few planks of timber supported by two barrels at each end. Drake ordered a circle of fires built a few feet from the table, to give light as he worked. Diego and I each held a lantern over Joseph's remaining stare.

"'Why not wait until morning?' I asked Drake.

"'It is best we do it quickly. The men are nervous,' Drake replied, 'and this, our science, is still young. It is a game of speed and shadows and a little luck.'

"Drake's hands were trembling. I removed Joseph's clothes, Diego helping. Drake watched the body of his brother glow in the firelight, his skin a sour lifeless white. 'Are you sure he's dead?' asked Drake. I searched for a pulse. There was no morsel of breath. I nodded my head. 'He's dead.' Drake held the surgical knife, whose handle and blade were slightly bowed, like the horns of a bull. He appraised his brother's chest, starring into the landscape of its flesh.

"'There are no maps to explore the soul,' he whispered. 'There is more a journey here on this one spot than all the keels of all the ships that have ever taken...and no maps...no sextant...no compass but the mind...,' he said. With that Drake walked to the hut. The crew at the campfire, their own clothes robed in the luminescent shadows of flames. Their eyes watched Drake in his passage. He disappeared. When he returned, he was holding curling sheets of paper, ink, a pen and a writing pallet. He called to the crew. 'As we venture into death, let us leave some soundings, some charts, so those who come after us may know its coast.' Drake held the paper above his head.

"'There is no death I would not die to follow Drake,' cried Oxenham. The crew cheered.

"At the table, Drake held the knife again at his brother's chest. 'Those were the words, and this is the flesh,' he said. He seemed to feel the pain as he drew the knife down between his brother's ribs. The flesh untied and separated."

"IN THE MORNING DRAKE SAT ON THE SAND, EXHAUSTED, HOLDING the drawings between his knees. He looked at them. 'There is a world in the flesh where some continents pump thoughts and others sculpt sight, where rivers flow in bile through caverns of bone and mountains heave in flesh. We have too crude a bark, too crude a lens, to sail those shores with certainty. We are still trespassers in our own meat. This I know—my brother and the others bled to death from some internal wounds. How they were caused, I do not know. How to prevent them, I do not know. All I know is I plan to stay and take the Spanish gold.' The crew around Drake nodded.

"'There is no mutiny in our resolve,' said Thomas Moone. 'We only wish that our courage will match your own.'

"Ellis Hixon, the *Pasco's* cook, whispered in my ear, 'There's nothing like a little death to spice the taste of profit.'

"Diego sat far off, carving a death mask. 'Where the spirits have been disturbed, the dead need protection,' he said, showing his work to Drake, the mask in hysterical grin. Drake thanked him.

"Behind the crew, beneath the sheet, lay the ruined instrument that was Joseph Drake, his entrails and those bits of self laid back into him by his brother's loving hands. We buried him in his mask, next to John, and Drake said a few words over him as the sea rolled its life against the shore."

Chapter Eighteen

A RIDER, A DRUNK AND A BATTLE IN THE DARK.

T JAMESTOWN the silence cut its lesions through the dark. Bereft of words, our surgeon, Thomas Wotton, placed another log upon the campfire, his face, a flickering haunt of scarlet, framed in shadows. "Could you disembowel your own?" asked one of Ratcliffe's favorites.

Wotton sighed his confusion filled with horror.

"All men may rage themselves into a sleep of pain." The old mariner's eyes starring as if through a hundred years. He spoke, his voice rising like a whisper beckoning to some hidden protocol, "Blind, yet the seeing eye finds a comfort in a familiar wound." He gave a little chortle to his demons in the air, then he continued his tale. "For the next three days we tended our sick and waited, despondent in our thoughts, exhausted by our memories, until, on the fourth day, Mandinga sent word that Spanish gold was on the road toward Venta Cruces. The weary crew, in rough shouts, cheered the news. Even the sick raised their heads to cough salutes.

"Drake knew that when the gold moved inland, the barge traffic along the coast near the city would increase. The Spanish captains would hurry to Venta Cruces to pick up the treasure to transport it to Philip's warehouses at Nombre de Dios, but Drake was going to strike before the gold reached Venta Cruces. He told the Cimarrones to return to Mandinga and say that he was preparing to join him, but that we needed assistance to carry our provisions and we needed guides. Nodding to Diego, the Cimarrones disappeared into the shadows of the trees. 'My people are of the land,' said Diego, looking at the wall of the forest. 'We move in its spirit and so are unseen. We shall teach all this, my Drake. Then you shall be of the earth and the sea.'

"Drake smiled, looking past the graves of his two brothers, then toward the sea, where the gulls in feathered squalls rose on the chartless winds. 'I am already of the earth.'

"Drake had lost more than half his crew. Our number was down to thirty-five. Of those, only twenty-five were fit for the march inland. Four days later Pedro Mandinga arrived with thirty Cimarrones. Drake divided his command, taking seventeen of his sailors with him, leaving Ellis Hixon and the rest to care for the sick.

"The crowns of the trees burned with the feathers of crimson flight. Flocks of macaws settled in the high branches. A few circled in raucous play through shafts of light that fell through the jungle growth toward the earth. We watched the flecks of light on the jungle's roof, an insinuation of day on our darkened path. Four Cimarrones led us. Twelve more formed a forward guard. We marched behind Mandinga with Drake and Diego, as they talked. Carrying our weapons, we moved slowly, balancing ourselves carefully on huge roots snaking in moss-covered spines on the jungle floor. We stumbled forward. To the rear, more Cimarrones filtered through the shadows, carrying the heaviest of our provisions.

"'On those shoulders and those alone rides the success of this our enterprise,' Drake spoke in admirations.

"Each morning we marched through jungle mists that hugged the earth as if the sky had bowed upon the land, praying to some eternal dark. Lizards clung to the bark of trees, their tongues tasting the air as we passed, their eyes peering through leathery patches, breathing, with their sight, the scent of men.

"From dawn we would march four hours, until the heat hung upon us in scales of sweat. Then we rested while the Cimarrones built crude shelters from plantain leaves and palmetto poles.

"At noon we would break camp and march again until four o'clock. Then we would establish another camp. The Cimarrones would hunt for extra food. One day they killed a wild pig, which they roasted on a crude spit. We sat in the night watching it cook, its own fat feeding the fire, listening to the logs crack and the skin sizzle, smelling our hunger on the wind. After eating, we watched the changing weave of vermilion flames, licked our fingers and heard stories of Spanish slaughter.

"On the third day we arrived at a Cimarrone town, which was a fort surrounded by a ten-foot-high mud wall, around which was dug a deep ditch. A drawn bridge spanned the ditch by the town's gate. We marched across into a land of sorrows.

"Children, dressed in rags, chattered at our feet, curious and friendly. They followed in our steps along the mud path that was the town's main street. Men and women, both black and a few Indians, stood by the road, silently watching. A woman raised a fist as she cursed the Spanish.

We stopped and rested in the town square, which was a landscape of ooze, around which fifty or so low huts huddled against themselves and the earth. In the center of the square was a large cross. Around it in a semicircle, impaled on three wooden stakes, were the skulls of Spanish soldiers, their metal helmets nailed to their heads.

"The Cimarrones walked among us, talking, patting our shoulders, happy at the sight of allies. Mostly they were dressed in rags, the clothing of their slavery, the very garments they wore, I thought, when they escaped the Spanish.

"Our Cimarrone guide stacked our equipment in a hut. We were given maize and sweet fruits and meat in all its plenties. We sat and ate and heard tales of their captivity and Spanish cruelty. They wanted us to understand. It was as if our new faces had unlocked tides of anger, which the familiar surroundings and the familiar persons of their daily life had choked to the sickening sameness and loneliness of a people under siege. Our presence had changed the circumstance of their suffering and oiled the flames of their vengeance.

"We were told how a year earlier the Spanish had attacked and seized their town, slaughtering, mutilating and enslaving men, women and children. A man, his hand held like a claw, as if he would tear the eyes out of the air, told of his baby crucified to a tree; his wife, her feet cut off, so she could never run away, dragged into slavery. Old men burned at the stake. Children hiding, hunted down, torn apart by hungry dogs. For the living of the town and its dead, the only mercy was in death that day. There was no limit to the Spanish frenzy and their lust for blood.

"Oxenham looked at the Spanish cross in the center of the town, mounted with a Spanish head. 'Why not battle Spanish in heaven as you do on earth? Convert to our God,' he said, looking at Drake, waiting for an approving nod. 'Seize their redemption, lay siege to their heaven as we shall seize their gold and despoil their towns. Let gods in commerce war!'

"Pedro Mandinga slowly replied, 'This at last would be war in its eternities. Our old gods are memories. They sleep in peace in a far country. Let them be. All your gods are one. Behind the one the many; behind the many the one.'

" 'I am unworthy," said Drake, knowing Mandinga's thought.

" 'Of course. That is why you are chosen.'

"The hills and mountains sharp about us, hooded in dark forest, silent, blindly bending forward like praying monks, watched, as Drake looked across his assembled flock and spoke. 'We are all in an alien country, outnumbered, surrounded. All our suffering has been authored by one enemy. We are together here because of him. Our agonies have made us one. One, because we have refused to yield, our skin to be stamped into another's coin, our blood made commodity, our flesh made goods. This sacred stuff, which is ourselves, we will not surrender. Here we sit at war's communion. Its church, these mountains. Its ministries, these our weapons.

"'If the Spanish had a king who had mercy, there would be mercy, but there is none. If he had compassion, there would be compassion, but there is none. He who would have chained your flesh would chain your souls and have you worship your own manacles as justice, your own suffering as a gift.

"'My father rebelled to have his own church, as you rebelled against the Spanish king. Let us together complete the revolt. Tie the two bloody cords of rebellion into one.' Drake raised his fist. 'As my father had a vision, so I, bereft of holy water, in words of baptism, create a congregation. Let the sea, thundering in its own cataract yet speaking not, now speak. Let the earth we clasp to our lip, soddened with last year's death, now blossom with life. Let the sky's egg crack…. Let the oceans be my trinity.'

"Drake bent his head. The Cimarrones followed. 'We are of another, but yet unchanged,' said Mandinga, smiling at Drake. 'You make good conversion.' Then he laughed. 'In a few days I will show you the body of your other god and of your cross,' Mandinga said. Then he was silent."

At Jamestown the face of the old mariner glowed like a flame, the sweat on his forehead reflecting the fire as he spoke. "The guide guides, the pilgrim follows, and who is who, as always beneath their feet the earth quakes in its deeper journeys.

"We refreshed ourselves among the Cimarrones for two days. On the third, Mandinga led us westward toward the uplands, its hills and cooler slopes. The Cimarrones still broke the trail. We followed, scrambling over the heaves of earth, the rolling convulsions of rock, the petrified earthen sea. Still we climbed, Mandinga at Drake's side, the trees sparser now, the clouds quilted in tremors, the fluted mountain rising like broken teeth.

"Next day we came to a high ridge, its sides bare and grooved by rain, its heights sloped in a skyward curve, like the edge of a stone ax. Mandinga came to Drake. 'We have come to the womb of vision,' he said, 'that place where gods consume gods, their divinities crumbling into dust.' Mandinga gestured with his hands. 'Here gods are born in whispers. It is the gate through which your life must pass.' With that he turned and beckoned Drake toward the crest of the hill. Oxenham went also, following Drake.

"'You coming too?' said Mandinga.

"'He is my captain,' replied Oxenham.

"'Two men should never cast the same shadow.' Mandinga nodded. Then, ignoring Oxenham, he led Drake up the slope of the hill. I followed. On reaching the crest, we walked along its spine for a few hundred yards. Below us, on either side, the jungle mists swirled above the grass in dissolving vapors. Flags of mist rose through the few trees to the level of the hills before abandoning all form in the crystal air. From the throne of this hill we could almost smell the breath of the clouds. The horizon lay hidden by a circle of lower hills that spread envalleyed below like monuments in a haze.

"Ahead of us on the bare hill crest was a single ancient tree, gaunt and gnarled with age, its bark twisted in convulsions, memories of a living past. 'A watchtower for stray travelers,' I thought.

"We approached. Mandinga led on. The trunk of the tree was huge. Vines twisted through its limbs like sleeping snakes. Blackness burned from its bulk. Maybe it was the first tree that ever was, a thing grown in the imagination, without the motherhood of a seed. It seemed to have wormed its way into the earth. It sat, devouring raw stone in its search for rest. As we came closer, I could see steps cut into the trunk, a living staircase ascending through the tangle of branches to a bower, a platform high between the fork of two great limbs. We stopped before the tree. Mandinga told Drake to follow him up the stairs to witness 'the flesh of the new sea slip over the bones of the old earth.' Through the leaves I could see Drake step onto the platform, Mandinga pointing first to the west and then to the east. 'Behold the eternity of oceans.' Oxenham and I rushed up the stairs. There, beyond the tree, the sun, in its westerly fall, called in whispering light, our brain crying, 'I am the sun, both shield and signet to a new sea. Follow my wheel to the beyond. Follow my wheel.' Below the sun, the Pacific spread to its far away reach, its waves in gentle swells, perfumed in distance, enticing us with imagined shapes to the world's edge.

"'There is eternity in a glance,' said Drake. 'Rocks roll back. Tombs belch forth. I am consumed in ages.' He stood and stared into his own sight, drinking with his eyes visions of the mechanisms of nations. 'Half of all the Spanish treasure is shipped on that sea, unguarded. The Spanish hold those waters as a private lake. To sail an English fleet out there and surprise the Spanish would bring gold in mountains and feed avarice far beyond its hunger. There, Oxenham.' Drake pointed to the Pacific. 'There is where God and war and profits merge.'

"And of the sea?' asked Mandinga.

" 'Oh sea, my trinity, whose arms embrace the eternal three…grant me life,' whispered Drake, 'that I would know an English deck rinsed in the rise and fall of your Pacific waters.'

"In that tabernacle of vision, Oxenham had begun to see his place. 'Drake, I am nothing but a servant compared to you,' he said, 'but if you will have me on that adventure I pledge my life….' Later, Oxenham would rebel against his own modesty, assuming whatever Drake could do, he could do also. There is nothing cheaper in the envious eyes of the learner than the accomplishments of the master. But for now, Oxenham started to kneel. His eyes filled with tears —though it was difficult to know from which overwhelmed aspect of his temperament. As he knelt, Drake caught him in his arms and lifted him into a hug. 'Together then, the two of us,' — he looked at me, offering me part of his embrace — 'the three of us. We shall be the first Englishmen to sail the Pacific.'

"There is that moment when separate flesh finds a certainty in a touch, a pledge of being, both eternal and eternally brief. We were all drunk on air. 'The journey is still far,' said Mandinga, after we descended the steps of the tree. As we left the ridge, he took Drake's arm. 'Wherever you fight, I shall fight too.' Drake took Mandinga's hand and shook it firmly. Then they embraced and faced each other. 'So be it,' said Drake. Oxenham smiled as he watched, grasping Mandinga's shoulders with both hands. All he could utter was 'And I too!' How simple are the words that shape a death.

"WE WALKED FOR TWO MORE DAYS, ALWAYS KEEPING TO THE HIGH ridges. The morning mist swirled about our knees. Winds rose against the earth, through the hillside at midday, bringing cool breezes and relief. We walked in ragged cohorts until the afternoon of the second day. There, below us, was Panama City, and in the bowl of its harbor, anchored, and at brooding rest, was the Spanish treasure fleet.

"Mandinga went to his sword. At their anchor, the Spanish galleons waddled in the tide, oozing waste and shadows across the sea. On the upper deck the backs of exhausted slaves glistened with sweat, sometimes mixed with blood. Others bore the red lines of many lashes. The Cimarrones chanted in low moans. We watched. Most of the oars of the galleys were stowed in its huge hull, but a few rolled extended in the swells, like the remaining legs of a broken water bug in its final balance before it drowned.

"Mandinga looked at Drake. 'We go,' he said. We turned again inland.

"Drake walked ahead with Oxenham, Diego and I a little to the rear, listening. 'The time of Spanish galleys as master of the sea is gone,' Drake said. 'They're old and slow, but, best for us, they are lightly gunned and fragile, a paper menace in an age of storm. Once in the Pacific, an English ship, with speed and with easy turns against the wind, could rescue the world with the profits of its Spanish plunder.'

"'The Pacific...the Pacific,' was all Oxenham could say.

"We marched for some hours, until, at a grove of trees, we lay down our burdens and made camp. The Cimarrones disappeared into the jungle to find food and palm leaves to make our shelters. It was a pleasant place. The sky was visible through the swaying fall of vines. The air seemed to rush upwards from the earth, as if we were in a natural chimney. Clouds passed across the sky's distant blue bowl. We watched them through the sliver of our only perspective, and wondered at the strange upward breeze. At night Mandinga sent one of his Cimarrones into Panama City to learn what he could of the movements of the Spanish treasure. The Cimarrones had many spies and sympathizers. Slaves may have chains, but they also have ears and tongues to spread news.

"In a few hours the Cimarrone returned. He had learned the first gold would come the following night, on the second of two mule trains. The first would be carrying silver and provisions; the second, gold and jewels. Accompanying the gold would be a Spanish treasurer from Peru and his family. Mandinga smiled. Drake turned to the Cimarrones and said, 'There is no night that cannot be swallowed by your day.'"

WE SAT LISTENING TO THESE WORDS, THE FIRE LOW. DARKNESS IN blanketing waves moved across the camp, dissolving us into nervous silhouettes. "There is nothing like the smell of gold to bring a man to his eloquence," said Russell, our stout adventurer, who had one of his servants throw another log on the embers of the fire. Sparks in flurries rose in ignited smoke. The log itself did not burn, but lay like a shadow on the glowing heat.

"How much gold…how much gold did he take?" asked Martin, who was no longer a visible form, but a voice.

The old mariner's skin in the fading light shone thin and translucent, like smoke behind glass. His words came in a whisper, as if it were the night itself that spoke, or some ghostly lips pressed to our ears. He answered with the strangest words. "Every age invents its own Christ. Ours wears around his neck a golden eye."

Reverend Hunt started to stand, then said simply, "A better word would be discovers that part that speaks to them. Every age is rewarded in its own coin…or damned."

The mariner acknowledged Reverend Hunt with a nod, then continued. "We were in the night, crouching in tall grass. The jungle throbbed with predatory life, maniacal screams and calls conversed in unintelligible banter. Unseen things darted through the bush. Around me, specters lounged or slept. Emaciated ghosts talked and dreamed of worldly joys. John Pike stumbled across the road, drinking from his private store of aqua vitae. Finally he disappeared. In our greed, no one cared. Drake had divided his company into two groups and dressed us in the white shirts he had to distinguish us from the Spanish. We were fifty paces from the road that led from Panama City to Venta Cruces. Two groups of men, one hundred feet apart, waiting.

"I turned and lay on my back. I was listening for the hoof falls of mules and the tinkle of the bells around their necks. I turned on my stomach and I wondered, would the jungle become silent in homage to the passage of such wealth? I laughed to myself. The land played with the darkness upon it. There should be little fighting. Drake's plan was relentless in its cunning. Let the silver train pass. Wait until the gold train is within our lines, then grab the lead and rear mules. Have them lie down. The other mules, well-trained Spanish mules as they were, would do the same.

"The air began to tremor with the mechanical beat of a horse in gallop, its hooves pounding in dull weight the darkness into the earth. 'It's the wrong direction. The rider is from Venta Cruces. Stay down,' said a voice. The night had now opened upon us like a mouth. The hooves were closer, sharper, more confident in their attack. 'It must be a messenger,' I thought. 'Just let it pass.' The horse now in full stride, its legs drove upon the earth in clipped thunder. A human voice. The horse screamed in idiot surprise, its hooves tearing the land into dust. Words in Spanish, then silence. I looked up and saw a form in a white shirt, one of ours, staring at a horse pawing the darkness, its eyes reflecting horror, the rider upon it clothed in shadows. Another ghost rose near the first, grabbing at its mouth. The two white shirts struggled, the second forcing the other to the ground. The rider cried, urging his mount forward. The hooves clipped sparks. The rider held to the animal's neck, closer to the thrusting power of wind and muscle, secure and low in his silhouette. The earth darkened again as the tremors faded, now indistinct from silence.

"'It was John Pike. He was drunk,' came a voice.

"'Are we discovered?' called Oxenham.

"'No man move. Hold to the earth as if it were your pillow. All is not yet lost,' cried Drake.

"We waited, time clicking in its hours. Then something human cried far off. There was the snap of a whip. The air cracked with the brevity of light. The darkness returned. Hooves, sharp in their falls, came toward us up the road. Bells around the mules' necks clanged as if luck itself were throwing coins into a pauper's tin plate.

"Through the trees mounted figures moved, their clothes hung in rags. Their bodies seemed of straw, rolling easily in their stiffness, lightly holding to their saddles, their horses unconscious of any weight. Some walked along the side of the mules. We let them follow the road.

"We began to crawl forward, slowly at first, then faster, the grass scratching our faces as it bent under our bodies. The mules began to disappear down the road. Drake stood, blowing his whistle. We all rose and rushed forward. The drivers turned, more exhausted than surprised. They surrendered in silence.

"Drake ordered that all the Spanish be kept together under a protective guard. Some of the Cimarrones wandered in small groups nearby, resting their swords on the earth. The Spanish backed away, falling against each other, as if they would have hidden in a pocket of air if they had the chance.

"The baggage of the mules now lay on the ground in twisted shapes. Empty blankets fell from their backs like ruined skirts.

"'Food and small silver,' said Oxenham to Drake.

"'We were indeed discovered,' replied Drake. 'This was all a ruse to keep us here while the gold fled back to Panama City.'

"'Shall we go back the way we came?' asked Oxenham, 'taking with us what we can?'

"Drake looked at the jungle, asking all that was his circumstance to be his guide. 'To do the same thing is always a little bit of death. There is no advantage to the hills. No surprise. We must make for the coast…and ships. I have already made a place there for us. The fastest way to the coast is through Venta Cruces,' said Drake. 'We must capture the town.'

"'This is not wise,' Oxenham started to protest.

"'Agreed,' said Mandinga, 'it has surprise and boldness.'

"'I will tell the men about Venta Cruces,' said Drake as he walked away.

"Oxenham shuffled his feet. He nodded and looked down meekly, arranging the rocks on the ground with his toe, the unimaginative cipher of a soul confused.

"We pushed on into the night, men grumbling at our ill luck. Two mules' worth of silver, twenty bars, but no gold. We had suffered for that gold. We had buried our friends for it. All our labors for nothing. Our dreams turned into statues of dust. Drake still urged us on. 'We have made some profit,' he said. 'Soon our talons will drip with gold.' But there was no gold. When men tire of gods, angels are cast into ditches. Silver measures its weight in shillings, gold in pounds. We drank our need from the mind's cup of salt, and only the golden wafer would sweeten again our tongue.

"The hard road passed under our feet. The trees hung with vines. In the night they seemed like silent judges, their branches filled with companion spirits, bickering, screeching their taunts.

"'Who goes there?' came a voice in Spanish ahead of us. A line of figures moved across the road and waited. Around their nervous shadows the red-eyed sparks of the firelocks' tapers swung like nesting bees. 'Are you Spanish?' came the voice again.

"'We are English,' was the answer. 'I am Drake.'

"'Surrender,' came the voice, the figures wavering in the gloom.

"'I leave that honor to you,' Drake replied. Our company formed behind him. Beyond, at the edge of sight, a line of flashes and the smell of burnt thunder stained the air. They volleyed. There was a cry among our ranks. We returned volley for volley. Arrow and ball fled through the pauper's light. We rushed forward, Cimarrones screaming their battle cry, 'Yo peho! Yo peho!' Ahead of us, figures crumpled to the ground, hands held to chests. The line reformed. A few pikes, like wounded teeth, were leveled at our hearts. We came among them, our swords cutting down the pikes. Sword met sword. A Cimarrone screamed, skewered on a blade like a ripe plum. He fell to the side, an alien weight in his chest, his agony beyond pain, his death on his lips.

"Drake, a slight wound upon his arm, swung his sword one last time before some Spaniard knelt in surrender, while others fled, their backs melting into the shadows like driven smoke. Four of their company were killed, several wounded. We lost two, and four others wounded. We tended them all as we could. Then we marched into Venta Cruces, the Cimarrones carrying ours, sometimes two to a man. They were the gentlest bearers I have ever seen. It was as if their ferocious blood could change to saintly milk at the turn of their mind. Our Spanish prisoners labored, carrying their own. Diego walked beside Drake, talking. 'For a wise man, my Drake, you make a foolish war. You take too many prisoners. The Spanish make a very happy dead, I promise you.'"

Chapter Nineteen

A SHIP OF MYSTERY. NEWS FROM FRANCE.
ALLIES AND THE DOUBLE WAR.

HE LIGHTS OF VENTA CRUCES burned in their window frames, bright and defiant, as if the universe had cut a hole into the night, and found, behind the darkness, the day. 'With an army such as we,' Drake said, 'we could seize this Panama.' There was a cheer. More lights were lit in Venta Cruces. Doors opened. Heads appeared. The Cimarrone and English were in groups, English to watch the Cimarrone and their fury, keeping the Spanish safe and at ease. 'We harm no one,' said Drake, looking at Mandinga. 'Only those who raise weapons against us. And even those, once they surrender, are protected.' Mandinga said nothing. 'We are made mightier in our restraint,' added Drake, almost pleading.

"Mandinga looked at our captain. 'You make your war in your mind…but it will be as you wish.'

"We raced through town, banging on doors, awakening the Spanish garrison, the town mayor, the citizens, a few slaves and some Indians. At a small shack in the center of town we found three women recovering from childbirth. At the sight of the Cimarrones at their door, they pulled their blankets to their necks and screamed in such hysteria we feared their tongues would flee from their throats, their faces red with tormented blood. Drake ran to the house to calm their fears.

"'I am concerned with your health. My men shall not harm you, I swear,' he said. But the sight of Drake and Mandinga only added to the women's grief.

"'I am posting guards at your door,' he said. Unable to soothe their minds, he left, letting them scream themselves to sleep.

"The next day before dawn we left, taking some food, burning two storehouses. Drake told the slaves they could join us if it pleased them. Most did, but a few remained, confused and uncertain. 'There are times when we become comfortable in our pain,' said Diego, with the reflection of a man who had already seen too much.

"Mandinga had already sent ahead three Cimarrones to bring Drake's fleet to the new camp he was preparing near the mouth of the Chagres River. We reached the camp in four days, stumbling through the last line of trees that framed the beach, falling, tripping over the tree roots that held fast to the earth like talons gripped in flesh. We lay in the white heat, smelling the baking sea. The Cimarrones had already built shelters for us, and were preparing a meal. They helped us up and gave us water. Some of our party too weak to stand, they carried, just as they had carried many of us through the heat for miles, tending us with wild herbs they had picked from the green mysteries of the jungle floor. The Cimarrones knew this land well. We learned from them that the jungle is a garden whose fruit can hold in its juice the kiss of life or the sweet and pungent nut of death.

"Diego, Drake and Mandinga were the last to walk from the line of trees. Oxenham rushed to Drake's side, wanting to know the plan. 'In good time,' he said. 'We will sit in council tonight, where all views shall be heard.' It was Drake's way to let each man speak his mind. The decision would be Drake's, but each man would feel he had a part.

"'I am still for the gold,' said Oxenham, anxious to be heard and impress Drake.

"'For us there is no choice but war,' added Mandinga.

"'I promised my crew this enterprise would bring us wealth,' said Drake. 'I promised this through all our trials. Why should I in safety now change my plans?'

"We ate well that day. Toward sunset our small fleet appeared, casting their anchors into the water near the beach. The crew rowed ashore. Their jaws hung low, their words denying to their halting breaths the reality before their eyes. 'We are not death,' laughed John Pike, 'just a counterfeit of life,' trying to amuse those who still held him responsible for the loss of the gold.

"'He is being punished for his crime,' whispered a voice.

"'That would be too simple,' whispered a reply.

"Pike looked at the thin sticks that had become his arms, and at his rags and the rags of those about him. 'We need new clothes,' he said, his eyes filling with tears too weakened to flow. 'Our bones have become our flesh.'

"At night, around the fire, we held our council. Some wanted to return to England while they still had their Christian souls. Others wanted to try for the gold again without delay. 'A soul without wealth is a pauper's bag,' laughed Oxenham. Mandinga looked at Drake and said, 'Your convert may have found the wrong apostle.'

"Drake smiled and stepped forward. 'The Spanish know we are here. We have lost our greatest ally, surprise. We should sail out and make the Spanish believe we have gone elsewhere to take our prizes. Then, in a few weeks, when the Spanish are convinced the treasure is safe, we sneak back and lay our ambush for the gold again.' There was a mutter of agreement around the fire. 'We will divide the fleet: Oxenham to sail south and I north. In two weeks we meet at Slaughter Island.'

"'Done,' said Oxenham, grinning, as he silently savored his rank as second in command.

"'He even begins to look like Drake,' said Diego to Mandinga.

"'He only knows the surface,' Mandinga replied.

"Later that night, when most of the others were asleep, Mandinga, Diego and I sat at the fire, breaking twigs and throwing their darkness into the flame. Drake sat watching the light playing upon the shadow, thinking. 'Some say my father stole horses in his youth and was saved from the gallows by an influential friend.' Diego looked at Drake. 'But in a revelation he was transformed. He converted, taking up the Protestant Bible. He spoke in public words of a new church, the sermon of a new salvation. This was the time of Queen Mary's marriage to Philip of Spain—England with a foreign king, an alien hand on the royal scepter—a Catholic. Then the persecutions came. My father was an exile in his own country, a Protestant, driven from his home. We moved from Devon to Plymouth. There he preached, while we lived in the deserted hulk of a ship. My younger brothers were born there. It was a strange place, England then. Protestants burned at the stake. Fifty in Kent alone. Hundreds throughout the country. Yet, on special nights in the woods around Plymouth, fires were set at the rising of the moon. The town still observed its ancient rites. Multitudes still danced and sang to see the gods made manifest on earth. We are in smallness all made large in celebration. And so the earth called forth its spirits. Even my father in his revelation drank this brew. To hold a rock that reflects the moon, to hold a book that reveals the words, to feel the voices rising in the sea—what's the difference? It is the ancient soul of my people.'

"Mandinga looked at Drake and said nothing.

"The next day the sun again walked its lightning across the land. Our anchors raised, we pledged to Mandinga our swift return. Ten Cimarrones asked to join us on our ships. Drake agreed.

"'They are pleased to be allied with you,' Diego said. 'They say among themselves their war now moves upon the water.'

"We left the Chagres River, parting company with Oxenham, who sailed south. The wind swung to our backs, the sails came full faced, their cheeks in a merry puff against the caught breeze. The masts creaked in their roots. The bow nosed the swells into a pelting mist, which, in its lace of watery diamonds, fell upon our decks. The enraptured sea flowed to the world's edge, its changing facets flowing in a living jewel.

"'Any sail?' called Drake to the watch.

"'Clear she is.'

"Toward dusk the red glow of the sun bathed the sea into blood. Darkness and a wedge of moon passing across the black water, burning it again into mirrors. After hours of sleep the day rose in a chase of green.

"'A sail!' the watch cried.

"'What flag?' called Drake.

"'Too far off.'

"Our ship, in cautious tack, set its wake toward the ballooning point of sail. 'What flag?' repeated Drake.

"'She's hoisted none,' came the cry.

"The ships now moved in their predatory dance, attempting to gain advantage of the wind for that last thrust before the cannonade.

"'It's French…the ship is French,' cried the watch. 'She's slackening her sails,' he called as he pointed.

"The sails slowly slapped into a flutter. 'The captain's signaling. He wants to parley.' The ships moved in their silent wash, slowly, closer, their masts almost intertwining. Hull facing hull, they dropped their anchors. The French ship was far larger than the Pasco and much better armed. The faded paint of its closed gun ports loomed above us.

"'Are you the Francis Drake?' a lone figure at the rails called across the waters.

"'I am. And who are you?'

"'I am Guillaume de Le Testu. I've been searching for your ship. We have, shall I say, the same occupation.'

"'And what would that be?' asked Drake.

"'Converting Spanish gold into personal treasure.'

"Drake smiled. 'I am but a poor vagabond, a pastor. It's true…I seek converts where I can.'

"'I appreciate the man who displays such modesty when a weapon is pointing at my heart. Could you tell your black friend to lower his?'

"Diego, who was hiding in the rigging of one of the masts, put up his firelock at Drake's signal. 'My crew is always nervous for my safety,' said Drake.

"'A wise crew. These waters brew strange encounters. But I am embarrassed that so early in our conversation I have another request. I have wine by the keg and much cider, but I am low on fresh water and food. My crew, she has a great hunger and thirst. Some of us are with the sickness. Can you help us?'

"'I shall have a supply rowed over to you. I have all the water and food you can use. And how do you know my name?'

"'The whole coast is in terror of you. We stopped a ship. We heard of your sport.' While they spoke, a longboat was lowered, then filled with water kegs and sacks of food. 'You are a generous man, Drake. I have heard this also and other tales of your doing, which make me to the belief that we should join as allies for the mutual profit.'

"Drake didn't answer immediately. He let Le Testu taste his own silence, Drake's way of asking questions directly into the souls of those to whom he spoke. 'I am not a common pirate if that is the question you ask in your gentlemanly silence,' said Le Testu. 'I have been to these waters many times. I accompanied André Thévet when he explored the coast of Brazil. Three different times we sailed to those waters. I was with him when he discovered tobacco among the natives, saw its uses and collected its seeds. And maybe you have heard that it was Jean Nicot, but it was Thévet the monk who first brought tobacco to France.'

"I looked at Drake. At the mention of tobacco, he smiled and played some casual charms as to gauge this man, Le Testu. 'Jonas, my alchemist, has bad feelings of the leaf. He thinks at its center there is a curse.'

"'Your friend is wiser than most. Tobacco is a rumor. It is a legend had in promises. It whispers hungers and feeds a want that seems a cure. But for those of us who love its taste, that taste is a pleasure that shields all consequence.'

"Our longboat had unloaded its provisions, Le Testu's men having carried the boxes and bales and water kegs up their rope ladders. Drake listened to the Frenchman's words, studying his larger crew and his more powerful vessel. 'He could be a threat,' I said to Drake.

"'Or a powerful ally,' replied Drake. The sea folded upon itself in sunlight. Gentle swells sighed their playful surges against the two hulls, while in the depths, beyond the sun's reach, shadows, in graceful hunt, swarmed in search of shadows.

"'I must seem something of a confusion to you, but I am something of a confusion to myself,' Le Testu continued. 'We French Protestants, we Huguenots, are made by agonies and betrayals loyal citizens in quest of another country.'

"Drake nodded his head, as if agreeing with some inner voice. Then he spoke. 'If you care to set course and follow me,' he said, 'I have a store of provisions hidden on the coast. I would be happy to replenish your entire ship, and there we can discuss an alliance.'

"'I am your servant,' bowed Le Testu as he spoke. 'Have you heard? Holland is now in revolt against the Spanish.'

"'Holland?' questioned Drake.

"Le Testu did not reply quickly, but thrust his voice across the canyon between the two ships. 'England may be the last refuge for us all.' Then he disappeared, ordering his men to make sail.

"Our longboat returned. Anchors weighed, sails lowered to their place, the ships that once by vision held to each other's sides now followed, sliding through each other's wakes. The sea flowed back against our bow, unchanging in its bite, as we changed our tack. The coast rose in towering shapes, the mountains of a continent across the sky, beyond which lay the Pacific, beckoning us to its mystery and to its lore of plunder.

"Through a break in the coast we sailed into Pheasant Bay. The ships nosed toward the beach and anchored. We lowered boats and Drake and I were rowed ashore followed by a party from the French ship. We led them to a stand of trees, between which, weeks before, Diego had built a shelter. The monument of sand, logs thrusting from beneath the blanket of white, looked like the burial place of an exiled king.

"With a shovel we dug free the door. Drake stood aside. 'Take what you need,' he said. The Frenchmen disappeared into the darkness of the shelter. Boxes began to appear, and kegs.

"Outside, a Frenchman approached Drake. He was carrying two

cases. 'For you from my captain.' Drake took the cases and opened them. In one were two firelock pistols and a silver powder horn. In the other, a scimitar, its hilt encrusted with jewels, its blade dipped in gold. 'My Captain says to give you this message: 'Let us make war as we make our lives, in style.'

"Drake said, 'Your captain has regal qualities. Tell him I have received his gifts and I will receive his friendship, with great thanks.'

"The Frenchman bowed, adding, 'My Captain sends his regrets. He will join you shortly.'

"Drake nodded. The Frenchman bowed again, walking backwards a few paces. Then he turned and walked toward the beach.

"Drake turned to me. 'In my cabin, under my bed, is a box. In it is a heavy gold chain. Bring it to me. Le Testu is a man whose hand sweeps in grand gestures. We must not be outdone.'

"When I returned, Drake was sitting on the beach. Behind him Le Testu's crew walked in line, carrying their provisions to their boat. I held the golden chain with both hands. It lay across my wrists. I bore it like a holy garment, a moving sacrament, in an open church. Its links were the thickness of a man's finger. It seemed more a shackle than an ornament. I gave the chain to Drake, who took it, hefted it, remembering the weight, indifferent to the chain's presence except for the purpose it would serve. He who had lost two brothers, risked all our lives, suffered, placed the gold on the sand. I swear, he almost forgot it was there.

"'What we seek,' Drake had said once, 'we should seek with all our being. But let us not be chained to it after we have it.'

"Drake leaned back, his arms supporting him. The sun wandered through some low clouds that framed it like an imperfect jewel. Le Testu walked up from the beach, laboring as he walked, the sand sucking at his boots. 'He is a man drowning in the earth,' said Diego, as Drake stood to greet Le Testu, offering him the golden chain in his hand.

"'I cannot repay, except with gratitude, your gifts, but I offer this small token to seal the circle of our friendship.'

"Le Testu took the chain and placed it around his neck. 'Our friendship was sealed when you gave us food. After that gesture, all else are trinkets. But what I sent you with that sword was not a pretty bauble, a blush to bring to the face of an empty head. It was the offer to join me in a holy war.'

"Drake started to speak. 'I have always…'

"Le Testu interrupted. 'That sword I gave into your hands was presented to me by Admiral Gaspard de Coligny. You know him, my friend?' Le Testu paused a moment. 'Yes, we all know him.' His words expired into breath that hissed through his lips like dry sand.

"'You received that sword from Gaspard de Coligny, the leader of the French Protestants?' asked Drake.

"'A martyred leader, my friend. Always the martyred. The lamented in my heart.' Le Testu looked at Drake strangely, then said, 'Then you do not know—I am the fool. You are how long at sea?'

"'We left Plymouth the twenty-fourth of May of last year…eight months.'

"'Our Europe has become a pasture of the dead, whose sheep deliver from their udders only blood,' said Le Testu. 'The French Protestants are murdered. Tens of thousands dead. Coligny and his son, women, children, old and young…no one spared. The slaughter went on for week after week.' Le Testu howled his words, as if trying to awaken himself from madness.

"'Coligny was having great influence over the king, that Catholic weakling Charles XI. His mother, Catherine, a she-devil of a Medici, made an assassination on Coligny to end his power over her son, but it failed. In the panic of a discovered coward, she lied to her son. Venom makes the mortar of this world. She convinced him that all Huguenots were traitors and we should be killed in slaughter. She refused her son even the moment to speak with Coligny. Her children are fools. How could they be otherwise, suckled on the poisoned milk of the Medicis. They murdered Coligny in his home as he made his healings from the assassin's bullets. They killed him in his bed and threw his body from a window. The next day, Saint Bartholomew's, Catherine released the mobs. There was no more law in France. The mob, they welcome no restraint, just a chance for wanton murder and for theft. What sacrament is a people's blood? They battered children's brains out in the street. They drew and quartered the living. Thousands, locked in their own houses, burned, smothered in the smoke. Others bound, thrown into the river to drown. It went on for almost two months. What church is this to find its salvations in a slaughter?'

"'Words are slights of empty sounds, and we domained here in our ignorance, while our world lies in massacre,' said Drake.

"'The Pope ordered bonfires lit to celebrate.' Le Testu kicked the sand as he spoke. 'He even had a golden medal struck to mark his joys at our extinction. We who survive fight on. France has the civil war. The Dutch are in revolt against Spain. The holy whirlwind of retribution has begun. We are in universal war.'

"The sun, in its westerly fall, had passed behind the mountains, its last light now casting shadows from the jungle peaks. 'Shadows,' said Le Testu. 'There is day and night and shadows, light turning to darkness at a touch. I am orphaned by murder.' He was silent for a time. 'I am without hope of a country,' he said finally.

"News of the massacre rolled through our crew in voices of rage. The French told their stories, the English were frozen in that sense of disbelief where arms and legs move of their own calling, searching for attitudes to console their own passions. One man blanketed himself in his own arms, holding his own flesh, his hands against his own back, seeking comfort in his own touch. Others held their fists like mallets, striking them against other open hands, causing in their grief more pain to themselves. A pain of flesh to counter the pain of grief. Our own world disintegrating into an agony of words and the fantasies of vengeance.

"Le Testu sat with Drake and Diego. The sunlight faded, as if it had exhausted itself in grief. Only the monkeys still chattered, terrifying the macaws, who glided through the air, squawking and raging to each other in savage replicas of human speech, as if they, too, wished to rise to the level of human murder.

" 'It must be said, in truth,' Le Testu spoke, 'that some of the Catholic nobles refused to allow the massacres in their provinces. They defied the invitation of that weakling King, and protected us. I have come in my own mind to know that God is honor, and man without honor has no God, no matter how he prays. Let the weak hug their churches and their holy writs. It is the oath between men like us, and our deeds, in which there is God. God is invested in the pledges between men. They alone sing psalms to him. Churches are confusions to nations. They are houses of vanities.'

"Le Testu rose to his feet. 'With the Huguenots slaughtered, France is without power. It has murdered its army. We Huguenots were its generals, its admirals. We were its children and France has murdered itself. Spain can be the only victor. It has no rival now in Europe. If I had my chance, I would cut the breath out of Philip's lungs with this my sword.' Le Testu turned, then turned again, not sure which way to strike. He fell. 'I am drunk with mourning,' he said, limp with confusion. 'If all is death, in what am I to believe? Only in England is there still hope. It is fitting, my friend, that you now own the sword of Coligny. You should know what I have given you.'

"In the cove, the last rim of light spread across the waters in a knowing grin. I thought of the Pacific and its water rising in thunderous waves of fire to the sun's bowl. Drake then stood. The sea, in its gentle affirmation, awaited our pleasures. 'Look,' he said, pointing to the last sunlight. 'The sea has opened its arms. It whispers in the breeze: You are blessed unto us. Oh humans, your time is brief.' Then he turned to Le Testu. 'Come to the beach and pray with me. We shall converse in one voice with the other half of God.'

"'You have a very particular way with the religion, my friend,' said Le Testu.

"'Everyone hears what it is his portion to hear,' replied Drake. 'You may set the Protestant Bible by your side, if it makes you more comfortable.'

"'I have no offense at this. If the Holy Spirit invests the world with its presence, why not a special presence in the sea, who, as every sailor knows, has by its own such whims that lord our histories. Speak to the sea, Drake. It is a better conversation than with most men." Le Testu spit, "Men, we are but the seep, the elixir that poisons on the lips. I, for my part, will not pray, but will sit by your side and keep you company.' "

Chapter Twenty

TOWARDS GOLD, THE PASSAGE OF MANY JOURNEYS
AND THE MARRIAGE OF THE STORMS.

 ARLY IN THE MORNING of the next day, Oxenham sailed through the narrow entrance to the cove, his sails an outline of white against the rising mist. 'We had good fortune. A good hunt,' came his voice from far away, as if imprisoned in a cave. With him was a Spanish prize, a ship far larger than his own. It moved behind Oxenham, echoing the silence of its ghostly lead, a shadow of sails, white against white. The color sucked from the sky, they moved in monotonies. The day breathing sameness, they sailed as if in a trance, the falling anchors voicing in their splash the end of their tack. Longboats lowered. Oars struck silent water smoothly, as if in sleep. Oxenham rowed ashore.

"'Fine catch she be. Maize and hogs aboard her.' Drake nodded. 'Large enough for an Atlantic crossing,' Oxenham added, awaiting Drake's praise. Drake looked about him—the sky, the mist, the sails, a turbulence of white. He breathed deeply and said, 'The world is bled of life.'

"Drake ordered the Spanish ship refitted with cannons and some fresh supplies, the crew kept prisoners. But, as always, he would provide for their well-being. 'You've done well, as always. Done well.' Oxenham smiled. 'But I see you, too, have had a good hunt.'

"'I have found us new allies who bring some ghastly news. Come.' With that, Drake led Oxenham up the beach toward Le Testu, who sat with his men around a small fire. They rose as Drake approached. Then all sat and talked, the color of Oxenham's face draining as he heard stories of the massacre. It was agreed that Le Testu and Drake together would steal the Spanish treasure, each taking an equal share. After a short time a Cimarrone runner was sent to the jungles to find Pedro Mandinga and his men. Our cove was kneading itself into a vortex for war.

"Diego was put in charge of the building of shelters. He picked his own crew from among the French and English. Watching us fumble with our hatchets, he laughed. 'You are soft, my friends, but soon your hands will be hard. You will kill many Spaniards then you will thank Diego.' Even our sailors' hands were raw as we cut palm leaves and palmetto poles. A few of the weaker men fainted from the heat. 'Faint, if you wish, my friends; Diego will carry you into battle on his back.' We laughed and cheered Diego, who answered us with a wink as he worked beside us. 'You sailors know hard work. Now you must learn how to sweat in the jungle,' he said, smiling, as we rested, eating our evening meal.

"Two days later, Mandinga, with thirty Cimarrones, moved from the jungle with such care and silence that, surprised at their appearance, Drake said, 'It is as if you do not move, but the earth creates you where you chose to be.' Mandinga replied, 'As your sea, the land gives up its love to those who respect its ways.'

"Mandinga and Le Testu and Drake sat beneath a small group of trees to hold a private council. It is said that, at first meeting, Mandinga stiffened in the presence of Le Testu, Mandinga having been a prisoner of the French pirate Nicholas de Isle for almost a year.

"'A scum of a man,' said Le Testu. 'It would have been a great favor to us all, if, in your escape, you had cut his traitorous throat. If it please God, I will do it myself someday and dedicate my blade to you, my friend.'

"'I was kept in France a year....'

"'You had luck to be returned alive,' said Le Testu. Drake told Mandinga of the slaughter of the Huguenots, 'brothers to the Lutherans,' Drake called them.

"'I am an orphan to the world, an exile by murder,' continued Le Testu. 'Even my faith becomes a habit of no consequence. I would pray solace and to any naked God, who, even in his indifference, might bring my vengeance. Death to the French assassins and their Spanish allies.'

"'Yes,' said Mandinga, nodding his head in recognition. 'The Spanish-French. We three will make war.' The Cimarrone then turned, his hand holding Le Testu's shoulder in a clasp of power. 'I have news of importance. My people tell me that the gold will soon be shipped to Venta Cruces. But when it reaches there, only part of it will be shipped by barge to Nombre de Dios. The rest will be taken by mule.' Mandinga looked up, smiled, then looked at Drake. 'Fools find mistakes a reason not to learn.'

"'How much time until the mules start for Nombre de Dios?' asked Drake.

"'Some five days,' answered Mandinga.

"Drake thought for a time 'We must be patient and determined, as we must be clever. We cannot attack the Spanish in the same place. That time has passed. We must become the unexpected.'

"Mandinga looked at Drake. 'It is said among my people that he who would dance naked with a feathered cape and a mask becomes the bird.'

"Le Testu looked at Mandinga. 'And he who has died with his people, yet lives?' he asked, 'What does he become in the dance?'

"'A man who eats his own soul,' answered the Cimarrone. 'The monster in the night who howls without a mouth.' Mandinga touched Le Testu's arm. 'In our war we need soldiers, not the sleepless dead who remember.'

"Le Testu was quiet. He nodded to Mandinga. 'Our attack must be as close to Nombre de Dios as possible,' continued Drake. 'The more dangerous it is for us, the more relaxed the Spanish escort and the greater their surprise. We will take fifteen of my crew, Le Testu in command of twenty of his and Mandinga in command of thirty Cimarrones. Our Spanish prizes, the *Minion* and the *Bear*, will land us at the Francisca River, five leagues from Nombre de Dios. We will march toward the town three leagues. There, at the Campos River, will be our *ambushado*. After we seize the treasure we will march back to the Francisca River. That should take two days. The pinnaces will pick us up on April third and return to the *Minion* and *Bear*. The large ships must hide. Our sails cannot be beacons for our enemy. The pinnaces, with their shallow draft, sailing close to shore, will keep us safe from any large coastal galleons.' The council of war at an end, the three stood.

"Orders were given, gear loaded onto the *Minion* and *Bear*. In days of work, the pinnaces were made ready. The ships moved through the cove, sometimes pulled by a pair of longboats, their crews straining at their oars. Beyond the cove, the sea, the wind's urgent push, our exhilarating race, the sea thrown back in foam. Clouds, in joyous upheaval, smoked skywards, flowing in exultant bloom. The thoughts in our heads were blown to dizziness, so consumed with life we were. And so we came to the mouth of the Francisca River. We organized ourselves quickly. The Cimarrone pathfinders were ahead of us cutting the trail, as before. Then we set out again, into the jungle, into the darkness, where monkeys still chided through trees screaming indignities at our labors.

"The Cimarrones had taught us well. We moved through the jungle silently, using the land to shape our paths, surrendering to the curve of the rocks and the roots of the trees, letting their strength guide ours. Le Testu and his men struggled in blind determination, as if will alone would assault the mountains into valleys and the ravines into gentle plains. Rocks do not crumble into sand by the gales of human breath, nor do the roots of trees claw the earth less tightly at the sound of a human cry. The land is a silent predator that ever lies in wait. We who had been taught by Mandinga and his Cimarrones had learned how to be cradled, exhausted, in its power; how to tell its food from its poisons; how to judge its spirits and its moods. And so our steps fell lightly upon the land.

"'You are strong for the jungle,' said Le Testu after climbing over the top of a large tree root. Drake walked farther from the tree where the land was more level, a greater distance, but with less effort.

"'Would you care to rest?' asked Drake, noting Le Testu's weakness.

"'No...I am impatient with my exhaustion. Your men and the Cimarrones are good with one another, respectful of each other. They move silently, even carrying heavy burdens. If there were more of us with the provisions, we could be an army of consequence. We could take all of South America and its mines—choke Philip with his own gold.' Le Testu walked, balancing on the top of a root, toward Drake. 'This, my friend, this jungle is the citadel of the Reformation.' Caught in the fire of remembered passion, Le Testu threw his hands toward the earth, as if he would cast away his own beliefs. 'If I could believe in any holy writ again, I would build an altar here of ghosts and lizards. I would worship bones.' Le Testu looked toward the sky, where light trembled beyond the canopy of leaves. 'There are opportunities in this place, opportunities we should seize.'

"We walked for two days to reach the Campos, which was more a flow of mud than a river. We were within two leagues of Nombre de Dios, so close we could hear the hammers of the workers in the shipyard, and at times the cries of children and the voices of provincial life. We sat and ate, hidden along the road, while Cimarrone scouts filtered through the trees, searching for the Spanish mule train.

"An hour or so passed slowly. Time fell about our shoulders like a cloud. Le Testu took from the pouch on his belt a small clay pipe, stuffed some tobacco into its bowl. As he rested against the roots of a great tree, he lit it. The white smoke from his mouth drifted across the encampment like spirits born to haunt the air, perfuming our empty wait, awakening us again to the thoughts beyond the frenzied slowness of time. Le Testu serenely leaned his back close to the dark bark of the root, which seemed to enfold him like a cape. 'A useless, driven habit,' he said, watching the lazy smoke above him rise to oblivion. 'A breath for the wind,' he laughed, offering Mandinga the pipe. Mandinga considered it. 'The Spanish have a use for this, as they do for all things,' he said, 'but they play with it as if it were dead. They are deaf to all voices except their one.' Le Testu placed the pipe in his mouth. He drew a breath of smoke, letting it sing from his lips as Mandinga spoke. 'In my old country we would light this and let it burn alone on an altar. No one but the holy or the mad would tend a spirit in its fire.' Little did I know then that that leaf had been brought to Africa from Spain.

"Mandinga took the pipe from Le Testu. I, hearing the mention of the leaf, walked and sat by Mandinga's side. He looked at me and said, 'I was once a slave in Cuba. There we grew the tobacco for the Spaniards and secretly for ourselves, the Indians showing us how to mix the leaf with the crushed seeds of other plants. These potions of the Indians would take our senses. We could not work. The Spaniards searched to find and burn our leaf. What pleasures to us were only pleasures to forget. It was but a toy, this drug that simpled us. We planted more tobacco. The Spaniards could not find it all. The escape we could not have we found by chaining ourselves to the tobacco leaf.'

"Mandinga smiled. 'Each earth tends its madness differently,' he said. 'There is a legend among my people: a man who thought he could defeat the poison of a snake by letting it bite him many times. He thought poison would kill the poison.'

"'And he died?' Le Testu asked with some amusement.

"'No,' said Mandinga, 'he became the snake. All things living give birth to themselves and all things are alive.' Mandinga put the pipe in his mouth and drew a breath, then handed it back to Le Testu, saying, 'Touch each rock as if it were the lips of your beloved. All that is created speaks. There are even voices in the smoke.'

"All this in my alchemy I do believe myself, but I was silent except to speak about tobacco. 'The leaf has always borne a lethal cure,' I said.

"Le Testu shook his head. 'There are no medicines in the herb. Its work is ever in its misunderstandings. I was with Thévet in Brazil. The savages there never used tobacco as a cure, only for its pleasures, or a gift to bribe a favor from the indifferent gods, nothing more. Thévet wrote this but was ignored. All our histories are but a confusion and a lie. We receive well our delusions. What serves the spell rules the written history. It was he who brought the first seeds of tobacco to France, grew them in his garden in Avignon, those the seeds of the Nicotiana tabacum variety, three years before Nicot sent the seeds of the Nicotiana rustica to France, and with them the rumors of all its cures. It was the Spaniard Oviedo, the murderer of the Indians, never learning the language of those he slaughtered, who confused tobacco with another herb, *perebecenuc*. Knowledge of that cure is now lost, the savages never showing their plant to the Spaniards, who cared only for gold. That plant forgotten, no one now can identify it. The gift of generations squandered. Blood to its regrets that it is but blood. Memory failed. Thevet's work ridiculed, ignored and slandered. Nicot the hero, the herald and the praise for introducing tobacco to France. Catherine de Medici, the murderess herself, became godmother to the leaf, using her influence to spread its use. And still I smoke the weed.' Le Testu, his pipe in hand, the smoke about his mouth, rose. 'And whose sovereign do I serve? Are all my empires but a trance? I have cast down generations, and yet I still love the weed.'

"The Cimarrone scouts returned and told of two hundred mules laden with treasure moving slowly along the road, guarded by forty-five ragged Spanish soldiers, some barefooted, lightly armed with bows and a few firelocks. Drake, Le Testu and Mandinga looked at each other.

"'The opposition is not so formidable,' said Le Testu with a smile. 'But the treasure, we cannot carry it all.'

"'First we have to seize it,' said Drake. 'Then we can curse our good fortune. Many have died to bring us to this wealth and many may die yet.' With that, he ordered the few men who had gathered around him to prepare. As news of the mule train spread through the whole camp, the tension of the wait twisted itself into a feeling of loneliness. We did not speak for fear of being overheard by a passing Spaniard. We sang our thoughts, filling our emptiness with brave gestures. We tightened the hammer springs of our wheellock pistols with keys, like the key that winds a clock. Darts were fitted into crossbows, swords lifted from scabbards. The tapers of our firelocks were lit with grand flourishes of the hand. Bowstrings were tested and plucked, biting the air with a darkening hum.

"Now a whole mass of men moved forward toward the road, crawling, letting the grass and vines again cover our human forms. We pressed our cheeks against the earth, listening with the skin of our faces for the soft pounding of many hooves.

"Far off there was the sharp crack of a whip, shattering the crystal silence of the air. I lick the tears of avarice from my lips. I taste their salt, alchemies now come to cleanse my dead, as through the earth far off concussions in lazy hammers fell. Closer now the hooves. We held our weapons to ourselves. The earth began to cry in low moans against our flesh. The dirt seemed to tremble, as if loosening itself from its own roots. We buried our eyes into the loam, hoping that if we could not see, we could not be seen. The sound of the mules grew louder. 'No mistakes...,' I whispered to the earth. I look upon my hands, which were covered in gold. I thought I was being blessed, anointed with wealth. It was only the sun. I could see the mules on the road.

"The soldiers walked by the mules' side, many dressed in no more than rags. Displaying their Spanish power, wretched, dirty, carrying their dignity all assumed, the Spanish moved into the web of our ambush. There were blacks and Indians, dressed in lesser rags, marching with them, some carrying weapons; others, less trusted in their bondage, drove the mules. Slaves watching slaves. I watched my gold and wondered, is a slave with a gun less a slave? I held my pistol and my sword, frightened, hating those who had the vanity to be the sons of Spain.

"Staring ahead into dreams of drink and escapades of the night, the Spanish soldiers passed in slovenly stumble, haggard, their eyelids drooped dull in expressions of exhaustion. A few Spaniards held their firelocks against their shoulders. The blacks carried theirs with both hands across their chests. The blacks with bows slung them over their backs. Each class of slave had its own colored sash at the waist. 'A mark of rank in a closed society,' I thought. 'A torture for the soul. A source of pride in their chains. They hate their servitude, but they love their honors. How like the titled Spanish with their endless lists of privileges. Suffocate the spirit in orthodoxy but indulge your powers.' Now their flesh would be strewn with my gold. I was ready to do service for it. The earth rotted on my cheek. The unseen jaws of our trap closed in a desperate silence.

"At Drake's whistle, we all rose with a cry. The dull eyes of the Spanish turned toward us, widening in terror. Mouths opened. Mules stopped in midstep. Weapons bore in our direction. Concussions of fire and shot flashed in scarlet lances. We were among the Spanish now. Sword bit sword in a contortion of limbs. Cries of agony drifted through the air. Human forms in twisted battle wielded savage blades.

"A Spaniard came at me with a pike. I leaped to the side, his blade and shaft passing my chest. I brought the hilt of my sword down upon his iron helmet. He seemed to feel no pain. My sword tore at the armor on his chest. I was surprised he would not die, until his face blushed in the bloom of fresh blood, as I discharged my pistol into the bridge of his nose.

"We pushed the Spaniards down the line of mules, the Spanish courage gone. With a last volley they fled, their resistance evaporating, the jungle molding the motion of their fleeing forms into its own darkness. Our crew began to tear the packs off the backs of the mules. Silver coins and bars fell to the earth. I ran toward the mules. 'No silver.' The arm of one of the Spanish slaves caught me. I almost left my feet. 'Gold.' He pointed to another mule. 'Gold.' He patted the bags as he loosened the ropes.

"Around me in savage quest, the crew ripped into packs. Gold avalanches fell to earth. Slaves ran along the line of mules, pointing to bundles that carried gold. 'Take the gold first. Forget the silver.' Oxenham screamed. Somewhere in space there was another cry. It seemed to float in a whirlwind of its own sound. I listened to the words, trying to understand their meaning.

"'Le Testu is wounded,' said a voice. My head turned, my mind not sure of any direction other than those of gold and retreat. By the edge of the road he lay, his face a mixture of surprise and agony, his hands holding his own blood. Several of his crew attended him, pulling away his bloodied shirt to unwrap the wound. Instruments were brought. Drake knelt by him.

"'He was shot by a slave, one of those they give weapons,' said Diego, standing by my side. Diego smiled. In his hand he held the head of a man, its last blood dripping on my feet. 'Let he who lived like a Spaniard die like a Spaniard,' said Diego, raising the head. "Let him look.' Diego held the head toward Le Testu. After a minute Diego turned the face toward me. 'Even in death, I see no regret,' he mused. 'Vacant are the eyes.' The skin of the head hung in limp folds. 'One death is not enough,' said Diego. Then he put the head by the side of the road, stepped back. 'I hope he feels the vermin eat into his skull,' he said. 'I have become a little of the Spanish. Have I my own enemy in me?'

"Le Testu cried in pain. He slumped into the arms that held him. A tree branch was placed in his mouth gently so he would not cut into his tongue with his teeth. Le Testu raged in his flesh, as if his bones would bloom from his skin to flee his pain. A short medical lance was probed into the bullet's course. He fainted as the wound was cut aside, the flattened shot removed, the threads to tie the meat pulled upward, pulling the skin. With some herbs and leaves and flowers, the Cimarrones and I prepared a plaster for the wound. The stomach wrapped, blood staining the dressing, Le Testu was placed against a tree to rest, exhausted, grasping the air with his hands, searching for words hidden in his own breath.

"The gold was lying on the ground in confusion, scattered by the avarice that had sought it. The heels that scratched among the remaining packs kicked dust upon them. The bells in Nombre de Dios began to peal, crying out their rage to heaven in a bank of sound. The commotions of the street we heard, and drums.

"'There is little time. Take only the gold. Bury the silver. We'll come back for it,' ordered Drake.

"There was, in the execution of those words, a slap to the mind. We worked in groups, some packing gold in bags, while others crawled on hands and knees fitting silver bars into the holes dug by land crabs. We burrowed under fallen trees, seeding the land with the nuts of our plunder. We worked in hysteria, our limbs never moving fast enough. Those who would have in other places kissed every penny with a miser's love now discarded a rain of silver bars as if they were dirt. It is said we buried fifteen tons of silver in two hours. We worked against the walls of our own passion and our own fears. When ready, we swept the ground with dirt to hide our orphan bounty. Then, with the gold and the wounded Le Testu carried between two of his own crew, we left, Cimarrones and freed slaves, English and French fleeing over the jumbles of roots and the crumpled contours of the jungle. Behind us would be the pursuing Spanish, the phantom's breath, simmering the idea of capture into our thoughts.

"'Where is that drunken Lorens?' called a French sailor.

"'He's lost,' called another.

"The jungle vines moved in tentacles, some along the earth, predatory in their lies, pointing nowhere. Drake walked next to Mandinga and Oxenham. 'If he is captured, he could be convinced by torture to reveal our plans.'

"'The Spanish will kill him fast,' said Mandinga. 'If not, the jungle will have him.'

"Oxenham nodded. 'The choice is not ours. We cannot search for him.'

"Drake, in his reluctance, agreed. We moved between the valley of the great roots, lizards trotting before us, their tongues licking the air at our passage.

"Le Testu was half in faint, his head rolling on his neck, trying to remember sensations other than pain. We stopped and rested. Drake and Mandinga knelt by the injured Frenchman.

"'I have become your death,' he said. 'Leave me behind.' Le Testu coughed, his wound still belching color through the bandages. 'I am weakened unto sleep,' he said. 'I must have rest.'

"Drake looked at the earth, which tumbled in convulsive riot, not a flat ground to be seen. It would not be a soft ride, even with the strong arms of the Cimarrones. 'Better die with us than alone,' whispered Drake in his ear. 'Let Mandinga's men carry your litter for a time. They are fresher and stronger than your own.'

"'No,' said Le Testu, 'I am too weak. The thought of it exhausts the little strength I have. I will make your travel slower. I will rest here, regain health and follow in a while.'

"Mandinga looked at Drake. 'You will be alone,' he said. Le Testu's two men volunteered to stay with him. Drake looked again at his friend, the scream of unseen things echoing through the mottled light. Vapors of mists swept around the trees.

"'My friend, I have learned not to believe the promises made between God and men. They are only fragile things the mind makes iron in our hopes. But between men, their words, their oaths, their allegiances must carry the divine light from the nothing before our birth to the nothing at our death. We are the nothings made divine in our promises. Go. If I die, become my life too, become the better part. At my death, become my vengeance.'

"Drake stood. 'He gathers himself for a final struggle with his own demons. He has made his choice. Honor it. He is still bleeding,' said Mandinga, watching the rosette of blood grow on Le Testu's side. 'The roughness of the trail would tear him apart. It is better to be left here in peace to heal.'

"Oxenham said nothing. The rest of the French crew talked in small groups, their impatient gestures framing the anger in their eyes. The English sat with the Cimarrones, eating and trading bits of meat and biscuits and flasks of water, sometimes mixed with aqua vitae.

"'The men want to live long enough to spend the bounty of God's gift,' said Oxenham, finally. 'You have no choice.'

"'All I have is choice,' said Drake. He knelt again at Le Testu's side. 'I will be back for you. Keep to the thick of the jungle.' He looked at Le Testu's two companions. 'Step away from our trail and hide. I will be back.' Drake repeated his oath with his eyes and a nod of his head, pledging his body, as he spoke his words.

"'Fools make the best kind of friends…eh?' Le Testu laughed, his hands grasping again his wound, the pain rising to his mouth. 'When you count out the golden eyes, those Spanish coins, think they are me, watching through their glow….Now off.'

"Drake held Le Testu's shoulder for a time. 'All I can do…will be done.'

"'Better still, give me an honest count of the gold, my English friend. The hordes in heaven are small against the hordes in hell.'

"With that we left him under a tree, weakly waving his hand, his complexion almost drained pure white with loss of blood. As his hand moved, ghostly vapors seemed to rise from his flesh. Darkness and distance interceding, his face became a coin of white, shrinking into a point, then a nothing. We walked on, our thoughts holding his face alive, until our own exhaustion bleached it to the hollowness of a spent idea.

"We labored across an earth of eruptions, twisted into silent agonies, lethal edges of rocks and roots and rise. We carried on our backs the gold of our own salvation, the anchor weight of our fears. The ghostly Spanish surrounded us in a curtain of phantom stares. We felt watched. We were pursued. Our muscles ached. We drank air, discarding food to ease our load. The jungle darkened as light was forfeit. The wind freshened through the trees. Clouds swept through the sky in menacing hurricanes. Animals no longer cried, but hid themselves in trembling hush. The heavens opened rain upon us. Winds raced lunatic across the earth, as trees bowed to demonic forces, some breaking, their corpses falling, expiring in a rush. We walked through the half-light, the clothes on our backs now a weave of water. We melted into rain, the earth sucking at our feet. Afraid we would lose our footing, we held to each other's hands.

"At dark the Cimarrones found high ground, and we rested under the shelters they prepared. We played with our gold coins, bouncing them in our hands, letting the clink of wealth sing static to our exhausted souls. We sat on mud, bowed with talk, staring into passing moments of sleep or watching the lightning briefly gesture in the night.

"The storm passed and night evaporated into day. Mist rose from the earth. We started again toward the Francisca River and our pinnaces.

"We walked now upon a land exhausted by rain. Drops of water fell from the high trees, cascading in earthy tears through the vines and leaves. On the jungle floor plants opened their foliage to the feast, holding in leafy wells pools of water that fed in silent rush their roots, and where creatures drank and vermin swam passions through the galaxies of their eggs.

"We pushed through the jungle's green chains, our feet slipping in the mud. The weight of the gold on our backs held us to the earth. Always behind us were the visions of our pursuers; ahead of us, the open throat of the Francisca River and beyond it the impatient sea.

"Toward midday the ground became firmer under foot. The crown of the trees spread yawning to the jubilant light. There were sea smells and sounds of water tumbling against the heat of white sands in a quenching hiss.

"'The river is close,' we cried to a man. We urged ourselves on. That last breath of strength we spent. We bit the air with our teeth, swallowing our gasps, the air eluding us, fleeing before us as we stumbled on in our race to breathe again. By the last line of trees between us and the coast, Drake signaled us with a desperate gesture to be silent and walk lightly in a softened step to the view of the beach. We moved with caution now, knelt, hidden by jungle growth. There, floating beyond the white thunder of the surf, were seven Spanish oared shallops, each mounted with a single cannon at its bow, which protruded like a trumpet over the water.

"'The sea has come as derelict to our aid,' said Oxenham. 'All is lost.'

"'Lorens was captured and tortured to reveal our plans,' someone sobbed.

"'What about Le Testu?' asked Oxenham, always suspicious of the failures of his betters.

"Drake gestured for us to move away from the line of trees, back to the shadow of the jungle. We crawled in panic, darkness covering us with its concealing tongue. We sat on the soft ground, the weight of gold on our backs. Some took out gold bars and coins, stroking them with their hands, caressing the surfaces with their fingers, as if hoping their whole bodies could penetrate the smoothness of its face, be consumed and hidden, eaten in a living death by the object of their desire.

"'The Spanish have our pinnaces and soon will have all our ships and all our provisions,' said John Pike, who now sat holding his sack of gold to his chest, rocking back and forth, clutching visions of terror as a dam against a swell of memories.

"'He wants to have his fears,' whispered Mandinga. 'It's easier than facing the spirits of his emptiness.'

"Drake looked at Mandinga and addressed his crew. 'I would rather face a wildfire than a panic. Fear feeds itself on nothing. You are your own enemies.' Drake's words came like stone tablets thrown at the feet of an errant tribe. 'We must think. There has been no time for the Spanish to attack our camp. Even if the pinnaces are lost, so be it. The coin that slips through our fingers still leaves the coins on our backs. The *Minion* and *Bear* are safe. We must in all haste reach them and bring them here.'

"'Overland is a long trek,' said Thomas Moone.

"'There is no time. I propose to go by sea, to build a raft, and I will sail it with a small crew.' Drake was then silent. The crew murmured as it considered folly.

"'We can flee into the jungle and hide,' said a voice.

"'But how would we get to England? Our gold is poorly spent when it only fries in this heat,' said another.

"'That can be a fifty-mile voyage on an open sea,' said Oxenham.

"'If we stay here, chained to safety and our fears, we will be captured,' said Drake. 'We must construct the raft.' Drake spoke quietly, letting the smooth force of his words reveal not only their meaning, but that he knew what he was about.

"With little to offer of its own, the crew finally agreed. We began to gather fallen trees, pulling them across the ooze of the jungle floor, their spent lives now only weight, their branches clawing the earth in a dead mockery of a protest.

"We lashed the logs together with ropes, trimmed the broken twigs, which were the last of their branches, and raised a crude mast with an unseamed biscuit sack as sail. A Cimarrone reported to Mandinga that the Spanish shallops had disappeared.

"'The sea is spread before us without a Spanish sail,' said Mandinga.

"'A good sign,' said Drake. 'Either they were lazy, or cowards, or never certain of our escape route. By truth, there are no Spanish soldiers coming behind us for now. Otherwise the ships would never have left and opened our escape by sea.' It was just like Drake to take a scrap and turn it into a meal. Whether he truly believed what he said, no one could know, but it reassured the crew and brought them back from the delirium of panic.

"'There is still the sea,' said Diego, 'and your voyage into mists.' Waves rolled against the beach, the smoke of quenching waters rising into the air like a spray of hair.

"Drake watched the emptiness of the sea before him. 'Where else should I in naked weakness go, a beggar to the fates, than on the salty wine which is my God?' Drake looked at Diego. 'I will need three others to man the raft, three expert seamen, good swimmers.'

"Mandinga said that he would go. Drake shook his head. 'I need you here. I want you and Oxenham to take command in my absence and if anything should happen to me, lead the men inland.'

"'I would rather, in that case, my life close with yours,' said Mandinga.

"'We have all spent too much blood in this war. For me and for your people it is best you stay. You have no experience upon the water.' Mandinga's hand grabbed Drake's arm. I thought there would be war among friends, but Drake added, clasping Mandinga's hand, 'You must serve where your spirits are, as I must serve with mine.' Mandinga smiled and said, 'We are both men who turn whispers into hurricanes. We are the shadow guides. There are no easy paths for us.'

"Diego looked at Drake as if to speak, but decided it was useless to plead his case. I volunteered, as did a Frenchman who looked both strong and burly. He had not seemed to have tired under the strain of his Atlantic crossing with Le Testu, or from the heavy burden of our ordeal in the jungle. 'You are not familiar with me, but I am much experienced and well fitted for this journey of yours,' said this Jacques Mahleau to Drake. 'I am of Le Testu's crew the best sailor and have knowledge of waters like these. I shall be more insistent than any here because I am more in confidence of my skills. On those seas, you shall need me.'

"Drake was uncertain. He did not know the man, but the Frenchman's manner said this was someone determined beyond the restraints of modesty. When Drake nodded his consent, Jacques did not utter a word, but immediately turned and walked to the raft, inspecting it, tightening ropes and adjusting logs. He tied new ropes to the mast to resecure it, and ropes to the logs for us to tie to our waists.

"While Jacques worked, Drake turned to his crew. 'I need one more sailor.' John Smith of our crew stepped forward. 'I'll have my chance out there,' he said."

Chapter Twenty-one

OF STORMS AND GOLDEN JOKES. OF DEATH AND MANY PARTINGS. OF PROMISES AND GIFTS, AND THE MARRIAGE IN THE WHIRLWIND.

T JAMESTOWN, around the fire, the voice of Ratcliffe burst into laughter. "With Drake too...Smith? A finger squeezed into every adventure, eh?"

"No, not myself," I said. "Just another with my name."

"Yes. If you were at Drake's side you'd be older than that wreckage who tells the tale," replied Ratcliffe. "They say time holds no mercy for a mutineer and a traitor."

There was a hiss from the company. The sound snaked through the blackness. Ratcliffe backed into silence, his hands raised before his chest, as if he would push in another direction the anger aimed at his soul.

"There are meanings in Drake's own life, this enterprise better know, because death was not the total suffocation of his fate. This earth still spins on whispers, my friends.... It still spins on whispers," said the old mariner.

Reverend Hunt apologized for Ratcliffe. "Please continue," he said. "Your history is more a garden than a tale. In it are many exotic apples to be plucked."

The old mariner looked again into the fire's jagged flames spitting their light in trembling brevities against the skin of the night.

"We dragged our raft to the ocean's edge, the surf rolling toward us in an expiring rush, the tip of the water's tongue just reaching our feet. Kegs filled with water were lashed to the raft. Some food and other provisions were placed aboard her and secured. The men on the beach muttered among themselves. The low groan of their murmur was like the hum of a lost soul. Drake turned toward the sound. Faces meeting his shrank from his sight, staring down at the blind eyes of the sand. 'Already the winds have gathered on the land to push us seaward, and still you gloom. The trip is dangerous, that we all know; but here, in this our own sunlight, on the lip of our great sea's altar, we are in our open tabernacle. The sea may rage, but it rages to test our courage, that we will be worthy of her gifts. Some of those gifts you now carry on your back.' Drake watched his crew nod their heads.

"As the sea fell rolling in its battalions behind him, Drake raised his hand so the crew could see the water race in its diminishing wash toward the beach. 'The roar behind me is our God's choir, mighty is its voice and patient is its gentleness. I shall not fail in the sea, and, with the help of its watery hand, and despite all the Spanish in the Indies, I shall bring rescue to this beach…as I have with its ministry brought wealth to your pockets.'

"Then Drake turned and our raft was pushed into the gentle foam. We rowed with our crude oars, the winds full in the sack of our beggar's sail. The breakers broke over our dark logs, washing them with the expiring lather of a white foam. The raft rose, twisting against the confusions of the surf. Still we drove our oars, our backs braced determined as we dug into the power of the water's bite. The raft, in humble float, leaped and fell upon the water's rush. Finally the sea gentled into a lake, the surf behind. The figures on the beach sat and watched. We headed south. The sun blossomed then slumbered into its own heat. We traveled on, losing sight of our companions.

"Drake was ever joyous. The sun rose beyond its height, painting shimmering pathways on the sea, all headed east, toward home. While standing on our wooden speck our faces burned. Our skin began to flame red. Dried of its life, it peeled in strips of white ruin. We drank in greed, our kegs emptying. We ate, fearing our food, now wet, would spoil. We sailed on. Toward night the moon's eye moved, half-closed, above the horizon's sliver of light, shrinking as it fled upward toward the sky's darkening bow.

"Even cupped in the ocean's hand, Drake saw in his littleness immensity. At night the dome of the sky flamed in blackness. Stars jeweled, floating their diamonds through ribbons of their own galactic smoke. When the sea ran calm, Jacques fished, letting his line trawl through the invisibility behind us. 'It's more for the mind,' he said, 'than for the stomach,' watching the small length of string for any twitch of success.

"Toward dawn the sea ran in havoc. We held to the mast and to our lines. The sea, in its lethal spray, cut pain through our injured skin. Water rose in mountains to tongue the air washing over our raft.

Floating in its surge to our armpits, we called to each other words drummed, their meaning lost in the water's crash. Lightning tore cracks in the warring clouds. We held to our raft, balancing her. She never sank, never capsized. We did as our experience told. We rode down the storm until she exhausted herself into a gentle rain. We washed ourselves in its sweet shower and bathed our wounds.

"At dawn we caught the coast again. Drake knelt and prayed. 'Oh God, my knees again on thy chest, a supplicant, gladly, that I might feel the heart that brought me forth out of the test of your storm. If I am worthy now in your sight, grant me my ships that I might be thy apocalypse on earth...thy dragon.'

"The sun rose. The sea smoked heat between our planks. In a narrow cove, resting safely from the storm, we saw our ships, the *Minion* and the *Bear*, and around them, their sails in flutter like nervous birds, our pinnaces.

"Drake did not make directly for his ships. There was always in him a twinkle in the soul that lit his eyes with the jest of humor. 'We shall have a joke on our wayward friends,' he said. With that he steered the raft to the point of land before the cove. We landed on a sandy beach and walked into the trees. It was cool in the shade. The damp held to our skins like a foul breath, but Drake, ever bright in his joke, urged us on. 'When we come to the ships look downcast and sad,' he said. 'Speak no words. I shall talk for us all.' Near the ships we walked from the jungle growth. No one saw us. As we advanced, Drake wrinkled his brow. His gait became weary. His face showed in its attitude painful thoughts.

"'Who walks there?' called a voice.

"'Answer not,' whispered Drake.

"'Are you Spanish?' called the voice again, as a bell began to clang aboard the *Minion*, the *Bear* answering in nervous alarm.

"'Who—' began another voice. 'It's Drake!' Behind the rails of the ships the crews gathered, watching our approach. 'Only four,' someone screamed. 'It's a disaster. Are all lost?'

"'We have been cursed since we were baptized by the sea.' The words now in their fearful conclusions.

"Drake mounted the rope ladder to the closest ship, the *Minion*. He went first, acting his gloom. We followed. The crew gathered about us, not certain they wanted to hear their captain. Drake bent his head, not speaking, his hands and fists before his eyes, the crew watching his face, waiting for his news. Drake looked up slowly, then he cast his hands in space, opening them wide as if they were sunbeams. From his palms gold coins fell to the deck, as he cried, 'Our voyage...is made.'

"The coins flung high now parasoled in their fall, struck the deck and bounced and rolled. Falling to their knees, the crew groped at air, trying to catch the golden wheels as they fled like cheerful mice across the deck. Drake stood apart, contented in his various humors. He laughed. Men began to stand, holding coins, their eyes fixed on the frolic of their curves.

"'I left a thousand of these golden eyes on a beach near the Francisca River with our crew as guard. We must now make our haste and bring them forth,' said Drake. The crew cheered, their words rushed into a song of plenty. The ships took to the wind and to their tack, as if they, too, would glory from a treasure in their hold.

"Drake was told the pinnaces had not made the meeting on the appointed day because of powerful and contrary winds which kept them far south. Drake listened, nodded. I am not sure he fully believed the tale. Later he said to me, 'The dreams of promised wealth make some men cowards. Safety...beware safety. It is the chains of thought that bind us to our own destroying rocks.'

"On the Francisca River our companions waved to us in frantic glee. We anchored, took aboard the sacks of gold and their tired bodies. They hugged Drake and swore in pledges eternal alliance with his soul. All loaded, we sailed forth out of Francisca Bay. Drake set his course toward our camp at Pheasant Bay. It was an easy sail, in a fair breeze, our thoughts of wealth dreaming oil on the sea, greasing our hulls in easy slide through the slippery waves.

"At night we entered our cove, lit fires, drank. Men danced through the fire sparks, holding bottles of aqua vitae above their heads, roistering with their own shadows. Others told the tale of their adventure over and over again, expanding their part with each telling, exaggerating their bravery. But with the gold now in hand and with the remembrances of their fears, the littleness of themselves came back into their thoughts. And so they hid in repetitions from themselves.

"Some men just raged in their joys, their souls squandering their life's power as they raced along the beach shouting for the love of shouting, jumping in the air for the love of jumping. Some men smoked tobacco, the Cimarrones mixing it with the crushed seeds of a sacred tree. What pleasure this that makes men mad? No place to store the whirlwinds in their heads, they blew their heat wide-eyed into the night until, exhausted, they collapsed alone, their arms embracing mounds of sand, the sea, in its incoming tide, tickling them in their sleep.

"In the morning we rose groaning from the sand, or the decks of ships, or the places we just dropped in mindless sleep. We ate if we could. Drake ordered the sacks of gold brought to the decks of the *Bear*. There, in bags and piles of loose coins, he began to divide our prize: half to the French, as was promised to Le Testu, and half to ourselves.

"The Cimarrones watched, indifferent to the gold; or sad, perhaps, that they were not a party to this kettle or that their allies cared more for the golden wheels than war. Each nation has its own coin; theirs was theirs, and ours was holy profit. The division done, two piles lay upon the deck. I am sure that some of us wished the division never done and we kept it all, but Drake was his word. Some of the French hefted sacks of gold in their hands, their ears against the cloth sacks, listening to the clink of wealth, as a child might hold a spiral shell to his ear, listening to the echoes of an imagined sea.

"'There is still the question'—Drake addressed the French—'of our wounded Le Testu and our buried silver. I intend to return to the Campos River and, if possible, retrieve them both.'

"'I have no interest in making the fights with the Spanish soldiers again,' said the new French captain, Henri Foré. 'The silver is yours. Take it with our compliments. Also Le Testu. We have received all we had wanted, now we must go. It is pleasing to make the profit with you.' The Frenchman approached, his hand outstretched in sunlight, its shadow moving across the deck like a dark sword. 'We are all for one thing alone,' the Frenchman said, grabbing Drake's hand, 'and what have we not given up to make sacrifice for this gain?' He pulled Drake's hand, jerking it up and down, as if Drake were a spigot of a well from whose mouth gold would vomit forth.

"The French began to gather the bags from the *Bear*'s decks. I wondered if Drake would allow them to take the gold and desert Le Testu. But what choice did he have? A war among holy thieves? They had fulfilled their part. The oath to Le Testu was Drake's alone. We all knew the risks. Only Drake had pledged his soul. Only his dreams gushed with the sea's blood. The French were a sadder version of himself. Drake had scuttled his ship, dissected and buried his brother. Drake could not make war of retribution on his own, even if they were only a pauper's shadow of himself.

"Mandinga wanted war against the French. 'They are not worth a death,' Drake said. Diego muttered under his breath as the French ship took the wind and moved through the rising white mist toward the darkening eastern sky.

"'Wealth can make cowards of greater men than us,' Drake said, addressing his crew. 'We are all baptized into different worlds. We will refit our ships and soon we will sail to find Le Testu and our buried silver.' Drake waved his hands across his face, as if pushing an unpleasant sight away. The French crew he would leave to its fate. He would stay and finish what we had begun, although it must be said that many of our own crew would have run with the wealth we had, rather than stay for the honor of another adventure and possibly another prize.

"For two weeks we refit our ships while our pinnaces gathered provisions from our hidden stores. We braided new rigging around our masts, rising vines of hemp, a spider's garden to carry a human quest. We repegged our planks. We sewed torn sails. Kegs were filled with fresh water. The ships, newly tallowed, rode now heavy on the sea.

"One morning Drake gathered us upon a beach. The sand, in its whiteness, blew in jeweled storm in the sunlight and wind. The sea rose and fell against the fresh breeze. 'It should be safe to return to the Francisca River,' Drake said. 'The Spanish should have quit their search and humbled themselves in their galleons toward home.' At that, the crew did not cheer, but stared at each other in silence, nervously.

"We manned our pinnaces, set the bite of our running keels against the oncoming wash, as once more we forced speed from bulging sail and moved through the spray of broken waves. The mouth of the Francisca River tongued its ooze into the sea, while its deserted beach echoed heat. Our sails flapped as they fell. The anchor thrown overboard to its place, we saw but emptiness.

A voice came from the beach. A figure ran toward the water's edge, his clothes in shreds. He waved, disjointed. His legs collapsed, no longer able to heed his will.

"We rowed toward shore. The figure was on his knees, his hands on the sand, supporting his frame. His elbows buckled. His head seemed to bury itself in the earth.

"'On what is he breathing?' said a voice.

"'Memories,' said Diego.

"On the beach we walked to the man, who was piling sand around his head. He babbled in French. Drake looked down at him, the sand encasing his head in a fort of wet sloping walls.

"'Where is Le Testu?' asked Drake. The man kicked his legs, trying to drive his head deeper into the sand.

"'The man is a lunatic,' said Oxenham. Mandinga pushed the man with his foot. He fell over onto his side then looked up. 'Light in blackness are you death?'

"'I am a spirit,' said Mandinga. 'I am blind. I seek the loan of eyes.'

"'Seeing is not the joy...for spirits,' said the man.

"Oxenham looked at Drake. 'He's one of those who stayed with Le Testu,' he said. Drake nodded. Oxenham kicked the sand, holding his impatience back behind his reddening face. 'Where is Le Testu?' asked Oxenham.

"The man looked at Oxenham, his head tilted to the side, like a bird drawing in its mind images of a worm. 'In many places,' said the man. Then he laughed hysterically in a confusion of tears and glee. 'His parts are bells. They peal in blood.'

"Oxenham struck the man, who fell back against the earth, his lips bleeding.

"Mandinga knelt by the man and lifted him in his arms. 'The man has agonies in the mind,' Mandinga said, pointing to his own head. 'Your fists will drive his spirits deeper into their own pit.' Mandinga washed the man's face with water, gave him a little food. The man watched the food. He must have felt some pleasure in its eating. His sight began to recognize a place. He looked up.

"'And Le Testu?' asked Drake.

"'The Spanish found us,' said the man, exhausted into truth. 'Le Testu they killed. They cut off his head and quartered him. They hung his severed limbs on a small tree then carried them back to Nombre de Dios, his blood anointing their path. I escaped. The other they captured alive...quartered him living.'

"Drake walked away, watching sea and sky howl inaudible in their lunatic of pain. Diego walked to his captain's side. 'He is dead, my Drake.'

"'How much death to quench an empire?' Drake asked. There was no answer. He knelt and ran his hand above the shallow puddles of the sea. Drake smiled. 'Well…there is still our silver.' With that he ordered Oxenham, with a party of Cimarrones, back to the Campos River to find what of our treasure could be found. They set out at midday, Drake staying behind with the ships.

"Two days later they all returned, carrying thirteen bars of silver and a few bags of gold. 'The Spanish did a fine search,' laughed Oxenham. They dug in the rot of the earth until you would think they ate the ground they dug.'

"The Cimarrones added little. 'So be it,' said Drake.

"At Pheasant Bay again we made ready for our partings. Drake visited the graves of his brothers. Already the wind had blown obscuring sand in storms across them, their rocks half-hidden, their mounds made level. The earth had returned to the flatness of earth. Drake stood above the graves alone. What Drake said was lost but to himself.

"He walked back to the camp, stood at the water keg, took a tin cup from the peg at its side. Opening the keg he lifted the top. The water in its satin waves rolled in its nest. Drake dipped the cup, feeling again the soft lips of the water on his hand. He drank. 'It is always the sea…always the sea,' he said, 'and the earth that holds us muling in our cradle.' Along the bay, the sea birds, in their heat, bled cries as they swooped across the jumble of the sea's waves. Above the tumult the fading light breathed its white horizons to the sun.

"Mandinga approached. 'Soon our war will be done,' he said.

"'Yes, this moment will close, it is true, but our war will go on,' said Drake. 'I want you to bring your men to our ship one last time. I would like them to chose from our stores any provisions they need. It is a gift for our battles.'

"That night the Cimarrones and our crew sat on the beach as Drake ordered the burning of the pinnaces. There was now no place for these aboard our ships. With all the gold, the silks, the plate, the barrels of tobacco we had as plunder along that coast, no room now upon our decks or in our holds for them. Servants die, their faithful service done. Even the *Minion* set to the torch, not enough of us alive to man that ship. The boats blazed before us, the shadows of their disintegrating masts melting into the rush of the flames; the smoking hulls, the pop of cracking boards, those which had borne us on their chests crumbling, expiring into coals. Some, in curious watch, smoked tobacco as the boats raged their agonies in flames. I thought of the *Swan*, sunk those months before. Eager my faithless lips kissed passion on the torments of your face. Most of our company now held a pipe, no passion there, just general regrets: just a spectacle and an excuse to enjoy the weed.

"In the morning the fires had exhausted themselves into smoke. The collapsed decks had exposed the bowed timbers of the *Minion*'s hull, which spread their burnt and blackened fingers to the sky, as if the stiffened wreck of a severed hand. Some crew had begun to walk among the ashes, looking for the metal fittings. These would be given to the Cimarrones for their use. Each time an ironwork was found it was tossed up the beach. The metal part flew black against the sky, trailing smoke, like the overdone meat of a fresh-killed beast.

"The Cimarrones came aboard our ship and did their search, taking powder and shot, weapons and food, clothes and domestic fare. Our crew in generous sadness of farewell opened bales and boxes, searching with their eyes for items to consider. Mandinga and Diego were in Drake's cabin with Oxenham and me. Drake had special presents for Mandinga. As he opened a wooden chest in his cabin to display fine silks and cloth for Mandinga's wife, the Cimarrone leader saw the golden scimitar, the sword of Coligny, the sword that Le Testu had presented to Drake, its jeweled hilt crying sparkling tears of light, even in the dark cabin.

"Mandinga touched the sword. 'The souls of men are enfolded in this blade,' he said. 'I feel their strength. I will have it.'

"'All who have owned this sword have died,' said Drake, trying to discourage Mandinga. 'It was Le Testu's and his slaughtered friend's before him.'

"'This edge,' said Mandinga, touching the sharpened curve. 'This edge can cut spirits in its wash.'

"Drake, longing for a memory of Le Testu he could touch, truly wanted the sword. He looked into Oxenham's eyes and toward the light flowing through the two bowed windows of his cabin. He looked at Mandinga. 'Think of Le Testu when you wield that blade,' he said. 'It is better served with you than on my wall.'

"Mandinga held the scimitar in both hands, swinging it through the shafts of light, cutting with each stroke phantoms in the air. 'I have a request of the Brother to the Sea,' he said. 'I have a son and a daughter, and there are twenty others. I wish you to take them from here and settle them beyond the reach of the Spanish on an earth still purified with spirits, an old place where life can renew itself. This I would have you do.'

"There are many captains, their ships filled with treasure, who would have laughed at such a request, or taken the black foundlings beyond the sight of land and thrown them into the sea. But to Drake, it was a duty to accept. "Done…by the powers of fate. It is done,' he said, holding Mandinga's hand.

"'And Diego, what of you?' asked Drake. 'What would you wish?'

"'My Drake,' smiled Diego, 'without you, war here may be small and a little dull. I would come with you and bring some help to the Spanish to speed their death.'

"'I am but a humble captain,' laughed Drake. 'I may retire to sleep and a life of ease. Diego, my friend, you may grow decrepit with dreams of a war that has passed us by.'

"'Where you go, Drake, there follows war,' smiled Diego.

"The Cimarrones piled their presents on the sand. Booty to field a small army. We kept enough shot and powder to see us home. We waited some days for Mandinga's children and the other Cimarrones. Meanwhile, Drake had all the provisions from the *Pasco* moved and stowed aboard the *Bear*, which was a larger ship and much better for an Atlantic crossing.

"The last of the Spanish prisoners were brought before Drake. 'I am giving you that ship, my *Pasco*,' he said, 'to sail it where you please.'

"The Spanish captain thanked Drake, adding his appreciation that his life was spared. As the Spanish captain spoke, his eyes glanced aside, watching the Cimarrones walk among the dunes, talking. The Cimarrones themselves watched across that distant yet shrunken landscape where enemies hold each other close in thought, and where all that is far away is just an eyelash to a hate.

"'It is with the gratitude of our gracious God that we thank you for your kindness,' said the Spaniard. Drake acknowledged his words. 'We are all sailors, no?' said the Spaniard. 'Both you and I, we share the same taste in our mouths, the same smell in our noses, sail on the same seas.'

"'We always sailed on different seas,' replied Drake. 'Even the waters under your keels squirm.'

"'Riddles. I am not too good at the riddles. Water is water. I do what it is best to do. To our king Philip, too much imagination is the original sin. Philip likes his people of one soul…like our dead Queen Isabella, who gave us Holy Inquisition.' The Spanish captain began to whisper. 'You have become the Drako, the Dragon. In your name is your mantle, the sign of the apocalypse.' Beyond the beach the sea's breakers rolled, glistening like the scales of a serpent's back. 'Isabella wanted the world one nation, under one church, to begin the apocalypse of the second coming,' continued the Spanish captain. 'What we have brought in the blood of our persecutions, it is not the dragon of our hope but you, Drake, the dragon of another kind.'

"'I am the dragon of my God,' said Drake as he rose. 'I am the apocalypse. What destruction is man when his mind is visions?' Drake's arms threw themselves wide, his fingers teeth, as if in the bony jaw of a great mouth ready in its gape to consume half the horizon to the sky. 'I shall feed fire to the wind.' His shirt blew into rolls of fabric on the breeze. 'That I am its servant.'

"The Spanish captain looked at his superstitious men. The actor Drake acted, sculpting fear in the hearts of his enemy. The Spanish captain would tell his tale. Madness was now the ally of our enterprise. Drive away the Spanish certainty and even when they came upon us armed, they were naked. It was one of Drake's greatest performances. How much he believed of it, even in his deadly jest, is ever in my thoughts. I do not know, but some of it I know he did.'

"The moment spent to its proper conclusion, Drake walked away. As he passed me he winked, then he stared ahead. How lightly he did step into the waters of his twin beliefs."

"THE MORNING OF THE NEXT DAY, MANDINGA'S SON AND DAUGHTER and twenty Cimarrones came walking down a small shaded path to our beach camp. I was surprised at their youth. Most were in their twenties. Some of the party were as old as their thirties, a few still older. They greeted Mandinga then sat apart for a while, talking. Finally Mandinga sought out Drake. By his side were two of the youngest of the Cimarrone party.

"'Into your hands, Brother to the Sea, I give you the blood of my blood. Take them to a place beyond the Spanish.' Drake looked at the two, hardly more than children. 'I will…as I can,' he said.

"Mandinga was silent for a moment, as if considering in his thoughts the shape of his private demons. 'You are the shadow flesh of the sea,' he said to Drake. 'In your hands the power of water dwells. On that place you find for my children I want you by wizard's nuptials and beads of earthly blood to join the spirits of sea and land, so that the new land will run with the ghost of the sea, so her rocks will be eager with life and her rivers tongue visions in the mind. This can be only if the spirits of sea and earth are joined as one. That land to have a double flesh of ghosts and so my children will be twice protected. I want you, Drake, to reforge with baptism what the gods have left asunder.'

"Drake tried to speak. His contesting thoughts ate at his words. He stammered. Oxenham looked at me, his eyes wide in unimaginative white. 'What does Mandinga want?'

"'He wants Drake to baptize the earth,' I said, 'then wed it to the sea.'

"Drake, now composed for the moment, looked toward the sea. 'What earth would be so joined' he said, 'no heaven is vast enough to hold.' Near the shore the watery hand of the waves opened into the gentle fingers of an outstretched arm. The surf dissolved into whispers, 'Come to me…come to me,' it said, as near the horizon's edge, light shone on the heaves of the nurturing bosom of water. I felt my head lying against its warm light. Drake turned to Mandinga. 'Another step. I am ashore. It is taken. It is done.'

"I heard the crackle of Oxenham speaking in my ear. 'What nuptial this? It is heresy. It is heresy.'

"Mandinga looked at Oxenham, hearing his words. 'To death, life is a heresy.'

"'The soul of the alchemist's stone is water,' I said. "Why not marry the bodies of the sea to a portion of its coast, some land? Are not their spirits one?'

"Behind us, the bales and boxes and barrels of tobacco were being loaded aboard the *Bear*. The *Pasco* still swayed on her anchor, unmanned. The Spanish prisoners on shore watched the lean of her rigging and heard the vacant flap of her rolled sails against the mast. The beach now was almost deserted of human things. Only the drift of man himself marred the white sands.

"Mandinga and Drake stood for some time together, drawn to the last breath of each other's words. Mandinga's children had rowed to our ship to see to their berths. They would return briefly for a last farewell with their father, before the separation turned into memories, memories into silence and silence into unanswered questions of disconnected lives.

"On their return, Mandinga hugged his children, who melted into the power of his arms, closing their eyes and their minds to any feeling other than the heat of their father's touch. They seemed to push themselves deeper into his embrace, clothing themselves with the last of his warmth.

"'We are love and we are memories. I have given you gifts of both. I am ever with you. You are all to me. Be strong in the memory of my love and be free.'

"The children were tearful, destitute even in the flood of Mandinga's words. 'You are not cast out, orphaned to the earth, or humbled by a parent's neglect,' he told them. 'You are on a hero's quest, not alone but with guides and spirits, searching for a new home. I must stay with my duty here. You are my messengers to another age and to another earth. Be in this proud. You and I are not of weakened flesh. Distance does not fade our love. We are forever one.'

"Diego and Mandinga embraced and said their farewells. 'The feather on the wind,' said Diego.

"'The feather on the wind,' repeated Mandinga, adding, 'We rise as one.'

"Drake stood and watched, his head slightly bowed. Mandinga put his hand on Drake's shoulder. 'You are the face on the whirlwind. You are a chosen,' he said. 'Among my people there is a saying, All gifts from the gods carry a thorn.' Then Mandinga whispered, 'My friend, the gods are like children. They break their toys just to see their parts at play. Beware, the gods give a darkness in their gifts.'

"Across the bay two birds raced above the water, dipping their beaks into the surf. Were they catching fish or their own shadows, I wondered as they flew on.

"The Spanish prisoners were released. They ran to their boat, falling over each other in their panic. Some swam to the *Pasco*, others rowed, their confused oar strokes turning their boats in circles in the surf.

"Mandinga laughed. Drake shook his head. 'Our enemy is not in a fighting humor today,' he said. Diego scowled. 'Such a waste. So much unused death,' he said, looking at the escaping Spanish.

"From our own ship a boat rowed toward the beach. When it landed, the crew stood, pulling their oars skyward, holding them at their chests. 'It is our salute to you, Mandinga, and your Cimarrones...but it is time for us to go,' said Drake.

" 'Return...and we make good war again,' said Mandinga.

" 'Soon,' said Drake.

"We gathered ourselves for the last time on that beach, then walked to the boat, boarded her, sat to our own places and were rowed over the smooth waters to our ship.

"We raised anchor. Our sails snapped wind into its harness. As we began to move, our embattled flag spread with glory across our wake. Mandinga still held to the beach. In the distance he became a dot, a pin of a man, who, for those who watched him disappear, held the turn of space around his very frame."

"WE SAILED NORTH INTO THE GULF OF MEXICO, KEEPING AWAY from the coast, Drake watching the watery horizon to the west as we passed the ghostly latitudes of San Juan de Ulúa. Drake said nothing. The sky became the dome of a great tunnel, the sea its floor. We sailed on.

"The sky sent down its barricades. Mist swirled about us, making in its toss the breath of invisible forces manifest. We sailed on by dead reckoning, Drake carrying in his mind the memory of charts, the ink sketches that define in their easy portraits the mysteries of a new continent. He consulted the charts he had, but they were old and almost useless. They showed a land bloated in its coast, bulging with amputated forms, stubbed and withered in its congress with the sea, a land drawn from rumors and ancient fears, the cartography of neglect, of voyages only half made good. Drake ignored it all. He did not need charts. He watched the movement of the sea, the slip of current over current. We heard the birds. We sailed ever north. Mists in shrouds, all distance closed in fog. The tops of the masts were lost in grays. Becalmed, the water lapped in its empty dominion against our hull. We lowered boats and pulled ourselves with straining arms north to fair winds. The fog dissolved into a fresh flow, our sails again like full sacks bulged with a relentless push.

"Now along the Spanish coast of Florida we sailed. Drake

watched the compass needle hold to its points, marveling always at the invisible tickle that kept it true. Our bow closed toward the west. The coast lay against the horizon, beaches in white sweeps hiding swamps and open channels. Birds screamed in lazy float above our sails. Gliding in nervous flight, they came to perch on our spars, calling their arrival as they fluttered into squawks and waddle and stared in momentary rest.

"We stood with small weights and lines, taking our depth, measuring with rope the cold fathoms over which we sailed. Drake made new charts, surveying the intrusions of the land that fell away from us toward the west. We followed. For hundreds of miles, Drake, with ink and quill, drew the shadow of this land on charts and tables of measured space, those mathematician districts of miles and of degrees. The land itself held firm to its roots, while we, in journey, painted its miniatures on our unfolding maps.

"'We are in search of a wide inlet with good supplies of game and fresh water,' he said, concluding with a final nod. And so all had come to this, a hunt for a break in the coast, a wound through which we could pass our human cargo and our human things. There was smoke at times inland, savages at work or hunt or devilish play. We sailed beyond their signs, we hoped. The sand bank that formed the coast fell away. Beaches sank into the distance behind us, their soft white curves slipping smoothly into the swirl of tide and surf, their hardness now no more than watery smoke.

"After a week's sail the land along the coast flattened into swamp, shields of leaves and vines forming skins of green ferment on the rolls of the current. We sailed steadily north. The land began to fracture into coves and the mouths of rivers and the wind came fair from the west, pushing with its invisible hand our ship farther out to sea. Drake took the wind in his tack, and with skill and sail held us to the coast. He fought the wind, ordering barrels thrown behind the ship, tied to ropes to drag against the sea, slowing our drift seaward before the breeze. Then, on the landward tact, the barrels were pulled aboard, easing our bow's cut toward the coast. From the perch on the top of our swaying mast we surveyed the sea rolling in its season, until the soundings we took began to deepen. The cheek of the land fell back. The continent opened wide a watery wound. The light lay in heatless fire on the tongue of the waters.

"'Come about,' ordered Drake. 'Come about.'

"Our bow cut to a new heading. The wind calmed. Our sails fell to the flutter of an empty sack. We waited, drifting in our search, head to head; the land watching the ship through the eye of the sun; the ship watching the land through the eyes of man; tasting the depth of each other's life; the immensity of a continent touching the immensity of a grain of sand.

"'Lower the boats. We'll row ourselves in,' ordered Drake.

"We pulled our ship into the bay. The water turned smooth, its surface glassed with shadows and reflections of the banks. The land rose about us in spirals of trees. Our anchor slipped into the water.

"'We are here,' said Drake to Diego. 'The Jerusalem of the leaves. The Eden of the reborn.'

"We spent the night upon the ship. In the morning we rowed Mandinga's children and the Cimarrones ashore. We explored the land, which conspired in its alliance with the air and sky to bring forth all kinds of berries and nuts and game upon itself. We hunted and fished, and laid in stocks of food for the Cimarrones. Diego saw to the building of shelter. What powder and weapons we could, we left. We shared our clothes and provisions. In all manner and in all things we saw that Mandinga's children would be given a good start in the grotto of that bay.

"'Fair current in a fair wind through a fair place,' said Oxenham, admiring the little town. 'We have done our pledge,' he said to Drake.

"Drake did not answer immediately, being far less easy with a pledge than Oxenham. Finally, he said, 'Vision is but a quest. By what thunder shall come its nuptial?'

"Before our leaving, Drake gathered our crew and the Cimarrones on the beach. He held in his hand a golden chalice. We faced the ocean; Drake faced the land. He dipped his cup into the bay. 'No more let the spirits of earth and sea conspire in separate might,' he said. 'Let there be no coast between your breaths. Let there be no chasm between your names. Join, alight, fathom in holy slide upon this new ground. Commerce as one. Intrude upon the other in lover's touch. Hold in unity. Earth rise in havoc's rest and sea in zealot's wash. Sing lightning. Crack thunder. Run in tides of earth and stones of water. Choir now in canticles of rain. In your baptism now, I baptize.' Drake began to pour the water from his chalice onto the ground. In the distance thunder groaned, the sky darkened as the light began to sleep. Rain swept upon us in purifying waves. The sky forked lightning. The earth set forth its perfumed blood. We stood and took our blessings from the air, the sea, the land.

"'Flame in watery fire,' Drake said, as the lightning flashed. 'Burn air. The sea wars in broken tide. It falls in heavens.' Drake opened wide his arms. He raised his head to the rain. 'Come to me, delicious, sweet sea.' He drank the air. The waves crashed upon the beach. 'Sea, bring thunder in this earth,' he called. 'Rocks in whirlwind rise. Let the fires join, let all contested graces merge, let spirits kiss. For thee I have broken laws, to make thee one.'

"The air was now awash in rain. The world rushed upon us in its fury. Somewhere there was a scream, as if a spirit giving birth. The edges of familiar things dissolved. There was a melt of visions. All things flowed into each other. Nothing could hold itself apart. Words lost their meaning; sounds spoke only wind. We were becoming one with the torrents.

"In the morning the mist rose in a spiritual drift. Hung shadows that might have been men floated in the air. The earth was hiding itself in an airy egg. In the sky there were cracks of light. Drake walked upon the deck. Soon we would sail. He looked into the swirl of vapors, saying to me, 'I shall never forsake this place. I shall bring more than orphans to this beach.' Then he walked away.

"With the sun holding to its noon, we sailed, the land trembling in its rolling hills, its plains sighing in its flattened washes. It was a new land. It seemed to speak in whispers just beyond the ear. What new voice, this land? What alchemies gossip in its air? What magics in its nervous silence? What wizard would presume the ear to hear its voice, if voice there be? And what had Drake birthed to stalk the jungles of our dreams?

"Drake sailed from it. He came home with fortunes in gold and tobacco pirated from Spanish ships. This was the second time Drake had brought the leaf, the second time to urge the English taste, and now with seeds to plant a London garden, amuse a guest. Small crops from a mighty adventure flowed. No one thought the weed was much. Nicot in Paris with its cures, England still indifferent and history in its lion smiled and had its wait.

"Drake returned the wealthiest man of his age. Drako, the Dragon, the apocalypse to the Spanish; the symbol of our nation to the English. Drake had his wealth, had powerful friends, gave counsel, became advisor to the queen on matters of the New World. Ten years later when Sir Walter Raleigh wanted to found a colony north of Spanish Florida, he came to Drake for advice, spread his maps upon the floor. History hid its shadow on the wall. Raleigh smiled. Drake stood, pointing to the place he left the Cimarrones and said, 'Found it here....I know the land well.'

"And so it was that Roanoke was born. Raleigh found no Cimarrones. Both colonies now have disappeared. We are all but fractures of the relentless lost," said the old mariner. Then he folded himself into his own arms, rocking gently as he sat, and was silent.

At Jamestown the only sound was the crackle of the fire. All looked at the mariner until Ratcliffe spoke. "Old man...if you had followed Drake all those years...why are you not at home, guarding your fortune?"

The old man straightened his back, behind him the tobacco smoke. His face glowed with the reflections of fire. "The land here is a haunted place...as we are all haunted. In Panama we were haunted by the getting of gold, but, getting it, we became haunted by it and the memories of what was lost and what might have been. I came here to find something of what I lost."

"You're raving, old man. Your wealth, if you ever had any, has made you mad." A few of the company laughed as Ratcliffe spoke.

The old man trembled, looking at Ratcliffe. "This land bleeds elixirs. They can intoxicate your mind. But be warned, this land eats its young."

PART THREE

The Fires of the Hunter

THE ALCHEMIES OF THE RIVER

Even in the night their lights reflect as fires in the waters. My eyes fill with the wash of my own heat. There is a new summer. My water moves in a nervous chill. Cold shadows float upon my skin. It is the flooding wash of their boats. There is a terror in the alleys of my blood. Their bullets tear heat through my healing currents. Sparks in their scintillations flee or are torn away. I know a new emptiness. Wet dust rises to my sight. Urgent, I am held in the thickness of my warmth as my fingers still cast themselves with life, desperate for the sea.

Chapter Twenty-two

SAT IN MY TENT, candles lit, pen in hand. I was to begin my narrative, a page before me, blank. How frightening are the white landscapes of the empty sheet, Italian paper for an English book, our words to bake a foreign grill, England not rich enough to have a paper industry of its own. And we in the wilderness to create marvels we do not have at home. Such was the folly of our task. The ink I brewed myself from berries and their juices, black and red, and the crushed charcoal of our fires, the powder mixed. The embers newly cold, I smelled the linger of its heat. Seeds of reputation are oiled in the black of ink. There the sooted bile waits upon the page to give us fame. My quill dripped dumb to the public ear; but my time is yet, the sands are not fully cast upon the page. *And now*, I thought, *I am to speak my soul in ciphers.*

My trial done, Captain Newport and Reverend Hunt had in words of great passion convinced Wingfield and the others to allow me to take my council seat. And so we are all confirmed in consent and faithful practice. Obedient to one another and to the whole, our quest this enterprise, each pledging our failing loyalties, derelict, in a shadow love. And so it is done with words. All language is a camouflage to hide the deeper need. Wingfield smiled. Archer plotting air to court a wanton law, always wanting power, its secret ever in his nose. Ratcliffe the sniffle to Archer's sneeze. Martin ill. But all this a fitted rainbow and I its chronicler. Nothing by nothing done. Jamestown still a ruin. No houses built, we slept in hammocks or on the ground. Lazy gentlemen starved, they would not hunt. Game was all about the forest and fish flooded in the rivers. Summer but the wait, soon the cold and winter's famine. And so I sought to have the power to save the enterprise. It was my right by forfit. Alone, I am myself alone. There was no one else. I am now begun. But was I born to grasp such consequence?

But Wingfield in his whispers still called me traitor. He would stare at me in his hangman's glances, for I have claimed there are decorums here beyond all flatteries. That I would call myself his equal was my treason. That I would act as such was my crime. Archer now bred plots with Ratcliffe against Wingfield. The company conversed with slanders and moved on rumors. Wingfield contented himself with extra food and indulged his powers, punishing those grumblers as he could. A few labored with me. Most would not. I was becoming the necessary treason.

Gosnold and Wingfield argued. Gosnold wanted the flogging stopped and Wingfield to share the food with all in equal portions. Wingfield decried the accusations as slander. Gosnold sickened. Wingfield and his favorites smiled, well-fed and healthy in their fat. Archer, the failed lawyer, held himself as judge, licked his bile on the company. Ratcliffe was his tongue. Wingfield knew of all the discontents, but held to his birth and to his rank as his armor. Iron is the tread on the iron path of they who will not learn. Sparks from their heels, the fires all about, the metal glows and in the heat the shield that once protected melts.

Wingfield was nervous with all the sport and whispers at his expense. Sailing soon, Newport tried to bring some peace, asking Wingfield if he thought himself settled in his government. "I fear none among the company except Gosnold who has friends, but he is ill," said Wingfield. "He is inclined to justice, but not to power. Archer would be lethal to my office if he could, and snare in all this discord my power."

Newport, who could oaf any good cause on a foolish practice, then told Captain Archer of Wingfield's words, trying to reassure Archer that he had power and was well regarded. Newport, ever the dull, forgot that the smell of weakness is the blood which urges our deadly sports. Archer, encouraged, stroked his grins and plotted smiles.

I SAT IN MY TENT THOSE EARLY DAYS AFTER THE MARINER'S TALE, thinking of Drake. Never would he sit his quill, its feather to rule his compass. Words were not his treasures. He left that for others. He had abandoned history to its actions. His voyages had absolved his generation, his riches came in daring. How saintly came his coins in England's resurrection.

Always too generous to his friends, too humane to his enemies, Drake came as a gift to the nation. His face is on our new land, on our company and on this whole enterprise. His is the vision behind our eyes, the color of our thoughts. This colony is him, cradled forever in the aims of a second birth.

And so I sat and wrote two histories: one a public dash to promote this colony as his legacy and to tell of its possibilities and my part in it, honestly giving complaint where it was due, but leaving by the way painful stories and hard truths. The Company had it printed as "True Relation, or Newes from Virginia." My second work is my private thoughts, a darker brood of words, wherein that which was left out of the former, for public and private good, can be told and the whole made right again. It is this work you read. Take now the traitor's hand, and let us enter again into our conspiracies of truth.

BY THE END OF JUNE OUR TOBACCO, PLANTED BY THOMAS WOTTON, our surgeon, had grown to the height of a man's knee. Its leaves in green wings rose as if to catch the wind, a vegetable leather it seemed, predatory in its float. The plants stood untended in marshaled rows, digesting light, little worms upon them, their eyes to the sun, feasting ruin upon the leaves, as they watched in delicate contemplation the completion of our fort walls.

Only Newport's sailors and a few of our laborers really worked. Wingfield idled in his official office. Mostly he spent his time taking new titles and medals and honors for himself. He organized the men less now than at our arrival. Gentlemen addressed their pins at bowls, positioning their fingers in the discussions of vast plans, their sweeping wrists the architecture of their works.

Tended by none, the few cornstalks had grown to wither. The earth, it seemed, was giving forth hints of its displeasure. And I in all this turmoil ever under threat. Disaster the only sovereign when authority plays only to its plots. The day before Newport's departure, the waters of the bay ran with shivering life.

"Worms! Millions of worms!" screamed Martin. We ran to the beach, watching the tide heave in flesh. "This land is a cadaver," Martin cried. Ill, his eyes had sunken into his head. "Worms... worms...everywhere worms...."

"Sea worms," said Newport. "They'll eat into the wood of the ships."

"One bit me," yelled a gentleman, holding his wounded hand in the air.

The worms circled upon each other in their rolling sport. The low waves brought them against the sides of the ships.

"They'll eat any plank not properly tarred," said the old mariner. "I've seen it before. Damn things bite like serpents."

That night Newport's ships were made ready for their departure. The council dined in Newport's cabin one last time. "I'm leaving you by the will of circumstance one final gift," he said. "That old mariner, Jonas Profit. He is something of an entertainment and a fine sailor in the bargain. He may be of use. True, he is a little mad, but his lunacies have their depths and even their histories."

"Is he then a seven-year indentured servant or a shareholder in the company?" asked Wingfield, always anxious to know the weight of a man's rank.

"A shareholder. He has the means." Newport placed a bag of coins on the table. "I will make final all the arrangements in London." He paused and smiled. "Jonas is peculiar. He himself never touches any moneys."

"He is the good fool of all our dreams," laughed Ratcliffe.

"Nor does he give it away," added Newport. "He is staying here to cleanse his memories. He has knowledge of this place; even his spirits can be helpful in their hauntings." Newport looked about the room. There was only silence. With no other words on the subject, Newport continued, "With luck I shall make a quick return with fresh supplies."

Each man toasted in his fair cups a quick return and resupply, but only I thought on the grieving numbers that would be our fate. We had by all reckoning thirteen weeks' supply of food. Newport pledged his circle voyage to England and to us again, twenty weeks. But guesses are not facts. To me, judging by our westward voyage of near four months, this swing of sails would be twenty-four weeks at best. Two and a half months without food. Winter and starvation at our door. Our hopes could be our graves if we did not plan for our urgent needs.

I spoke my warnings. Wingfield sent his silent curses in deadly stares. "Some will always eat," whispered Archer into Kendall's ear. By any quarter, by any means, Archer would sour this company. Kendall, whom we presumed the crown's spy, nodded, remarking that there were Spanish supplies close and to the south in Florida.

Newport repeated his smiles and said, "It is only twenty weeks.

Certainly our English gentlemen will not lose their crust in twenty weeks." There was hollow laughter in the room. Captain Kendall then spoke. "There is our pinnace, soon to be ready. With some few we could sail for aid to England, or north to the French, or south to a Spanish fort." Kendall looked at Archer who smiled an anonymous consent. Ratcliffe's face was blank, as though awaiting some inner prompt.

"Why should we set one hope against another? There are better chances here if all will share in equal toils," I said.

Kendall made his own reply. "We are alone upon this bay. What wide embrace is here to hold us to this place? We have our pinnace. In hunger we could sail north or south. We have informations that may prompt a good reward." No one thought on Kendall's words but I. Was there some Spanish treason in our Sandys cousin? My suspicions went unsaid.

Still weak and sick, Gosnold spoke. "We are pledged. No matter the cost, we stay."

The company cheered and laughed salutes, and raised their cups of aqua vitae and drank their drinks. Some lit pipes.

Martin handed Newport a small pouch of yellow rocks. "It is our gold, I am sure," he said, holding tight his gleeful laughs against the tremors of his greed. "By certainties I am sure, but the final assay must await a London chemist."

Lord Percy gave private letters to Newport to deliver in England, as did Gosnold and Kendall and Archer. Mostly the worst speak first, assured to have the easy ear. The council sent its reports signed by all to London. The words not mine to unfold the tale.

After our meal and our farewells, we left.

The candles at Newport's table still glowed through the tobacco smoke, while beyond the ship's hull ten thousand years of night stretched in its blackening holocaust through the world.

AT DAWN ON MONDAY, THE TWENTY-SECOND OF JUNE, 1607, Newport's three ships cast off their anchors and began their long, lonely sortie home. Reverend Hunt blessed their passage and us all: "Faith is the iron of our flesh, goodness our resolve. Pass over us, oh time. Your moments will not find us wanting."

The full sheets of the sails now in place, the ships, in their diminishing race, passed under the sun, beyond the sunrise.

"We are alone to blasphemies and such our fears," said Captain Archer.

"And free to eat our fill of this," said Ratcliffe, his hand sweeping the air. He danced in circles, laughing. "It makes a man's loins quiver with plans...doesn't it, Smith?"

"Here climbs our desperation and there sails our extra food," I said, ignoring Ratcliffe.

"We still have the pinnace," said Kendall, half under his breath, watching me from the corner of his eyes.

We stumbled back to the fort. Most of the tents had collapsed, their fabric flapping about the dirt in a mild breeze, like the wings of a heavenly angel in the throes of death. Men dragged themselves, pushing forward, as if the air itself gave much resistance to their flesh. One or two fell. "What is this new ordeal?" asked Reverend Hunt. "Has the mind made murder of the soul, or is this some fresh disease?" Men walked to their spot of ground, sat in groans. Some buried their faces in their hands, crying. Foreheads began to sweat in fever. Some just lay back, rarely to move, their flesh becoming filth and another mound of earth. It was as if the vapors of despair had crushed our will and sickened our flesh.

Within a week most of the company lay in fevers. Each day more succumbed. They cluttered the open ground, clutching their bedding to themselves, embracing rags. Some, in hallucination, called for water or for lost loves. When the water from the wells turned to slime, we brought the half-salted water from the bay. We drank its brine. Tools rusted. Barrels of food yawned open to the air, to the rain, to inquisitive worms. We grew thin. Thomas Wotton, our surgeon, worked good deeds with potions; Reverend Hunt worked his own with words and kind intentions. The old mariner, caught in his own dilemmas, swore his help was death. After all those years, he was a man still salted in grief.

Healthy gentlemen still bowled and conversed with each other, or lay relaxed on the grass, the bright hues of their garments staining the earth. Mostly they ignored the dead. Wingfield never showed sickness, but grew fat. Men grumbled. Archer and Ratcliffe held to each other, plotting with those still not in delirium. I organized work parties, but, with sickness and privilege, little was done. Kendall whispered the dreams of mutiny in the ears of all who would listen: "We should flee. Wingfield would be king and have us vassals if he could."

Archer and Ratcliffe nodded and encouraged Kendall. They kept their own plans silent, while pushing Kendall to a frenzy.

Martin, when not sick, thought only of gold, even as his own son began to weaken into fevers. Gosnold, a friend to all, brought some unity; but he, too, was very ill. Only Reverend Hunt's counsel held the others to our disintegrating enterprise.

SEVEN DAYS AFTER NEWPORT'S DEPARTURE, OPECHANCANOUGH SENT a deer as present to us. His ambassadors bore it on their shoulders, and with them came words of peace. With our company so weakened by disease, so many of us ill, lying on the naked ground, and so little done to house ourselves, we feared to have our condition seen. We kept the emissaries from entering our fort, but with great ceremonies we welcomed their gift of food. Speeches done, the Pamunkeys asked of our ships and when they would return. So casual is the point brought to the throat. I said our ships were but south to seek our lost colony of Roanoke, and soon would be at our fort again. The Pamunkeys showed no concern, but played their words casually, as if a distant whim. We were told that Opechancanough and his Pamunkeys and the *werowances* of the Youghtanund and the Mattaponi were our friends, and would make peace between us and those who were our enemies: namely, the Weanocs, the Appomattocs, the Kiskiacks and the Quiyoughcohannocks. "Sow your fields without fear. If those who are your enemies make war upon you, we shall make war on them together."

I said to Wingfield, "We cannot discern one tribe from another. Opechancanough knows this. He is trying to involve us in one of his wars."

Wingfield didn't answer me, but gave the messengers all kinds of toys and trifles, which pleased them greatly. A week later Powhatan himself sent us the dressed meat of a buck, with words of peace and an inquiry as to the location of our ships.

"They fear our fleet and cannons. A blasted tree makes a great monument," said Reverend Hunt. Wingfield told the savages that our ships were still close and would be returning very soon.

Two days later, without a present of food to oil his good intention or veil his sneer, the *werowance* from across the waters of the James, the king of the Quiyoughcohannocks, sent his emissary to seek a parley with our president. Wingfield, always disposed to please, did consent, and so sailed our pinnace and a well-armed company to have their display, our president to have his interview. This *werowance* too asked again of our ships and the days until their return. Nothing was spoke to him that was not spoke in courtesies and lies to all.

And so it was that every few days we would receive questions from the *werowance*s and some gifts of deer or beaver or turkey, which we made great use of in our camp. We gave copper in return to encourage peace. A small trade developed. "They will be our Cimarrones. You shall see," said Reverend Hunt. In weights of copper, prices for the deer rose each day. Wingfield was over-generous, the savages understanding now our need for their food. Then in July all trading stopped. Our allotment of food came only from our common store or kettle. It was one boiled cup of wheat and a boiled cup of barley, our meal for an entire day. Mostly it was filled with worms and vermin, so it did move on the spoon and shiver on the tongue. Finally we just boiled it all into a stew with some fish or sickly game and tried to forget what we ate. I complained to Wingfield that our gentlemen were the cause of our empty stomachs. "We should hunt or fish, not laze in ease." Wingfield turned to me in angers.

The discussion ended, the old mariner saying to me, "We are a colony. Here, who works for one, works for all. Too much is general. There is no benefit. No motive yields no gain. The yield to profit is more discipline than the whip. Think on Drake."

- Our corn withered in the fields. Weeds strangled the earth where gardens should have bloomed. The tobacco was almost dead. Worms still crawled upon their dried flowers. Unpruned leaves ate each other's life. The plants shriveled into chaos. Even the savages would not walk near them. No smoke would ever rise from these to appease a savage god.

THE FEVERS OF OUR CREW INCREASED. MEN BEGAN TO BABBLE IN delirium, their eyes widening into internal night. In August the deaths began. We died in scores. Each night we dragged our dead from the fort, wrapped in the loose gowns of their bedding, to a small hill, where we, the dying, dug the graves for the dead. This ceremony only for the dark, so the savages could not see our loss.

The colony was now sucking death from its food and water. The sky turned gray like the ceiling of a jail. Archer wandered between the beds of the delirious making notes in a book. Rumors were heard of Wingfield cooking chickens in the woods, stealing food and asking privileges from the cape merchant, Thomas Studley, who guarded and dispensed our food from the common kettle, or sold it to those who had the rate, the moneys as profit to the London Company to pay their expenses. But most went into Studley's own pocket. And so, all the world stumbled from its path. Martin's son died suddenly. Martin, in his own delirium, cursed our prospects and swore vengeance on Wingfield, whom he blamed. I fell ill. Archer fell ill. Then Ratcliffe. We lay on our blankets, the screams like the calls of lost birds in our ears. Thomas Wotton tended me. Finally, his fears in war, the old mariner gave me potions.

The breeze sung in groans. I was weak, but recovering. Captain Gosnold was dying. There was no restraint. Wingfield and I argued in his tent. Sabers now rent the air before him in his fever. I asked Wingfield from where came all his extra food. Wingfield said from his private stock, and that I was no better than a beggar with a name so low. I swallowed his insults and waited for a better time to spit them back. I cared only that our enterprise succeed. I crawled to bring water to the sick. I nursed Ratcliffe in his fever. I wiped the sweat from his face. He looked at me and screamed, "God is flesh!" There was no hope. Then the savages brought us baskets of their strange harvest.

We had never seen green corn. Without tasting, we thought it poor, not knowing unripened corn was at its best. What heralds there were in those ears of grain. Our enterprise reprieved, but still there was death. Gosnold died. The whole company grieved. His greatness was his life. Emptiness brings no circumspect. Death shall not bribe me of complaint. Then Thomas Studley died. Then for a time, death no more. The savages brought us meat and berries and oysters, nuts by the basketful. We ate and began to regain our strength. There were only six healthy men in the entire company. Sixty-six had died; forty-one still alive.

Yet still the council fought over spoonfuls of beer and the last barrels of oil and aqua vitae. Wingfield wanted the council and a few sick favorites to have extra portions of food. Kendall and Martin accused Wingfield of withholding their daily allotment of meat and giving them bad corn. Ratcliffe spoke in private to Archer of having food distributed in proportion to social rank. Archer smiled his ambitions into poisons. There was no authority. No action was taken that was not reconsidered and set aside. Everyone intrigued against the other, and we all intrigued against Wingfield. The council was chained by pettiness and circumstance. We fought over scraps and the honor of dying last.

IT WAS THE LAST WEEK OF AUGUST 1607. EACH MORNING THE DAY would open the new sack of its heat upon us. The air was gray with water. Our clothes were heavy upon our backs, so thick their fabric hugged its wetness against our flesh. Our armor rusted against our chests. All movement was weight lacquered in a constant pain. Our landscape was despair. How low the horizon lay, the river a suspect in all the deaths. Causes are everywhere when cures are few. Reverend Hunt, who never had been ill, was whispered to hold the contagion that brought the disease. On our crossing only the ship on which he sailed suffered loss. Eyes in rumors, all sight upon our pinnace. Our enterprise now was rescue, the company whispered of abandoning the colony. A few, so despaired by hunger and the council's abuse, escaped into the woods to try the mercies of the savages. Kendall talked openly of rebellion and of abandoning the colony and of the sanctuaries of a friendly Spain. He was deposed from the council by Wingfield, who imprisoned him on the pinnace under orders never to return to the shore, except by permission, and then only under guard. Archer and Martin wavered, held by an ambition which bravery knew as greed. Wingfield, blessed by office, grieved for Gosnold but generally ignored the dead.

We who would save the world must ourselves be saved. Such confession is too much spleen. The stomach knows many a truth the eyes decline. In the nations many a crime is not a crime, but too much honesty.

IN EARLY SEPTEMBER RAIN WASHED ACROSS THE LAND. THE HEAT dispelled. A comfort now cooled upon our limbs. Those who had survived grew stronger. We had more food, but not enough. Nor war with the savages, yet even a small trade. A boy named Samuel Collier and a laborer, William White, who had run to find sanctuary with the savages in the woods, returned, and the moment had its joy. We all knew now the savages were not cannibals, and would by custom never permit a guest to starve or die by bloody murder. The council showed a mercy of its own and did not flog the two. But when four others who had deserted were brought back, each was tied to a tree, his back laid bare, flogged until the flesh was cut to such a depth the bones hung open in the wash of blood. The one punished by Ratcliffe died. The others, so broken by their ordeal, were never good for work again.

Reverend Hunt decried the punishment. "Free Englishmen in free association cannot be beaten like dogs! Not in England, not here! It is monstrous that we should forget."

The council took its pleasure in petty licenses. Even petty mutinies were flogged: a stare, a scowl, a chance remark, a joke that soured in our president's ear. Men were becoming beasts to men, and who knew the head that carried all the horns?

Samuel Collier told stories of idle savages at their ease all day, and at night, in their dances, raising howls to the moon. "Still, they lounge in their plenty while we starve," he said. "If the savages idle for their earthly reward, why should civilized Englishmen toil?"

It was a question that made even the savages' gifts of food seem a taunt. We angered at each other and cursed all charity.

"The lazy are always a rebellious lot," whispered the mariner in my ear. He wanted to say more, but I cautioned him and walked away.

Our justice sickened as our camp. We were on our own. The threads of English law could not stretch this far. They broke mid-ocean. Even Reverend Hunt couldn't contain the rot. His sermons still spoke compassion, but hysteria deafened the ears. The council nodded, but no longer heard the words and the dream of English sentiment. I mutinied with the rest.

ON SEPTEMBER 10, SECRETS COULD KEEP THEMSELVES NO MORE. Martin, Ratcliffe and I went to Wingfield's tent with a signed warrant and asked him to step down. He refused. His station was but title birthed in air, but we, by the powers granted us in our charter from the king, had the right. Our warrant spoke of Wingfield being unworthy as a president and as a council member, and so was discharged of both. I, who had held all these months his slanders down my throat so hard the rock of them had turned to pit, now rose on the spit of vengeance. Uncertain I stood, lost upon a failing hope. Martin had grieved his son's death into rebellion. Ratcliffe wanted the presidency. Archer was the puppet master, Ratcliffe on his string, he the jest ambition made.

Wingfield still refused. We assembled armed guards to have him yield by force. No riddle now, his medals could not thwart his circumstance. His power had passed. The colony convulsed on rumors and stood before his tent. Wingfield was given to an armed sergeant. There were shouts of anger as our company called for our president's blood. So released the tremor through our colony. "It seems I am at the mercy of your pleasure. Do as you will with no further noise," Wingfield hissed.

Martin asked Wingfield if he would ask the king to bring grievances against us. Wingfield refused to answer.

Ratcliffe threatened to hang him unless he did.

Wingfield said in his exhausted breath, "I am satisfied. I shall make no complaints."

Ratcliffe wanted the pledge in writing. After it was given, Wingfield was imprisoned on the pinnace with Kendall, much to our late president's pleasure, for so near the council he was in fear for his life.

Gosnold dead, Kendall and Wingfield deposed, Newport gone and well at sea, the council was now only three. Ratcliffe was chosen president, as was the plot. I on the council, the only chain around Ratcliffe's vices. Martin grieved and ill. Archer, who always acted as if he were on the council, — commanding authority from the air, posturing to him being more a fact than titles — was denied a seat, but made recorder for the colony. Ratcliffe and Martin passed a resolution that new council members could only be seated by unanimous vote. Archer was angered but kept a silent vengeance in his smiles.

Ratcliffe now charged me with all things abroad — the fort, its work. "It is your portion to command as you see fit," he said.

I organized the men anew. We began to set our tents, repair our fort walls, clean the rows of stale and withered corn. We tore out the tobacco stalks, which so crawled with worms one might think their dry leaves did heave in walking flesh. The few flowers that still survived peered towards us in surprise to be so consumed.

Our fort began to become a town. Our tents billowed in ordered rows. No houses yet were built, but our men were now drilled to the necessity of labor. Most would still idle in their stare and sit, not seeking their own relief. They complained and fought against the constraints, but with our meager supplies we ate. Always I took my own share last. My tent not set until the others done. My food the smallest portion. I would be the example for them all, differing from Ratcliffe and Martin and the others. My skin would be our Jamestown's second fort. Good deeds are safety only to the fool.

WINGFIELD WAS BROUGHT BEFORE THE COUNCIL AGAIN TO HEAR charges read to the entire company. His insolence so polished to offend. I asked Wingfield if he would prefer an armed guard to protect his life. He sneered as if talking to a bug. He would stand alone. Archer read the articles of mostly frivolous complaints. The whole story was lost upon the words. Archer spoke of slights and refusals to allot spoonfuls of beer, of having favorites, of taking extra food. It was an insult waged against insolence. And what of our disaster? Wingfield's true offenses were: no food grown, no houses built, no good well dug, and with that most of the company dead. Archer spoke of Wingfield plotting with the Spanish to destroy the colony. A strange accusation, I thought. Mostly it was a charge about how Archer himself was not well served. Sometime we accuse not from suspicions but from the prosecutions of an inner guilt, and so Archer spoke his vengeance in its slanders. I watched Archer spit regal to justify himself. After the articles were read, Wingfield grieved that we were not better born, then he was sent back to the safety of the pinnace before someone cut his throat. Kendall was released upon his pledge of a better conduct.

The next day Ratcliffe came to me, his face smudged with pasty sweat. "You shall now be in charge," he said, "of the gathering and apportioning of all our food. You are the new cape merchant with Studley dead." Ratcliffe smiled and asked me to follow. "Your men's respect will last only as long as the food." We walked to the tent that was our storehouse; mostly empty barrels overturned beneath a cloth. The smell of rot transfixed the air. I looked into a barrel drum, into the vermin porridge underneath its wooden lid, inspected the full of our supplies. "Eighteen days of food is all we have," I said to Ratcliffe. "At most," was his reply. "You were chosen to secure a miracle so you have your chance." Newport's arrival with fresh supplies was at least twelve weeks away, if he was not detained. Lord Percy suggested a month, but I thought not. When the company learned of our common plight, Archer and Ratcliffe had one of their minions propose they be appointed to sail the pinnace to England, or south to find a new supply of food. It was but a veil to hide the gesture and for them to escape the colony. I objected—"With the savages having their new harvest, let me make a trading voyage along the river." Martin agreed, believing all the rocks he had found around the camp or along the river were flecked with gold. And so for Martin the more we explored the deeper the mines of his expectations. Archer and Ratcliffe were overruled. Kendall smiled in whispers and held aloof in secret strategies.

And so I was to try my hand at trade. I put old Jonas in charge of preparing the newly built shallop for our journey. He said, "That bay already has the taste of us upon its tongue…and how are we going to explore down the belly? We don't even have proper sails."

"Make them," I ordered.

He made them from tents. "We'll lose a little here and there before the wind but they should do."

There were no maps nor much food, nor did we have much strength against the savages, but still seven of us climbed into that small boat. What was to be done? Fear behind as fearful as fear ahead. We passed beyond the sight of land, the day sunless, the waters gray like sour milk. Our wake turned. The water rolled, now resembling the back of a serpent. We found the far side of the river, the lands of the Quiyoughcohannocks. There, we spied a savage sitting under a tree and came ashore. He did not attempt to flee. He sat and watched us approach. We made signs of friendship which he returned. When we asked him of his people, he told us this strange story. Two children had died in his village and were mummified and buried. Shortly thereafter the children came to their parents in a dream saying, "Come and behold us. We are alive. . . ." The parents went to the place where the children lay and brought them forth from the earth and saw in their eyes the bright seeds of life. They called the whole village to come and witness of the miracle. They came and beheld the eyes. But there was no breath, no heartbeat, only eyes. They left the parents to those eyes and returned to their houses. Soon the parents and the entire village were dead but for this one savage, who sat under his tree, telling his story to all who passed.

We gave him trinkets and left him, sailing across the river. Further south we came to a small village. I went ashore. With a few of his court, their *werowance* approached. His face was painted blue. I made signs of friendship, my hands and wrists moving through the rags of my cuffs. I said that I had many magical trinkets to trade for corn. The *werowance* replied in sign saying that he would gladly trade—not for trinkets but for our pistols, firelocks and swords, for which he would give a handful of corn each. *He who cannot feed himself is a beggar. You clothe yourselves in the rags of your own dead. Take what is offered and be gone.* He sneered as his hands moved, lifting his chin, looking down along his cheek at me. I turned and walked away. I would be no beggar in Eden. I would not be insulted by a snake guarding his plenty. If there had to be one will to sculpt the face of this new earth, it would be mine. If I had to be a little Spanish to bring the savages into the English fold, so be it.

I reached my boat and ordered my men to take their weapons in hand and follow me. We charged up the hill, screaming like playful hounds to bluff a battle, running toward the *werowance*, who promptly turned in his terror and fled with all his court. We entered the village, the savages gone. There, avalanched in mountain piles, were corn and pumpkins and squashes and nuts. I told my hungry crew to touch nothing. "We are to trade, not steal. We want allies and unity in our enterprise. We want Cimarrones. Harm none, that we will not ourselves be harmed." Our mouths watering with memories of the food, we walked through the village, abstaining even from touching what was not ours to touch.

The bushes before the village now shook, as if some beast were sharpening its horns. Howls rose skyward in the wind. We stood in wait, and loaded pistol shot into our firelocks' mouths. Some of the small trees bent and broke as savages in squares of military order advanced. "What savages are schooled to fight in civilized rank?" said one of our company.

Jonas Profit looked at me. "Remember that Don Luis, the savage educated by Spaniards whose story I have told?"

The savages came screaming in their ordered march, their faces painted; bows and arrows, swords and clubs; shields brandished in all threat. Before them on a platform came their idol, sculpted from wood and moss, covered with the skins of animals and the claws of birds, dressed with beads and pearls and pieces of copper. Four savages carried it like a hideous cross.

"Aim above their heads. We don't want massacre, we want friends. Practice power only with restraint," I said calmly.

Our ranks fired a volley of smoke so dense the sound of its report was almost smothered — fighting to break free, it boiled through its own cloud toward thunder. The smoke trailed away. Many savages ran toward the forest, while others crawled on the ground shaking in their fear. Their abandoned idol lay on its side. We walked toward it, straightened it, smoothed and ordered its heathen works. Its eyes stared back at us, its mouth smiling, as if at some old friend.

We stood watching the field for signs of what would come—seven of us, alone, like the single point which marks the circle's depth. I felt huge in my circumstance, the point on which the compass wheels. I stood, drinking air in gulps. Soon, one of their devil priests came from the wood, giving signs of friendship. We made signs to him to approach, which he did, asking now for peace and the return of their idol, Okee, their rude god of mischief. The idol stood at my feet, contemptuous of all, except his conception of himself: his hair made of moss, his ears the curio and claws of other skins. His appointments were pearls of the sea and the copper of the earth. He sat now dead on the ground in thought, smiling.

The savages wanted him. "I shall return your Okee," I said, "and I shall give you friendship, besides beads and copper and hatchets, if you will give us corn and venison and turkey and other foods. We want your friendship and we want to trade."

The devil priest made signs of agreement. The woods filled with the songs of some savage dance. Our shallop was loaded with sixteen bushels of corn and much meat as well as nuts and oysters. The savages now danced about us. They spread tobacco on the ground in circles and they thanked the sun for all life. We left them friends and well pleased with our encounter. None was killed and none abused.

WE SAILED AGAIN ALONG THE BAY AND DISCOVERED THE TOWN called Warraskoyack, where the savages, thinking us in famine, would give us nothing but contempt and little for our weapons. I treated the *werowance* with my own disdain. The children in the town were so pleasant and pretty that I gave them toys for nothing, as a kindness, and returned to our boat. There we decided to spend the night, riding like a fallen leaf on the flowing bay. That night a savage named Amoris swam to us. He said that he was our friend, and not to be fooled. His people wanted to trade. I gave him copper as a kindly gesture, and then he disappeared through the moonlit waters and was gone.

The next morning I went ashore, but before I touched the beach the whole town was by my side with baskets of corn and nuts, each with hands in imploring signs, *Come and trade with me*. Trading we did. So much food was gathered to our boat that it would suffice the needs of Jamestown for a month.

I wandered on the land to judge its wealth, and there, in a small clearing, was Amoris, his head lying upon a rock, his skull so fractured it had no shape but wreck, the bit of copper I had given him sewn to his mouth. Next to him was another body, I knew not whose, but some nameless friend to us, I guessed.

"This land is not subtle in its angers," I thought, "nor easy in its absolutions." I knelt by the bodies, but I could make no prayer. I was becoming some other Drake.

Our boat filled, we sailed. "I can feel the land's jaws on these waters," said the old mariner, his hand on the tiller. "The shadows of the currents have a nervous edge." The old man's back stiffened in his rags, straightened as if it set itself hard against some invisible rest. "We should find Mandinga's children," he advised, "and we all can coax this land back into its ease."

Chapter Twenty-three

TREASON FLOATS ON PROMISES AND FAIR TOMORROWS. I ADVENTURE FOR FOOD AND THE WESTERN SEA.

T THE Jamestown beach, gangs of our fellows walked along the fort walls, calling to the air in gestures of confusion and disbelief. Some stood in groups. Others sat alone or talked in pairs. All stared toward the pinnace, which floated like abandoned suds offshore. We landed our shallop.

"Kendall and Wingfield and their disloyal few have seized the pinnace and are to quit this enterprise and sail for England." Lord Percy, brother to the Earl of Northumberland, spoke, nervous in his uncertain stare.

"Where is Ratcliffe?" I asked, leaping to the shore.

"He is taking council with Martin. Archer is whispering we all should leave and many do agree."

I called to Anas Todkill and the others I knew to be loyal to follow me into the fort. *Why not, I have brought them food. Without me they all would starve*, I thought. An idea to bribe faith and action. We walked to the cannons. "Load them all," I said, "and tell the others to get firelocks."

"What of Ratcliffe? Certainly he should be informed of your doings?" asked Percy.

"All things abroad are in my command. If you, my lord, wish to inform our president, you may have the honor." Then I turned.

The cannons loaded, I brought six gentlemen with their firelocks and forked rests to the edge of the beach, saying. "Plant your rests and point your weapons toward the pinnace." Then I walked to the edge of the water and called, "Wingfield, Kendall! Bring your company to the beach or I shall sink you where you sit." With that I ordered a cannon fired. Its smoke broke in clouds over the land. A plume of water rose in momentary geyser near the pinnace's bow. Kendall appeared at the ship's rail. "I am not in fear of he who was a beggar among the Turks," he called back. Others joined him at the rail. I saw Wingfield.

I had our firelocks volleyed to strike the water about the hull. Our shots fell in scatters on the river. Kendall disappeared from the rail. I ordered another cannon fired. It broke in fiery lance across the sweep. "Come ashore, or next it will be your lives," I called. A white flag now waved above the pinnace's rail. Wingfield came ashore. "Why such war when all we did was stand in wait of the council's decision to sail or not?" he said, smiling his double strategies through his teeth. "I have offered a hundred pounds of my own to pay for all to abandon this curse and tomb of a place, or to sail with Ratcliffe and Captain Archer to acquaint the London Company with our plight. I stood in obedience to our council's will." Archer and Ratcliffe now approached and agreed they had thought on adventuring some to find us aid. "England...or somewhere south," Archer said. And so, nothing came to nothing. Martin still held to have the colony stand its place, but Martin was ill. Ever his lunatic to have his gold, he set a weakened keep. I alone was the first that gave us resolution.

OUR ENTERPRISE WAS STILL INTACT. MY LIFE WAS STILL FOUNDED in its mission. We unloaded the victuals we had in trade from the savages. Archer and Ratcliffe plotted vengeance on my name. Some have condemned me for refusing to wisely yield the ground, but you cannot understand the adventure unless you understand the dream.

Even in my day's absence, all things had gone adrift. Not a twig was thatched, not a board was nailed to build any house. The company sat and complained, which was for them the same as planting food, or having shelter against the rain. This crew, without my will, would, for their own devices, talk themselves in pleasures to their deaths. How obstinate they were, to remain in helpless rest. With good example and marshaled threats, I chained them to our colony.

Ratcliffe, like Wingfield before him, all too ready to be our common law, to author all conceits and to father pleasures and intrigues, mostly stayed to his tent. When he went abroad, he had men whipped for small infractions of the peace. Mostly it gave him pleasure to exercise the hollows of his will. Power is the one phantom privilege that can manifest on earth. Martin weakened. In desperation, our surgeon, Thomas Wotton, made plasters and waters from tobacco to have a cure. "The French have always used the leaf as a medicine," he said, "with some good effect."

The old mariner objected, saying, "I've learned from my cruel history tobacco has no cure." Wotton smiled and disagreed. Medicine warred with itself, but Wotton had his way. "Belief held long enough soon seems the truth, no matter how many skeletons rise in contradiction," replied the mariner as he walked away.

Martin seemed better without the salve, but he swore it gave relief, so Wotton sat by his bed, pressing ground tobacco on his back until the stain would have you think that half of Martin's flesh had risen from the same mud as his foolish gold.

FOR SAFETY IN HIS DISGRACE, WINGFIELD STAYED TO THE PINNACE, except when summoned. A small group of the company was with me, besides Anas Todkill and the ever-loyal Michael Fettiplace, born of an old Norman family. For weeks we worked while others complained. "An English gentleman is provided food by his officers. That is the law upon which we agreed. So go, crawl, provide," they would taunt me, I having power, they having rank. They laughed as they ate double shares, as Ratcliffe smiled and approved.

I worked and hoped, by will and by sweat, to bleed my life into this enterprise. Ratcliffe sat in his tent, stared and talked of mutinies and the savage women. "Here is all authority on my fingertip," he told me in his cabin. "Watch it point. It carries daggers in its sweat." Ratcliffe never went so far from the fort but that the crack of a twig would send him to our walls in a run. He started carrying a bag of beads and some copper with him at all times, hoping that if caught by the savages in *ambushado*, he could buy his life.

With only fourteen days' food on hand, the pinnace still not fully rigged or provisioned, Ratcliffe and Archer assembled the company and told us of their plan to sail it to England for relief. "Most of the store of food will go with us, and all things that provide our needs," said Ratcliffe. "But we will return many times what we take." I saw our enterprise hatching dust if this were allowed. Cowards make themselves their only cause. This rescue was for the few that sailed.

Martin, who was still ill and could hardly make the trip, boomed objection. I agreed. The company stood, its knees wading deep in revolt, knowing this was a charity to bring their deaths. I stood unyielding, marshaling the rest. "It is a better use of the pinnace to send it in commerce to Powhatan," called Todkill. "Our only salvation is in trade. Send Smith to deal with the savages. He's brought us corn and victuals before." The company cheered.

"Didn't Archer want to desert this enterprise before we ever saw this coast?" I said, telling all the tale. "That day, lost at sea, Archer panicked and begged Newport to turn about. No cur ever had a longer tail between his legs than Archer. The next day we heralded land." The company laughed. Archer and Ratcliffe would not have their way.

IN OCTOBER I SAILED NORTH WITH A CREW OF SIX, LANDING AT the village of the Paspaheghs. We were hailed by their chief in signs of friendship, but Wowinchopunk's acts made devices of his words. We traded, loading twelve bushels of corn into our boat. The savages were always close, always near our weapons, their eyes in hunger for our firelocks, their hands tentative to touch their lethal edge. And so the savages. They made their plots and small diversions as a ruse, so we would let our weapons lie unguarded, to be stolen from our sides. Seeing this betrayal in their spirit, our trading done, I took my men and boat offshore for safety. Their plans to seize our weapons at an end, they called from the shore, pleading for more trade. Now in the current of the river, we ignored their howls. We passed along the riverbank, the coming night having shadowed the air to darkness, the shore swift behind us in its silhouettes and voices, all distant in their echoes.

We sailed on to Jamestown, where the twelve bushels of corn

were received with scowls and disappointment. "Only twelve?" said Archer. "Hardly a feast for all our efforts." I told the council of the Paspaheghs' treachery. But those savages being close, and well supplied with corn, Martin was sent again to trade with them. Todkill was sent along as advisor and as an anchor to all recklessness. Two journeys Martin made, bringing back eight to ten bushels each time, plus quantities of yellow dirt, which Martin swore was gold. The hoard was hid in Martin's cabin, I am told, where he examined the piles on his desk all day and by candle all night. His hope gone maniac, his mind could not turn the page to see the story's other side. Some say he carried a pouch of his foolish gold around his neck. To me it was common dirt which the earth, in its humor, had made yellow to provoke the fantasy of men. The corn Martin brought sustained us while Jonas Profit readied the pinnace for a longer trading voyage to Powhatan, which the company had agreed would be our salvation. Behind that word, in all our desperation there moved a passion transfixed in its urgent call, the image of that savage girl, that daughter of Powhatan.

With winter close, Newport was not expected for at least two months. It was November. In the days before my departure the sky began to fill with geese and ducks and swans and all manner of water birds. They floated down upon the bay in the swirls of a feathered cloak. It was as if the earth, in its autumn hush, had clothed itself in life against the winter cold. We hunted them in boats, or standing on the shore, firing our weapons into the clouds of those passing flocks, so thick with numbers we did not aim, not marksmen enough for a single kill. But we knew our shot could not penetrate that shadowed mass without at least one hit.

We piled our kill upon the beach so high they were to our waists. We filled our boats. We cried for joy. One fellow dove into the water from a boat to grab a wounded duck. He wore his heavy clothes in ruffled weights, which drank the bay to fill his second skin. His clothes so overfilled, he began to sink. Holding the wounded duck above his head, screaming to take the food, he drowned. Such loyals we are to the passing lunacies of our pleasures. We ate until our fill belched forth peace and throttled, for the moment, any thought of mutiny.

.   .   .   .   .

"COLD WIND BRINGS FAIR DESTINIES," TODKILL SAID TO ME ONE day, eating the shattered wing of some bird.

"The worm in his bed never sleeps," answered the old mariner.

The darkness of another's darkness we can never taste. Ratcliffe paced the fort, encaged. Archer, the master of the prompt, sovereigned in his whispers behind the throne. Ratcliffe was a vapor seeking substance to be a fool. Food scarce. The ducks now fled. The company in fear, their tempers ran hot. All protocol devised to whims and slants of violence. James Read, our blacksmith, at his forge ironed in hammer falls the small metal chisels we used for trade. Ratcliffe, seeing him at rest to ease his back, called him lazy and unworthy of his food. Words rushed fast to gorge the space where the anger fills. Ratcliffe offered to strike the man. Read in defense raised his hands, a violence more in gesture than in fact. But Ratcliffe, as president, held himself as king. Read ordered before a jury to be tried for mutiny and for his life. The judgment passed, Read was to be hung. A ladder set beneath the thick branch of a tree, a rope there tied, its noose waiting in an empty swing. Read must have thought some rescue close; he climbed the ladder, insolent in his contempt of Ratcliffe and his court. No words came from the assembled company. Read's eyes now searched in fear, his disposition changed. "I know of mutinies and plots," he screamed. "I wish to speak alone to our president." Ratcliffe took the man aside and heard that Kendall was a traitor and a spy who planned to steal the pinnace and sail to Spain to inform them of our colony.

Kendall before a jury admitted all, bragged of his plots and gloried in our suffering, his own arrogance the sentence upon him. What is it in a cause that men do think their death no death? Few ideas survive the conceiving skull. Read was spared. Kendall could have easily denied it all and saved his life. For Sandys' sake, I argued mercy for his cousin. Myself in warring parts, my loyalties to me in all my humane self-portraits, and the memory of the Willoughby's and our friend, but Kendall was a danger to this enterprise. I swallowed caution, vented conscience, perhaps for some better good. But the burn still wounds to the deeper meat.

We tied him to a tree and shot him, as befitted a gentleman. His head broke in splinters from its mold. We buried him in a sack. His life is blanked to ghost my mind. Remorse no resurrection, regret no salve, but still he would have betrayed. Let furies bathe in their wars, their kisses lunatic in the shadows of love and hate. I wanted him dead, I wanted him saved. I war in violence upon myself. I am the counter-clock, I tick against the grain. Never shall I follow that path that discretions to the grave.

CONFUSED AND NERVOUS FROM ALL THE TALK OF MUTINY, RATCLIFFE and Archer's one desire was to abandon the colony and seek safety on the sea, but I was the dam to that. Ratcliffe ordered me to make discoveries along the Chickahominy, a river we had seen on our first sail six miles north on the James. "Have our Smith explore to its source, so far he may be lost, or have some sweet *ambushado* take away his life," Archer whispered to Ratcliffe.

Sour, in a grayish blush, Ratcliffe said to me, "Trade food along that flood, make maps, bring us geographies." It was a lure, with it a squander of an excuse. I was being sent to die. I understood the murder behind their plan.

The pinnace ready, I sailed my shallop north; the pinnace was to follow the next day, if she ever sailed. Our intent was to meet Martin where the Chickahominy flowed its currents wide into the James. The day in its decline, the river yawned and broke, divided in its course, and the sun did set its reflections in a double tongue—two suns rolling in a single coin. Are we not the same? What liberty comes by the flogging post? What freedom comes by slaveries? The contradictions, and yet we execute our will in a divided course. Rude winds do sweep the plaintive leaves. Can ghosts cleave their spirits into twins? Am I the soul that seals the gap? A bird, no matter how high its flight, is still no measure of the beast. Should our enterprise be forgot? I would have rather died, having mysteries as my nameless epitaphs.

At dusk we reached the village of the Paspaheghs. We anchored, keeping offshore for safety. I was in the center of the confluence. A group of savages approached the beach, calling to us, asking our purposes. I told them I was sailing north to discover the lands of a great people, the Chickahominy, of whom I'd heard. One of the savages said he was of that people and would gladly guide us. I told him to come and join our crew, and so he swam to us. On the shore the Paspaheghs angered. They howled and chanted sounds that groomed contagions in the night. What I did not know was that the Chickahominy were a nation independent of Powhatan, ruled by a council, not a king, and always jealous of their freedom. Peace to them had become an uneasy sovereign. The Paspaheghs feared that a Chickahominy alliance could have them between two enemies. As we pulled our anchor from its throat, our guide threw tobacco upon the water as a sacrifice. It floated across the dark blood of the river, through the waves of moonlight upon the folds of the current, passing southward toward the sea.

For three hours we sailed north, the boat groaning as the river's rush swelled against its side. The race of water still wide. Ahead of us lights floated, rising and falling on the darkness, as if a spirit had made campfires in the air. We sailed toward them, the fire casting shadows and streaks of light across the plains of water. We came closer. The darkness glistened diamonds. The earth birthed stars. There were savages on the river in many canoes with fires set on logs that hung over their bows. Above the fires savages held spears, watching through the river's course for fish, attracted to the light. We saw them plunge their spears many times into the water, only to raise them swiftly again, wiggling with sturgeon, trout and bass, and of many fish for which we had no names.

The Chickahominy turned at our coming. Our guide hailed them. They followed, laboring upon their oars. They pushed their canoes into our wash, our trail now set in fires. I watched them, feeling here I was truly the law to all light. For me to only speak its name would bring the birth of a nightly sun.

These are the Chickahominy, my people, signed our guide. *We are close.*

Some in the boat lit the tapers of their firelocks. I smiled. I saw little chance of war that night. We arrived at the village, a circular stockade with twenty or so cabins, or wigwams, as they were called, protected by its log walls.

We thanked our guide, giving him many gifts, and walked with him ashore. One of the *werowances* of the Chickahominy met us, along with a priest who wore a shirt which completely draped one of his arms and shoulders. With his exposed arm, he spread tobacco on the land and chanted praises to Okee for our safe arrival. We did not smoke the ceremonial pipe that night. The *werowance* asked if I would like to be kindly entertained as his guest in his village that night. I said I could not leave my crew, who would follow after me, so great was their love and loyalty. *All of us would be too great a burden but perhaps one of mine could go in my stead.* I looked at our small company and said, half in jest, "Who would like to feast his braveries on entertainments of our friends?" Todkill stood and said that he would try the pleasures of such diversions. Before he left I told the *werowance* that, as a kindness to himself, I would similarly entertain one of his sons on our boat that night. "Fair hostages bring good morrows," I whispered to Todkill. The *werowance* understood the bargain. His son accepted our invitation. So with guests exchanged, we gave such entertainments we could, then we pulled our blankets to our chins and slept, our eyes half-closed, vigilant until the dawn.

When the sun gave hints of upward float and the darkness had turned to gray, there were in the village cries and chants and the sounds of running feet. We all now stood in our boat, our eyes still glued in sleep, the tapers of our firelocks lit. There, down the slope of the beach, rushed the entire village — men and women and children, even babes in arms — all naked in the autumn cold, without modesty, in a jumbled mass. They came to the water's edge and entered, sending the water in geysers with their hands. They jumped and dove and swam, washing water upon themselves in delights and cries. I groaned in my mind to think of the cold; we, who wash only once a year at most. It was a horror to see even savages drown and lose the natural oils of their skin in such an unhealthy and wanton sport.

Their bathing done, the savages ran up the hill to the village, the girls in their slim and naked flesh. How in water bejeweled. How in wetness they glowed. It was a test. I knew it was a test by some darker heathen will, to excite the savages to this sport; to excite me from my enterprise; to seduce me from my destiny. "I am the seed from which all history springs," I thought. "I must be more protective of myself, more selfless, strangle desires in the mind. There is no immortality for the weak. There are no praises for the lost."

When the eye of the sun appeared full above the horizon, the *werowance* came to the boat with Todkill. Todkill said little of the night except that he was kindly treated and well fed. There may have been some hiding of wantonness in his silence, but I never fully asked and he never fully said. While Todkill was a good friend, he was no forge of destiny, no Smith of history. So if he took some pleasures, there would be restraint and little harm.

We followed the *werowance* to the village. There, we traded to our content. I took in moderation, and always in good value to both sides. Pleasure there is in a commerce that gives each an equal portion. I traded with all, not letting the savages know our true want, or our famished state. Thus, I took less than our need, but so holding prices down and keeping our secret safe.

We left all in fair spirit and headed north again, coming upon many villages with eager and friendly savages. Many towns I discovered on that river of the Chickahominy: Oroniocke, Mansa, Apokant. All geographies are but profiles of a face. All Europe the red lips of Charatza, her arms of grass, her fires the warm light of suns. I searched the pastures through to grasp the phantoms of her embrace. And in this new land we are called by London to seek upon the thighs of waters for a western sea. All continents diminished to a glance. The distance to the Pacific not well known. A river might, by its gentle tongue, lead us west to a lake, a marsh, a further bay, a brief passage to that foreign sea. The dimension of the world slighted to a hope, but within that hope a path to China and so to fame.

The most beautiful village was Manosquosick, a quarter of a mile from the river on a high plate of land, containing forty or fifty houses surrounded by a stockade. On one side of the town was a great wood, watered by many streams which passed around the settlement only to fall in great showers over the side of the cliffs toward the river. On our approach, the town seemed to float above the cataracts as if supported in the rising smoke of a watery flame.

The largest village was Mamanahunt. There we traded with two hundred savages, filling our shallop in such a time that I could have loaded a ship with what I could not take. Our boat now filled, we sailed south, back toward Jamestown. Canoes followed us in fleets, savages begging to trade. I took all I could while I wondered, where was the pinnace? The fear of sinking was in my mind, so great was the plenty. So much we could have had if the pinnace only came.

We traveled on, hoping around each river bend or riverbank to see the pinnace's sail. There was none. The only whiteness on the river was clouds and they blew across our paths like crafts of fancy. All the way back to Jamestown we came upon nothing. Finally, on a beach not fifty yards from our fort, we saw the pinnace floating, her bow stuck on some sandy spit. "Well caught, I would say," came the voice of Todkill. "It is all a device…a device," was all I said.

· · · · · ·

NEAR OUR FORT, MARTIN AND OTHER GENTLEMEN WERE DIGGING in the riverbank, searching piles of mud in their sweat for gold. The tents of our village lay unfurled, benches sat mostly idle, guard posts abandoned, the pinnace left alone to ride on the lonely waters, gray with the reflection of the clouds, while on the riverbanks gentlemen soiled their clothes with streaks of dirt and their foreheads with thoughts of gold.

As we landed, those not searching for the metal rushed to our boat. The others followed with broadening grins. They all helped us unload the six hogsheads of corn. They gave me praise. The corn was carried to our common store. Ratcliffe came, seeing the bounty and hearing of my esteem among the company.

"And you did not find the source of the Chickahominy...if I am to understand," Ratcliffe said. Threats around him empowered the air. He would send me far to send me to my death, but I would boldly dance upon the rack to have a chance at a better name.

"I did not have the pinnace to offload my corn," I replied. This was no game to be lightly played. Ratcliffe and Archer wanted me dead so they could abandon the colony. I wanted the Pacific and its fame. My explorations would be a hard vise upon their throats. My words moved in reputation. One risk for all, my life in counterweight.

"We do not ask for excuses; nor are we bought with food and petty meats from a favorable commerce with savages. We ask you to fulfill that which is your duty." Then Ratcliffe turned and addressed the entire company. "There are many ways to rebellion, but this is the first I have seen paved with food. Insolence may make a better cowardice to some, but not to me." With that said, he left, pushing his way through the crowd, throwing some of the more sickly aside with such force they fell.

I rushed to Ratcliffe's back and pulled his shoulder so he spun about. I grabbed his throat. I stood above those he cast aside and said, "What of you there is, is but for you. I beat you once to save this colony"—I held my fist against his face—"this time for the pleasure of it." The men cheered.

"Do it!" called a voice. "We'll set the dogs to lick his blood."

Ratcliffe pulled himself free and said, "The council will meet in an hour."

.   .   .   .   .

The Fires of the Hunter 277

THE COMPANY ASSEMBLED. A TABLE WAS BROUGHT TO THE OPEN air. Behind it three chairs were set. Ratcliffe, a sickly Martin and I took our places. Archer then stepped forward and asked to be made a member of the council. Ratcliffe stood and said there were other matters which would bear on the proposal, so, for the moment, he asked Archer to be seated. Ratcliffe spoke again, saying now that the company was better supplied with corn, it would be a prudent gesture toward our enterprise for Archer and him and a small crew to sail the pinnace for England. "We will take in stores only what wisdom would call necessity, leaving the rest for you."

"Your demons sing fair homilies," laughed Jonas Profit, "but it is the only song they know."

Martin stood, thundering objection. "We are so close to the discovery of gold," he screamed, "all our efforts should be turned to that. We have food now. Newport will arrive. For me, I would tear the riverbank with my teeth, so sure I am that wealth is at our hand."

Famine's ghost, its toothless smile all about. I spoke then to the crew. "The food we have is not enough by half. We need the pinnace. We must trade while the savages are well supplied. We must harvest now, for soon the winter will be upon us."

Ratcliffe was in a rage. "Captain Smith does not need the pinnace. He has failed to map the source of the Chickahominy River, which I intend he find. Smith will take our shallow-drafted barge now newly built and complete his mission. Then we will talk of the pinnace and more trade."

There was then a general argument that fouled the day. Ratcliffe was so called down that he leveled his intent, tabling his plan for England. Those who wanted expeditions to find gold served their silly cause well, and in the end went back to digging with promises of future consideration. I was to make one last journey for trade, and after my return was to reembark and voyage on the Chickahominy to its source.

Chapter Twenty-four

THE FOREST BURNS. MURDERS IN THE WOODS.
A COMPASS BRIBES A FATE.

 SAILED AGAIN to Mamanahunt, where two hundred savages had gathered with hundreds of baskets of corn. I traded, filling the barge to its full. Toward the end of the third day, I saw the savages had little more to trade and less desire. As I prepared our barge for its return, the *werowance* came to me and requested that we fire one of our pieces, which they had seen us do each day in our hunt for waterfowl. As a gesture of friendship and of wise display, I had one fired. Its flash smoked lightnings across the smooth waters of the river, so smooth, those waters, that the burn and mist could not be told from its reflection. A few savages threw themselves into the river, some in fear and some to drink in breath the remaining power of our smoke.

When at Jamestown once again we unloaded our corn, yet few gentlemen acknowledged my return.

"Let savages truck with savages," said Ratcliffe. "It is a poor diversion until gentlemen decide to have their way." He looked at me and smiled. "Tomorrow, try your insolence on the Chickahominy."

I looked at Ratcliffe and thought, *If a map they want, I am the map. What geographies my blood! That river's source I shall bring them upon a page, even if I need die. And all those western oceans I shall hand them in a cup.*

Nine men were chosen to sail with me on the barge, among them Jehu Robinson a gentleman well disposed and allied to me in my struggle with Wingfield; Thomas Emry, one of our carpenters; George Cassen, a laborer not much for work, but whose ear was ever for adventure, even when his mind was blank.

Before I left, Jonas Profit, who was to stay behind and attend to the pinnace, came to me and said, "Remember the tale of Don Luis. He may be still about."

"And so to destiny…we shall see," I said as I ordered the barge.

This our fort, shallow its draft, its broad beam, its square corners longer than it was wide, the flat roof of a small central cabin with a single sail. With poles and oars we took again the river's bite.

"Shall we throw tobacco upon the water as a sacrifice for a fair voyage, as the savages?" laughed George Cassen, ever giddy to move, the surface flow enough direction to make him drunk.

"The shadow of each god casts demons into the world," called Profit. "Beware. This the savages know. It is their Okee."

FOR MILES OF OUR SAIL THE SKY BOILED IN GRAY CONVULSIONS. The air seemed angered and turmoiled, and yet no rain. The land swelled with hills rolling to the riverbanks. How vast the expanse, now thick with low marshes. The landscape gloomed to weeds. The water turned to a muddy ooze. Grass, in brown wands, hissed in the wind's drying breath. We stayed to the deep channels. The river divided. We followed the Chickahominy north. Birds rose at our passage, quacking annoyance as they fled. We hunted duck and kept ourselves well fed.

The land became steeper. We saw towns on the roll of hills, as sloping cornfields rushed towards the river's bank. Black sand and red cliffs, canyons of yellow clay and white rock. After miles we passed among a place of many bare islands, lying like overturned plates upon the water's run. I watched them pass. The highest point of land in that place was called Apokant. On its hills a small village. We sailed it by. The river narrowed and angered, flowing swiftly against the bow. With oars and ropes we fought its will. The land now low in sandy plain, pressed upon us, strangling our passage. I would not yield to any beast of sand. We labored until a great tree, like a gnarled and ancient finger, blocked our path. From bank to bank it had fallen across the river. We pulled our barge to its edge, roped ourselves in place, and with an ax I hacked at its bark and wood. Its inner flesh was the whitest I had ever seen. It seemed of bone. I hacked and cleaved it in two, but when it fell, it still blocked our path. We decided to return to Apokant and hire a canoe.

We arrived at Apokant, anchored in the bay, then ate and watched what night we could. The north sky glowed a dismal red, as if, now that the sun had fled, the darkness itself seemed to birth a distant fire.

"Some great blaze," said George Cassen, "now bloods the sky."

The air smelled of ash. "It is natural for these woods to sometimes blaze," said Jehu Robinson. We thought little of it. We slept.

AT DAWN, AFTER THE SUN HAD RISEN THROUGH THE SMOKE, I WENT ashore. The savages seemed kindly. They moved about me, staring. One danced before me, as if he were a holy man. What supplications come by tint? Do they think me to be a priest? Small I am, in giants do I walk. They spread circles of tobacco on the earth and chanted to their Okee. We passed a pipe and let our mouths breathe our spirits to the whiteness of the wind.

We made some small trades. Then I hired a canoe and two guides. Returning to the barge, we anchored offshore, the river to act as a natural moat. No dangerous shots of arrows would reach her there. I told the company that they were to stay aboard and not to go ashore for any reason or by any summons.

"Friendship here," I said, "mutinies at the slightest breath. Be on guard."

George Cassen said, "A small walk on shore cannot be any harm. I shall stay to the beach and well in sight."

"Stay to the barge," I said again. "What is by common done is not always wise."

I chose Thomas Emry and Jehu Robinson to accompany me north. I thought our three against their two fair odds. I kept my French pistol loose in my belt and well to hand. We traveled upriver again, the savages at their paddles, their faces painted on one side red, on the other black; half their mouths in shadowed hues, the ridge of their noses the dividing line. Their bodies were covered with a yellow oil, which was a mixture of an herb called poccoon and bear grease. It was said to keep them free of lice and fleas and other vermin.

Not ten minutes after we were gone from the barge than George Cassen decided to row a small boat to a sandy beach and wander by himself to enjoy the trees. His pleasures sang to him for what? So slight to his own consequences, and he so warned, his head so filled with emptiness. In a glade he met twenty savages who saw our barge and saw me leave by canoe, and wondered where I did go? Cassen said he would not tell. Arguments and scuffles, orders and angry words. Cassen seized and tied to a tree. Sharp mussel shells and dried weeds cut wounds as swords on naked flesh. Cassen screamed, tormented, his fingers torn by amputation from his hands. Blood came in torrents on the grass. His toes hacked from his feet. Choking, he told my plans, swallowing on his agonies. My direction was up the river to find its source. Signs of weakness intoxicate the already frenzied mind. Cassen's cries brought not peace but wild unrestraint. A fire was lit. Cassen watched his pieces die by flames. The savages cut away his scalp and threw it in the blaze. His face severed from its flesh, his neck carved down in strips. Living, he watched his flesh broiled into flames. They skinned him to a howling meat, no form but a silhouette in human blood. His stomach open, his intestines hanging to his feet. Soon the savages tired of their sport, set the tree alight, a shadow blazing in the rising avalanche of flames. The savages danced their victory until he was a smoking wreck. Then they sent two runners north.

All this I did not know. The six on the barge, hearing Cassen's screams, panicked and sailed south to find some safety, making Jamestown in a day, abandoning the three of us to whatever was our fate.

IN A FEW HOURS WE HAD PASSED ALONG THE RIVER'S NARROWING race. The great tree I had hacked in two we left behind, and the river closed to a strangling space, its torrents swift, the bottom of the channel hard with stone. The trees held their branches across our path. Twigs, unbloomed like predatory claws, tore our clothes. The forest had turned hunter and willful with its brood. I guessed that we were near the river's source. Some lake, I thought, some wide majesty of water, with flights of birds rising in broad tiaras across its sweep.

We pulled the canoe ashore. I would go ahead with one savage, so sure I was our goal was at hand. I told Emry and Robinson to light their tapers and keep their firelocks close. They sat on the ground, their heads laid against the shell of the canoe, as if to sleep. I told them to be on guard. They did not rise, but bade me fair journey. Emry joked about strewing tobacco before my path. "Such a flower shall be the leaf before your procession...like a Roman conqueror. Your advance guard shall be naked savages," he taunted. "Your rear guard shall be of corn." Robinson laughed. I did not smile. "Fire your weapons if you need me. I shall be close." I ordered the savage to follow me. We moved into the forest. I looked behind. Soon I could see nothing.

I wanted the source of that river. I wanted oceans. I was desperate and I was brave beyond wise counsel. The savage seemed friendly, my purpose close. I smelled smoke in the air. Victories are not left to whim, only monuments survive. I wanted the maps of my discovery to sculpt my fame.

We pushed through a tangle of vines and tall grass, my savage and I. The land, a quagmire, oozed in water, bubbling in the breath of unseen things. We walked carefully, feeling for hard ground. Behind me in the distance was a human cry, but no weapons fired. I looked back along our trail. I saw nothing. I looked at the savage, whose face was now twisted in terror beneath the mask of paint. I grabbed his arm, put my pistol to his head. He told me to flee and hide. *Let the shadows be your cloak*, he said. I tied his hands behind his back, then roped his hands to my belt. I pushed him forward. He was pleading with me to run. I wondered if the price of his freedom would be my betrayal. An arrow cut through the ruffled balloon of my pants at the thigh. It did no hurt. Two more arrows fell around me. I turned. At the edge of the clearing where the noonday sun frosted the cold trees in light, a savage stood raising his wooden sword. Beside him three more savages crept, arrows at the ready, held to the bowstring. I raised my pistol and fired at the savage with the sword. He was thrown back against a tree, blood on his chest, more surprise than pain on his face. He slumped to the ground. The other savages fled. I pushed my hostage ahead of me. He stumbled and whined. I turned. Moving from the trees, a hundred savages in a living rank stalked my path. I held my savage close like a shield. *No, they will not murder you. You are a priest*, he said. I fired another pistol. A savage fell, much hurt. The others threw themselves on the ground. Some crawled away.

My hand at the throat of my living shield, I stepped back carefully. Now from the woods came the full snake of the savage power: two hundred warriors with bows and swords; ahead of them, their leader and second emperor, Opechancanough stood and looked at me curiously with his lethal smile. *All yours are dead. You, I will spare. Throw down your weapons.*

There is a jolt of energy when facing such a might. The whole situation was now known. "I will return to my boat," I said. "And I will keep my weapons."

A savage stepped forward. "I am war," I cried, "my hair the riot of its heat." I fired. The whole horde threw themselves on the ground again. Only Opechancanough stood and folded his arms about his chest. *A leader, making a legend out of a moment*, I thought.

I walked backwards into a line of bushes, no direction safe, pulling on the rope of my hostage, who cautiously followed. He had no choice. I reloaded my pistols. I watched everyone, the eyes of the savages on me. I was now standing in water. I pulled one foot up with difficulty and stepped back. The water was cold and at my ankles, then at my knees. It was at my hips. I was caught, the very earth sucking me into its bowels. I felt its intestines ooze in muck. I was held as if in the irons of an icy mud. The waters had betrayed me to the earth. I tried to free myself but could not. The waters at my chest, soon I would drown. All my mercies now came in a choice of hazards. I threw my weapons toward the shore and surrendered to chance my life with the savages. None of them would approach until Opechancanough picked up my pistols. Then they grabbed my arms and pulled me free, cold and shivering. I felt as if my blood had iced my bones. The savages rubbed my legs to bring them to a comfortable warmth.

I was dragged back to the canoe along the lands that once I walked. There Robinson and Emry lay, their bodies porcupined with arrows, their open eyes staring upward.

The savages built a fire, sat me near it, though its heat felt far away, as if its warmth had somehow been reflected by the cold. Opechancanough sat across from me, staring, indifferent to the death behind him. I looked at the two bodies. Opechancanough followed my eyes, turning his head. I pretended no anger. War here was waged for vengeance. I would show no concern.

I signed and spoke in the words I knew. *We are all born to death. All things pass away, and still they do not die*, I replied, answering a question not asked, as if I could read his mind. Opechancanough nodded and ordered four of his savages to take the corpses away. He looked into my eyes as if plumbing in his gaze the depth of a lake. Behind him the forest burned, its smoke rising into the air in balled fists.

"The forest here seems to be taken in fire," I said, strangling my fears into the coolness of an assured power.

We were hunting, Opechancanough said.

"Me?" I joked, putting comedy on the plate of terror.

Hunting deer, he replied. *We set fires to the woods in a great circle. The flow of flames and heat drive the animals toward the center. We follow behind, until, at the narrows, where there is no escape and the animals are trapped, we use our bows.* Opechancanough paused a moment. *Where there is no burning, no man can walk. The fire keeps the forest clean and makes the great trees. They are born to children of the smoke.*

"We have then met by chance," I said.

No, we have found one of your men walking on the shore. He came from your large boat.

The barge? I signed.

Opechancanough did not answer, but told me of the manner of George Cassen's death. He looked at me, awaiting my reply, savoring his power and his pose.

If I am small and a priest let me, by some altar trick, play easy theology and bring hesitation to my death. From my pocket I took the only instrument I still possessed, a compass. I showed the savages how the little arrow always came to the same direction, toward me. They watched, amazed, not knowing I the north, my iron buckle the pull that fed the pin. They tried to touch the needle; the glass face of the compass barred their way.

"In liquid I have turned the light to frost," I said. "And so prisons are made in these clear confines."

Opechancanough sat silently. I handed the compass to him. He turned it in his hand, thinking, and saying nothing. I showed him the calligraphies of all the winds written on its face. I showed the savages, using the campfire as the sun, how the turning earth provided night and day. How come the seasons, and how the moon revolved around the earth and the earth around the sun. The planets in the sky and the stars I explained. I spoke of them in words and signs as if they were my kin. My voice spoke amulets. I sang the universe in a tale. Opechancanough smiled.

I said to him, "It is as if you already have knowledge of this."

I am, he responded, *contemplating the significance of what you have told. What magic is there in you that is in our Okee, who is the bearer of all strange events?*

"We English, as did our Captain Drake, use these compasses to sail around the world, whose sphere I have described."

A round earth in a flat land? Opechancanough questioned, as he rose, holding the compass. *And so every Englishman has these?* My talisman divined but to a common art, it was time for blood. The savages grabbed me. Their faces painted red. What brothers are we by tint? Red by red, its flames but flesh. My own beard and hair still wet. And all my priesthood is blown rainbow to the wind. Lifting me to my feet, they dragged me to a tree, tied me there. They stood in front of me in marshaled rows, their bows raised, their bowstrings drawn tight, the arrows at their cheeks. My execution at hand, I screamed, "The same compass Drake used to destroy the Spanish invasion fleet, its Armada, in our English surf. It is what Don Luis would want to know!"

Opechancanough stood in silence. He raised the only magic that I had. He raised my compass to the heavens in both hands, as an offering to the sky. The savages murmured and put down their bows. They untied me. I wondered what was the cause, what spice had healed the wounds? Which word did they understand? Was it my magic or some politics or Don Luis? Was he still alive? We left the camp in careful procession, three savages holding my arms, six in lines on either side of me walking with arrows held to their bowstrings. In front of me all my weapons were displayed in the arms of other savages, all my might just decorations to flatter the devices of a savage king. I smiled to myself. I had survived to live another death. In what sanctuary do I serve this mystery? And who is this cunning savage? I am resolved, if I must eat of my own ashes before it's done, I will know the truth of who he is. Opechancanough walked between two files of his men, advanced in front. I to the center, with a rear guard behind.

And so we marched until we came to a small hunting village of some thirty or forty cabins made from mats. That place they called Orapaks. There the women and children pressed in a staring mass, fingers pointing inquisitively. I, with Opechancanough, stood in the center of a savage guard. The three still held my arms, the others kept order about the town.

A priest threw tobacco in a fire. Painted a yellowish red, clubs and arrows at their backs, fox and otter skins covering their arms, with spread-winged birds hanging their feathered mummies upon their hair, the savages chanted their hellish notes, dancing in circles. They beat the earth with their feet. In snaking lines, in hellish undulations, they danced three dances, at the end of which I was led to a long house. There I was left with thirty savages as my guard outside. I was given enough meat and fine bread to feed twenty. None would eat of my food. When I had finished it, they tied what remained in a basket they hung from the ceiling above my head. Then they left, as I wondered if today I was being made well fit, that tomorrow my flesh would be harvested in cannibal savagery. I had no reason but fear to suppose these savages cannibals. Thoughts now indiscretions in my head, I covered myself and shivered to sleep.

In the middle of the night I cried out from cold. A savage named Monacaster brought me a heavy gown, saying it was for the presents I gave him when first I came to Jamestown. And so I went to sleep again, thinking briefly of Don Luis.

I WAS NOT TO BE A MEAL THE NEXT DAY OR ANY OTHER. EACH morning three women brought a great platter of bread and more venison than I could eat in a week. They would take away the food from the previous day, which then they would eat. It was their custom to feed a guest. This vast plenty was more than I had seen since my arrival in Virginia. As I ate, the blood rushed from my head. I began to faint. I could think only of the abundance here and the starvation in Jamestown. *We are aliens here,* I thought. *What England can there be in such a land?*

I made a great effort to improve my understanding of their language. I spoke to my guards and observed the village. Everywhere there were chains of tobacco. It hung from the poles of their wigwams. The savages carried it in their arms, like vestments. When someone died, it was burned in their campfire. When the priest chanted, it was spread on the earth. Its smoke was the horn through which their gods spoke to their own, the geometry of its leaf their book of prophecy. Tobacco was the face behind all.

What the savages could do to content me they did. Opechancanough came to see me. We spoke of Newport and when he would return. "Soon," I said, "with many ships and many cannons with their frightful ordnance." Opechancanough smiled. Then we spoke of ships and sails and the stars, the lands of the earth and, when approached with gentle curiosity, the politics of Europe.

"And tell me," he said, "of your nations and their tribes." He would reveal nothing of what he knew, or if he knew anything of us.

"Father Newport, who is the *werowance* of all the seas, and I, his son, and all the people you call strangers, were caught in a mighty storm, and so came to your land by accident to repair our ships. But we, the English, are called to a great struggle with the Spanish, they who have a colony south in a place named Florida. If they come, as I believe they have once, they will bring your people suffering, slavery and death. Father Newport and I wish in our love to be at peace with you, and you to be one of those many powerful nations who have joined in mutual protection against this Spain." Opechancanough considered as I added, "We wish to practice our strength in distance. We do not come to hurt or rule. We come to be your friends. This is our enterprise."

"My people believe this earth is flat in a circle." Opechancanough's fingers swept around in the air. "We believe we live at its center. And you believe the earth is round, like a ball."

"Yes," I said.

"A ball's surface has no center. You must think your gods do not love you to disperse you so adrift; or do you invent your centers in your mind?" He smiled.

"I was told a story once," I said, "about one of your people who was taken and educated by the Spanish, who, by his craft and wisdom, returned here, renounced all he had become and then rose in a mighty war against the Spanish and their priests."

Opechancanough nodded his head. "Of all our people, only Powhatan and I survive from the old time. All else is dead. So what happened in the past is only known to the past." With that, he asked me to join him in a walk.

I smiled and said, "Aren't you afraid I might escape?"

"You know as well as I," he said looking at me, "this land sharpens its teeth on the bones of fools."

We stepped outside. My guards held my arms, and formed two lines by my side. We walked behind Opechancanough. The children of the village and some of the men and women followed, softly murmuring questions and bits of conversations. We walked a short distance beyond the wigwams of mats to a small cabin with bars at both open ends, watched by two great savages. There lay a fire near it, and an old woman sat weeping, throwing tobacco into the flames and praying. In the cabin were about a dozen boys of thirteen to fifteen years of age. We stopped. The youths crawled over each other to get a better view. Some looked beaten. Others, their eyes wild, reached their hands beyond the wooden bars of the cabin toward nothing but the imagined spirit drifting in the sunlight. I looked at Opechancanough. "And what is this?" I asked.

"The end of the *huskanaw*," he said. "the beginning of the return.

These, the most beloved and strongest of our children, those who may be naturally wise, we have them drink of a brew from the maddening leaf. For nine moons they drink and are kept far away in the woods, apart from all they know and all they own. This is known as the *huskanaw*. This is the time of forgetting. A child casts out all memories. His past is lost, his possessions taken away and given to others. After nine moons he is brought here and given less of the elixir each day until his reason returns. This is the time of the great demand, as it is named. The child must forget who he was, his parents and his possessions. He must become nothing, so he can rise reborn."

"And if he doesn't?" I asked.

"Once started, that knowledge must be consumed. This is our way. Okee will take in death those who are unfit. With those, he will be satisfied, sucking the blood from their left breasts. The others he will leave be. How else"—Opechancanough looked at me and said—"can our leaders be purified from the loyalties of blood and memory? Are those you follow so pure?"

"We are selfless in our service to our king and country. All that we are is forfeited to that one great cause, and to this, our enterprise." Opechancanough smiled as I added, "Are you saying you can recall nothing of your childhood?"

Opechancanough stared into my eyes as if he sought the legions of my heart and said, "Isn't your history but a toy played in memory? What would you not sacrifice for the greater good?"

What witchcraft is this, that these savages taunt me with my own beliefs? I raged as I returned to my cabin. They sacrifice their children's memories to make them wise without restraint, to make them action without spoil. But nothing that is of human thought ever sleeps and when the whisper comes, to what end my childhood no more? Man's memory is his fate. An infant at his mother's breast, that is where our life first becomes us. All that lost? And what remains but a ghost that haunts itself? These savages are a strange twist of humankind. But wouldn't I crush all my memories under my own heel if I had the chance to be pure to my own season, for my rank to outrank rank? For this is joy rejoiced, without regard to sovereignty, confines or power. But Don Luis was no child when he was taken by the Spanish. If Opechancanough were he, then he would remember.

.   .   .   .   .   .

THE NEXT DAY, AN OLD MAN TRIED TO BEAT IN MY BRAINS WITH a cudgel. My guards subdued him, preserving me for other matters. Later I learned he had come to take vengeance upon me because it was his son I had killed that day I was taken prisoner. In the evening I was brought to the wigwam of the old man, where he lay unconscious, his face gray and solemn in the firelight. A priest sat by the fire, watching the tobacco smoke rise through the chimney hole in the roof, tracking the ebb of the old man's life. He rose and passed a tobacco leaf above the old man's face, crushed it and spread it upon the ground, examining the patterns of its ruins. He chanted softly, gathering it again in his hands, and once more cast it upon the ground. Three times he did this before throwing the weed into the fire, writing again in smoke the future of the old man's death.

When the old man had struggled with my guards I was told he was afflicted by some seizure of the limbs, some disease that feeds on rage that an ancient mind cannot abide, and so it snapped.

"I have elixirs and good ointments at Jamestown that might cure him," I said, "if only you would let me get them and bring them here."

"We are not as children," said Opechancanough, "no matter how you wish it."

"What I tell you is true," I said. Opechancanough clothed himself in silence again.

THERE WERE GREAT COMMOTIONS IN THE VILLAGE AT THIS TIME, talk and threats of attacks on Jamestown. Wowinchopunk, the *werowance* of the Paspaheghs arrived and told me, "I have gone to your fort and around your campfire sorrowed with your friends of your capture." Such is diplomacy in its double face, both its mouths speaking in opposite directions at once. Before our cannons he was talking peace, but here, in the wilderness, the Paspahegh counseled only war. The Paspahegh, the tribe closest to us, felt most our breath. Other tribes under Powhatan, more solicitous of our weapons, counseled peace. Some few would have stood and waited and seen if time itself would have been a better ally than any treachery. "They want Jamestown to starve," said one of my guards.

"If you want us dead, why do you trade us food?" I asked.

The savage looked at me. "The winds around the fire blow in many directions, but there is only one storm that fills the night with lightning and thunder."

"You want our weapons, but your *werowances* argue how to get them," I said. The savage said nothing more, but he left the cabin. He threw the mat that was its door aside as if he had won some victory.

Opechancanough and Wowinchopunk came to the cabin shortly thereafter. They sat on mats and looked at me through their paints and their oils and the animal carcasses that laced their hair. "We have treated you kindly, have we not?" Opechancanough began. "I would give you more, all I can, in generous love, land and furs and women, even the freedom you so desire. All this I can do."

I acknowledged Opechancanough's power. "You are wise," he continued. "Like our conjurers, you are small and cunning. Your hair hangs in fires, wild in its animal. You hold the spirit of the world in your hands. We want your wisdom," he said. "Tell us of the weapons at your fort and how we can attack them...for attack them we will."

"Of course I will tell you, Opechancanough," I said. "You saved my life, both at the quagmire and here your guards stopped the hands that might have slain me. And so now, I will give to you your life and the lives of hundreds of your people. The cannons of Jamestown in one thunder could crack the trees to their roots, scatter to the earth the limbs of a whole tribe of men. There are mines whose explosive flames tear the earth from earth, leaving canyons where once deer grazed and grass grew. Our firelocks will cut men's flesh, killing them, throwing their bodies great distances. It is brave of you to face such ruin...but not wise. I wish only for you and your people to live your lives with us in peace. Our magic can protect us both."

Opechancanough and the Paspahegh listened, as I continued. "There are those who love me at Jamestown who may fear me dead, and who may take some wrongful vengeance on your people. Let me send a message to them telling of your kindly ways, and so assure them I am alive."

"How will you send your message?" asked Wowinchopunk.

"I can make this paper speak my words." Holding a small book of navigation tables, I tore out a blank page. I made some ink. Simple words now would battalion magic at my needs.

"No conjurer ever known can make such speech," said the Paspahegh. Opechancanough sat regarding me in silence, afraid to show whether he understood writing or not.

"If you take this paper to the fort, give it to my brother Anas Todkill," I said. "Thereupon, you will see my friends fire a cannon and rush from the fort, armed with all their weapons. If you come again the next day, I have told the paper to tell them to give you presents and such articles of clothes as I may need." Opechancanough nodded his agreement. "It is a three-day journey at this season," Opechancanough said. Outside, snow was falling. The ground was covered with its white lake. Through the bent trees the air was filled with the floating silence of its cloak. Three messengers were dispatched to Jamestown immediately with my letter, which also reported the savages' intent to attack our fort, the deaths of Robinson and Emry and Cassen, and how our company must follow my instructions as holy writ to avoid disaster. I hoped those that escaped on the barge, and my few, might have the weight to hold the others to my plan. Otherwise, all my moments now would unfold to be my death.

OPECHANCANOUGH SAT IN MY CABIN. WE SMOKED TOBACCO AND watched each other through the curtains of our breath. We talked of Powhatan's empire and all the peoples of this land. I asked of Roanoke again. He said there were a people he called *Ocanahonan* who wore clothes like mine. "They live far away and have ways that are different. They could be who you seek."

"Perhaps, but what more can you tell?"

"Little more but they are known. You can ask others of them. Tomorrow we leave, for your safety. There are those who would take vengeance on you...as you have seen."

I nodded calmly, relighting my pipe with a twig from the fire. I drew in a breath and let the smoke drift from my lips. "Your tobacco is bitter," I said.

"Why should the gods make it pleasurable to see our own souls?" Opechancanough smiled.

AT DAYBREAK THE SAVAGES LED ME FROM MY WIGWAM. THE EARTH was still in frost, the air sharp in its cold. The winter sun flowed its empty heat onto the land, as the snow sparkled in its ease in the crisp bells of light. They took me by the arms again, files of savages about me, Opechancanough with his legions. We passed from the village into forest, crossed the snows through the newly burnt hills of the hunt, some trees and earth smoldering still in their charred landscape of white. The smoke rose through the snow in a few places, as if the earth were breathing spirits into the wind.

We forded the branches of many rivers and stayed in the villages of many tribes. Always I was treated kindly and received with awe. I was Opechancanough's captive, a great king's greatest prize, the red-haired wizard, the man who held the thunder in his belt. My weapons displayed, I walked with my guard of forty.

Each day I gathered news. I spoke their language with greater ease. I heard that Powhatan had left the town near the falls and was about. I slept in his hunting lodge at a place called Mattaponi, then marched four days to a town called Menapacant, where their king, in appreciation of some kindness from me at our fort, feasted me in his council house.

And so I sat and ate of their kindness, around me this king, his court, his women and his lands. "Will you show us the effects of your weapon?" the king asked. I said that I would oblige him. My forty guards rose with me. I was given my pistol and my powder. A target was set in a tree at some thirty feet. The pistol loaded, I held the winding key. Wound like a clock, its spring forced the hammer to its fall. I turned the key to bring tension to the hammer. The key clicked in its seat. But as I pulled back the hammer, the tension now full, it snapped in two.

"I cannot fire this," I said. "The weapon is fouled with accident and is broken." I showed the king the parts of the pistol. Bows were thrown to the earth. Savages stamped their feet. Howls were made in such chorus I thought my life would be forfeit.

The king stood, raised his hand. The voices murmured into silence. "That which brings death has its own death. I have learned much," he said. After he had spoken, his people cried still in their disappointment. He let them sorrow. His power was for order, not to chain their souls.

The messengers returned from Jamestown and reported that all I had foretold had happened, there being a moment for me of some masked smile. The garrison had rushed from the fort with all their weapons ready. A cannon had been fired which blasted a tree into a cloud of wood and falling ice. The next day presents were given to the three messengers, along with the articles of clothes I had requested.

"You see, we can make the writing on the paper speak," I said, hoping to impress Opechancanough as I had the others of his tribe.

"Our nations have similar words," said Opechancanough, "but it is the writing of flesh." I looked at Opechancanough as if to ask him a question. "One day you shall understand," he added.

WE CAME TO THE BANKS OF THE PAMUNKEY, WHERE OPECHANCAN-ough was king. The Pamunkey called themselves by the name of the river along which they dwelled, as was the custom. Opechancanough in his village again, his women and his children surrounded him, showing their merriment at his return. I was taken to a long house and fed, then I slept.

In the morning the savages spread mats across the floor, built a great fire in the center of the house and placed one special mat before it. There, they bid me sit, which I did. My guards left the room. I was alone with the fire. One of their priests entered, wearing a shirt which hung from one of his shoulders. His face was oiled with black grease, his eyes haloed in white. Along his cheeks were red strokes of paint. He looked at me, his head tilting from side to side to the rhythm of some unheard chant. In his hair were the skins of weasels and snakes stuffed with moss. Their flesh hung over his back and shoulders and face. On his head, their tails tied together. Feathers were woven into his greased hair to form a crown.

With contortions of his limbs and hellish cries, he began to dance about the fire, stamping the ground, as if his feet could persuade the earth to give answers to his calls. *Invoke your passions,* I challenged through my thoughts, *and your strange powers, and would you know me in all my depth?*

Three more savages joined the first, their faces painted half red and half black, their eyes rounded in white. They all circled me in their dance, laying corn and tobacco on the ground in a ring. Three such rings they drew before three other priests joined them to howl in their hideous laments. These too had masks painted on their faces. Each struck his rattle in wild gestures through the smoky room, chanting and singing songs of tortured words.

Soon they silenced. The chief priest, his face black with coal and oil, spoke. The others groaned. The chief priest laid down five ears of corn, straining his arms in such a gesture of fatigue that he began to sweat. His veins bulged. He spoke again. His words ended with another groan. This was done until all the circles surrounded me with one great ring of corn. Tobacco was spread over the ground. It was thrown upon the fire. The smell of its smoke filled the house, purifying the air. I breathed it into my lungs. I felt joined to its flavor and to something else. The air widened into silence, yet I felt apart. The priests left me then. At night we feasted. I in my enforced new purity, they in a festive mood.

"What songs did you sing of me and what answers sought?" I asked Opechancanough.

"To see if you come as friend."

"And?" I questioned.

"You have too many faces to be seen as one."

With the dawn we marched. I was flanked on each side by twenty savages, their bows ready with arrows. My arms, grasped and supported, my weapons held by others — the empty trophies of my vanquished power. And so I came again to Powhatan's village, his capital, Werowocomoco. As we began to climb to its stockade, its rude wooden battlements, this derelict citadel gave forth people. They rushed to the edge of our march, talked and pointed, speaking secret whispers in each other's ears. As we passed, the savages walked along with our parade. Like a gathered host they came, a carpet of woven human forms.

There was one who joined to me alone. Our glances touched, as if sight could steal a kiss. That young girl, Pocahontas, who months before had passed me in silent stare. What imaginations in an imagined kiss. What embraces in the imagined warmth so locked. Her lips so frequent to my eyes—her dark hair about her face perfumed her mystery. My lungs breathed rocks. I could not speak. She walked, watching me across the phalanx of my guards. I called to her in unspoken whispers I should have strangled in my mind.

Our procession reached the sides of the circular stockade. We walked along its walls a short distance, entering the spiral of fences where one overlapped another, forming a small passage about six feet across. Once through, I was in the village, the largest I had ever seen.

I was taken into a house a hundred feet in length in the center of the village. At one end sat Powhatan on a platform raised about a foot high, covered with decorated mats. Powhatan himself was covered in a great coat of raccoon fur. Chains of pearls hung from his neck, his chest cloaked in flashing crystals of their armor. The royalty of great birds were tied into his hair, rising above his forehead in a feathered coronet. How strange, as if he were inheritor and master of those pilgrims of the air. At one shoulder stood a young woman who appeared to be eighteen. At his feet sat another. On each side of the room sat a line of ten savages and standing behind each was a young woman—all with faces painted red, in their hair the carcasses of birds with wings outspread. About their necks hung strings of pearls finely woven into delicate falls. All looked my way, their eyes glowing in their painted masks. There was a fire in the center of the room. The room glowed crimson. Shadows were its jewels. I was greeted with a great shout. How much this custom voiced to me in messages I could not understand? What execution now awaited but for the final judgment of a savage glance?

Red-haired and small, I was strange to them as they were to me. I was brought before the fire and before Powhatan. He seemed grayer, but still his muscles coiled as snakes beneath his skin. A mat was placed on the floor and I sat. Apposuno, the queen of the Appomattoc, approached with a bowl of water, in which I washed my hands. A fan of turkey feathers was brought to dry them. Powhatan straightened his back and drew his power about him, then looked at me and spoke.

"Why have you come into my kingdoms? Why have you taken my lands?" He spoke slowly, weighting each word with the medal of his authority. Every gesture claimed sovereignty over all, both by a tradition measureless in time and by force of arms. This was a power patinaed in the well of his rivals' blood. This was a savage majesty from whom even the kings of Europe could learn some splendid pomp. "Why have you displeased me?" Powhatan asked after a silence, after toying with the quiet as if it were his jewel.

"It was not our wish to displease," I said. "We sought only refuge. We were blown off course by a storm after we had defeated in a great battle our enemy, the Spanish. We would have left a while ago, but our father, Captain Newport, had to do service elsewhere, and our pinnace was too leaky to follow. He will soon return for us," I said, wanting the savages to think Newport was close, and I was his child under the protection of his magic.

"Why have you come so far upriver, so far into my domain?" asked Powhatan, not caring whose father Newport was. My dice rolled blank.

"I have come in search of those who first attacked Newport's ships and our company, and who killed a youth," I answered.

"Those were the Monacans who I shall take vengeance upon

myself," Powhatan lied, as they had been Paspaheghs and others of his own people. This sport gamed war, and all our contests had come to play its swords in banter. "When first you came I asked you twice to make a war upon the Monacans," he said, "but you refused."

"We seek not war but only to punish those who have harmed us," I answered unwisely with words worn too smooth with overuse, remembering in a shock of recall the deaths of Emry and Robinson. Would Powhatan think I would come again in vengeance if he let me live? Would Powhatan speak of them? He did not. To us both they were momentary casualties, death on the periphery, someone else's price of service. To history, all death is like the wind, the pressure known but never seen.

"Tell me of your kingdoms," Powhatan asked. And so I spoke of Europe, its peoples, its wars, its weapons, of its metals and of its science. Powhatan listened, asked me questions. Opechancanough had told him of our astronomy and of the earth in its ball, of the moon's race around the earth, and of the earth's and the moon's race around the sun. All this Powhatan wanted to hear from my own lips.

When I finished, Powhatan told of his kingdom and of the peoples upon its borders, those who dwelled in the place of fire, the Potomacs. He numbered for me his enemies and the legendary tribes he had never seen. He spoke again of the Ocanahonans, the mysterious ones so much like me, yet different. "They are the dark ones, but they are far away and I know little of them other than that it is said they were born of the water."

"Of the water?" I repeated.

"So it is told. And their god is a great snake who breathes fire."

"A dragon?" I asked.

"I do not know the word," said Powhatan. "It is not a word of my earth."

I sat my curiosities near my heart. Asked more but heard less. Powhatan then told of the Anone, who had much brass and many houses like those at our fort, of tribes who ate human flesh and of those who sailed the sea in many ships and made war along the coast. He told me of the lands above the falls where ran rivers west into salt water bays. I wondered at his tales. Were they to frighten me or to make him more powerful in my eyes? I did not know, but it was important that Powhatan mentioned the Ocanahonans.

Powhatan asked me about the paper and how I made it speak. I told him of writing. "And so we are able," I said, "to speak to each other and tell of our adventures through the ages to those who will only hear our voices in these frozen lines."

"We, too, have writing, but it is flesh." The very words Opechancanough had used. As Powhatan stood, all rose. "Follow me," he said, bidding me and Opechancanough to walk behind him.

We left the long house, into the gold glow of the sunlight, my guards following behind me at a distance, across a small open square to a long cabin. Powhatan pushed aside the animal fur that hung as its door and we entered. The light lay upon the room in smoky gray. It seemed to dissolve through the faded air. There was a small fire tended by a kneeling priest. He turned in surprise as the sunlight fell into the shadows of the smoke, then he stood. Another priest knelt on a platform about three feet high, canopied in mats. It seemed a giant bed where sleep was offered to the gods. The priest upon it had a feather fan in his hand. He was dusting and oiling what had been human things, the flattened skin of mummies, whose bodies sprawled in the outlines of their final rest, their corpses filled with sand to bring them almost full. How flat and darkly gleamed the landscape of their death. At the feet of each mummy was a covered basket which held its heart and lungs and innards.

"What once carried their life is now before them," said Powhatan.

Behind the bodies on a recessed ledge stood an Okee. Its face was sculptured in a surprised grin, its arms upraised, whether in salute or demonic laugh, I couldn't tell.

"These, the bodies of our great chiefs, speak their flesh to us, as the marks of your writing speak to you. These are the stories of our tribe. This is our history. These are the whisperings. These alone are granted by the gods eternal life. All others pass away to nothing to be forgot. But these are memories. These are who we are." Powhatan's arms swept across the foot of the platform. "This is our language in its eternal flesh."

I looked at the bodies and thought, *In this sand the tree of nation is pushed to bloom. These savages are not so far from Englishmen if we could but wean them from their calligraphies. Here tradition is tended skin upon the bone. Ours is our tombs, our heraldries. All laws command in memories, and we, my savages, are closer kin than you would think.*

We left. Outside there was that girl again, whose living flesh sang of pleasant suffocations. *I am for my enterprise here a monk*, I thought. *Would you seduce me and make me traitor to myself?* I was lunatic. I was losing who I was. I bit my lip to know again the pain of me.

Powhatan sat again in the long house. "It is my wish," he said, "that all you, our strangers, quit your Jamestown and come live among us here. I will supply you with venison and corn and all the food you need. In this I declare our friendship. What say you?"

"It will be done," was my reply, my too quick reply. Hesitation would have shown my strength.

THAT NIGHT I SAT IN MY CABIN. OUTSIDE, MY GUARDS AROUND me like a cloak. I stared into the fire before me. The flames, in their serpentine dance, waved like silken veils in the morning's soft chill. Embers burned, rising in the air in flights as winged jewels. I watched the pillars of smoke ascend, then boil, confused in a cold draft. Someone had entered my wigwam. I turned. It was that girl, Pocahontas, who walked soft lightning upon the land. I rose to speak its firmaments. "And why have you come? Are you carrying a bowl of food?" I said, feeling small and afraid, a melt of flesh before this girl. Where I would have spoken other words, I spoke in insults, a puppet to my fears. She stood and did not answer. "Powhatan might be angry if he knows you are with me," I said.

She began to sign to me, not speaking the language she must have known I understood. I think it was a returned insult. *Powhatan's anger is more your concern than mine*, she said.

"And you are familiar with the character of his moods?" I asked.

"I am one of Powhatan's moods." She now spoke to me, her lips letting breath flow over their own moistened rims. She looked at me like a quizzical bird, amused at some pleasant bit of worm. I thought of the luxuriousness of wiggling in the cast of that warm breath, surrendering to the passing touch of that smooth flesh.

"Are you here with a message from Powhatan?" I asked

She smiled. "Are you a great warrior?"

"I could tell you lies."

She laughed, an interested smile upon her face.

Oh that I had said, "Girl...there are no truths in my words that the light of your eyes could not spike." But, instead, I told my coward's earnest truth, a tale from bravery. "I have battled in many places. Once, between two great armies, I slew three champions of my enemies, the Turks, while thousands watched. I brought their heads as trophies to my camp."

"And?" she asked.

"How much blood is blood enough to drown your curiosities?" I replied.

"Who sings the song of your victories, and who does their dance? Are yours so small they are not of legends?"

"Would you hear all my history in a day?" I smiled. "Are all the girls of your tribe so sure and forward in their society?"

"Kings here descend from sisters. Powhatan's power upon his death goes not to his son or his brother but to his oldest sister's oldest son. Through me are the roots of emperors."

"Are you, then, Powhatan's sister?" I said, knowing months ago Naurins had told me she was Powhatan's daughter.

"No. I am his daughter." Her eyes flashed.

I bowed. "Then, my princess, you find me impoverished but for a future service."

She then giggled like a little girl and bit the tip of her finger, looking down upon my bowed head. She leaned back into the shadows, as if light itself had pressed her to some safety.

"So tell me more," she said, her words washing warmth over the cool waters of my soul.

I did not want to betray her with the truth. I did not strut words, like fancy horses, dressed to parade down a serpent road. I wanted no harvest from this Eden but her lips parted in admirations. I told of my wars against the Turks and against the Tartars, of massed armies in their forged iron vests; of cannons, of cavalry, of crossbow's darts that can pierce a tree the girth of a man. I bled wounds on those fields. I gave my blood in victories. Men followed me now, Fettiplace and Todkill, one who served me then. But in my truth, in all truth, there is in its seed, enkerneled deep, a treason waiting to spread its leafy weed and breathe free. She was a royal of the blood, even in savage rank her station far above mine. Would I seduce with words what I could not allow myself to take in flesh? I would not be Ratcliffe, or Spanish, or call license a liberty. I would, like Drake and the Cimarrones, make allies for a common good. But first I must wrest survival from an angry land, eat dirt. I told her that once I was captured, held as a prisoner by the Turks, but escaped with the aid of a daughter of a great lord. I bled history to my cause. All I told was true. A seed grows to its leaf and then to bloom, flowering into its seed again. Who knows what return there is by the telling of a tale? But what I did not tell was that I was sold as a slave, beaten and chained as to the dead.

At the end of my tale she turned without a sound and left, taking with her the heat of the room.

Chapter Twenty-five

ADOPTIONS IN A GIFT. A TRICK BY CANNONS. I AM
CONDEMNED TO HANG BY A TRAITOR'S ROPE.

N THE MORROW I was given a bitter drink that sank me into a strange drunkenness. I was brought before Powhatan again in the long house. He sat on his crude throne, his women, his court about him. A priest sat on a mat, throwing tobacco into a fire, running his hands in hellish gestures through the smoke, praying to the rising idols of whirling ash. Across from him sat Pocahontas, her face a painted mask of red, her eyes in painted white. They blinked. Her head moved stiffly on the pivot of its neck, as if in some pantomime of life. She seemed in solemn dream, her beauty now disfigured in its paint. I felt betrayed, treasoned by a hue, sullied, made coward by a rouge. I wanted to run, escape. But I was held by grotesque chains of an angel, made monstrous in the flesh. Still I stared, wondering what else could come of this girl. Whore or virgin? Angel or fiend? A priest brought me a bowl filled with the same potions I had drunk in the wigwam. "Drink," ordered Powhatan, "it is the brew of Okee's leaf." I looked in the liquid. "Have you fear? There is not enough for half a death." I drank the bowl, threw it at Powhatan's feet. "Good," he said. I was given another, which I drank, and another....

"Is this the *huskanaw*?" I asked. "Am I to be no one? Is a nothing to be your prize?"

Powhatan now stood. "Are you ready to be reborn in voices?"

"I am always ready to meet my death, but I will not die easily," I replied, confused.

"Struggle in that passage then between birth and death, and be with us." Powhatan lifted his arms. I started to move forward. A host of savages grabbed me, held me fast and dragged me to my knees. Three priests brought a large rock before the fire. They chanted. Tobacco was thrown in the flames. The smoke danced in the breath of their howls. I was brought to the rock. My head was laid upon it. Hands set upon my shoulders, pushing. A savage stepped forward with a cudgel. I screamed defiant words. I rebelled, my limbs screaming in the memory of their strength. The savage raised his arm and waited, as if for some secret sign.

Powhatan nodded. I closed my eyes, waiting to feel the execution of my own life. Around my head I felt the cradling fingers of two hands and the soft pillow of human flesh, warm breasts against my cheek. I heard words spoken. "So as I am given so do I give." Words ritually spoken. "So as I am birth so do I await the giver of life." What play is this? Am I the bit player who frets upon the stage, never knowing of the plot? The chalice of her arms about my head, her words rehearsed through these long years. I looked up and I saw her face contrived in its paint look down at me in gentle glances, her eyes confused. I was pulled to my feet. Pocahontas sat back before the fire, as if she hadn't moved.

Powhatan looked at me and spoke, pointing his finger. "You now have no name. You are as you were before your life…death not death. Newport and his ships can seek no vengeance. Soon you shall have your only birth…no longer orphaned to the earth. Ours shall be your mother and your tribe. Drink light and wander upon the river sleep. Soon is the gift of voices."

They dragged me by the arms into the daylight. The earth breathed waves of motion through the land. I drank the landscape, then all went black.

When I think of all those years gone by, three births I had and with each I laid a treason by the womb that sought to have me new. Did Pocahontas speak and save me for my life? Was it all a savage game? I do not know. Love pleads to me. I am eaten by its thought. The years have made me simple by the memory of a touch.

FOR TWO DAYS, THEY SAID, I SLEPT. ON MY AWAKENING, THE SAVAGES led me to a large wigwam in the forest. They lit a fire in the center of a large room, and sat me on a mat facing it. They removed my shirt.

I was naked. There was a curtain of hides drawn across the room in front of me. The savages left. I sat, ever alone again. My head ached. I shivered and sweated. The world rolled on in dust. Something moved behind the hides. They billowed. There was a scream. The curtain pulled back and Powhatan and two hundred savages, all painted black, danced into the room. Naked they were, save a cloth around their waists. Such noises they made with rattle and chant to suffocate the air and bring the crush to any spark of light.

Around me they danced and called and howled, spreading bits of tobacco upon my head and shoulders. They gave me ears of corn, and placed colorful gourds in my hands. They danced in pounding rhythm, rising, falling, swelling in its thunder. They burned tobacco in the fire in such weight as I could have smoked the air. Then there was a snap of light that cracked the air as if the sun had flashed in angels at my feet. The chanting came in waves. Feet upon rhythm's dust. Rocks were placed in the coals. Embers glowed their heat in bated fires. The rocks baked red. Water cast upon the heat. Steam rose upon the smoke. All that was was turned in mist. My hands sweated rain. My face streamed. A voice came in from far aways. I was lifted on many arms. I was afloat in flesh. A scream swooned upon a deeper chant. One voice above all. I was laid upon the earth. Tobacco clothed my skin. I fainted. Cold water on my flesh. Then they stopped. Powhatan bid me rise. He cleansed me with a tobacco leaf, rubbing it as a cloth about my chest and back. "You are now a *werowance*. Through you the secrets and the voices," he said. "I am your guide and father. You are of my tribe, adopted as my own." I acknowledged the savage and his words. I stood in my grateful monuments, my skin smudged in the juices of the tobacco leaf. Powhatan, this man, was priest. His miter in a double crown. "It is the earth's leaf that clothes you in its color," he said, "as voices now clothe you in their silence. Soon they shall whisper to you ever in their only voice. Soon you shall hear the river. Nothing that is, is dead."

Powhatan stood, watching me. Then he said, "In what drink the cool elixir flows, its wash in secrets to the tongue? All wisdom holds some mysteries even from the wise. We are to water born. We are its sorceries. We are, as the fire, no broader than its flame. Only tobacco makes all spirits manifest on earth. Its smoke whispers secrets to the gods. It is our sacrifice. It is our messenger. Council with it only in holy dread."

Holding me by the shoulders now, Powhatan looked into my face, the oils of his forehead glistening. "The voices are wounds that will not heal. They come of the third blood." With that, he cut my arm with his knife. "This is the first blood. Two more wounds and you are birthed, the voices of the river in your ear. The third will be your birth. You are now a *werowance* and to me as my son, as my Nostanquid, and I am as your father. And so on the fourth day you shall be returned to Jamestown. I am your lord. I require gifts to repay my gifts. I want from your hands two cannons and a grindstone, to seal in earthly treasure our bond forever in its blood. Will you do this now as my new beloved son?"

"This I will do as it is within my power." The air sat dead upon my ears. All consequence had fled. I ignored that I was now a savage priest to some unknown god. I thought of the mariner. Would he take up the gift that I cast down? Am I adopted only to be damned? Two chops, two spurts of blood and I am voiced. The novice gone in alchemies. I to be a wizard, a heathen to a heathen thing. Some gifts not always wisely given, better to the mariner, but he is not the plan. His soul not forfeit in the act. Neither mine, for I do not seek the gift, or know it real. But if it comes, let wounds wound silence. Does the river drone its wisps like cobwebs in the ear? If there be a voice like Drake's, I'll grasp its heresies. For without the golden pea could the rattle make its noise? I smiled and sorrowed in my prophecies.

"Good," said Powhatan. Then we left the cabin. The land in smoke, the snow outside drew whirlwinds in the cold. We all went to the long house, where we feasted on fine meats and nuts and corn, smoked tobacco to seal our pledge, our words rushed on the holy vapors. I sat before Powhatan. Pocahontas served me bread. I looked again into her eyes. She called me "warrior and almost brother." As she spoke, she glanced to me in her eyes of womanhood. Then she walked away.

We feasted late into the night. Outside, the savages chanted and danced. The rhythms pounded into the darkness, as if the blackness had a beating heart. I returned to my wigwam at dawn, just as the horizon began to glow with sunrise. I slept the day and rested for the next two. I saw the girl each day when she brought me food, but still I could not come to caress that which moved my soul.

·   ·   ·   ·   ·

ON THE THIRD DAY, TWELVE GUIDES AND I STARTED FOR JAMESTOWN. From Werowocomoco to the fort was only about twenty miles, but the savages made a dawdling haste. We had made little progress by evening. I wanted to travel on, but they decided to spend the evening at one of Powhatan's hunting lodges. Rawhunt, one of Powhatan's skilled advisors, had accompanied me. We sat by the fire, teaching each other our languages, giving names to mysterious forms and forms to mysterious sounds. And so the night progressed, lit by firelight. The other guides threw logs in the flames and talked of hunts and legends and their ill-tempered gods.

I asked Rawhunt about Powhatan's empire and his power. "He is more than king," Rawhunt replied, "but somewhat less than god. Through him Okee's power flows. He is like the green tobacco leaf in its growth, gathering within itself ghostly presentations."

"To what law is he subject... god's or man's?" I asked.

"Powhatan is a priest's priest," replied Rawhunt. "The river beneath this island plate, this earth, sings in its hollow voice to him. The legend says that Powhatan stands on two legs: one upon the earth and one in the voices of the smoke. With only one, he falls and so do we all, the world to fail. It is said that the forest will return to thicket so full that a man can no longer hunt but only stand in place, snared by the tangle, its bushes vines and wreck. So legend tells."

"One good burn should clear a thicket. Fire has always been your path. Ashes feed your forest groves. That has always been your way," I said.

"The legend also says that three strangers shall arise on the Chesapeake to challenge Powhatan's domain. Twice he shall overcome them. The Spanish and your colony at Roanoke. At the third, he shall be overcome. Are you the third?" asked Rawhunt. I gave nothing more than a look. I cobbling a smile on the silence, and played the moment slight.

WE LEFT AT SUNRISE, ARRIVING AT JAMESTOWN BY MIDDAY. MY absence was little on a month, but still the logs of the stockade wall listed in the jaws of the earth. Some leaned forward, others somewhat back. Some were missing, having fallen to the ground. They seemed like ruined teeth in a beggar's mouth. But these beggars were in Eden. We entered the gate. The thirty-nine survivors of our band of one hundred and seven walked with labor or limped or half-crawled to greet me. There were true marks of happiness at my return. Only Archer and a few of his band watched me silently, their eyes cold in already-persuaded plots.

The old mariner whispered in my ear, "In your absence we despaired. Sloth is the poison, idleness its spoon. Now the only law is license. We are English only in name. Archer is on the council, elected by Ratcliffe alone, without Martin's consent, in defiance of our law. Ratcliffe's tyranny is a tantrum in a willful child's feast. You, my exile, have returned as the exile in his own land. This year December came in a bitter cold so nothing was done, but now the ice on the river thaws. And where is our hope, in what direction does it lie?"

"I am the authority that binds this company to its pledge," I replied. "But I have my own promises to Powhatan I must fulfill," I said, "before we can tub this stupor and seal it in its own pot. Powhatan has given me my life and made me as his son but I, in my filial duties, must give to him by these guides two cannons and a millstone. We must do this if we are to have peace."

"But two cannons?" asked Martin, overhearing my words.

"Two cannons where?" said Ratcliffe, half hearing my whispers.

"I pledged two cannons and a millstone to Powhatan," I said to the company. "It is our trade for peace and goodwill, for which we will have food and other gifts."

Ratcliffe smiled, his tongue licking the edge of his lips. "Have you betrayed us to the savages? For what favors?" asked Ratcliffe, drooling his words. His own words betraying his guilt.

"Your own words confess you," I replied. "Which do you favor more, food or war?" Would Ratcliffe now wreck the woods in argument?

"Commerce as you will," Ratcliffe spoke softly, then his voice broadened. "Smith may have found the heat to fire the savage heart. Maybe more shall come of this than food and peace. I shall not object."

I called to Rawhunt to follow me with his eleven savages. We walked to one of the half-moon corners of the fort where the guns faced outwards towards the land. "I wish you all to see the dominion over the earth I give to Powhatan." With that, I ordered the cannons loaded with stones and fired at the fluted branches of a great tree, which splintered, raining dust and ice. The savages fell to their knees and held their ears. Then they ran from the fort, the laughter of our company trailing at their heels. I ordered silence from our men and coaxed the savages back into our walls with words of peace and friendship. "Powhatan wishes these cannons and a millstone. As it was my word to him, now take them."

Rawhunt ordered two of his strongest savages to lift a cannon. They walked as if their legs were held back, standing half in fear before the still-smoking tube. They touched it quickly with the tips of their fingers just to feel its heat. Satisfied that it was cool and patting its shiny bronze as if to calm its angry spirit, they moved, one to the nozzle and the other to the rear. Then, with exertion that turned their muscles to the wires of taut ropes, they began to lift. They groaned, their faces strained in the call of agonies. The cannon did not move. Rawhunt ordered four to lift the cannon, then six. Finally, all. The cannon rose but inches before it fell to its wooden carriage.

"It cannot be done," spoke Rawhunt, waving his hand before his face as if fanning air into his mouth.

"That displeases me, for it was Powhatan's wish to have them, but, in friendship, I will find other presents which will bring contentment." I gave them hatchets and toys and other presents for the guides, for Rawhunt and for Powhatan and his wives and children. And to that one, my Pocahontas, whose flesh in silence speaks forbidden voices, I sent a locket of my own, a sacrifice to forever quench those unspoken breaths that sang to me in their eloquent chastities of heat.

A chance that day I had to be alone with the mariner. I told Jonas Profit of my adventure and of that girl who held my orphaned head in her hands and shielded me. I told him I was now a *werowance*. By dance, potions and magic words Powhatan had anointed me a king and something of a priest. "After a third wound, he said I shall hear the voices in this earth. Through me the secrets of this world are tongued. Is that not some devil's alchemy to put into your tale?" I laughed and stood in silence for a time.

"And where and when shall we search out your wounds to hear our voices? You could be my other Drake," was all the mariner said. I smiled and thought, *My father's father I am not, but I sing to a fearful wilderness in a tarnished child. And what resurrections are we to become for all the damned?*

TOWARD EVENING, WITH THE SUN IN FULL DECLINE, THE SAVAGES left, having let many hours pass. I walked outside the walls of our fort and watched the pinnace offshore bob on its anchor, its masts like naked trees, dead to the wind. The lapping of the swells against its sides, the creaking of its boards, were like the beckoning of home, and I wished I were traitor enough to go. But he who would be history could be traitor to all but his resolves. Ideas are the only loyalty. My name I swore would ride in hurricanes.

Now words in distant whispers to my ears. "Beware Smith, and his suspicions and the cannons of the fort."

There was a sound far off that echoed across the water, a puff of smoke from the pinnace's deck. In the river a small geyser rose and splashed upon my boots, another sharp crack which broke to clarity my haze of dreams. "We are under fire," I yelled. Sails now unfurled, the pinnace was alive with crawling ants, their fists raised, their smoking firelocks brought to bear upon me. Lunacy had packed its fears in violence.

"We are in mutiny!" Diving into the fort, shots tearing at the walls, the loyal few at their stations: Martin there; Ratcliffe and Archer not about. The cannons of the fort pulled back from the wall to receive their charge, Todkill ordering loads of bar shot. "Demast her!" he cried. Our cannon spoke in smoked violence against our ears. Plumes of water rose about the pinnace, her mast by shot torn loose, falling across her side, her sails descending in mortal flutter about the deck.

"Never…Smith…never…shall we come back," Archer screamed, his words and the reports of his weapons splashing in designs of war upon the waters.

"Put a shot on her bow," I ordered Todkill. The cannon's fire echoed the sunlight. The bowsprit exploded into splinters. About the pinnace the water plumed in violence. Stunned in her silence now, her weapons quiet, her voices still, she seemed to wait, as if exploring in herself the edges of her pain. Ratcliffe spoke now.

"We are coming about." His words drifted in from far away, as if he spoke disembodied from the far side of the sun.

"Do not fire again," called Archer. Behind the sadness of his defeat there was a determination and a resolve.

"Beware fools in cowards' clothes," Todkill said, "for they are ever vicious in their pursuit, even to their own destruction." I nodded.

The pinnace turned in suffering slowness toward the shore. The crew rowed her, dragging her mast and sails trailing in the water like the innards of an exploded gut. Near the shallows they dropped anchor. Archer and Ratcliffe and their six lowered a dinghy.

"By what cause," Ratcliffe said, "do you, Captain Smith, discharge your weapons in the direction of the president of the council and one of its members, our Captain Archer?" As Ratcliffe spoke, he and the others advanced upon me. Todkill was at my side. "By what cause?" Ratcliffe repeated as the space between us closed to the thinness of a breath. "I am here by agency and charter as a second king. I have risen from obscurities to now sit thrones upon you. Why do you play treason in my camp?"

"There is no law on earth that discretions mutiny," I said. "War against our God if you wish, but not against my enterprise." My tongue slipped. I had now heresied against God. Ratcliffe's flesh had dragged me into its loop toward what I did not know.

Archer needled accusations toward me in a smirk. "How many interferences have we tolerated? The council cannot act under your constant threats, Captain Smith. If we wish to sail to England to find supplies, the president has the right under law."

"And you would abandon the colony to starve, to save yourselves," I said. "The law is a thwart. It betrays convenience. What you call your right I call a coward's treason. And all that you are I oppose, by worlds and heavens I am ever at your throat."

"I will not disfigure all our warrants to please your whims," hissed Archer. "Never again shall you meddle in my plans. The law has its ways to serve my many needs. It is the writ that will tear out your heart."

Ratcliffe then addressed the crew. "Our Captain Smith wishes you all to die. Supplies are but short months away in England. I, who would bring them hither, am delayed. By king and council I am the law. My pleasure is to see you fed."

"Ratcliffe's crimes have made him fat," shouted Fettiplace. The company laughed. "The council should be overthrown." Words once thought, their conclusions in the air. Ratcliffe's and Archer's weapons pursed beneath their hands. Violence ever taut, pending on the casuals of a push. But Archer, tasting defeat, his will deflating, baked his courage in a cunning pie.

"I'll have none of this," he said. "The council shall meet."

"The moment now is well pruned for it," I demanded.

"At my discretion," Archer smiled, puffing his venom.

Ominous sleeps the cat with watchful eyes. I went to my tent, set Fettiplace and Todkill as guards, asked Jonas to prowl and see what he could learn. It was January 2, 1608. The days had begun to have some warmth after many frigid weeks. Four hours later I heard Archer calling in an inviting voice from outside, asking if I would join the council in its deliberations. I rose, hand on my sword, suspecting something foul. I brushed aside the curtain of my tent flap and walked into Ratcliffe's breath.

"Look well about you," Ratcliffe smiled. Todkill and Fettiplace had swords at their throats. "Your head may soon be bleeding brains." I felt something hard touch my head. It was Archer and two of his crew holding pistols to my ears.

"Hear death in the iron seashells?" laughed Archer. "I arrest you, Smith, for the death of your two companions, Jehu Robinson and Thomas Emry, who died by your bad judgment and for whom you shall pay with your life." Archer spoke his milk in venom, his eyes glistening with joy. "How sweet the verdict's rope about your neck, my dear Smith,"

They took the pistols from my belt, held my arms as the savages had done and led me through the fort. And so, I had become again a prisoner. I wondered what invisible chains bound my life to hold me convict to every whim. Those of my crew who might have tried a rescue were disarmed. Lord Percy would not speak to me. Reverend Hunt seemed strangely silent. What war now could be my defense? A table was set in the center of the dilapidation that was our town. Collapsed tents blew and bellowed like defeated flags upon the ground. Cabins stood with ruined roofs and broken walls. Light and the smell of darkness showed through their cracks.

Ratcliffe and Archer and the reluctant Martin sat before me at the table, I before them awaiting the judgment which had already been judged. Archer stood first and spoke, holding the Bible in his hand. "By this book, by the chapter called Leviticus, this man"—he pointed to me—"has taken two lives. By God's law, his life is forfeited. It is an eye for an eye and a tooth for a tooth."

"I did not kill Robinson and Emry. It was a savage *ambushado*," I interrupted.

"In Leviticus, when Aaron's two sons died, although Aaron did not kill them, God ordered him punished."

Reverend Hunt rose and spoke. "God asked for atonement. He asked that the sins be placed on the head of a goat, and the goat with the iniquities be set free in a solitary land, and that the goat should go forth into the wilderness."

"I ask for Smith's death!" shouted Archer. "So that his bearded and horned goat shall not pollute again this our land. I ask for the same cleansing as God himself has asked. The oils of atonement are blood and only with his blood shall he atone. This, our council, shall eat of his flesh in vengeance to purify itself."

"It was God's will that man not eat of blood." Reverend Hunt stepped toward me as he spoke. "The life of the flesh is in the blood, and God ordered his children not to eat of it but to reserve it for offerings in atonement or to bury it in the dust so that life shall water life but not eat of it."

"And so it shall be," spoke Archer, his mouth now cruel in the taste of power. "Smith shall hang. He shall be buried in the earth. His corruption shall feed this ground." Archer paused, looking at Ratcliffe. "All who say guilty and so bring death to Smith, raise their hands."

Archer and Ratcliffe raised their arms. Martin shook his head no. There were cries of protest. "Is this mutiny I hear?" Ratcliffe said, rising to his feet. "Our trees can bear many a harvest of bitter fruit." There were no complaints now, almost everyone disarmed, only an angry silence. The mariner sought to come to my defense but was restrained by Archer's friends.

"Shall we hang him within the hour?" asked Archer. Ratcliffe looked at me and smiled. "No sooner tried, no sooner hung," he said, "and we then to sail."

They put me in a tent with a guard at the door. I walked about the room, its emptiness and its dust my only companions. Archer came to see me, bearing a clay pipe and some tobacco. "It's from Ratcliffe. A last pleasure for the condemned, I was told to say. His idea. I myself have just come to watch you exhaust yourself in fear." He lit the pipe and took a puff and handed it to me. "Soon you shall be dust. Why not eat of its waters now." I took the pipe and toasted him with the smoke. I inhaled. "What a wasted pleasure is this sacrament," I said. My fear no fear, I played the moment spiced.

Archer smiled, "A savage pleasure, with no atonement, no rescue. Only for you a little time." The cabin now dressed itself in shadows. By the open door was there a rumor of light. I walked to it and looked outside. Beyond the walls of my prison were the walls of the fort. Beyond the fort was the narrow cage of the land. Beyond the land, the waters of the bay reaching to the horizon and the gray fence of the sky. I stood my point in the great axis of a circle of walls. Where I stood I imagined space began.

"A SAIL! A SAIL!" A VOICE BEYOND THE FORT'S WALLS, ITS CRY weighing on the thickening air. The company ran toward the gate. My guard left his post. Archer rushed past me through the door. I was forgotten and deserted, but for my life. I walked from my prison. The only chain that bound me was its idea. I crossed the town alone, through the open gate, touching elbows with some of Archer's men. They ignored me as they would the ashes of yesterday's fire, staring into the bay where the gray sails of a ship held a distance before a gray sky. The sails seemed to rise from under the roll of the waters. They came forth from a low line of mist.

"It's Newport!" someone shouted, as he danced behind his pointing finger. The sails now buckled pride in their crests of bloom. The flags, visible from her masts, filaments of our nation's might, sailed colors across the sky's empty plate.

Newport's voice hailed us even before he made the shore. We sang to him joys in tears to chase back our griefs.

"There are no storms at sea," Lord Percy cried, "that this land cannot match in trials."

We gathered by the stumps of several cut trees which served as the ship's dock. Newport came ashore, his crew following with disciplined pride. We gave them all fair welcome. To us it was as if the earth had birthed angels from a watery nest. "There should be another ship," Newport said, looking to sea. "The *Phoenix* should be along soon. We were separated in a storm. But where are the rest?" he said, looking at the twenty-nine of us who still remained of those hundred and seven he had left some six months back.

"Gone by death, its famine, its diseases, by judgments badly made, by idleness," Reverend Hunt answered. We then gave thanks on bended knee, while Ratcliffe and Archer whispered in each other's ears. Reverend Hunt coughed through his prayers as the sky blackened into the grip of a seamless night.

After we had tasted the soup of our evening meal, eaten the spoiled barley and its worms, while sixty new adventurers, half too weakened to come ashore, sat in the foul air of Newport's ship, breathing contagions in its stink and drinking bad water from rotting barrels, Newport rose at the head of the table to speak some apologies. "I have some blame in all this death. I should have returned from England by November last, but was delayed by faults not wholly mine. Martin's gold was not gold at all, but dirt. Rumors of its being pure and wealth spread in wild certainties through the London Company, even to the king. When the truth was known, Martin and this company were all accused of being cheats and hoaxing to gain rewards. The company wanted investigation, and so too the king. Thwarted hopes blamed beyond all reason. Rage wants pain to redress its pain. Those at court in secret dealings with the Spanish won delays in my departure. I sought only to protect, but made the matter worse. I said that perhaps I had brought the wrong ore to be assayed. I was then accused of being a cheat and a fellow with this fraud. I swore to the king and council, to save all our names, that from this voyage I would return with gold, or never go into their presence until I did.

"All our names lie dirty on the block. Greed has fermented its poison, all our reputations are now tied to finding a better gold."

Martin bit blood upon his lips, smashed his fists upon the table and cursed. Newport said that the fast pinnace *Phoenix* that accompanied him was to return at once to England with the fresh ore when it arrived.

The council met again. Martin, Archer and Ratcliffe sat behind their table. I still under accusation. Two great fires burned on either side of them, casting light on the folds of their clothes, on their faces, so the hollows of their eyes and their cheeks were sunk in shadow and their skin made marble in the flickering glow. Martin stood and protested Archer's presence on the council, as he was seated by Ratcliffe's vote alone, without the approval of either Martin or myself. "It was agreed that only those with an unanimous vote would serve," Martin said. As he spoke, his eyes watered in the golden sun of the reflecting fire.

Ratcliffe stood, saying, "Martin always sees his yellow wealth, where others of less lunatic see only dirt. And what fruit has all this borne for us in England? The vote is done. Let it be." Archer's company of a solitary few spoke to his defense. Others parried in anger, gesturing with closed fists. Words were thrust forward from mouths to pointing fingertips, as if aimed on darted breaths. There came then a confusion of angers, gestures and purposes. It would seem that words had hatched cataracts in the night air. Newport stood, a man desperately seeking to save his reputation, raising his arms to bring order, to bring silence. All had a grudging respect for Newport, who represented a true power, enforceable by his ships, by his crew, by his cannon, by his circle of authority which we knew pressed beyond this noose of our Chesapeake to the larger realm of England and its courts. Finally, after we ordered ourselves again, the company spoke of the deaths of Robinson and Emry, and of my trial, of my conviction, of my sentence.

"There is no law here," said Todkill, "that is even a ghost of our English practice. We have in our license turned ourselves into savages."

A stranger rose to speak, a gentleman by his dress and demeanor, one of the new supply of men who had the strength to come ashore. "I am Matthew Scrivener," he introduced himself. "What we have heard this night is a dialogue of the lost. We are lost not by continents but in ourselves. We stray into words, waifs to their meanings, blind to their intents. Yet we are the lamp that our England has set down in a darkened world. The Spanish main is to our south. Forget your wars of pettiness among yourselves! The stars themselves have given to our lips words to break forth in cataclysms. I am a soldier as most of you, a gentleman without calling, but to this call I am given. For earth, for England and for Saint George." When he finished, our company cheered.

Newport stood and offered Scrivener for the council. We all approved. Ratcliffe hid his reluctance before the mass. He had little choice, for both his and Archer's heads would have surely fallen that night. My conviction was set aside. Archer was deposed from the council to be our recorder once again. A man of title without power, as he would ever be a power without title, Archer fumed in his discontent, but few cared or noticed.

Chapter Twenty-six

A TRADE OF GIFTS AND GLANCES. THE NIGHT
OF FIRE. POWHATAN'S QUESTION. A MEETING IN
THE SHADOWS. THE POWER OF THE BLUE BEADS.
OPECHANEANOUGH HAS A BOOK.

T DAWN when the vapors of the night still hung close to the earth, a savage walked from the line of trees before our fort. A cloud of frosty mist swirled about his feet. He shouted my name, asking if he might approach. I walked to the wall and saw that the savage was one of those Powhatan trusted most. I shouted back, "Approach without fear. If you come in love, it is my love you shall receive."

The savage advanced. Behind him seven others appeared, each carrying some offering of either food, a trinket or an animal skin. One of their number who had been toward the rear in the line of march ran forward, taking up the lead, as if command had now laid its scepter's kiss upon her cheek. It was a girl, and a child of Eden. It was that daughter of Powhatan, Pocahontas. She walked into Jamestown ahead of the group.

With so many new arrivals to the company and so few houses built, many of us had slept outside on the cold ground that night. Many now rose in their blankets, in their rags. Drunk with cold, they staggered in search of warmth.

That girl—her eyes swept in one glance the destitution of the place. Her head tilted on her neck silent in its questioning, sorrowful and amused. She was not shy or afraid, even among us. She stood in front of me, her face, her lips, her very self a gesture to a dream. "My people come to trade," she said. Newport and Ratcliffe approached and heard her words. "You may take what you like and set any value you think is fair, but first I have brought you presents."

"Captain Newport has returned. My father,' I said, Newport at my side. He was acknowledged with signs of peace from the savages. The young girl also touched her heart, then raised her hands, opening them in silent blossom to the sun. "You are welcome in love," she said. "I have brought your son, your warrior, presents to keep him safe." She then unrolled six skins of fur upon the ground, two of bear and two of deer and one each of mink and otter. The crew who gathered about us groaned in amazement. Newport, who first wondered at the high regard in which I was held, now begged strategies from the blaze of his own ambitions for reputation and gold.

"These would bring a price in London," one was heard to say. Even Martin was asked if he would prefer a gold that brought warmth with its wealth, instead of one whose riches were always cold. Newport's eyes hardened at the mention of the metal. Martin did not answer, but Ratcliffe asked the girl, more stern than in a joke, "And none for Newport and myself?"

"There is trade for you, which is as a gift," she said, looking at our disheveled crew. She paused, looking at Ratcliffe. "Opechancanough, my great uncle, says he who would force from a present more than is offered can never be a wise or trustworthy friend." Ratcliffe's face boiled red, as if his blood had been fired by a slap.

"Teach your little conquest," Ratcliffe said to me, "that there is a stinger in this thicket she sees only dressed as a trifle."

"Now, now," said Newport. "Let us have trade with these people and not seem as a war unto ourselves." He paused and turned toward the savages, not even looking at the girl, as he asked, "And what do you carry for which we might trade?" The savages stood in their watch, their eyes searching mine for my approval.

"Does Smith now appoint this time for trade?" asked the girl, embracing my will as her sovereign, even before the great *werowance* Newport.

"Yes," I said as I nodded. The savages unrolled their mats upon the ground, placed baskets of nuts and turkeys and ducks and venison on them in fair display. Food to add to our common stores. To we who had starved, it was a generous mercy. "Nothing metal," Newport whispered to himself, counting his salvation in golden weights. Thus do paths divide. Then the savages placed a chain of tobacco and eight furs and a handful of pearls on their mats. I gave them a few copper trinkets and two hatchets.

Pocahontas took the copper from me, smoothing the surface color of it in her hands, warming the iron of its heart in her touch. She looked at me. "I am content with this," she said.

"But I have more," I said, taking a string of copper beads and placing them around her neck. "For you, a gift from Newport and myself."

"Half given, but well received," she said in laughter. I wondered what she meant. Was it an insult or crafted subtle taunting? I watched her eyes, as her lips bled sweetened moons.

"WELL CONTENTED, I THOUGHT," SAID NEWPORT AFTER THE SAVAGES had left. "Only food and trifles, but disappointment may yet herald some good conclusion. But why a present to the girl?"

"Perhaps our traitor has private forest conquests in his plans," said Ratcliffe. The company laughed. Ratcliffe acknowledged their approval.

"She's Powhatan's favorite daughter," I said. Newport, in shock, jumped as if to leave his skin.

"A savage empress! An empress," he kept repeating. "An alliance there could have golden consequences. Does she wear any golden trinkets?" Newport asked. "We should have been more generous."

"There is no gold. Their wealth they count in food," I said. Newport, persuaded to a different hope, ignored me. Impressed with any rank or any royalty of the blood, he had given his soul in loyalty to too many English nobles for him to treason his obedience before even a savage of exalted station. Our minds manifest themselves in chains, not only to their links but also to their shadows. "She would know where is the gold, or more certainly, her father," said Newport. Martin wagged his agreement with a nod.

WE BEGAN TO UNLOAD THE SHIP THAT DAY, JOYOUS IN OUR NEW store of food and our metal provisions, those tools to bend the land to our labor. We met in better greeting the new arrivals to our fort, sixty in all. The London Company had now sent men of some skill: goldsmiths, refiners of metal, gunsmiths, tailors, a maker of tobacco pipes. The beginnings of industry as London saw it. But men of skill, by our custom and our parliamentary law, only had to practice their own trades, and would not work at some general labor, even when there was a need. I wondered how much they would be gluttons to our food rather than allies for our success.

Martin's health returned and with his strength he spent his breath on talk again of gold. Nothing but of finding gold. He and Newport held their council. Greed led an alliance into friendly plots, all for gold. Newport sought a vapor. He became an idolater in his mind. It was a disease of thought, its contagion spread in words. Soon half the camp dreamed his dream. My work was left to idle.

Newport talked of great exploration and great excavations. I talked of food. We played against each other. Every few days Pocahontas and groups of savages came to our fort with presents and to trade. They would call to me, asking if they might approach our walls. "Come," I would say, "come in love," a word I now spoke in hard ritual, as if I wanted to drain its meaning and forget its soul. Words have souls that ring like angry spirits when betrayed. Always she came to the fort first. Before all I would receive my gifts and a few for Newport. She was close again. I felt the soft nest of her breath. I set the value of their trade, gave them copper. I cast down my better heart. I should have licked passions on her lips and enfolded her in my arms, but I did not.

She would leave and return. Newport was always at my side, ingratiating his strategies in kindness. The savages would trade only with me. What I bartered went into our common store, the food and the many valuable furs to be sold by the stock company and divided among the shareholders, who had paid for our provisions. The others of the company grumbled. They told the savages of their own greatness, saying they would give more for the furs and the food than I. They plotted against our own interest. They played treason to our future.

And they complained about me. "You have no charter to be sole agent to these savages," spoke Archer to me in his venom. Others agreed. Ratcliffe gave the sailors permission to trade with the savages. Newport smiled in satisfaction at his words. Now he could please the savages and gain a stronger trust, doing a subtle violence to our supply of food by his quest for gold...but that was not Newport's concern. The members of our company took to themselves the rights that were first granted to the sailors. The trade became general. All wanted the furs. There was profit now where once there was only death. When only I traded with the savages, I set the prices and the prices were low. Now the prices rose. Soon we could not get for a pound of copper what I once got for an ounce. Hatchets and other tools began to disappear from Jamestown, stolen for the trade with savages. Soon it was hammers and swords. Then guns. We had become locusts in our own nests.

Our common store, which had begun to fill with food, now began to dwindle away. The public trade with the savages almost ceased. It was all in secret now. There were rumors of what could be had for copper or swords or guns. Sailors made fortunes in a single trip, while our company was destitute. We hated Ratcliffe, who became the cape merchant. He managed our common store, charging us fifteen times what anything was worth, pocketing the money which should have gone to the London Company. He lived well on the proceeds of our blood, as if it were an inheritance. We traded what we could with the sailors for extra food, who then traded with the savages and made the profits.

Newport's ship became our tavern. Newport pleasured only in his avarice, found no gold, but grieved of nothing else. Men of our company would stagger on his deck, drunk, vomiting over her sides.

For weeks after Newport's arrival we built huge campfires at night to keep us warm. Flames leaped into the sky. Sparks rode above the madness on darkened heat. Men wandered before the fires, dancing in the memory of drink. Logs cracked in the flames, sending sparks like gusts of meteors through the black, until the winds one night blew tempests across the earth. Gusts in riot raced, their spirits carrying frenzies across the waters of the bay. Spray rose in thunderous swells. The world a faceless mouth screaming its inundations upon our fort. Flames and sparks of our campfire raged, its heat quenched as it was swept away. Our marrows froze, our bones turned ice. We shivered on the scarecrow frost. Flames leapt sparks in their ignited hurricanes. Cinders in their crystal fires rode the wind, some of them falling, catching on the thatched roof of the storehouse. Fumes soon smoked, exploding into fire, other houses burning, tents, hammocks, our blankets on the ground. Flames danced conflagrations in their taunts as we ran frantic in our silhouettes. Wind had wild spread the fire and there was nothing we could do. That night Jamestown was mostly burned to ash.

AS I WALKED THROUGH ITS RUIN THE MORNING AFTER, I TRIED TO push away the obscuring vines of smoke with my hand. Men sat on the ground, coughing, soot smudging their clothes. Most had lost the little that they had. There was a seventeen-foot breach in our walls. Our church, our tents and most of our few buildings gone. The earth had swallowed us.

Scrivener came to my side. "Is this the end?" he said, looking at the weight of the smoke upon the wind. "Do we abandon it now?"

"We will rebuild," I said. "And we will rebuild again if we must. There is no spoil that can take me from this place. I am here in granite."

Some wanted to leave, but I would brook no desertion. Reverend Hunt, who had lost his books and all his clothes, spoke of his resolve to stay. He never complained of his loss. He moved men by his example. We would remain. He energized the lazy and gave cheer to the wretched.

We slept on the ground, building great fires during the day. At night we spread hot coals upon the earth, warming the hard frost, laying our blankets upon the expiring softness of the heat. And so we would sleep, the earth seeping its fever through our covers to give us rest. Some would have their beds on the boat, but lack of space made that impossible for all. Some were in the few tents still unburned. We would change our place of rest each night—from earth to house to ship—conserving our health, as we could. Still, we began to die. The new, the seasoned, all equal in our congress of death.

Trade with the savages continued more frantic than before. Crumbs now meant life; skins, the robes of warmth; fowl and meat, the weights of hope. The prices the savages demanded increased. We paid them. Newport sent Powhatan presents to dazzle his mind, ever wanting to learn in confidence where lay the golden treasure in their vaulted rocks. But all the presents bribed only a strange silence. They only fired Powhatan's imagination and exaggerated to him his own worth. This extravagance confirmed to the savages Newport's greatness. If only it had been his wisdom. Newport was now speaking in flattery in a land where only strength and resolve had bite. He had cloaked his weakness in eloquent signs, but who would pay the price?

POWHATAN SUMMONED NEWPORT TO HIS VILLAGE A FORTNIGHT after Jamestown burned.

"I shall take sixty of us as protection against the savages' treachery," he said. That was most of our company.

"You only need a dozen and me," I replied. "But if it gives you courage, we shall take twenty." It was not the subtlest of my pronouncements. Newport's eyes froze in their stare, as if all thought had ceased to grow when it came to me. "The savages respect courage. If you come to them with an army, they will know you are afraid."

"Or that my greatness requires I come with vast legions."

"I have been among the savages alone and have brought them to my will. Twenty shall serve us nicely. We cannot spare the other men." I gestured to the pillars of charred wood protruding from the earth that once were our homes. "We now store our food in a roofless hut. Men are dying from the cold. The enterprise here must be set right or this entire company will flee to England or desert to the savages for rescue."

"No Englishman will traitor himself for a forest hut or a heathen's meal," said Newport, holding his anger close.

"They have before," I said, "and even now this company ministers to its cold with warm dreams of the savages' firelight."

"Not this company!" Newport's voice rose.

"Men change their gods to smooth their course. Men worship what they will for what they want," I said.

We walked out amidst the ruins. Men, wrapped in blankets, shivered even in their cloaks. They huddled in groups. A few worked, carrying blackened logs. Scrivener and a party were rebuilding a half-burned house. Martin sat before a few, whispering sermons of bright wealth. Men listened. Newport smiled as we passed.

That night I sat in a cabin of Newport's ship, paper before me, blank. I stared into its flatness. I began to write my public book, the narrative of this place, a call to England to join my dream. I told the expedient truth, that of our failure and our weakness. I told of our deaths. I made disasters into adventures, my hand and my quill passing through the shadows of the swaying candle flame. I did not tell of the girl. I could not. I told she was but a child. It was as if my life were hiding behind my future name.

WE SENT MESSAGES TO POWHATAN THAT NEWPORT, WITH A GUARD of twenty, would soon come to trade. In the meantime, messages from Wowinchopunk arrived at our fort with word of a group of men dressed like us on the bay further north. "For love and a few hatchets," the messenger said, "we will guide some of your Englishmen to them."

I told Newport of the stories I had heard of the Ocanahonan during my captivity.

"And you believe these legends true?" said Newport.

"I believe the savages told what they knew. What the truth of it is, who can say?"

"It could be an *ambushado*." Newport spoke, his cautions hiding personal fears.

"There are strategies we can use to prevent their treacheries." As I spoke, I wondered how I would make his vanity an ally. "What a garland would come to this enterprise if we could find the people of our lost Roanoke." Newport thought, then nodded his reluctant consent.

"Tell your king we shall come in love, bearing ourselves and hatchets and resolves for the journey to seek our own," I said to the messenger.

RUNS OF ICE WERE ON THE RIVER WHEN OUR BARGE CLEARED the last of Jamestown's beach. We sailed into the Chesapeake, into its frost and shifting plates of ice, sailing toward Powhatan, first to make some visit to seek our lost. How strange our lot, our company cast to the wind. The barge's small cabin was filled with presents for Powhatan: robes and plates and things from England, including a white greyhound sent by King James himself. We fed the animal on our scraps. The dog lived better on our bits than we.

Our bow, in a fresh wind, tore flesh from breakers. We headed north. We stopped at the village of the Paspaheghs, gave two of our company into their hands, they to be led by Indian guides to find the survivors of Roanoke. We took three of Wowinchopunk's children against their safe return. The savages were not pleased by our mood, but they agreed, asking that the hatchets be given first, as a sign of our love, which we did.

The wind now freshened from the south, the sky so gray it spilled its milky pallor upon the waters so there seemed to be no joint, no horizon where they met.

"Do we sail on earth or across the sky?" Scrivener joked. The wind blew such cold we almost shivered into frozen bricks. With waves that swelled in race through broken frost, besides some groaning of the ice, the river was silent, no strange voices in my ear. I felt some disappointment as we made our perilous course to find some protection from the storm.

Now through the bay, the sky broke into floods of snow. We sailed into the shelter of a cove, its hillside white, its waters almost black with cold and shallow draft. We raised sails over our heads as a roof and lit a fire, resting our heads and hands against its light and vacant heat. We froze, well packed. We smoked some tobacco, passing several pipes among us. Robert Cotton, our newly arrived pipe maker, stared at the deck of the barge, breathing in the vagrant smoke as it drifted across his face. I handed him a warm pipe. He tapped the glowing coals with one of his gloved fingers. His face winced in a dart of pain. "There be a better way to tap the leaf," he said, taking from his pack a tobacco box, "without the burning of a fingernail." In the box was a small metal ladle called a snuff spoon. "To bring the powdered herb to the nostril to have a whiff." Cotton smiled. "We need the priming iron to bed the glowing leaf proper in the bowl and the tongs to place a coal upon the herb. We need not the balance to weigh the pudding, our sweet tobacco, or the pick to clean the bowl. We are as set as any English gentleman." Cotton put the pipe to his mouth. "This Virginia leaf is not of quality. There's a bite to the taste that kills its price in London," he said. "Not worth the trouble to plant, maybe half a shilling for ten pounds—worthless. The West Indian leaf brings ten shillings for a pound, but that's a better climate, better water, better heat...but still, this fills the pipe." The company laughed as the mist and snow drifted on the wind, mixing with and obscuring the tobacco smoke.

"Why are you here then?" asked a voice, hard, shaken with its own shiver.

"Improve the leaf a bit. If I can. Make pipes for trade with the savages or for sale in London." As he spoke, he turned and pulled from the box a clay pipe with a small bowl and long, thin stem, which curved gracefully to its head, like the neck of a bird.

"Think the savages might approve this," he asked, "instead of their heathen ones? Put a feather or a few beads here or there and it would make any savage proud. Our English dandies are well pleased by our English clays. Why not these savages? London, Bristol and Winchester all are centers for the trade, Queen Bess herself giving us protection by a grant of monopolies but six years past. So England serves its own, they to serve the world."

The snow slid through the air, obscuring land, turning the world to white. The night came again.

AFTER SOME FEW DAYS, THE TWO WHO HAD GONE TO FIND ROANOKE returned. "It was all a trick to get our hatchets. We went but twenty miles, then were brought here. They think us fools," said one. There were those who would have killed Wowinchopunk's children in vengeance, but Newport and Scrivener objected, and I said, "No, they have brought ours back in safety and we must do the same." We released the boys. "Tell your father our word is ever true. He has bested us once, but to the forfeit of our love."

When the sun rose, the storm had passed. The land glittered in the sharp crystals of a cold dawn. We sailed north again. Newport, anxious for his gold but still uncertain of Powhatan's love, asked me to take part of our company overland to test his intentions. I agreed. We anchored at the head of a large river. Newport was to wait twelve hours before sailing further north to Powhatan's village at Werowocomoco. I was to march across the country with eight of our company and ply our best hopes against his bite. I to take some presents for Powhatan, including the white greyhound, who for most of the trip lay on our deck in a coil of fur.

The bay in which we anchored was filled for a mile with frozen muck. Three small creeks cut icy veins through the waste. We set out as we could, the thick ice supporting our weight. It was a treacherous path toward shore, with all safety an illusion, and solid ground only a willful promise.

The dog sniffed the ground as we walked. At times he wandered away, but a rope around his neck held him to our path. Occasionally he would bark at unseen things.

As we marched, my mind turned not to the dangers that might treason the very ground I walked, but to that girl whose name, even her very name, was a logic that poisoned thought, a potion that drank its sounds into my ear, into my history. Would I break the shell to birth a manhood I would not want to be…for her, for the certitude of a caress that tongues no blessings for my fame to come. I was nervous at the thought of seeing her. I'd rather not, but I'd rather yes.

AT WEROWOCOMOCO WE MARCHED TO THE DOOR OF POWHATAN'S great meeting house. Before it on a mat were fifty plates of fine bread. I smiled. Each sovereign displays himself in the currency of his nation's coin. I remembered my hunger. Was this a subtle taunt to remind me of our want? As I entered there were tunes of joy sung for my arrival. Powhatan lounged on his low throne, cloaked in a large fur wrap, forty women reclining at his head and at his feet, as pillows on a divan. Lines of nobles sat against the walls, their heads and shoulders painted red, jeweled, as always, in pearls and copper.

Powhatan leaned forward at my approach. I did not see his daughter. I presented the savage our gifts of a coat of red cloth, a hat such as King James wore and the white greyhound, who, as fate would have it, licked his emperor's face, then curled himself on the throne in a groan of relief and peace. The nobles laughed. Powhatan smiled. "I wish all our English were so well behaved." I laughed as well. I sat and was handed a tobacco pipe. I drank deeply of its smoke, tasting its heat. The queen of the Appomattoc brought me bread and wild turkey and water. I ate until refreshed. Then Powhatan said in a merry mood, "I am always pleased to see my English Smith, but where is your father, Newport?"

"He is out on the river on our barge. He will come ashore tomorrow." Powhatan thought of this reply for a moment. Deciding it was satisfactory, he asked, "Why have you not sent me the two cannons and the grindstone which you promised me?"

"As was my promise, I offered the cannons to those you sent with me to Jamestown, but they seemed not to want it." At that, Powhatan laughed. "Perhaps next time you will offer ones which can be carried," he said, as his laughter silenced. "Are there others with you, Smith, or do you come alone?"

"I have a company of eight," I replied.

"Well, have them enter and let them be refreshed with our food."

I had told my company to remain outside with the tapers of their firelocks lit. Friendship here feigns convenience, until it is time to prompt a war. Together, closed in upon each other in the confines of a small room, surrounded we could be overwhelmed. Powhatan smiled in his expectation, willful in his cruel magnificence. Always was there a balance here of safety against offense. I stood, saying to Powhatan that his request would be quickly granted. I called to my company, ordering two men to enter the meeting house, present their bows to Powhatan, then quickly depart before the next two were to enter and perform their homage. Powhatan thanked me for each bow, granting each of my company a plate with five pounds of bread. And so it was that at no time were we all so confined as to make a neat slaughter.

I sat again. Powhatan came casually to his deadly point: "And as a sign of our love and friendship, have your men place their weapons at my feet. Who needs such things when we meet in peace?"

I looked at the wily fox and into his treacherous eyes. "That is a ceremony only an enemy asks, never a friend. You have nothing to fear. Tomorrow, Newport will give you one of his sons, a youth of fourteen, Thomas Savage, for you to school in your ways and your language."

"And I shall give you one of my advisors for you to take to your England and be similarly taught." Powhatan gestured as he spoke. And so we fenced with smiles and tugged with pleasantries to test each other's strength.

"You see, we grow close in our exchange, but why have I not received the corn you promised when I was last your guest?" I asked, changing the subject. Powhatan looked at me, his eyes in thoughtful stare.

"You shall have it soon," he said. I did not like the thrust of those words, and so I said, "Newport also comes to make alliance with you against the Monacans."

Powhatan's eyes now watered in joy. "We shall," I added, "bring their women and their children and their domain under your rule. So it is Newport's wish," I lied. Newport wanted to explore the land above the falls where the Monacans lived, searching for his silly gold, as he ever was, and for that passage to the west, that mysterious sunlight quest to the riches of the Indies. So I clothed his dream in a lie. Newport would have no wars with Powhatan or the Monacans.

Powhatan now rose and spread his arms, the fur cloak about him lifted on his arms like demon wings. "I declare to all assembled here," he said, "that this, our Captain Smith, was made by me some time ago a *werowance*, and that all the English are from this day forth of our own people. No longer strangers but of ourselves. So may none deny them what they need—neither corn, nor country, nor women." So saying, he led me from the meetinghouse to the river, his people and my company following. At the banks of the flow, frozen plates of ice passed us in faithless rush. Powhatan said, "Go to Newport. Tell him of our love." Then he threw tobacco on the waters, as sacrifice for our safe passage.

I turned towards the river, but there was no sign of the barge, only the cold wind and its low hiss through the trees. The clouds came thick and bottomed from the sky. Rain fell its icy sorrow on the earth.

"The river is in its ebb and has carried your barge far down the stream," Powhatan said.

I had warned Newport about the tides in this river, which,

apparently, he had forgot the moment my words were said. After a time in the cold, watching for the dark line of the barge, we walked back to the village. "It is no matter," Powhatan said. I was led to a long wigwam. Inside was a fire on the floor before some mats. From the roof hung hundreds of bows and arrows, which swung in the drafts of the room, their swaying shadows intertwined. "It is a sign of our friendship," Powhatan said. "I have ordered my people not to injure you or your company in any way, or to steal your weapons."

"They are weapons only to our enemies," I said. Powhatan repeated my words. "Your company is being given a hind quarter of venison to cook as your evening meal," he continued. "They will join you soon." Then he threw a few logs on the fire, watching their sparks die as they swirled in the upward smoke. Then he left me to myself.

I looked about the wigwam, bows and arrows swaying like nervous things. The day being overcast, the room was dark. Shadows danced on walls as they drank the light. In the darkness something moved. It walked forward, blossoming into glow. It was that girl, that daughter, Pocahontas. She knelt by the fire, looking at me, breaking twigs, casting them into the flames, always looking at me. I could feel the softness of her glance, as if the distance between us had been made flesh. The alchemy of her touch made the fire bloom. Sweat was on my cheek. She stood, walked past me, her hand lightly caressing the coldness of my hair. Then she departed, my mind holding to the memory of her touch.

I am caught by hungers, by a passion am I snared. I am a haunt of loneliness. To a memory I am wed. Would I by forest nuptials tear breath from her sweet breath? Play coarse by love's rough sport? I dream a tenderness upon a space of air. I kiss at nothing but an idyll in an emptiness. But it will not cease. I am wormed by thought. My phantom arms seek a shadow. Its apparition has her name. Her profile speaks in worlds, their landscapes suffocations. I tongue her lips. I steam in a cold heat. I am by pain. My passions will not hold me as a rock.

THE NEXT DAY THE SUN SHONE WITH HOLLOW LIGHT UPON THE land. The air was cold. I walked with Powhatan to the river's edge. I saw many canoes on the river and on the beach. Savages were unloading furs and corn and copper and pearls. "From all my lands I am sent this tribute," Powhatan said. "You see." He pointed to canoes so far off they appeared as dots on an empty page. "They go for more, a five-day journey to bring all this to me. So large is my empire. I am as your European king, am I not?"

"And how do you know of European kings?" I asked, thinking of Don Luis. Powhatan smiled that smile power has when there will be no answer. "All kings ask tribute," he said. "Your barge comes with Father Newport." On the horizon's rim there was a blur and a sail. "So it does," I said. Powhatan left me alone, walking back to his village to prepare himself for Newport's arrival. Soon the eight of my company joined me, the tapers of their firelocks lit. I smiled as I whispered to myself, "Caution...always caution."

Newport landed. We left five of our company with Scrivener at the barge as a precaution. "What we have here is a nervous peace," I said to Scrivener. Our possible retreat respected, fifteen of us marched into Werowocomoco. Before us went a trumpeter calling his fanfares to the sky, as if his instrument would mate with a brass goose. Our ears throbbing, we marched to Powhatan's lodge, where we were received with all the savage dignity and respect which was their custom. We smoked tobacco to seal in signs our friendship. Newport presented the youth Thomas Savage to Powhatan, who received the child with warmth and affection. "Your son," Powhatan said, "is now as mine." Orations were given. We ate. The next day was set aside for trade and so we spoke, I as interpreter, being the only one fluent in their tongue. Some of our crew grumbled at the importance given my place. "He brags their tongue into his own dominion," one said. I heard but did not want to listen. Why do they tear down with their hate what they cannot build with their hands? Without me, who would feed them? Not themselves. They'd rather eat each other. That night we returned to our barge. I went to sleep, covered by the humid dark, its coldness more a blanket than our sheets.

THE DAY FOLLOWING WE SAT BEFORE POWHATAN'S FIRE AT THE time appointed for trade. Powhatan rested on his throne, draped in his fur and his women, regal and savage in his bearing. He looked at Newport and said, "I am a great chief, as are you. Let us not be petty in our dealing. Let us not bargain. It is a rudeness to our station. Why not place all the hatchets and copper that you have before me and I shall set a value on all, rather than on each trifle."

I translated Powhatan's words, adding my own commentary,

"This is an old trick of Powhatan's. I have been warned of this by the Chickahominy, who are his enemies. We should not do it."

Powhatan sat forward now, awaiting Newport's reply. "I will do it," Newport said, dreaming his hollow dreams of gold. He was a man who wished to buy a convenient love for a desperate purpose. "I wish to show this savage our greatness and our wealth. What are a few trinkets, more or less, against the value of this, our grand project? And with his love may come some greater prospect golden for us all. He knows where there are mines, I am sure."

I cautioned again. "I would bend him to our will. Make him please us. For us pleasing him, there will never be an end. His demands will increase as he sees us yield. There will be no bounds to his avarice."

Newport waved his hand at my face, as if to chase my words from the air. "Tell Powhatan that I agree," Newport ordered. "I will bring no hurt upon him or have him think I am a cheat. As the king himself decrees, we bring no harm, no matter the cost." Newport was a man who saw the world through London's parchments. The company's hand before his face swept all to doctrines. Adventure not his soul, initiative not his practice: he once let a Spanish treasure fleet slip pass him in the night because he had not the courage to seal his caution down his own throat. "You are playing a fool to a savage," I said "who kills fools as a sport."

"We are not the Spanish," Newport replied. "A friendship sealed with a little more profit to a savage is not a bad friendship. They will love us for our largess."

"You are being shammed and to put this right again may cost us blood. I came to this savage with nothing and brought back baskets of corn. Now you throw that away to prove you are a fool, which you call your greatness."

Newport answered me by asking if he should not consider my advice an incident of mutiny. I told him he could consider it what he wished. Powhatan, understanding our tone though not our words, smiled under his painted face. "If you wish this disaster," I said to Newport, "translate for yourself." With that, I rose and walked from the wigwam and returned to the barge, where Scrivener and the five of our company stood on guard, smoke circling above the lit tapers of their fire-locks. "Be ready. We may see some treachery yet," I said. "Although with Powhatan having all he could desire, it is probably no longer worth the blood." I told him of Newport's folly. Scrivener sighed.

In a while, Powhatan's son came to call me back to the council. "My father likes his Captain Smith always close to him. And bring your friends," he said, gesturing to Scrivener and the guard.

"No, they must stay, but I shall come," I said. Once in hazard of their plot, I would not be so again.

When I sat by Newport's side, he diverted his eyes, as if he wished not to see a fearful truth. His face, even in the yellow glow of the fire, looked drained of color. It seemed like a smudged white, complexioned like a nose rubbed in the dirt.

"He gave four bushels of corn for all the hatchets and copper. It would be cheaper to buy the corn in Spain than from these savages."

All the value that I had set was now swept away. "I will change the trade and set a new account. We will have the better of him," I said.

Powhatan leaned back into rest on his throne, his women arranging the drape of themselves on the platform around him to best display their beauty and to make most comfortable his ease. "We shall have our feast now," he said, not quite making an order, but letting all assembled know that was his wish. Powhatan smiled as his words brought forth food. In the crowd, half-hidden in a halo of sunlight falling from the open door, I saw Pocahontas. She cast her shadow through the light as a seal through hot wax, the stamp ever imprinted through that daughter of the silhouette. She carried a single plate. About her neck hung the copper beads I had given her. She walked, her purpose careful and direct. She held the plate to herself. I was embarrassed at my own sight for seeing her. She walked to me and knelt. I would not have it, but I would. She placed the plate in my hand. She smiled, looking through my skin. She seemed to caress with a glance my thoughts. I died then in exquisite pain. "Would you whisper secrets," she asked, "if we had secrets to whisper?"

"I would," I said. "I like the copper beads about your neck."

"It was given me by a warrior, who, afraid of the cost, took back the sweeter half, but I kept it all," she purred in a whisper. Then she rose and left, Powhatan watching her as she walked away.

WHILE OUR BARGE WAS BEING LOADED WITH BASKETS OF CORN the next day, we gathered again our company to visit Powhatan for one final morning of trading. As we walked to the walls of Werowocomoco, Nostanquid, one of Powhatan's sons came to us. "It is my father's request that you keep your guns and your swords from our village. They greatly frighten our women and our children."

"This is the request of an enemy," I said to the son of Powhatan. Newport looked at me and said, "I see no harm in it. It is just to prove our love."

"Do as Powhatan asks and he will cut your throat." I spoke in hardened tones. "Love in this wilderness is a fatal spoil," I said. "These warriors do not carry bouquets of flowers in their hands like wanton gentlemen. Those are hatchets. Would you have us die by treachery?" I looked at Newport who wore the saddles of his two masters: gold and London. I took some pity as I said, "In our purpose shall be our history."

Newport saw my determination for our weapons, and after our discord the day before he reconsidered. "Tell your father," Newport said, "Robert Cotton, Smith and I shall come unarmed. The others of our company will stay by the barge." Newport looked at me. "Agreed?" The land fluttered in its nervous light. "Not of sufficient good to keep us safe...but better," I said. Robert Cotton nodded. In his hand he carried one of his tobacco pipes.

Powhatan arranged himself on his throne and greeted us. His demeanor was different this day, more attentive to the points of thought he made as he spoke. Gone was the brew of congenial talk. Now Powhatan had clothed himself in naked power. "I wish to trade for guns," he said. "Love in firelocks—our alliance would be sealed. Our war against the Monacans would go well, very well, indeed."

Newport looked like a man lost at a crossroads, choosing which uncertain path to take. I would not be demeaned by imagined certitudes. "I have told you many times, Powhatan, we have not enough guns for ourselves to trade even one," I said.

"Where are the firelocks Father Newport promised would be mine?" asked Powhatan.

"When we have a new supply and enough for ourselves," I answered.

Newport whispered in my ear, "A single firelock for an emperor is not a hazard."

"Our weapons have more bite in their terror than in their effect. Let these savages sport with them and in that familiarity their terror ends, and we are much weaker than before, even with twice our strength. Power," I said, "is an idea."

Powhatan, understanding our determination in this, soon changed the composure of his face, a congenial laugh and a ready smile upon his lips. He leaned forward toward us and spoke in the low voice of an ally making serious plots. "And when begins our war against the Monacans?" he asked.

"When we are ready," answered Newport.

"That is good," said Powhatan. "This is how we will accomplish our war. I shall send spies beyond the falls to discover their villages, know their strength. With a hundred of your English, armed with guns, and with a hundred of my warriors, Captain Smith and Opechancanough will carry our war to the Monacan lands. Newport and I shall wait here and receive words of your exploits. But one law must be observed by all." Powhatan looked us in the eye. "Women and small children will be spared and sent to me, the others let free or killed, as Okee will decree."

"And beyond the falls," asked Newport, "what is there? I am in search of salt waters in another great ocean. It is my wish to hear its lips wash upon its shores." He was half drawn to madness by the vision of the sun dripping a path of gold across the Pacific West toward the Indies and its plumed and spiced citadels.

"The sun nests in the mountain that is seen," Powhatan said, "but of another ocean? I have heard of bays that follow rivers to a salted reach of waters, great lakes in passages west. That is what is told. More I do not know." The wily emperor added, "When we have the Monacans' lands, perhaps we will know more."

Newport might have agreed at once to seek those Monacan lands beyond the falls. His equal less to Powhatan's. He asked about the yellow dirt. "There is tell of places where yellow rocks are taken from the ground. Do you know of such?"

"I know of the rocks. They come from a great distance," said Powhatan. Newport asked if he might have a weight of stone to show our king. "There are none close," said Powhatan, "but perhaps when we have our war with the Monacans."

"It is a fiction that reels a trap," I said to Newport, who sought to equipoise his wisdom with his greed.

It was agreed that an expedition would go forward at the earliest and best time, but as for a war, it was only said that we would explore before there would be any decisions about wanton bloodshed.

"You English wage your promise as if it were a war," Powhatan snapped.

"We, like great Powhatan, make our wars carefully," I said. Powhatan leaned back on his throne, angered. Robert Cotton presented him with a tobacco pipe. "For you. It is my gift, but would your people desire to trade for ones like these?" Powhatan looked at the thin pipe. The gently curving neck seemed fragile.

"What voice to what god would arise from this?" I asked myself.

"I could," Robert Cotton added, seeing Powhatan's displeasure, "add a few special blue beads on yours to befit your rank." Powhatan nodded his agreement, handing back the pale vein of clay. "When you light it, the smoke draws easily through its stem," added Cotton.

"Easy smoke does not rise far," replied the emperor.

I waded with my thoughts into Powhatan's eyes, seeing through his sight. He glanced at a pile of blue beads. The time was now to set the balance and the new account. "These were not among that which was traded," I said. Newport and Powhatan acknowledged that truth. "These are almost too valuable to trade at any price." I translated my own words. "They never should have been shown." I looked at Newport as I continued to translate. "You should never have brought these," I said to Newport angrily. Newport submissively agreed. "These are the rarest of all gems. Only the greatest of chiefs and his women may wear them." Powhatan's eyes drooled their desire for those beads. "Any price that is not an empire I will pay," Powhatan said, letting the common blue beads roll through his fingers, his reason lost to the pebbles.

"Three hundred bushels of corn," I said. "We are friends. I seek only what is just."

Seduction is but a haunt of will...self-done. "Agreed," said Powhatan. Our trading at an end, we feasted, Powhatan giving us more food than would feed twenty. We sent most of it to our company at the barge, or it would have gone to spoil, as the savages' custom was never to take back food once given.

TOWARD DUSK, WE WALKED TO THE RIVER, THE BARGE NOW LOADED with corn, the blue beads safe in Powhatan's hand. On the rude beach we pledged our friendship, gave some trinkets to our host. Newport walked on the ice sheets toward the deeper flood of the river. From there he waved his hand and stepped onto the barge. When we had left the shore behind, Newport said, "Why do your certainties always come so forward fixed in mutiny? Never again dispute with me before a savage or my crew or anyone on the earth. I shall give my report in London."

"Are all admirals spit from lesser men?" I answered. "You should be thankful to those who saved you from the slaughter brought by your own folly."

"Your words, Smith, may yet hang you on their tongue." As Newport spoke, the men on the barge pretended to work as they listened to us clash. A breakfast was prepared of corn and water, a little Indian bread and venison. We sat on the rough boards of the deck, wondering at the fruitful plenty the savages possessed. "There are no hills in all of England that can bring forth such bounty, with such ease," said one, pulling his blanket tighter on his shoulders. "This summer we shall see green miracles in stalk and stem when our English farming science comes full to this land." A few said, "Hear, hear," but mostly we ate and coughed and tried to keep away the cold.

WE TRADED UPON THE RIVER THOSE WEEKS. THE SAVAGES SHOWED much pleasure with our goods. There was little treachery. Newport and I hardly spoke. We sailed the few rivers we knew, visiting the tribes along their banks. The weather held cold, the shallows of the waters hard with ice. Sometimes our miseries came in rain, sometimes in snow. There was sickness and coming deaths. At times we ate only corn and water. Our own water gone, we melted snow or took cupfuls from the river. Then the deaths came. Most of the crew were sick. We were almost despaired of life when we landed at the Pamunkey village.

Opechancanough received us with great dignity and reserve. He gave us food. We sat before him in his wigwam and spoke of trade, then spread our blue beads on his throne and told him their tale. Opechancanough sat back and examined us with thoughtful eyes. "Before we trade," he said, "I have a question to ask you. There is something which was found many years ago." He reached into the shadows of his throne. A shadow moved. He brought it forward in his hand. A blackened bulk, its leather falling in strips. Opechancanough handed it to me, its covers torn from its hinges. I took the book in my hand, opened it, its pages browned and glued with mold. "It is a Latin Bible," I said, "Spanish."

"Book?" questioned Opechancanough with a smile.

"These signs we call letters speak words if you know how to read their lips. It would be like the message I wrote to Jamestown when I was captive," I said, adding, "How is it you have this book?"

"It was found."

"Where?" I asked. "I have been told one of your people was raised by the Spanish. Is this book his?"

"This book is kept with the bodies of our chiefs. It is a trophy, a memory and especially a warning to us all. Now let us have trade." Opechancanough took the book from my hand, placing it in the shadows again. "What I desire," he continued, "are hatchets, iron tools, guns and swords."

"We offer beads, copper and hatchets. We do not trade in weapons," said Newport.

"There have been others such as you but different who have come to these lands. Perhaps we should wait and trade with them," Opechancanough replied.

"Your book is old," I said to Opechancanough. "We do not want anything given in trade today that will be at our throats tomorrow."

He laughed. "You speak well for your cause, Smith, but remember the stomach ever rules the sovereign of the throat, the tongue." And so we sat and traded for a day. Opechancanough had his hatchets and copper and, in a final thought, some blue beads. Robert Cotton offered him a tobacco pipe, which was refused. "Smoke your own pipes to your own gods," Opechancanough said. "Here, the pipe is as sacred as the smoke. Yours was not made in our way. To break the tradition is to lose the meaning. We are all called by our own mysteries," he said.

I thought again of Don Luis. Opechancanough agreed that Robert Cotton could come in the spring and see the tobacco planted and tended in its growth.

WE SAILED BACK TO JAMESTOWN, STOPPING ONCE ALONG THE riverbank to dig some yellow-streaked rock. While we dug in the cold water and mud, Newport was rowed in comfort back to the fort in a canoe. He would not sit in his discomfort for any of his lusts. We labored for two hours loading the rocks and dirt into sacks, then departed. It was a shameful waste of time. Men coughed and fevered and supported themselves on their shovels. The only gold in those rocks was dreams. Men wandered around the ice flows babbling of wealth and women and fine clothes. They shivered in their sickness and sweated in their toil. A few collapsed, half drowning in the muddy soup which had become the riverbank. I had had enough of this silly sport. I ordered the crew into the barge, taking the sacks we had, and sailed on. Men froze on our decks, holding to those wet sacks, which in the cold now drained themselves to ice.

Chapter Twenty-seven

NEWPORT SEEKS AN ANSWER AND A SEA. THE LOSS
OF THE SECOND SUPPLY. POWHATAN'S REQUEST.
DANGERS, WAR, AND A CHICKEN CLUCKS.

AMESTOWN WAS STILL a ruin, its walls burned away. The logs that remained bit at the wind like chipped and blackened fangs. Through a wide gap in the palisades could be seen the town, a landscape of ash. It was now March of 1608. Men in bright colors crawled like maggots over the darkness of its spent coals, searching in the blackness, laboring to turn over clumps of frozen debris, only to find more blackness. Beyond the town, the wind-driven smoke had stained the land with soot. It was as if the ground had been burned with shadows. There were small fires on the rise nearby the town, newly set to thaw the frozen earth for graves.

We landed and tied the barge to a tree. The other ship of Newport's fleet, Francis Nelson's *Phoenix,* had not yet arrived and was now months overdue and, we presumed, lost. We needed those supplies desperately. Even with our trade with the savages, our provisions had to last until our first harvest. "Two weeks," I said to Matthew Scrivener as we stepped onto the shore. "Two weeks. That's all Newport required to unload his ship and refit her for the sail to England. Two months it has been, eating our scarce supplies and charging the London Company for an unnecessary stay." We were in danger of being starved by the very hands that fed us.

We walked into Jamestown. Men knelt on the ground hitting the earth with sticks, as if their madness had brewed a strange sport.

Some stood with brooms, dusting the ash and coal with angry sweeps. Others cursed, brooms over their heads, striking the mounds of soot, screaming, "Rats! There, in the grain! Rats!" Before the blows, flocks of brown panic ran upon the earth. Men chased behind their twisting carpet, which turned and bent in its race, to avoid the hysterical blows.

"We make fine shepherds to them vermin," called a voice.

"Those are ship rats," cried the old mariner. "They're in the storehouse now, eating away our lives, grain by grain. I've seen them take half the victuals on a long cruise." I looked up at the storehouse, which was hardly more than a charred shell, burned and roofless. A sail had been draped over its wreck.

"It has not been rebuilt?" I asked old Jonas.

"The sail leaks. There's water in the grain," was his answer. I kicked the earth. Soot in black dust rose in clouds. I walked through its ghost, searching for Ratcliffe, who smiled when he saw me, as he coiled a rope in his hands. Before him, tied to a table, a man lay face down. He was shirtless. His back bled in streaks. He moaned. "And this?" I said to Ratcliffe, pointing at the figure.

"He stole from the London Company." As Ratcliffe spoke, he admired his work.

"How?" I asked.

"He purchased from a sailor what could have been bought from the store, thus depriving the London Company and the cape merchant of revenue which is mine by right."

"Why should anyone buy from you what you will only steal?" I said.

Ratcliffe touched my nose with his bloody whip.

"There is leakage in our barrels of grain. The grain will spoil, we will starve. Why was that storehouse not rebuilt when Newport and I were at trade?" I pushed the whip away from my face.

"You, my Captain Smith, are in command of all our outdoor work. I gave you that authority. I have my own commerce with the savages now. Organize your own rescue but do it out of my sight. I am made lord in my own kingdom; small powers ever gather to my great advancement." Ratcliffe said no more but walked away. He spoke in the echoes of Archer's voice. The beaten man screamed as his friends wiped the blood from his back. Some of it had almost frozen in the wounds, whose flesh was dark green with cold. They carried him to the fire to warm his back. I heard two days later he had died.

Later on the night of our arrival, we buried three of our company in the charred graves on the small rise. The graves were shallow because of the frost. We wrapped the bodies in blankets or sheets. With shovels of earth they passed from our sight. Reverend Hunt spoke his words flatly by memory. The sky clouded itself into frowned choirs and sang winds of special pleadings for their souls.

WITH SCRIVENER, I ORGANIZED THE REBUILDING OF THE STOREHOUSE. Men grumbled at their work, complaining of Ratcliffe's portioning of food. I tried to mend the situation but could not. Those who were favored rallied to Ratcliffe. Their station made their privilege. I could do nothing, even with Scrivener's backing. Newport wanted gold. Martin talked only of gold. He drank its vision in the dry wind. He smelled it on his hands. He thought of nothing else. Men sat about him, refusing to work, camouflaging their minds in gilded hopes.

The goldsmith reported that the rocks we dug along the river were not gold. Martin accused him of treason, and of wanting all the glory of the discovery to be his own. The refiners of metals reported it might be gold, but they were not certain. Men now tore at the banks of the river as beasts into flesh. Those who would not plant food to save their own lives now froze and labored and died tearing the earth from its very bones to harvest a yellow mud.

"Everywhere is madness and a dirty art," I said to Todkill. "Our company dies its death of no consequence."

I who would have brought history to this place now saw my instruments squalled in mud along the bay, digging pies of dirt, loading them into our few sacks to freight a ship. When the sacks were all used, they shoveled the raw muck into the ship, washing down the decks with rags of their own sleeves to be sure clumps of yellow earth found the ship's hold.

I wanted to freight the ship with cedar and other valuable woods, or sassafras, which was a medicine, the only cure for syphilis, which some call the French pox. But Martin would not listen. Newport agreed, needing any gold, staring ever west into the declining sun, imagining the sparkling light on the western sea. I watched Newport close his eyes. His lungs drank the air as if his nose could smell the rumor of it in the air. And where was the quest at hand? Which golden chalice was quest enough?

"Drake found it once," Newport said. "It cannot be far. All the seas are one."

The old mariner turned to me his weathered face. "Mandinga said to me years ago in Panama that he who would embrace the one to the forgetting of the many is mad. He who would embrace the many to the forgetting of the one is lost."

THE LAST WEEK OF MARCH, 1608, NEWPORT'S SHIP RODE LOW IN the tide, her hull and wooden barrels filled with yellow mud. Over half the new supply of men were dead. The weather warmed. The earth broke green through patches of winter's straw. "And soon it will be time to seek our voices and make discoveries," said the mariner when we were alone.

All things revised to a different ruin, our own guns were uncertain. Todkill split his hand, his musket exploding while hunting duck. A finger lost, his palm ragged to a burnt and bloody stew. He fainted, pain echoing through the chambers of his meat. His own agonies blanked his mind. Our surgeon tended the wreck that hung his wrist, paring with a knife to bring some healing and some ease.

The council still voted to follow the phantom gold. Martin, Newport and Ratcliffe sat their balance, while Scrivener and I spoke wisdoms to no consequence. A fearful, vengeful Archer ever libeled merit and slandered all interests not his own and all power not his. Finally he drank a portion of his own venom, gaining a justice in our hate. He was ordered by Newport to leave the colony and return to England before our company cut his throat. Wingfield also was to leave for the safety of his rude estates.

Hearing of the certainty of our ship's sail, Powhatan sent twenty turkeys as a gift to Newport, who returned the gesture by sending twenty swords. I argued against the gift, both its extravagance and the wisdom of trading weapons to the savages.

"We trade them hatchets," Newport laughed. "If I am to be great, I must display greatness." Newport had learned nothing. In a final gesture, Powhatan sent a savage, Namontack, to accompany Newport to England. It was an exchange for the English youth, Thomas Savage, who was with Powhatan. But Namontack went as a spy, carrying with him a stick on which he made a mark for every Englishman he met. Yet, on reaching Plymouth, it is told, he threw away his stick.

. . . . .

ON THE EIGHTH OF APRIL, WITH A FRESH BREEZE FROM THE mountains to the west, Newport's sails bloomed in full cheek, their canvas stretched, swelled by insistent winds. The ship threw off its moorings and took the bay in brave farewells and spray, taking with her both Wingfield and Archer, and some disgruntled few. I would have ridden discoveries in Newport's wake, and sought the lost of Roanoke, but I stayed and planted. The mariner disappointed. "You must search for your wounds," he said. "Never forget what was given us." Desperations beneath his words, clawing for their own salvations.

Scrivener and I organized those we could to refit our fort and begin our planting. Martin and his group still whispered and dug their fingers into the yellow earth. Ratcliffe portioned our food to serve himself. Around us the hollow light of an early spring now filled the air with rumors of a coming warmth. Bees came as single vagabonds in search of flowers. Birds exercised their anxious wings on the bending branches of the trees. The warm spring came sweetly to our hands. One day I was in our fields, standing among the low, rolling lips of newly plowed furrows. The land waved in the heat and moisture of the new dug earth. I had not seen Pocahontas for weeks. I stood contemplating the emptiness. I was alone, except for the earth's tremulous skin offering its darkness to the air. I felt a chill.

At noon the council met. Five savages arrived with a present of twenty turkeys from Powhatan. They lay the dead birds at my feet. I gave them trinkets and beads as reward for their efforts. To Powhatan I sent a copper plate, and thought no more of it. Two days later Rawhunt, a savage of much craft and shrewd wisdom, appeared at Jamestown with a message from Powhatan requesting his twenty swords as a present for his turkeys, "as Father Newport had given."

"I have not my father's purse," I said. "And Powhatan knows it is a poor friendship that begs its own gifts." Rawhunt scowled his displeasure at my words. I gave him trinkets, which weaned him enough from his avarice to have him smile.

The world is a sweat of appetites, and we the morsels on its plate. For the next days we worked the fields, preparing the furrows for the seeds Newport had brought. The savages came more often to watch us plant. They would cluster at the ends of the forest and hold their long, oar-shaped wooden swords and point. They moved among us, either in small groups or alone and stood at the gates to Jamestown and talked and waited. By the end of the week we noticed tools and all manner of objects had disappeared. We well knew that what a savage stole, his king would soon receive. We were in a war of motions, Powhatan its ghostly general.

The thievery became more brazen. Our men were set upon leaving our own gates, their weapons stolen. A successful thief one day would bring three the next. Soon even the forest murmured spoils. The council met, but fear of offending the savages kept our responses meek. Foul policies sometimes make cowardice a remedy. Ratcliffe stayed to his house, Martin to his golden foolishness. Ratcliffe would only venture as far as the fort walls. There he would trade with the savages and hide his words in whispers. One day he disappeared for a few hours. When he returned he only smiled and, seeing me, removed some lascivious drool from his mouth.

The evening shadows moved in stains of hunger across the earth. The land set its black in silhouette. Men guarded each other and themselves. The work had slowed. Scrivener walked to my side and told me of a savage who that day had stolen two swords with nothing done to contradict the fiend. "Tomorrow he will return with others if the council will not act." Angered, Scrivener said, "These savages will thieve us into war. Shall we stumble into massacre?"

My own dark sermons brought me thoughts. Men avoided my glance, walking away if I approached. I wanted to be clothed in faith. I looked toward Ratcliffe. "There shall be no safety for any," I said, "if the fault's not healed before there is blood."

Ratcliffe nodded to the cowards in his consent. "Correct the savages if you can, but no abuse. We will have law." So saying, he walked away, adding, "Let's try to have no treasons, Smith. We wish to have them allies."

SCRIVENER AND I WERE FELLING TREES THE NEXT DAY IN THE WOODS some distance from Jamestown. The bell at our fort began to clang its nervous throat. We grabbed our weapons and ran toward our walls. There, on the beach, most of our ragged company stood staring into the bay, trying to glimpse the far-off cast of a flag above a distant sail.

"A ship! A lone ship!" someone cried. "Is she Spanish or English? Is she Spanish or English?" twittered a voice hysterical and birdlike.

"Shall we ready our cannons?" Todkill asked.

The wind fresh in our faces, the ship bore down upon us without tack or drift, the only point of height echoing against the horizon's flat expanse. "It's the *Phoenix*," cried Jonas Profit. "It's Nelson and the *Phoenix*." The long tube of his spyglass thrust forward as he held it to his eye.

"Months overdue and still afloat," came a joyful voice. We cheered as the *Phoenix* made our beach and dropped her lines upon the shore. We hauled them taut, closing the last space between ship and land. Four fathoms deep, the water caught in the breach, fretted and jumped in that final squeeze. Nelson's crew gave back our cheers as we tied the last rope to our tree. Down the ramp they came, ragged but well fed, Nelson in the lead.

We greeted all in this new supply of men, almost half of Newport's now being dead. Death was such a common store, life seemed the treason in our blood. In her holds the *Phoenix* had brought us grains and salted meat, which were in desperate need, and tools, most of ours having long since been traded to the savages, or stolen.

We feasted that night. Nelson told his tale. He had followed Newport from England, the two of them spreading their twin shadows across the sea. But on nearing the Chesapeake, Newport had sailed ahead. The *Phoenix* had caught the coast, her bow spreading wake. Soon the skies were turmoiling, the clouds boiled into storm. Fierce winds blew the *Phoenix* from the sight of land, chasing her through heaving seas, her masts splintering against the gale, her sails in torn sheets falling to her deck. She rode the cyclone east, then south, following the great wheel of its winds. The waves still came in mountains' crests. The ship rolled and heaved against the avalanche. Sailors were swept away and lost. Rigging in ruined webs lay about her deck. But with the ferocious speed that gave it life, the storm had passed, evaporating into clear sky and sun and only a few friendly balls of clouds to ride behind, chasing the demon east.

The *Phoenix* was a wreck. She sailed south to the nearest coast, the scattered islands of the West Indies. There she refit her masts and sewed her sails, filled again her water casks, and her hold with food for her crew. "Never did I touch, nor did we feed from your supply," Nelson said. "My vow was what was sent to you was yours—each tool, each grain of wheat. I did not want to seem a traitor in any eye." So Nelson spoke his tale and his adventure, his crew nodding their heads in the silent pleasures of his truth.

· · · · ·

WITH THIS FRESH SUPPLY OF FOOD AND MEN, IT WAS DECIDED THAT Scrivener and I, with a company of sixty, should explore the Monacan lands above the falls to seek what understandings could be had, whether of Roanoke or the western sea. Nelson gave a considered yes, far m__ore considered than it was a yes. He would lend a complement of his marines and his ship. For six days I drilled and trained our troops on open ground to march and shoot and bring, in ordered devices, war to any who would be our enemy. Even gentlemen who would not work in the general labor gladly gave their sweat to our practice; they being soldiers, such work was to their station.

But there were murmurings among our company that the exploration above the falls was to no good cause, offering little profit, or any outcome to assist our work. Further, it was said that we had no commission from the London Company to make such an expensive discovery. I watched the company bicker, drowning our fair prospects in their stew of words.

Many came forward to speak of Newport, saying, "He who brought us victuals and wise counsel, it is to him that all rights of explorations and discoveries belong. Is he not our admiral?" The stomach swells as the mind forgets. They taste the air. They speak the whim, as if the moment were the clock. And who am I? It was I who had kept them alive with food. Newport had overstayed our dock, lining his pockets with the company's gold, while eating our scarce supplies. And to him go all discoveries? What season pollutes our minds? What madness rides our cobbled stones?

And now the final thrust—Nelson caught the penny tide and changed his mind. He would not allow his ship or his marines to accompany us, unless he was paid for his time. He who would not steal a crumb from our mouths would gladly strangle us in our beds. I wondered why the greed came so narrow and so late. I thought of Ratcliffe and the London Company. By what discretion does our document read us small? And still I argued for the plan's safety and its ease, but even so, it was set aside. I had the proper instrument at the proper place at the proper time, and they let it lie; and so we settled back into our ease and pretended work.

"After all this, no voices yet," said the old mariner to me. "Perhaps as a gift I should give you wounds, but then, it is not wise to counterfeit a fate."

For a time the savages, fearing our ships, stayed to the forest and the tall grass and did not steal. Spies about the fort watched and traded talk and occasionally food for an eyeful of plenty. Mostly they asked if Newport had returned, and would there be swords for presents to Powhatan? Ever the uncertain prospects of our uncertain peace, and still we played our hopes hesitantly against tomorrow.

We divided the company. Fifty toiled in the fields with me, planting corn and cutting trees to remake our fort and our houses. Mostly they wandered through their work, idling often at their hoes or axes, staring, their eyes filled with the sights of their distant thoughts. Little was done, though more than nothing, a few houses built. So it would seem that five, well disposed to work, would have accomplished more than our fifty. The others of the crew labored with Martin, clawing at the riverbank in search of gold, dirtying themselves for a waste of time. Those who were left worked for Ratcliffe's pleasures, mostly fetching and mending, seeing to his ease, bearing the bite of his beatings for imagined slights. He was our sovereign and our law and our bastard king.

AND THEN CAME THE SAVAGES AND THEIR THIEVERIES AGAIN. Consequence could hold no reason in their minds. They were as deadly children. Scrivener chased one who stole an ax across our field, to the very boundaries of our point of land. Finally the savage threw down the ax and ran some distance away, where he stopped, his bowstring drawn to his cheek. An arrow flew in its lethal arc, missing its mark. The savage disappeared. An hour later he returned, secreting himself in bushes and behind trees, crawling toward our fort, rising to menace with a drawn bow all who passed. What a willful feint is this war of slights, and what pretense is in its fists! But where the truth?

That night the incident was not much thought upon. Martin called on the council to allow the *Phoenix* to be freighted with his yellow dirt. His dream was ever a prelude, but to what? While we rode complaints against the other's wisdom, some men smoked, the white ghost of the fumes drifting about their heads. Furs not enough near Jamestown, I suggested a freight of red cedar wood, which had a small value, but more than that forged coin of dirt. Soon the colony would need a commerce to support its expense. The matter, after much argument, was left unresolved. The *Phoenix* was now clear of our supplies and ready to sail. Nelson dined with Ratcliffe at his table most nights, where, after meals, they negotiated about something in whispers and pounding fists. Once I heard Nelson shout, "I cannot stay here much longer. This situation must be reconciled...and soon."

Secrets upon secrets, the drama vapored emptiness. I and my party stayed to ourselves. Matters continued their imagined footprints upon the air. Some days later Scrivener and I were in a cornfield near our fort, hoeing the ground. Six savages approached, making signs of their friendship and their love. Their faces, though, brooded dissuasions, their eyes in other intents. They carried cudgels with stone heads.

"We must return behind our walls," I said to Scrivener. The savages in their fearsome masks of paint, oil hideous in design, scowled. We brought our pistols from our belts, walked toward the fort, the savages following. I wondered what causes brought them to our gates to do their worst, as if immune from punishment. We walked into the fort, the savages at our heels begging our friendship, saying, "Why do you fear us? It is not you we would beat, but any of our tribe who have been discourteous. Show them to us."

Now, in our fort, the savages sought to surround us in a murderous ring. I turned and said, "If you have spoken the truth, there is one who is impudent." I pointed. The savages saw the form of one of theirs sleeping by our walls, well known by all to be a harmless spy. "We will beat him," said the savage with the cruelest face, his skin yellowed by herbs and glazed by the oils of the rancid bear fat they used to keep free of fleas.

The sleeping spy, whose name was Amocis, stirred. His eyes opened. He pulled his blanket to his chest, counterfeiting safety by giving himself warmth. He crawled against the fort walls, cowering. The savages approached him. "It is not my pleasure to have him beaten," I said, "so do not do it." Amocis began to moan. The savage looked at me, striking his sword against his own hand in practice blows. His pride grew on his vanity. It swelled his chest. It twisted his face in thoughts of violence as he said, "I will do what I will. Perhaps it is you we should beat."

Jamestown was not deserted at that hour. Gentlemen idly bowled or tended fires. Martin sat at a table whispering with some of his band, singing to themselves the songs of phantom gold. Savages were such a common sight at our fort that even at these times no one glanced a thought upon the scene. Those under strict law to bring no harm always believe no harm will come to them.

And so the savages faced me, cudgeling the wind. I smiled my intentions to mask their purpose. "We are not an easy *ambushado*," I said. Two more savages entered the fort through the gate in the opposite wall and joined the hunt. I saw Todkill and Cotton look our way. Ratcliffe stared at his hands. Before me now I saw the painted face of venom. I called to Todkill in a natural voice, so as not to alarm our guests. "Get others and close the gates and have it done quickly. We will trap these fiends."

While Todkill gave the silent alert throughout the fort, I danced distractions before the savages' eyes, Scrivener in mock battle with the other three.

Quickly done by whispers, two groups of our company ran in desperate race to the gates and slammed them closed. The savages, seeing their escape now gone, dropped their swords and bows and arrows, giving up their fight. Robert Cotton and his company approached with ready firelocks, their tapers lit. We tied the savages' hands. Then our own crew ran from the fort and captured eight more savages who were lurking nearby our walls. All these devils we brought to a house, which, after we nailed its windows closed, put a lock on the door and set guards at its corners, we named a prison.

The council was called to hear of these events. Ratcliffe was displeased. He wanted the savages released without discussion. Others of the council and of the company remembered well the savages' first attacks on us. "These devils always make war by feigning peace," someone cried. Ratcliffe sulked and threatened; losing even the small favor he had with our crew, while I wondered, "What secrets play in all his treacheries? And what me in all of us must now revolt? What seems this man that our company has not cut his throat? His is a tyranny by bits, a squander by rewards. Favors to hold just enough to stay the axe. The swing is rank, authority is our rope. We are claimed by the certainties that have no name. We are what is given, we become what is taken back. My power spoons on the power underneath. Ratcliffe stirs the pot. The heat unseen is almost felt. The current rises. By fascinations we play our part. The words ghost in our head, and still we hold back. A lesser king is nonetheless a king. Rank supposed is rank indeed, and so our knees are bent. The mirror alters to be a church, the *we* we worship is but ourselves. And so I am a feather in service to a qualm, and so I will act my hesitations until possessed, frantic in my lunacies."

.   .   .   .   .

IN THE MORNING THERE WAS SOME APPROACH TO OUR FORT. FLOCKS of birds began to race above trees, scattering across the sky, as dust blown across a path. Two savages came to the edge of our fields and called my name, asking to speak to me. I bid them come closer and gave them leave to enter our gates. As they stood within our walls, a well-armed company of our own at my back, the older of the two spoke, his eyes watching the smoke of the lit tapers of our firelocks. "Why do you have such anger with us, that you steal away our warriors and hold them captive?" I said nothing, letting the savage have his full say. "Will you release all that are ours? In your greatness we beg of your love." The savage was silent, awaiting my words.

I felt my anger steam. I smiled it cold as I tasted the sharpness of my words. "You have since the sailing of Newport stolen in such brazen thievery, even plotting to murder me," I said. "I want all our hatchets, swords, shovels back, all that was ours returned, or tomorrow the captives hang." So saying, I had the savages thrown from our fort. I posted guards on the walls. I walked away, Martin at my heels.

"You're not going to hang them?" he asked.

"We have tried forbearance. Now let's stroke them with a little fear," I answered.

As I walked by Ratcliffe, he waved in mock salute. "Ah, fair traitor. More abused savages, I see. You may yet hang in England."

Our men wandered through the gates to their morning work. "Stay close in the fields. Be warned," I called.

The sun, having risen to its height, began its decline. The shadows on the earth retreated, then pointed east. "The savages…the savages," someone screamed, "dragged two of ours away—the savages did!" Men from the fields came running. I met the rush at our gates and heard, in the confusion of their words, the single tale. "Richard Potts and Thomas Coe went exploring near a woods. In minutes we heard them scream and saw them carried off in struggle with twenty savages."

"Why did you let them wander? I told you to bind yourselves to each other and to the open fields." But there were only blank stares and a velvet silence. I looked toward the company who understood a consequence only as a retrospect.

I made the council meet. I had the spy, Amocis, stand close so he could hear my words. He was always about the fort, so familiar he slept in the shadows, unnoticed. He now to rise into his silhouette, become the prop to prompt the play and be of some fair use, perhaps. "There is no choice," I said. "We must now man our barge and our pinnace and this night fall upon every village in a two-hour sail, and destroy and kill and ruin all." And so I rose to slander reason with a whim. In desperation I broached the final ploy. I left the gates of our fort open, so Amocis could practice some escape and bring the report to his king. Shortly after I finished speaking, he disappeared.

Our president, Ratcliffe, was grim. For the moment he no longer scorned me but called for action. "There must be expeditions. There must be something done, or no one, not even the president, will be safe, even in the fort." Then in his fear he turned his wrath on me. "This is Smith's consequence for not allowing thieves to thieve in peace. This was a law given us by the company, and Smith should have let the savages have their content."

"We are under no law to be abused," I replied. Upon the thought, *Ratcliffe is a coward, but never plays the fool. There is some plot here, the drama I have missed.*

Ratcliffe spoke, his words weighted beyond their rounds, the meaning doubled upon a riddle, the moment confounds, the puzzle smiles, its grin a maze.

"Do as you wish. All matters abroad are yours to resolve. So go and befit your treasons," he said. Ratcliffe sat, mumbling to himself, drowning in his cowardice. Sensual ease now in its panicked pleasure rioted at the thought of pain. "His treachery is against all law. He should have hung. He should have hung." Ratcliffe slowly sulked into silence, as Nelson rose to speak, looking at him. "Understanding your situation as I do, I will hold my ship ready for your service and will stay here for a time awaiting the president's pleasure." Ratcliffe nodded self-consciously to Nelson, the weight of the gesture seeming to say more than it said.

DUSK FAILING ITS FINAL LIGHT, I SAILED WITH MY FEW NORTH in the pinnace. The night howled in its dark combustion, invisible hunters stalked the wild escapes in the specter dance of their prey. We rowed on the hollow waters. We lit torches and burned a small field belonging to the Paspaheghs to prove our grave intent, then fired our weapons once to plead our cause in noise. Fear breeds a kinder blood than war. Then we returned to Jamestown, holding ourselves to the agonies of the wait. None we killed or hurt, our hope ever for the sign of the elusive dove.

Many hours we sat waiting. Then at dawn Richard Potts and Thomas Coe stumbled from the woods. As they ran, they fell forward once or twice onto their hands and knees. They crossed the fields to our gates, slipping and flailing with their arms at some phantom vision, as if they swam through ghosts. "They set them free!" a sentry called. We clamored around the two as they entered the fort. "The savages released us. They told us to go," said Coe.

Richard Potts fell to his knees, his eyes wide, staring as he spoke. "It was Amocis who had us freed," he said. "He came to the savages. Those who were our guards heard his words, howled and threw down their swords. They counciled among themselves. They untied us, gave us food, pushed us from their camp, making signs for us to go."

I smiled, staring at Ratcliffe, "A little threat waged in a bloodless clash…"

The council met again. Scrivener gave a speech. "We must discover what plan the savages intend," he said. There was much agreement.

"And how do you propose?" Martin asked.

"Torture," said Ratcliffe. "Let Smith have the captives. Let him abuse them. He seems efficient in that kind of revelation."

"But the law, our orders?" said Todkill.

"Smith grooms his own dictates from the law," said Ratcliffe with a smile. "Torture for the company's good is not torture. It is not abuse if we ourselves are made safe. Captain Smith will follow the order of this council and the president or he is in mutiny and he will hang." There was a silence around the camp. Then Ratcliffe spoke again. "Your own actions, Captain Smith, have braided a noose upon the wind. I shall release one of our captives as a pledge that love to us barters a return of equal love. All other savages are Smith's, to do with as he pleases."

With that, the council ended. As I walked toward Nelson to make a request, Ratcliffe came to my arm and whispered in my ear, "Build your world on your legends. My tabernacle is the flesh. You and I are one. What serves us serves all, and I shall bring death upon my other half. Then I alone shall rule."

Jonas Profit, who was at my side, overheard Ratcliffe's words and said, "All men build the altars on which they sacrifice themselves, even Drake. Be warned, Ratcliffe, how you choose another's death."

Ratcliffe walked away, entranced, as if the old mariner's words were never said. "He follows his own ghost; its anguish and its howls he confuses with his pleasures. Beware, but let him go." So spoke the wrinkled lips of Jonas Profit, and so I listened. "Man is an alchemy, all voices of all things through him." Jonas nodded his own agreement to himself when he finished speaking.

NELSON WAS AMONG HIS SAILORS. HOWEVER CHANGEABLE HIS disposition toward us, he was ever faithful to his command. When he saw me approach, he almost stepped back into the circle of his men, their flesh a shield against my presence. "I wish to use your ship," I said, "as a prison for a few of the savages."

Nelson regarded me, nervous with the silence of secret words. There was less trust in Nelson's eyes than there was in Ratcliffe's. I saw Ratcliffe's face in Nelson's. The novice is more the puppet than the master, even as he speaks in hesitation the other's song. Nelson swallowed as he thought.

"Well?" I asked.

"I have declared my ship at your company's service. It is as you wish."

"Good. I want your crew to put some stones in an empty barrel and seal it, but have it ready on the deck near the main mast. Also, I will need a chicken with its beak tied shut, so it cannot squawk…and your main mast, where I will tie the savages for their torture." I looked at Nelson, who nodded his agreement.

I had the company armor itself to the full with heavy breastplates, helmets and firelocks. Then I had our captives dragged from their keep, tied their hands behind their backs and marched them to our afternoon prayers. The savage who would have beat me sneered and paraded his ridicule. His demeanor gave the other savages a spice for mischief. I took him aside with all those who were known to have stolen from us.

While our company gathered under the covering sail that was our church's roof, to sing the songs of jubilation and to speak the excited mumble of our prayers, I took the savage who would have beat me and I beat him with my fist, the psalms giving rhythm and exultation to the blows. The savage groaned blood upon my hand. He stumbled, confused, his face swollen, his red blood washing over the red dye of his skin in a fresh yield of paint. The songs behind me coming to an excited bloom, I pulled him to his knees and brought a rope to his back. Then I threw all the savage thieves, each in his turn, to the ground, the dust rising to powder the air at their fall. I whipped them until my arm was exhausted with whipping. I exalted in fatigue, stumbling drunk and glorified.

The prayers now hushed to their close, I ordered six soldiers to bring one of the unbeaten savages to the *Phoenix*. They carried him, struggling, then dragged him through blood-stained dirt, which caked on his feet in red mud. We brought him to the ship and tied him to the main mast.

"Light the tapers of your firelocks," I ordered the six, "and aim them at the savage's head." The savage fought against his ropes, twisting to hide his face from our guns. He cried and whined. I walked to the savage's side and faced him, saying, "I want to know why you bring this war upon us. What are your plans? Tell me." The savage forced the convulsing muscles of his face to obey and give him speech.

"I know nothing," he said, breaking the words from his lips in distorted sounds.

I walked back to the line of soldiers. "Fire a volley over his head." The volley discharged. The smoke rolled across the body of the squirming savage, who seemed to collapse at the touch of its cloud. The thunder echoed upon the plain of the water in diminishing report.

"I am not the one to ask," he screamed, "but there is one, a member of the council of the Paspaheghs called Macanoe, who is."

I had Macanoe dragged to the *Phoenix*. From the deck I watched him being pulled through the grass, his hands tied behind his back. He did not resist or scream, but came heavy, staring at the ground. When he was before me I cut the first savage free of the mast and had him led away. I tied Macanoe in his place and said, "See what befalls those who defy me." I walked to a place on the deck where I knew Macanoe could not see me. There I told the other savage to lie down. We tied him and stuffed a cloth in his mouth so he could not scream. Then I ordered a volley fired in the air. "He is dead, and soon his blood will wash my hands. His body I will give to the river," I called behind me. With that, I pushed the barrel filled with stones over the side of the ship into the river. Its splash sounded like a report of muffled guns, the plume of its rising water appeared as a cannon shot.

I took the chicken in my hand. It twisted mindlessly in its demon will to be free. I cut its throat, the blood rushing through its feathers in a red stain. With one hand I held its limp body up, letting the blood wash the other in its thick, warm ooze. When I was finished, I gave the chicken to one of the company and said, "Show it great respect. It's tonight's dinner."

When I was before the mast again the savage watched my hand cupped to hold the blood. "I want to know who among you hates us and why there is war." As I spoke, I wiped my bloodied hand across his chest. "See the last of his life is painted on your chest. But for a few words, he would have lived. Now fill my ears with those sounds that will give you life." I bent my ear to his mouth. There was silence. I walked to the line of the crew. "Ready your firelocks. Reload," I ordered, adding, "but slowly. Let the savage think on it."

"The Pamunkey and the Chickahominy hate you and they plan to steal your tools," the savage screamed. "Powhatan only pretends to be your friend. When Newport returns with Namontack he will invite you to his village with a great feast, seize your weapons and cut your throats."

I walked back to the savage and looked into his face. "Is this true?" I asked.

"Most of what is stolen is given to Powhatan as his due. It was he who brought the thievery upon you, because you would not send twenty swords for twenty turkeys."

And so all their diplomacies are but a ruse for murder, and all their gifts turn on plots. Their gestures are but the rising of a fang.

Chapter Twenty-eight

STORMS AND WARNINGS. A MAP AND EXPLORATIONS.
MANY MEETINGS BY PEACE AND WAR.
AND I AM JOKED BY GOLD.

 HE SAVAGES in our prison again, the council met. It was decided that the freighting of Nelson's pinnace with red cedar wood should begin, Ratcliffe saying that there was too much talk of war for any fairer prospects. I wondered what better trade had been blown to ghost.

Two days later, Thomas Savage returned to Jamestown carrying a gift of five turkeys from Powhatan. What food was this to coax a peace? I took the birds and sent the boy to Powhatan again with a message: "I wish only harmony between our peoples. Any who says otherwise lies. I desire to come to Werowocomoco to find stones to make hatchets. I would like your servant Weanock as a guide. Will you send him to me? We shall come in peace, but if one arrow is loosed upon us, I will destroy you."

Two days I waited for Powhatan's reply. At dusk Thomas Savage returned to the fort, carrying the small bundle of all he owned, saying, "Powhatan and the Chickahominy hold many councils, also the Pamunkey. There is whispering in the village, and I am sent from the wigwam when there is talk of these secret things. I was afraid. I am thought to know too much. I am thought dangerous. Powhatan has sent me to you. He wishes me no more. He says he wants another of Newport's sons." I sent Powhatan many gifts, but no more of ours. Our strength now contested in our wills. For three days I awaited news.

"All things that were divided now flow to their return," said Jonas Profit. The night bloomed from the dark waters of the bay. Our company prayed. I thought. Dawn came again, heralded across the sky by a chariot of green flame. I watched it pass. Near noon, with the western light in our eyes, Rawhunt and Pocahontas led a party across the field toward our fort. Her head and neck were painted red, the surface then overdrawn with fine swabs of black and white, masking her delicate grace. I wondered why anyone would forfeit such beauty to such an art. There was my copper necklace at her throat. Was she just a savage after all? It being May, and mild, the furs that blanketed her in winter were gone. She was naked to the waist. In rounds of flesh that curved on the excited air, she moved upon smooth landscapes of her breasts. Breaths breathing breaths. Her life in open soliloquies to my sight. I touched her fire with my distant glance. I was drowned in the open air.

Two savages carried the carcass of a deer tied to a tree branch into the fort; another, a plate of bread. Such offerings to thaw my wounds that they would bleed again. "My father sends you gifts and words of love and peace," she said, looking only at me. I listened, my skin quivering, nervous in its lie. Lightning danced in my pores. She stared through my eyes, whispering continents. I thought of her lips, her words speaking in my head. By what seductions do we seduce ourselves? What lips ghost our haunted choirs?

"My father asks that the boy Thomas Savage return to our village. My father loves the child and will do him no harm." A concession with a double face is no victory in a war. And where the profile of the plot? And what trust would I have that would not hatch in blood?

"He teaches the little ones as we teach him. It is in what we share that we are bound together." Pocahontas opened her arms as she spoke, pleading with the accents of herself those meanings that have more meaning than a word. "Be bound," I thought she whispered. "There can be peace."

"How can you speak as you do? Our hatchets and shovels and all manner of tools have been stolen. That is not peace. I have beaten those thieves we caught. That is not peace. I have beaten those of your people who would have beaten me. That is not peace," I shouted, attempting to veneer in sound that part of me struggling in revolt. By what warrant shall I surrender to myself?

The daughter of Powhatan softened her eyes into a gentle glance. "My father has made you a *werowance* of our nation. By our law thieves can have their bones broken and their bodies thrown into a fire. As a *werowance*, you can execute that law, but you did not. What you could have done by death, you did by beatings. Powhatan will have no argument with you. But now that the punishment is done he desires his people returned."

"And what of our goods?" I asked. "What of an end to this war?"

"Make a gesture to the peace."

"And what gesture will you have to my peace?" I asked.

"What gesture do you need that you cannot have?"

I looked at Pocahontas, her face placid but intrigued in answers, while through my brain demons raced whirlwinds in their fits. By what have I become to play myself as pawn to my own flesh? I am sexed in war against a better need. I lied in my public book. I wrote that she was ten years old. I wrote too much of her beauty, of that in her which consumed me in my spite. Some in England might have guessed what I hid in my words. My narrative wandered, thundering in its contradictions. I heard them in my sleep. Insistent is the whisper of the truth, oozing through its voices the soliloquies of the relentless beast.

Rawhunt stood his ground, silently awaiting my answer. The others of our crew were not far off and could not understand our words. Pocahontas was poised in the hues and cacophony of her face. I showed nothing of my torment. The girl's eyes spoke in subtle temper. The sky swung wide its arc as chains of clouds puffed full in white wander, floated trailing wisps across the air's blue cheeks.

Rawhunt handed me some folds of leather. "These are Opechan-canough's war gloves and guards for his wrists. His bow and his arrows he has cast down in submission to your law, asking only that you release our captives."

The council met, the balance now for reconciliation. I brought Rawhunt and Pocahontas to our gates behind the walls of the fort, its logs—some leaning forward, some back—like aged teeth. The captives were unchained from their prison, those that were whipped showing on their backs the claw marks of the rope's slash. Those that were not, more humble in their ways. I told our company that the council was releasing our prisoners as a sign of peace, since Powhatan had sent his beloved daughter, who had fed us and had been kind to us, to beg for their return.

Ratcliffe walked to my side, and looking first at the half-naked girl, then at me, said, "One day, perhaps, we shall all share in the bounty our Smith has brought."

So saying, the crew sang a few psalms, which frightened some of the savages, who thought more whippings were at hand. I gave Pocahontas some copper plates, which was a generosity beyond all necessity, a well-intended gesture to signal all things but to mean none.

Pocahontas took the plates in her hand, smoothing their hard surface in between her fingers. "Can a hot fire rise in a cold smoke?" she said, looking to my mouth to see its answer.

I gave the savages their swords and bows, all that they had had, which pleased them. Soon they left, walking in a single line across the field, a strand of living beads upon the earth's throat, with one true jewel. I watched them disappear from sight, myself contagioned with the pain no disease could sport, as if losing part of me. I agonized again to be made whole.

IN THE NEXT DAYS THERE WERE SIGNS OF WAR, BUT NOTHING CAME of them. Powhatan sent again a messenger to ask that Thomas Savage be returned to his court. "There is little danger to the boy," I said, "as we still have Namontack with Newport, if Powhatan has any mischief in the wind." But the boy refused to go alone. So it was decided that Robert Cotton would accompany him to see for himself the savages' method of tending their tobacco. They left together with a guide Powhatan had sent. Thomas Savage was reluctant in his bravery. I thought when he said farewell to me he whimpered through his words.

We now worked our fields in full plow, Scrivener and I wanting our crops planted before June. Those that would work had rebuilt and rethatched our houses. We started the final mend of the fort walls. Jamestown rose on her ashes. Powhatan returned some of our tools, as promised, but not all. Considering the lack of war, all weight with the savages seemed in balance. The company became more restive with Ratcliffe's favoritism in distribution of food. His service as cape merchant was a constant source of whisper and complaint.

At a council meeting he was told to divide the food equally among all our company or be removed from his office. By vote and by threat, we placed Scrivener at Ratcliffe's arm to watch his honesty. Ratcliffe fumed, his eyes angered in their sockets, darting in their rounds like caged things. In the end he agreed, swearing our actions would bring a vengeance upon us all, but he quickly silenced when he saw our resolve.

Even Nelson's patience with Ratcliffe had gone sour. "I plan to leave you in a fortnight," he said. "How do you wish to finish freighting the *Phoenix*?"

Martin called again for his yellow dirt, I for cedar wood. "We have sent that yellow muck with Newport," I said. "If it is gold we will hear soon enough. If it is not, let's waste no more time upon it." The council voted for the cedar wood again, having had their fill of dirt. Martin raged, saying, "I know dirt from gold. If you cast slander on those rocks I found, I shall go to England and take all the credit, all the fame, for its discovery." Martin then resigned his council seat and prepared to take his passage on the *Phoenix*. His health was not strong. He also wished to address the slander to his name at court after the mistakes of his first shipment of yellow dirt.

All things now in order, I set to finishing the writing of my first public book, which I called *A True Relation, or News from Virginia*. My tongue now the liquid on the point of my quill, my thoughts riding the lines of dark, the sounds, the scratch of the page, the music of my unfolding fame. As promised when in London, I drew a map of the Chesapeake for Henry Hudson, telling him of the savages' tale of a great body of salt water west and north: "It is the source of a river that tastes of brine." Hudson would follow my letter and my map to his discoveries and to his death. Thus we are each of us a whisper for another's fate. Martin came to see me one night and said, "I know from Nelson of your book. Write of my exploits too, of my sail to the savages. Let it not be only of you."

"I will mention your three adventures at trade with the savages, even if you never would stay a night with them."

"I was sick and had to return for my very health."

I nodded. "I will mention it all." He stayed a while, breathing behind the shadow of the candle's flame as I wrote. Then he left, unseen, the words before me the barricade to the noise of his going.

MY WORLDS DIVIDED INTO THEIR TWILIGHTS. SCRIVENER AND I now were left to be some hold on Ratcliffe, Scrivener's vote counting only one against our president's two, as the charter so devised. All things held to some account, I sought my liberties in discoveries and adventures upon this new land. I decided to do some exploring with six in company and our barge. I would take Jonas Profit and follow the *Phoenix* to the conclusions of the bay, then turn to our own head and map the Chesapeake.

On the day of our departure the sea ran in plaintive swells. I gave Nelson the manuscript for my first public book. He was the messenger at hand, why not? The book was done. It was time to first bloom my claim in ink, my fame in paper monuments. "Is it history?" Nelson asked.

What could I answer? I spoke some general truth which bit against my own written words. "There is no history without the words of those who lived it. Blind as we are, we are its only oracle."

IT WAS THE SECOND OF JULY 1608. THE WIND IN CONSTANT DRAFT took the sails of the *Phoenix* in full blow. We, in our small barge, were towed behind, bouncing on her wake, rattling on the division of her surf. The line that held us to the *Phoenix* pulled taut in extended sweep. Water dripping from her coils, she creaked against the resistance of our bow, plumed spray above the rolling of our decks. Near Cape Henry at the entrance to the bay, we threw off the line, waving in the joys of our sad partings the strips of rags in flags of farewell.

"Beware Ratcliffe," called Nelson. "There's a treachery that goes beyond the fort walls." Then we fell behind the *Phoenix*, losing her to the distance and the slow curves of the earth.

We turned, sailing toward the eastern shore, toward Cape Charles, wandering through a play of small islands which we called Smith Isles, the first print of my name upon this land. They were low and uninhabited, barren but for the waves of grass bending in eternal weave and rustle before the wind.

We passed close to many brief shores, the cut of our wake rolling in its splatter and hiss, as it disappeared among the beds of reeds.

On the eastern arm of the bay we found the Accomacs, whose *werowance* treated us kindly, giving us what food he could and whatever we desired. He sat us on a mat before a fire. We smoked tobacco to celebrate the peace between us. Then he discussed the bay, its islands, its rivers, which was an important help for us. I asked if beyond the edge of the bay there was another ocean to the west, "which we call by the name, Pacific."

"Of this I have never heard," he said.

"That ocean is far off," said Jonas Profit to me later. "It is but an idea whose shadows still run with memories of Drake."

"But Newport thinks it is close," said Walter Russell, our company's other surgeon.

"Newport," interrupted the old mariner, "is a fool, who canvases the earth with the smallness of his own mind."

· · · · · ·

THE SKY TURNED ITS GRAY FACE UPON THE WATERS. CLOUDS PASSED close to the earth, trailing through misty plumes in downward sweeps. A false night came in fists of rain. Then the sky dawned again, moving in wind-pushed tumult. We sailed through waves that rolled low against our bow, weighted, it seemed, with the color of the sky. We held to our crude sail, searching each inlet, each tongue of water, for the promise of a good anchorage or a savage habitation. We found little. I mapped the jaws of the land through which we passed.

After holding to the coast for some time, we saw a spine of islands in the center of the bay. As they seemed like eruptions on the earth's skin, we in jest named them for our surgeon, calling them Russell's Isles. We sailed for them, the sky darkening in the west. Rain fumed in sheets and mist before the blackness. Lightning tore solitudes through the onrushing storm. The wind came upon us in such force it snapped our mast and ripped our sails from their stays. Our barge now listed toward the overblown mast, which floated in a confusion of torn canvas on the pounding swells. With axes and knives we hacked at the tangles, trying to cut ourselves free. The waves about us shattered in white foam. The spray on the wind stung our eyes.

"It be strange," cried the old mariner, "that with Drake I would round this world in English sail only to flounder now in the ocean's tiniest tub." His rain-stained face glistened in the gale. His eyes came full white with abundant sight. His ax fell upon the halyards and sheets. Their coils began to sever and twist and fall free. The waves rolled against us in their heaving wash. With our oars we turned to face them, riding upon their surge.

Jonas Profit still wielded his ax against the last rope, which twisted wet on our rails, glazed as if in a serpent's skin. "The mast! It will pull us down," he screamed, his ax above his head again. He brought it down against the rope. The wind, in sheets of rain, closed its curtain about our barge. We could not see five feet. It was as if we labored half-blind in the hollows of the surf. With frantic blows Profit now struck, raging and sweating in a merciless ecstasy of fear. "I shall not die in this that baptized me," he said, his words tearing holes in the wind. The sea ran toward us in swollen cliffs. "I am guilty and faithless in my quest but Drake's hands are upon these waters. I hold to that." With a last swing of the ax the rope was cut through. The barge came right in the water in a rush. The old mariner fell to his place. We now bailed as we rowed, water oversweeping our decks. "I'll take the rudder," he screamed. The barge seemed to climb straight up upon the breakers as we sat. The old mariner smiled. "Every storm sings its winds in its own dirge. Listen to the landscapes howl. The tattler is telling the tale in meanings no one hears." He looked toward me, his taunts a knife thrust in provocations.

As around us the storm gathered, we wandered upon its fury. The face of the old mariner now glistened in the rain. "The world has a reluctant conscience…and I with Drake would know it best," he screamed in a voice not quite his own. By chance we found the coast and a small bay. Rowing through its entrance, pushed by the wind and surf, we landed, anchoring in the shallows. We built a fire and warmed ourselves as we could. Our food was wet and would surely spoil, our water mostly gone. We ate and shivered and passed the night as the storm lost itself in the distance, the lightning becoming an infrequent glow, the thunder a lost refrain.

In honor of the storm, we called the waters between the islands and the coast Limbo, that sorcery where men battle to map their souls to find a port. The old mariner talked of Drake again and the Cimarrones. "I was with Drake when he rounded the world in the *Golden Hind*," he said. "What vastness, such vastness spoke in centuries. There is always a longing in an emptiness. And you, Smith, no wounds. Bloodless is a silent fate, when riches lie wizard two small cuts beyond the ear." Then he calmed. He just looked into the tangle of darkness and thought.

The mariner's words, those accusations, conscienced in my ear. My smallness flaunted to me as small. He would spend my soul to buy his heavens. The circumference of ourselves is drawn upon the compass of a thought. My world a cup and Drake the walk of giants on the sea. Is the inheritor always but the prodigal? Am I a masquerade, the borrower who follows the lesser parallel, as old Jonas would have me think? Imagination cautions ever to itself. It is the thief of worlds, and who will hear the voices voiced on the river's lips, those silent choirs that wound with trepidations the willful magics of the air? Spirits war in histories. My coward comes by thought; too much births a suicide and yet I must die by parts to be reborn. Three wounds and I am different but again. Yet, I am pursed. My coin is me, flat the surface misers minted to its issue all debased. I have designed myself to be, my treasuries are a counterfeit. I cannot divine my salvation in a heresy. If three wounds come, they come by chance. I'll grasp no part, take the middle path. Affirm by strength, deny by craft. Let me sport with law and gods. I'll take my fate, playing an indifferent part. All my consequences now will cut by accident.

In the morning we hewed a new mast from a small tree. We sewed our shirts into a new sail, and again we set forth into the bay. Our search this time was for fresh water. The kegs we had were almost dry. The salt on the wind burned our lips. At a hand's length the waters of the bay were brine. We sailed along the coast upon the ruined plenty we could not drink. The sun now at its height filled the sky with heat. Then we left, spending the next two days digging in various places on the main or on small islands, searching for a fresh spring. Nothing we found but to note that the islands were a good place to fish and hunt.

AS WE CONTINUED IN OUR SAIL, THE LAND BEGAN TO CHANGE, rolling in hills in broad sweeps, high enough to cut shadows upon their long valleys. We went ashore, walked some miles and found a pond, its silent waters aglow at its edges with reflections of the earth and, at its center, the sky. It flooded through the turns of the hills to places past our sight. I knelt and tasted the water. It was sweet, but very hot. "It's like a bath," I said, "but fresh. It is as if the earth does cook its own."

We drank to our contentment, then filled our barrels with the sweet heat of this soup, carried them back to our barge and set sail again. The coast on the main was becoming woods. Islands were still flung wide off its shore, low, in waving plains of grass. We sailed. I made my maps. The rain came toward evening, which made us wretched. Our clothes held to us in a cold glue.

We opened three of our empty water barrels to take their fill of the deluge. "So it is sometimes on this earth," said Walter Russell. "That which makes us miserable may sustain us."

We shivered through the night, ate our soggy food, most of which was destroyed before this new rain. We cut away the mold on our bread and the places of rot on our salted meat. We chewed, hoping our tongues would become numb to the taste.

The morning dawned in warm sunlight. We sailed. Along the coast the waters broadened into a large river and sweetened. Now one shore came full with running savages, who darted in zigzag flocks like frightened birds. Arrows began to fall upon the river. Savages climbed into the tops of trees, pulling their bows wide to their cheeks, letting free their lethal darts, which fell into the water with small splashes, like the sharp beaks of darting birds. We kept ourselves close to the opposite shore, then we anchored, making signs of peace.

The next morning four savages rowed toward us from the bay. The course of the river was calm and silver flat, smoothly reflecting trees and sky and canoes, as if they all were painted on the waters. We treated our visitors with much kindness. They said they had been fishing on the bay and did not know what had passed in violence that previous day. After some discussion, the savages told us to wait and they would return with others, which they did. Twenty more canoes surrounded our barge in a while. And so we seemed to float on our own little island, men sitting, facing each other, making signs, floating on the podium of reflections on the cool water. Some savages agreed to be our hostages, others had their weapons hung from the trees as a sign of their friendship. When all was done, we came ashore. There some three hundred savages danced from the trees—men, women and children—all in song, clustering about us, painted in their red, black and white nakedness. Each came with some small gift—a piece of bread, some meat—bringing contentment to us with the pleasures in their hands and the smiles on their faces.

We smoked tobacco, sitting on mats facing their *werowance* in the center of a human ring, the savages wide about us, the tobacco pipe three feet long. It seemed some great clay horn of a yet-undiscovered beast.

We refilled our water kegs, traded for food, became such friends with these, our savage hosts, that there was nothing they would not do to please us. They were the people of four tribes in loose alliance, unlike the Powhatans, who were, to our eyes, an empire. They were the Sarapinagh, the Nause, the Arseek and the Nanticokes, who were the finest merchants of all the savages we met.

They told us of a river named the Potomac, and a great and terrible tribe called the Massawomekes, who inhabited along the coast near the place we called Limbo. "If they be great then I must find them and take their measure," I said, "for I am of a mighty tribe." The *werowance* told me more tales and histories of the Massawomekes, his words igniting the fire of their greatness, drawing me to them. Then he smiled on his subtle strategies, hoping, perhaps, that both his trespassing moths would be consumed in each other's flames.

·   ·   ·   ·   ·

THE FOLLOWING MORNING WE SAILED AGAIN INTO THE BROAD
reaches of the bay, lines of clouds on the horizon almost touching its
waters, golden ribbons of sunlight flowing in broadening immensity
west, toward a fathomless distance.

"There, beyond sight, may be the shore of the Pacific," said James
Watkins, one of our crew. The old mariner pulled at his oar in silence
and scowled. "This could be our straits to the west and to China—the
great northwest passage," Watkins mused.

"I went through the Straits of Magellan on the southernmost point
of South America with Drake. This vastness comes too small. The
northwest passage, if it be, is elsewhere." Inspired in his wizard, the old
mariner spoke. He touched the water, lifted it in the cup of his hands.
"This bay if it sings of oceans at all, sings not of the spices of the East."

We sailed and rowed through the channel between the islands
again. The world in its closed immensity came upon me. "Still no
voices?" asked the mariner.

"No," I replied. The mariner nodded. I thought of that savage girl and
of those secret matrimonies I held within. Ratcliffe could leer in his slander
at her nakedness. I would still love her in the calumnies of her flesh.

As we sailed beyond the islands heading west, I hid from my
choices; perhaps there is not enough god in me. I did not think of
voices. The earth displayed to us its soul in another guise. The bay
widened to a sweep of water so full the horizon did not show the
other shore. We held our course toward a dark line low against the
sky. For hours, we sailed, the sun in its decline, the sky coming to its
night, the line in the west rising into the cliffs of the western shore,
high, like battlements against the ocean's crushing surf. We called
them Rickards Cliffs, after my mother in her maiden name. We
anchored off their shore.

Having been at their oars and on our small barge for almost
fourteen days, the crew began to feel their discontent. "This bay
is endless to the west," cried Robert Small, a gentleman who held
himself in his own arms, giving himself warmth against the exploded
shivers of his fear. "We will wander until we are lost."

I turned our barge east again. Our bread all wet and spoiled, we
ate it like a moldy paste. The crew sickened. But the flesh is only a
servant to the mind. Weakened, they called in canticles of complaints
to return to our fort, to our Jamestown hovels.

"I will not return to that rash upon the coast until I have seen the

Massawomekes and that navigable river the savages call the Potomac," I said. "We still have food. True—it is spoiled. But we can eat it and it will give us strength, so much do I believe in this enterprise. There is, in truth, as much danger to return as to advance. The same storms, the same distances, can break us in our retreat as in our discoveries. But none of this will happen. This I swear. This land can lord its terror upon us. I am as wet and miserable as you. I starve by lips the same food as you; I am as despaired, but we must nest hard in our agonies, hold against the manacles of our whims. This land makes its memories of the weak. Yes, there is no soft place for us to rest our heads. Here we are as orphans born of no seed, but here we must be resolved and stand for who we are."

So saying, we continued, reluctant to the bone, the crew in shame and fear, and I in desperation. Two days later the rains came upon us again, the land hidden by its torrents. We were made blind by water. The crew was beyond misery. No words could hold them to a course. I had been bowed to failure by the winds and rain. We started our return. The bay was now broad in gray haunts of mist. The flats of storm ran upon each other in darkening violence.

"We move through the mist as the soul of the earth moves through its stones. No voices yet?" asked the old mariner, softly was the lunatic of his passion so restrained. "If there are wounds," he smiled, "hold to the pain, it is our philosopher's stone."

We held to the western coast until the weather cleared. At the point where we turned, the bay was miles wide. All about us it seemed endless, but for the hold of the coast. We found a river with a seven-mile-wide channel, which in the storms of the previous day, we must have passed. This day being fair, the crystal of the noon lit with a warm sun and ripening with the pleasant odors of the main, the crew agreed to a short detour. It is a fair day that brings fair temperament in men. The crew less sickly in their spirits, we turned our course through that broadening sweep. The sun in its plate lay upon the waters.

"We shall this day place a new name upon our map," I said.

For thirty miles we sailed along a wide wood, its trees so spaced in their immense pillars we could see for miles through the tangle of light adrift upon the pollen. No savages did we see to tell us the name of this place or of its waters. All about us the world bloomed sweet. We were in a dream of flowers.

There we sailed alone through grace, the only human things to foul the scent or disfigure the reflections in a pool. After some hours, we came upon two savages sitting on a beach. They led us to a small bay where a creek under the shades of the overhanging trees flowed in silver rills over rocky falls. All about us was quiet and stilled, as if the earth had hushed its breath. The savages pointed up the creek, making signs for us to come ashore and follow it like a path. The woods about the creek being thick and congested with the growth of obscuring vines, we held to the center of the river.

"This place is made for suspicions and surprise," said Todskill. "We have no hostages, no reason to believe these savages are at peace."

"Tell your people to come to us unarmed," I said to the savages, "and we will exchange hostages and be friends." As I spoke, I noticed the branches of the trees, which seemed to sweep low in the breeze, as if burdened with more than leaves. There, sitting on the boughs, small branches held before them as a thicket of disguise, painted savages waited in grim watch.

"We are in war," I cried. The sound of my alarm sent spasms through the crew. Firelocks were taken into hand. "Load with pistol shot," I ordered. Tapers now lit, the smoke rose about us in languid swirl. Our guns bore upon the woods, our aim still general with few targets yet. Just a sign to tell the savages that we were ready and in defiance.

Now from the woods came such screaming howls and cries of rage, one would have thought the earth itself had cracked its lips from its own steaming throat and called fury upon the world. Savages in the thousands ran, masked for war, to the water's edge. In their fisted hands were bows and arrows in threat at us. Some had swords, others cudgels topped with sharp stones. In killing rage, they raised their weapons above their heads and smote the air.

"For all their bravado, I don't think these savages are for war," I said. The crew looked at me with such strange expressions. "See," I said, "how they loiter their arrows in their bows. They have not fired upon us. There is more fear here than war." So saying, I ordered the barge to come about and bring its bow to face the savage hosts. "Let them think we are more for war than they. Let us jest war." The crew now stood as I had told them, aiming their firelocks at the river. We gave the savages a volley, skipping our shots on the water in leadened hail. Seeing the water tumult in the convulsions of a new tide, the woods in echoing thunder, the savages threw down their weapons as they called their words for peace.

Three savages swam to our barge and gave themselves as hostages. The rest hung their weapons from the branches of the trees, well out of easy reach. It was a strange harvest we saw swaying from falling vines in those boughs. Thin, like emaciated ghosts, they swung, their violence now at rest.

We rowed ashore, the savages moving back at our approach. We gave James Watkins to them as a hostage. He stepped into his confinement, a smile upon his face. The savages came about him and led him away through the broad plain of the forest far beyond our sight. Six miles they took him to the village of their king, where they contented him, purging him of all his needs and satisfying his desires.

By the river the savages gave us the name of the water I had followed for hours in its namelessness, drawing its line upon my map. "In our language it is called the Potomac," said one of the *werowances* I added its name in ink, a place changed by the sounds of a voice from a whirlwind of images to the landscape of a word. The savages called themselves the Potomacs after the river, as was the custom. Living at the farthest edges of Powhatan's empire where he was weakest and only recently subverted to his will, they were by spirits ever seeking allies to free themselves from his power. Such is the shadow politics of tribes, conjuring as in the nations, and we the new power on land. From the savages we learned that they had been ordered to ambush us by Powhatan, who was in league with a group at Jamestown.

"It is said that those Englishmen would have left our country long ago, and have tried many times, but were prevented by their Captain Smith."

I had come full course to stare again at nothing. The only power is the power of my own hand.

"There is a secret trade at Jamestown," continued the savage, "where Powhatan will buy guns and tools for any price that pleasures his commerce."

"Ratcliffe," I cried to Todkill and the crew, in their disbelief as I translated. "He is the treason, the scar upon this treacherous land. Even the air is filled with him. That is why Nelson would not leave these two months. He was awaiting my overthrow. Then all would leave. From deceits Ratcliffe has made his own Cimarrones." I would have sat upon the earth and cried my soul into my hands had I not feared the earth itself would vomit me in violent heave into the sea.

· · · · ·

I WALKED AWAY, WANDERING INTO THE FOREST, WATCHING SHADE
and sunlight interweave in a patient sway upon the ground. Cool in
my own reflection, in the animate peace of living things, I became
again what I always knew I was—a thing apart. Treason's only
treason, that disloyalty that brings us naked to our selves. Either
Ratcliffe or I would never leave this land alive. I knew it again, as I
had known it a thousand times. Wisdom comes to us in repetitions,
as we live our lives in squanders. And I swore I would not be such.
I thought of that daughter of Powhatan, her golden blush upon the
land, while I wondered where were her true loyalties, what were her
true loves? The silence still, my wounds not deep enough, suspicion
ever brings haunted wisdoms in its lies.

I returned to our crew and our barge. "Well?" asked Todkill,
"What are your plans?"

"To sail upon this river as far as the barge can bring us. Then we
shall walk overland and see what can be seen." We took ten savages
as guides. One, a bearded fellow named Mosco. He was an unusual
savage, being of great size, with a huge black beard which fell halfway
to his chest in thick twines of hair. Generally, savages do not have
hair upon their faces, so Mosco was quite proud of his. We always
believed him to be some Frenchman's son. If he was, he never said,
and if he said, we never heard. Mosco was loyal and most friendly to
us. "We are of the same people," he said. "We all have great beards."
In the wilderness such things mean loyalties. We gathered ourselves
onto our decks again and rode along the channel, following it north.
Some of the savages walked on the riverbank for a time. Then they
disappeared into the thickets. We journeyed the river, coming to a
great flat that lay in green pastures along the beach. What congress
of phantom citadels had swept the forest back I did not know. We
passed the place in silence, sailing for miles until coming upon huge
thrusts of rocks that rose from the river's channel like the submerged
horns of giant beasts. We sailed around them. Colors sparkled in a
jeweled wash upon their surface. We sailed on. At a waterfall we saw
rocks gilded in the rushing surf, encrusted where they lay with fairy
tinctures, the land in its sleep conjuring rainbows on her own skin.

There, we came ashore, we dug in the earth, finding the clay mixed
with worthless yellow rocks. We hailed savages, their canoes filled with
the meat of deer and bear and other beasts. They shared their bounty
with us just for the pleasure of easing their own paddle home.

The Fires of the Hunter

The keel of our barge touched the riverbed. Our planks scraped in sounds of gravel and sand crushed against their own beds. We turned again south. The king of the Potomacs, met us and brought us up a small tributary where we left our barge with six of our crew and several hostages. We traveled over land for many miles to a mountain whose face rose in steep cliffs and naked rocks. Water in white rushes plunged down its side, refreshing us in its cooling smoke. No easy climb did I see. We pulled ourselves up the mountain's cold cheek. Our backs against stone, our faces fanned by the endless breeze, we walked the narrow paths. We followed the savages in single file to a hole dug into the earth, around which were seashells and crude hatchets used for digging. Nearby, a small stream fell and twisted in crystal ribbons toward the valley below. We walked to that hollow in the mountain's side, bent to our knees and began to scoop out the dirt. The earth came to our hands in black chalk mixed with gold flakes. As the savages showed us, we washed this confection of dirt and chalky gold in the stream, the mud disappearing into the water's flow. What remained we put into cloth bags.

"Do you think this gold?" asked Todkill.

I had no response. The savages traded this crude black paint along the bays. For hundreds of miles around it was used as a wash upon their faces, which made them appear like blacks with yellow sparkles on their skin. It was a sparkling dust the savages called *matchqueon*, which meant "something pretty." We took all we could carry. But once on the barge again, impelled by other hopes, I threw the bags into the river. I would not bring a golden slander on my own name. I am no Martin. Mosco tried to stop my hand. "That which you cast away is of value." For years now I have regretted what I did. What stations do we forsake in our small wisdom, and what the jest? That which Martin sought may have been all the time on the savages' faces.

I did not think on it until years later, when gold was found near that very spot. What small conclusions upon a great consequence. We now rowed down the stream, visiting for a final time with the king of the Potomacs, who had, in all ways, contented us. We treated his people as they had treated us, with great kindness. We saw their wealth in furs, bear and otter, lynx and sable. Where once there was almost war, now there was a friendship. Patience, with a reserve of strength and much caution, could make these savages fair allies and reasonable Englishmen.

And so we traded for some furs and corn and shields to decorate with fair protections and raise upon the sides of our barge. Our food almost gone, we took our sails south. Streamers and flags we nailed to our mast, letting them unfurl at the joys of our discoveries. It was a play against what lay ahead, Ratcliffe and all his treacheries; but we had found a land rich in furs and game and fish. To our disappointment, there were no mines of gold and precious things, or so we thought, for what these savages would call a treasure, we just called a pretty stone. The rare so commonly rare, perfection so overlooked, why not in dirt as in men? The counterfeit more valued than the coin. And always Ratcliffe, the foul by foolishness made to seem so fair. But we had begun to map the legendary demon of this land. We lived our first prospects, which was the course. And so all ambition decays to some contentment.

Chapter twenty-nine

WHAT ASH IS THIS THAT SALTS OUR EDEN?

ITH PAINTED STREAMERS and our flags wrapped upon the wind in the furl and bright plumage of our joyful displays, we landed again at Jamestown on July 21, 1608. The company straggled to the shore to greet us, cloisters of the walking sick. The land about was stained with ill usage, burn marks where the tall grass was fired to give us views of all who would approach. On the untended fields, our corn was dead in its brown husks. Weeds in ruinous riot spread on the unplanted furrows. "The work was never finished," I said, my disgust so practiced it almost brought relief.

Jonas Profit looked at the corn in the distance and said, "They didn't make the height of a man's knee."

There were patches of tobacco lately planted, and half abandoned. Their purple flowers had begun to close upon their final bloom. "Robert Cotton must have returned to Powhatan," I said, watching the tobacco leaf wilting toward the earth, as arms stretched backward, as if seeking flight. "They need water and work." The stalks of our tobacco plants were choked with many small leaves, not like the savage's plants, which were pruned to only a few healthy ones. All this land in its heavens, yet all our efforts have pressed us to a doubt. When a savage killed a bear, he placed a lit tobacco pipe into its mouth as a gift to the bear's spirit that its flesh is taken, and I stood looking at this cemetery in its twigs. "What spirit here will rise on us to have its vengeance?" whispered old Jonas, possessed of his alchemies and his secrets. In our distance our disaster we could see so clear. Why could not the company see it close at hand?

"I will not let us be ruined in Eden." I swore my words upon the winds. The barge was moored to a tree. Streamers and flags drifted in their decline, supported only by the weakened draft of the breeze. I stepped ashore into a crowd of men too sick to cheer. They only groaned complaints about our president Ratcliffe.

"He has us building a palace for his pleasures in the woods. There are secret doings there at night," said one who bore the marks of Ratcliffe's whip upon his back.

"He beats us at a whim," said another. "He has broken men's bones for making complaints. He has cut away the tips of those tongues that have defied him."

"He has driven us with cruelties. Even the sick must labor on his palace," said one who spoke through a ragged beard. "In vengeance today we have set upon Ratcliffe and beaten him."

The company gathered, their voices rising into the hysteria.

"Ratcliffe is alive because those who share his wanton riot protect him," called a voice from behind a fist.

For a while the few can dominate the multitude, when the multitude is starved, weak and leaderless. *Authority is the only hope that worship gives to the hopeless, and so the most beg a favor from the fates, or from the knee crushing upon their necks*, I thought to myself. As guilty as any, I should have acted sooner.

I looked at Scrivener, who had forced his way through this crowd to my side. Knowing the question behind my glance, he said, "Ratcliffe has thrown away all reason. He has stolen most of the food. The rest starve. The company must work on that house in the woods, a refuge for loose sports. Savages are seen there at night and even their women."

I spoke to Scrivener, the crew listening. "The Potomacs told me there is a group of discontents among us who are in league with Powhatan. They wish me dead so they can escape in our boats to England. I know that one of the traitors is Ratcliffe."

"Death to Ratcliffe," came many voices. "Smith must be our president! Smith must be our new president!"

Men now leaped into the air, calling to me. They rioted, screaming the sounds that were my name. I had become in one simple word an emblem for this place. I was born of my own mistake. I was now the only human point for this my compass, my continent. For the first time I knew beyond all the pities of the truth this new land would speak its histories through me.

A MEETING OF THE COUNCIL WAS CALLED. RATCLIFFE'S FACE WAS bruised and swollen from his recent beating. His eyes, sunken into their darkened sockets, darted about like birds, nervous in their cages. Scrivener stood and read the charges. Most of the company lay upon the ground, exhausted in the summer heat. A few gentlemen sat on chairs. Scrivener seemed to me weakened, but he held to the table and called the charges in a clear voice.

Ratcliffe rose and protested the meeting. "I am the body of the law and I do not approve of these proceedings." After speaking, he sat again, touching the hammer of his pistol to emphasize his opinion. But we were all armed and smiled in the conclusion that we did not care. Members of the crew spoke. "If Ratcliffe be president, I will not work. I will no longer be abused and tortured by him that only feeds himself." All who rose to speak in the wreck of our town spoke the same. The roofless buildings, their gutted windows staring emptiness into the sunlight, held their own silent jury. Torn tents and ruined hammocks littered the ground. Men still slept in the grass with rags of canvas as blankets.

Scrivener asked for a vote of the council, then as a gesture of peace, for a vote of the entire company. Ratcliffe was deposed by the testimony of his own ruins. I stood and walked before the table to address the crew. A call of "Smith! . . Smith! . . ." came in cheers. As I raised both my hands to bring some silence, Ratcliffe stood, withdrawing the pistol from his belt. Aiming at me, he pulled back its hammer, which came to its reach with two successive metal clicks. "You, Smith, have brought this slander upon me. Die now by the voice of this my gun."

Ratcliffe held the weapon at arm's length, the dark cyclops of its gaze staring at a place upon my brow. I could see his eye rest along the barrel's sight. Some of the crew stood, their hands fumbling for their weapons. Ratcliffe turned toward them and held them motionless with a hellish look. His face sweated. He shivered, convulsed in pain, as if his blood were boiling in his heart.

"And now for death," he said. His finger locked itself upon the trigger. Its flesh bulged with the force of the pull. I saw the hammer snap sparks upon the powder. An instant echoed in silence. Then the gun flashed, exploding itself into debris, as it tore the barrel from the wooden stock. Ratcliffe screamed. He brought his hand to his face, searching in disbelief for the cause of his pain. Ratcliffe's trigger finger and thumb were missing. His blood pulsed upon his face. With the remains of his hand he held the weapon, his eyes wide, staring as if not sure of what he saw.

Ratcliffe let the pistol fall, howling in his beast. Walter Russell, Anthony Bagnall and Thomas Wotton, our surgeons, were at his side. They sat Ratcliffe in his chair, bound the wound with dry grass, lint and cobwebs to stop the bleeding. A rag was wound tight, to hold it all in place. The hand still bled. An iron was brought to burn the hurt so it would not bleed.

Smoke rose and flesh sizzled when the glowing point touched the skin. Ratcliffe bit his own lips to blood, then he fainted. Russell dressed the wound with fresh grass and a new rag. The unconscious Ratcliffe was brought to his cabin and left with Wotton to tend his pain.

Such hatred there was for Ratcliffe, the company still wanted the council to meet and decide on a new president. I was asked, but refused. "I am set upon different waters. For some weeks I have sailed upon this great bay. These courses may be the entrance to the great northwest passage, which all our maps say does exist. Or, this may be a small spit upon the earth where the water comes to rest in some few miles. I have decided to voyage again and to make discoveries on these last secrets. I may be away for some time. It is not good government to have a president so far from the fort. Therefore, I suggest Captain Scrivener be made president to serve until September tenth. Then I shall take up the presidency, if you agree." The company cheered and Scrivener became president. A new cape merchant was appointed, and all of Ratcliffe's group deposed from their offices. And why did I not attend upon this presidency when it was offered? Sometimes indirection is the law that rules the wise. I was not sure Ratcliffe would sit well his fall. I did not want to depose a war. By charter the president could serve but one year. Ratcliffe's term would be done on September ninth. A vote then seemed an easier throne. Besides, I wished my fame, and saw it in my explorations. And so I gave away that which I dearly sought, only to have it again on better terms.

Before we disbanded for the night, one of the company found the remains of one of Ratcliffe's fingers. He held the bloody twig for all to see, then tossed it, with a laugh, into the fire, where it burned to cremation for our warmth, its cinders mixing with the cinders of this new earth.

Jonas Profit tried to stop him. "Ratcliffe's ashes will be the seeds for a bitter weed," said the alchemist. "All transmutations come in fire." The company laughed again and ignored the wizard in the old man.

Chapter Thirty

I AM ALMOST TO MY HISTORY.
A VOYAGE IN THE CLASH OF WORLDS.

 HREE DAYS LATER, July 24th, the barge refitted, I sailed again with twelve for a crew and Jonas Profit at the tiller. We set forth that day on a dark blue water, whose color held within its surface the reflection of sun and sky. What depth there was beneath our keel the dazzling spray flung wide. Our speed, the race across those waters, held us transfixed in its urgent hungers for more speed.

We tacked on the changing winds, leaving our wake to wash upon the channel of the Potomac, sailing further west to a river we called Bolus, where a week before we had begun our return to Jamestown. This time, though ill, our crew was more honest in their braveries. They were mostly of the new supply and not seasoned to the country. Of the twelve, seven were already weakened by disease, which worsened by fits in the past days. Now they could only lie upon the deck and sweat in fevers.

The bay still lay before us. We sailed into its flat reach, the horizon a twist of dark clouds upon the distant line. Not far from the Bolus we saw the bay divide into two branches. Our explorations now on a freshening wind, the bay unrolled its secrets to our rush. We could see the two divided into four.

"There is no passage," said Richard Fetherston, a gentleman of promise and one of the sick.

"No, not here," I said. The two of the western branches that I mapped were hollow and uninhabited. Wild beasts grazed and prowled in search of other beasts. Birds in countless flocks rose in their winged landscapes. Fish turmoiled in the nervous water. Thrusting their heads along each other's backs, in their rush they sought the drowning air as they climbed above their wake.

On all the lands we explored we cut crosses into the bark of trees, bored holes into their sides, and placed notes in them saying that we were there. In some of the inlets we nailed brass crosses onto dead stumps of trees, marking now the world with our sign. We sweated and disfigured the land with our progress.

"A shallow alchemy brings but a shallow good," smiled the mariner. "Your wounds are all misplaced."

"Let's not sour our Eden with the claim of imagined gifts. The river drifts, its voices mute. In Jamestown, Ratcliffe may not long sit the idle of the dispossessed. He has friends who still have hands to tie a noose about our necks."

We discovered the river Patuxent, whose people were gentle and in their savage ways most gracious. We promised we would take vengeance upon the Massawomekes for them, thinking they too lived in fear. But they were at peace and in friendship with that tribe, which led to some unpleasant moments.

We came upon the river we called the Rappahannock, and were treated well by the savages there, the Moraughtacunds. It was there we met our old friend, Mosco, from the Potomac tribe, who had led us to the mountain of black chalk and uncertain gold.

Our chance reunion with Mosco eased many of our concerns. He was a shrewd and knowledgeable guide who knew the whole bay and all its people. For a savage he seemed to have traveled widely. We the English mice ever playing in the sleeping serpent's mouth. The tribes we did not know, or their shifting alliances, or what shadow emperor smiled upon us his wars in subterfuge.

Our company still heavy with fevers, Mosco tended the sick. He worked for us as he could, bringing wood for our fires and water for our refreshment. In foul weather he would search the forest for other savages to pull our barge along the coast against the running of the tide or the blowing of the wind. He told us to set the shields we got from the Massawomekes around the front of the barge, to fort a better protection, those shields being made of twigs and reeds, sewn together with hemp and silk grass so tightly that even arrows could not pierce them.

I decided to venture upon the lands of the Rappahannocks, which lay across the river. Mosco begged us not to go, saying, "Stay here where you are safe and trade in peace."

With a smile I said to Todkill, "I think our friend Mosco wants all our trade." Then I turned to Mosco. "I will have explorations on the Rappahannock land. Whether they come upon me in the thousands, I shall have my map."

"There is only war where you go," replied Mosco.

"I am set. My mind is fixed upon that ground." Seeing there was nothing to dissuade me, Mosco agreed to accompany us across the river.

We crossed near its mouth, being there about three miles wide. The day reigned its calm in sunlight. The waters held flat to its broad reach. Our barge making an easy progress, I stood at the bow surveying. The opposite shore rose opened-mouth from the water, widening its grin as we neared it. The lines of trees fanged their reflections on the surface of the river. We came closer. Sixteen Rappahannocks awaited us, giving us signs of peace and friendship, which we likewise gave. They asked for trade, directing us to a small creek where there was a fine beach for a council and a good anchorage close to shore. As was our custom, we wanted a hostage. On hearing this, the savages whispered among themselves some distance from the beach for a time. Then they agreed, coming to the river unarmed to assure us of their friendship.

One of their numbers swam to our barge and gave himself as hostage. I had Watkins with a lit firelock in his hand watch over him. We rowed toward the beach where other savages stood. It was on the side of a long hill which rose easily from the shore some hundred yards. Above the crest of the hill we could see little but the tops of trees. The savages waited impatiently on the beach, nervously walking across the sand.

"There is something I don't like here," said Jonas Profit. "It is very quiet for a wood." Mosco, lying flat on the deck so as not to be seen by the Rappahannocks, said, "This is an ambush. Do not trust them. We must go." About the beach there were four canoes.

"I will go and have an adventure," said Todkill, "and see what can be seen beyond that hill." We called to the savages that one of our crew was coming ashore to gather some wood, but was not to be harmed or taken hostage. The Rappahannocks agreed, gesturing to us to bring our barge closer. We did not. We floated upon the moat of waters.

Todkill lowered himself into the canoe, unarmed, and rowed from the barge to the shore. We knelt, resting our firelocks on the side of the barge to steady our aim. Stepping from the canoe, Todkill was on the slope of the beach. The savages stood in groups, agitated, discussing, hiding their words behind their hands, glancing at our barge. Todkill walked easily from the canoe, as if he were on a quiet country lane in England. He ignored the savages, stopping every so often to pick up a fallen branch. Around him the air was steamed in summer's glow, a bellowing heat in a radiant shower of light. Todkill was almost at the crest of the hill. He stopped suddenly, looking at the trees on both sides, then he turned and walked back toward us. "We are betrayed," he screamed. "There are hundreds of savages all in wait."

As two savages rushed from the trees, our firelocks spoke. The savages fell, rolling like rags upon themselves. They furied in their wounds as if casting out agony; their arms and legs flailing as they screamed. Todkill ran. Our hostage tried to escape by jumping into the water. Watkins shot him in the head as he swam. The yolk of his brain, blown from its shattering skull, spilled upon the waters. Now three hundred savages howled in the woods, the earth echoing to the throat of their growing rage. From the trees to the plain a shadow painted its darkening sweep upon the earth. We fired into them to hold back the dusk, the sparks of our powder and flash of our shots burning bright flames into the horde. Savages in bunches stumbled. Others, in race behind them, tripped, falling, carpeting the ground with a confusion of limbs. Arrows in waves flew in hawks against us. We moved to the bow and knelt behind the Massawomekes' shields. Arrows fell in fleets upon us. They struck the barge. They pinned themselves to our deck and to our mast and to our barge's side. But against the shields they bounced in harmless thud, falling back into the waters.

Todkill ran before the savages, tripping and stumbling, as if his legs would not yield quickly to his will. The savages were upon him. We fired to cover his escape. Savages dying as they ran. Our guns hot with use, we loaded our weapons with pistol shot to bring murder in leadened hail.

"Anas," I called. I gestured as I stood, "be flat on the ground. We are firing pistol loads." Todkill dove onto the grass. The savages rushed upon him. As Todkill crawled frantically, we fired. Blood exploded into the air in crowns of spray. The savages, amazed at the proof of our power, retreated into a quickening run.

We came ashore. Todkill was soaked with the blood of those who had died about him, but he was unhurt. We gathered up the thousands of arrows that had been loosed and gave them to Mosco as a present for his services. We also made him gifts of the four canoes. In appreciation, he stamped his celebration in a dance about the clearing.

The many Rappahannock shields we found we nailed about the sides of our barge, until it was encircled in a protective garter. We saw much blood and many slain. We buried their dead, debating if we should say prayers over them. That we did, Mosco chanting his own tunes in his own way. We spent the moonless night riding on the black waters, listening to the distant cries of unknown things.

IN THE MORNING WE TRAVELED ALONG THE RAPPAHANNOCK. ONCE ashore, we posted a sentry and set brass crosses into the earth to mark and claim this land as English. A few began to cut their names into the bark of trees, I among them, with knife and hatchet scarring through the folds of tough bark into the moistened center of the raw wood. Letters of my name in bright wounds upon the forest. We stayed for hours so marking the rows of trees, tall like living gravestones, with our script.

"How many summers do you think, Smith, before the bark grows over our names again?" asked Todkill.

"Before we all are dead." I stabbed my knife into the tree between the letters of my name, thinking of Jamestown and the coming winter without food. "Famine stalks the predatory of this woods," I whispered to myself. "The colony falters upon itself. Would this, our last Jerusalem, fall upon its own ruin? Lazy pleasures greed our will. Contrite by law, our legal treasons seize by license the shatters of our grail." There was a cry from our sentry. Arrows began to fall into the grass about us. We grabbed our weapons. Some hundred savages sneaked in stealth in their agile war, slipping from tree to tree in their flight, firing arrows on the run. Gaining a tree, they disappeared, holding against its back, so our shot could not assail them. Here it was Mosco whose knowledge of the savage ways did us great service, firing his arrows in such storms as he too circled among the trees. The savages kept to their hiding places, believing they had encountered a force far larger than they had thought.

Mosco continued his sneak among the trees until all his arrows were spent. Then, in desperate and heroic race, he ran to our barge to gather more, while we knelt in the shadows of the trees. Our firelocks bloomed smoke and spit fire at dark motions passing through the light. There were cries of pain. Mosco returned, his quiver filled with a bouquet of feathered sticks all in full plume. In his hands he held more arrows. The woods seemed silent again. Occasionally there was a lone volley of a gun echoing through the forest like the wail of a lost child.

"I think they're gone," said Mosco. "They ran away. Those were Manahoacs." He began to walk forward through the trees, slowly at first, then faster, reassured of the Manahoacs' flight. We followed almost at a run, coming out of the woods onto a long, grassy plain, the Manahoacs in the distance ahead of us. We were losing ground, the space between our bands growing. In their speed their bodies appeared as agitations on the horizon, low to the round of the earth. Then they disappeared.

Mosco walked back to us, disappointed that the race was over. We began our return to the barge, Mosco sullen. Lying on the ground near a tree was the body of a savage, his knee torn open by one of our bullets, the flesh in exploded tear still oozing blood. He seemed dead. I knelt to test the depth of his hurt, pulling his head into my arms. He groaned. Furious at seeing him alive, Mosco grabbed his hair. The feathered crown woven into the hair of the wounded savage broke between his fingers. A cudgel rose into the sky in Mosco's hand, its shadow passing across the earth. The Manahoac revived and screamed, as he aroused himself to battle for his life but Todkill held Mosco's arm, staying the blow. Anger now came in exploded fits across Mosco's mouth. He would not be stopped. Three of our crew held him, dragging and pulling him away. Mosco fought against these restraints like a wild beast in chains, his feet struggling upon the earth, tearing the grass up by the roots. Dust in clouds rose about him, the dirt stuck to the phlegm at his mouth. Two more of our crew came to hold him, wrestling him to the ground and kneeling upon his arms, his head still twisting against the violence of his unseen thoughts.

We carried the wounded savage from Mosco's sight. He quieted. Todkill brought some of the Manahoacs' arrows to Mosco and laid them in a pile at his feet. I left Todkill and the others to search the ground for other arrows while I returned to the barge to see to the Manahoac. Our surgeon, Anthony Bagnall, was busy at his work, sewing the wounds to stop the blood.

The Manahoac told us that his name was Amoroleck, he was a Manahoac of the Hassinunga tribe, and all his people not at war were hunting these woods. We asked him why they had made *ambushado* upon us.

"It was said"—Amoroleck looked away as he spoke—"you are demons of the underworld who have risen from the sea to take away our world." He patted the deck of our barge as he finished his words.

Why in all the world do men come to grieve their superstitions into a war? I asked, "And how many worlds do you know?"

"I know of those that are under the sky: the Powhatans, the Manahoacs and the Massawomekes, and others who live among the mountains."

"And what is beyond the mountains?" asked Todkill.

"The sun," he answered. "But more I do not know." I asked him about the Ocanahonan, those people I believed might be survivors of our Roanoke. He said he knew of them but that they lived far off and it was said they were eaters of their own souls. There was little more he knew. We gave him toys for his narrative, and asked him to stay with us, to prove to his people we came as friends. This he agreed to do.

THE NIGHT BEGAN TO SULLY THE DAY WITH SHADOWS. THE DECLINING sun bloomed huge in its orange blossom. Swirls of evaporating heat rippled its face with agitation. Night was coming to land. Above our decks we had built a canopy of shields to protect us better from flights of arrows. We cleaned our firelocks and sharpened our swords. Mosco arranged his arrows in convenient bunches around our deck. Amoroleck happily ate some of our salted meat. We cast off, moving slowly at our oars, the river in its dark lacquer held images to its surface in an illusion of profound depth.

Threads of white mist began to rise from the water, searching it seemed, in their undulating columns for a form. Onward we traveled, the mist curling about us, its eddies following behind our mast like ghosts in their voiceless smoke. On one side of the water sheer cliffs began to tower. The river narrowed and flowed against their stone walls. Trees from the other side overhung the barge.

"If the savages assail us now from either side, they can do us much harm," said Todkill.

Mosco stood to the rear of the barge, listening. A twig snapped in the night. Branches rustled against each other, as if caught in an exercise of some fury. Mosco looked at me.

"There is a stealth along the bank tonight." He signed to me to keep silent. "It has weight and determined path. It follows."

Somewhere behind us in the dark something howled and was answered in choirs spread along the river's bank. Arrows began to fall behind the barge. They hit the canopy of shields in torrents, falling across the stars in blackening arc.

I called to Todkill to bring Amoroleck to the side of the barge. Mosco gathered his arrows and a bow in his hand. Our crew knelt behind the protection of the shields along the barge, the lit tapers of their firelocks burning like angry eyes.

"Call to your king. Tell him we are friends. We come in love," I said, Mosco translating, as I threw my voice against the cries along the shore.

Amoroleck stepped forward, calling into the night, his voice almost fracturing against the force of his breath. The night still rained arrows upon us.

"Call again," I ordered. Amoroleck screamed into the unseen, horror now upon his face, his eyes wide.

The cries came closer to our barge. Flocks of arrows fell about us as if some clan of nesting dart. "We must have the savages keep their distance," called Todkill. "Can we send a volley upon them?"

"Fire at the noise," I ordered. The report of our weapons cut the night into lines of flames, the roll of our smoking thunder quieting the earth into dread. The world was in hush, the smell of our burnt powder evaporating on the breeze. Then the savages came once more in howls and cries and taunts and lascivious screams. Again we fired, another hail of arrows at our shields.

We kept the barge to the center of the river, to the faint shine of her surface, volleying into the unknown in desperate battle with the unseen, only a phalanx of sounds to guide our aim.

AGAINST THE SHELL OF THE SKY THE DAY DAWNED, THE DARK decayed to an anxious gray. Safe at last from the savages and their arrows, we had sailed into the center of a wide bay. We anchored and ate breakfast, hardly speaking to each other except to cough. We rested for a time. Then I stood looking toward the western bank where the savages gathered in small groups discussing no doubt their lethal plans to pursue us in their hunt.

"Arm yourselves with swords and firelocks," I said to the company. "And each man is to have in his hand one of those savage shields. Tear away the canopy!" This done, I said, "Now display yourselves as I." As I spoke we all stood, arms thrust wide, holding our iron plumage like sunbursts. Amoroleck stood with us and called to his people, "These are my friends. They tended my wounds. They stopped the hand of the Potomac who would have slain me—this Potomac who loves them more than he loves his own life." His voice cried in echoes across the water.

"You cannot do hurt to these my friends. Their shields are metals we do not know. Be at peace with them and they shall be your friends," Amoroleck called.

The savages talked upon the beach, their heads bobbing in the gloom of their words. Finally, one turned toward the barge, lifting his arms toward the sun in that familiar gesture of peace. Then the savages hung all their weapons from the branches of the trees. Two swam to the barge, carrying as presents one of their king's bows and a quiver of arrows tied to the locks of their hair. I received the gifts with great kindness, I giving them such rewards as would seal our friendship.

I asked that the others dressed as kings send their weapons to me as their own gestures of love. When the bows and arrows were on our barge we came ashore, reuniting Amoroleck with his people, who now in merry celebration danced upon the beach, saying their prayers for our good fortune.

Some came about us, their hands on our clothes in tentative yet curious touch. How friendly these lethal children. How forgotten were the wars of last night. A tobacco pipe was brought before us.

As we sat and smoked, the scent of the tobacco curled in waves upon the wind. The savages asked about our pistols, the grips of which protruded from our belts. I pulled one free from the cloth that held it to my side, displaying it in my hands, the sculpture of its curved wood and metal in delicate twist. The dark nozzle of its barrel delighted the savages. How much this instrument is of doom, yet it was thought a wondrous tobacco pipe. "And where walks death," I smiled to myself, cynical in my rejected divinities, "there walks the shadow of our God."

WE SAILED TO REJOIN OUR FRIENDS THE MORAUGHTACUNDS, WHO raptured in joyous dance when hearing of our victory over the Manahoacs, with whom they had warred many times. We all now being friends, the Moraughtacunds counseled us to consider making peace with the Rappahannocks, whose anger they feared, and whose terrible reprisals they expected, having recently stolen three Rappahannock women.

"These Moraughtacunds are not fools." I smiled. "They know the power of our guns, a power that can broker a general end to war. It is a peace only we can bring. If we become the arbiters, we could be the balance that wields this land"

Messages were sent then to the Rappahannocks to meet with me and all the nations along the river at the place where first we fought. "No wounds have yet been given that cannot be healed by peace"—I told the messenger to say this to the Rappahannock king as a personal greeting from me.

WE VOYAGED ACROSS THE RIVER THE NEXT DAY, HAVING RECEIVED word from all the tribes that they would be at the place we had appointed. The canoes of the Moraughtacunds came in flotilla around our barge, savages straining with their paddles to keep pace with the glide and roll of our keel. We unfurled flags and streamers from our mast. Proud we came to that council. On the beach there stood all the *werowances* of all the tribes, surrounded by their nobles, their warriors, their interpreters. Great tobacco pipes were held by their priests, who wore strange one-armed shirts and all their devilments. I by Powhatan was made a *werowance*, inheritor of voices, the voices I still could not hear. And where are you, my haunting, with your lips? My wounds not steeped, the pain but slight, my service had not yet gained the prize. My prize is fame, not heresy. If voices come, they are fated to my ear. Maybe this land had played a madness with my mind, a cruelty to make a comedy of us all, even the mariner, his chance forever lost, who still seeks, his only resurrection.

I sat across from the Rappahannock, a tall savage with a face that prided itself in power. He had the bearing of all the savage kings, regal and certain. A natural and courtly manner informed his speech.

The Rappahannock presented me with his bow and his arrows, passing them to me as I passed a tobacco pipe to him. We exchanged puffs in flights of smoke, looking into each other's eyes, human sight trying to fathom the mysteries of the human soul. I placed my pistol next to the tobacco pipe. Let smoke be smoke, intimidation wrapped in its theology. Looking at the pistol, the Rappahannock stiffened into a fearful courage and said, *Your friends the Moraughtacunds have stolen three young girls . . . my wives.* The Rappahannock king drew closer to my face. *All things must be balanced in their regrets if there is to be true peace.*

"If the three girls were returned would this bring friendship between all the people of the river?" I asked. The Rappahannock signed that it would.

I turned to the Moraughtacund king and asked, "Will you have peace?"

He who wanted peace most answered, "No." Words now to desecrate a land. "We have had our own women taken. Some now live with their husbands and children as Rappahannocks, forever lost to us. Who shall make compensations for them?" said the Moraughtacund king, adding, "War is always easier than a bad peace."

"Then are we to have war again?" I asked as I put the pistol in my belt again, as if readying myself to stand. The kings were silent. "The peace is its only gift. How much blood is ransom enough to have an end to murder? If I could bring a treaty of equal good balance upon the tastes of some regrets, would that satisfy you both?" To this they both agreed.

"It is done," I said.

Simple justice comes only by wisdoms balanced on a threat. Mosco was at my side. I had the three girls brought before me. I turned to the king of the Rappahannocks and said, "Choose the one you love the most." His eyes upon a passion. He brought one of the girls to his side.

I the wizard's mite, a crumb bought stale in a groundling's shop. I spark the dance of the scarlet from my hair, divinity presumed in a flame congealed. Now I wield myself, my theologies in a tint.

I told the Moraughtacund king to make his choice of the remaining girls, which he did. "She will be the foreign wife of a sovereign king," Todkill whispered to Anthony Bagnall, our surgeon, "a royal marriage arranged by our Smith."

I touched my beard and my pistol, "These are ever in defense of the peace we make today. He who breaks his word is my enemy."

Both kings nodded.

The last girl I gave to Mosco, who in war and friendship had always stood by our cause. He joyed of my present. The girl went timidly to his side. Mosco whooped and howled, stomped his feet. He ran to the barge, gathering in his arms all the arrows and bows and shields that we had given him from our wars, which now he gave as presents to his friends. Such luxury and wealth showered from his arms that even his new bride began to look cross at the extravagance. These savage girls are far more forward with their voices than our English women, and are far more free. But Mosco would not be halted. He paraded his delight among his friends, announcing to them that he would change his name to Uttasantasough, which means stranger in their language, the very name the savages call us.

I, who would bring peace unwrapped a new history at their feet. But I am the trace of moments, an echo in a hue. How long would this alliance hold? *The savages fear war,* I smiled to myself, *but what is this terror that I know? It is a whim that passes beyond remembrance.*

"Now that each of you has chosen his love, have we accomplished peace?" I asked to reassure my own doubt. The kings gestured that we had. With night coming soon and the beaches deserted of canoes, the nations dispersed to their towns. We to the center of the bay. The land as ever in its silence, speaking through the eye. The day streaked in crimson across the few high clouds.

IN THE MORNING WE WEIGHED ANCHOR AND SAILED ALONG THE coast. The drawing of my map, an expectation seized in the ink of our autumn search for trade. Thoughts of Jamestown ever a frightful vapor. In days I am president. Has Ratcliffe mutinied with his own? Am I displaced? My death lives graved in contemplations. The colony's landscapes a cemetery ever in my dread. Gray, the forest

I imagine gray, the branches twisted cold like granite stones. And where the brambles wither the grass grows white around the chalk of our finger bones. Seventy-five of our original one hundred and seven already dressed in their coffin sacks. Ten of the new supply dead as well. Three each week. A hundred by the next supply? As we hold by falter to the land, our willful hopes a comfort so tenuous, so brazen in their mortuaries.

"Can a splinter be wound enough?" the mariner seeing my hand on the crude wooden tiller. I looked, no wounds upon my skin.

"The deepest blood comes sweet. It oozes in a silence that I know," I replied. "We are all hard against the pike. Play the philosophies of your ear. But the blade is in our throat. The colony needs food. I am the doubter that will not grasp the wizard's staff."

"Harvest the air," the mariner cried. "It will feed more than breath."

AT THE RIVER OF THE TOCKWOUGHS WE HEADED OUR BARGE INTO the current. A few miles up, canoes in fleets came upon us. So numerous they were, it was as if parts of the river were covered in a wooden drift. Their bows darted on the current in angry thrust. I stood and called to them in the language of Powhatan. The canoes still came upon us, but no arrows yet were shot. I called with the only savage language I knew. My hands touching my heart, I gestured, throwing my soul to the sun. "We are friends," I said.

The savages circled us in their hollowed logs. It was a great flow of wood that surrounded us—two or three savages in each canoe, arrows in their bent bows, strings pulled taut. A voice came from one of the canoes, speaking the language of Powhatan. Other voices argued with each other in a tongue I did not know, an obscure debate, held with arrows aimed at my heart. I held a Massawomeke shield before my chest, then I raised captured bows and arrows before me as an offering of peace.

"How have you come by the weapons of the Massawomekes?" called a voice in the language of Powhatan.

"In battle," I lied. "In battle with your mortal enemies, the Massawomekes. We have come as your friends to take vengeance upon them."

With that, the Tockwoughs motioned us to come ashore and council with them. They brought us to their town, fortified all around with a wall of logs, armored with a covering of tree bark, the strips of the bark held to each other in overlapping plates. From a distance it appeared to be a giant tree stump. Within the walls were hung scaffolds for the Tockwoughs to stand upon and shoot arrows at enemies, with little fear of their own hurt. In places there were mounts like crude towers, their high platform walled around with bark and woven reeds. To us, the whole construction seemed as a child's dream of a great castle. But these children carried lethal toys, and welcomed us as allies into their endless wars.

The savages, as was their custom, spread mats upon the ground for us. Their population then danced and sang in celebration. Food was spread before us and we were given gifts of furs. All that they had was ours for the asking.

These Tockwoughs were different than the other savages we had met, for they had iron hatchets and knives and pieces of brass and all forms of metal tools. "Where did you find these instruments?" I asked. I was told they were traded from the Susquehannocks, a great and powerful people who lived along the chief river of the four branches of the bay.

"It is a journey of many days to their land," said the king of the Tockwoughs, speaking through an interpreter, the only savage of the tribe who spoke the language of Powhatan. "It is two days beyond the place where the river falls over a rocky slide. It is a place your barge cannot go. The land of the Susquehannock is a land peopled in giants."

"I would meet with these giants, these Susquehannocks, as with you, in friendship and love," I said. "Can messengers be sent to have them come here? We are all at war with the Massawomekes. Is it not wise for those with common enemies to meet as friends?" altering the truth for a necessary gain.

Two messengers were sent as interpreters: the one who spoke the language of Powhatan to bring my words and one who spoke the language of the Susquehannocks, which was different from the Tockwoughs. So close these savages to each other, and yet, in this new land, no voice do they have beyond the ears of their own kind.

FOR FIVE DAYS WE AWAITED THEIR RETURN. ON THE MORNING OF the fifth, the winds brought gales upon the bay. The waters rose in white crests, spray blowing on the gusts, swells tumbling in confused lines. My crew were at their morning prayers. I stood upon the beach, looking west into the rain. Through the mist in dark wash upon the water I saw many canoes. At their oars were people taller than any I had seen. And now I had come to see these giants who walked my earth. The canoes came in battalions. More than sixty Susquehannocks, their muscles straining.

The Tockwough messengers had stayed behind, being afraid of the storm. The Susquehannocks walked from the beach, carrying presents of venison and baskets of fruits and nuts; two of the savages, marching in deliberate stride, carried on their shoulders a huge tobacco pipe. My men watched, their prayers forgotten. I, who was smaller than these savages. With me the halo flames, shiver the earth in my cold fire, red hair and beard, a sunset dawns upon the teardrop of my face. Armored myself now in guile. The Susquehannocks came before me, their five *werowances* in the lead. They all looked at my crew, then at me, making conversation among themselves in a language I did not know. Then the *werowances* raised their hands and sang to the sky, addressing their prayers toward the directions of the rising and setting sun. *I am the mask*, I smiled to myself. *I glow in the fete of reflected bounties.* The Susquehannocks now touched my clothes with embraces and supplications. I was being worshipped as a god. Has the world a different crush to force the drink of voices to my ear?

"Are your voices with you now?" asked the old mariner. I did not answer.

The savages brought forward a great bearskin, which they draped about me, while around my neck they placed a necklace of white stones. The strands weighed upon me like chains. All the time they caressed my neck and hair, calling to me as if calling me forth into my power. At my feet they placed gifts of weapons and a great fur cape, sewn from eighteen different pelts. It was as if the Susquehannocks were offering me the inheritance of all their history and all their sky. I stood regal in my moment, wearing in my mind this earth as my ring. My own crew grumbled to themselves. I raised my hand. They silenced. The wind washed over me, making me shiver in the heat. The mariner stood in a wide-eyed frenzy as he watched.

The Susquehannocks signing to me their intentions as they anointed me their god and king. I felt naked, even in the softness of that fur robe. I was cold in my flesh. The savages begged me to stay among them and protect them from the Massawomekes. I was to be their divine vengeance on earth. They were at my feet. I was truly power. But there was still Jamestown. *My history is to be played for another stage*, I thought. *In England I am a nothing of no rank, and now this nothing is made a god. It is the human curse to war by certitudes against the certainties. Shall I hide in a savage truth and be a forest sovereign?*

The mariner's eyes were maddened, his words soft. "Around us the spirit quests to gain that perfection that was before our Eden's fall. Wizards were seekers of the way. But I am old, I want my Edens now. My absolutions in their heavens. Grasp the wounds! The voices may be our only chance." The mariner's words pleading in their force. "The world's soul flows in stone and water," he whispered. "I sought in my alchemies once to hold the recipes to chain the spirit of the world. To hold that knowledge as a man is to wield it as a god. Do you have the courage to grasp that heresy? Could you dare the world, your soul as chip? Heresy is a wound of sorts. Clasp the blade, your blood is almost voiced."

I gave reply. "Why push the chalice to my lips? The consequence may be soon enough. The world wounds us in its careless sport. Why all the prompt? I am not a monk to my own vision. To my own demons I am sin."

"Are you Drake? You have something of his face, you have a shadow of his voice, but are you him? He would have grasped the heresy, played the sacrifice. Would you as Drake trespass for a better fate?" A savage raised his hands to the sky and began to chant, as I wondered to what depths does my soul rebel? Am I son? Is all my inheritance but to take this lethal step? A father gained for a father swept away. To what do I claim, by what hesitations am I birthed? A child in his manhood bowling tantrums at the moon. But does my soul mint coins to spend against its heaven?

My crew, seeing me so approved, came almost to revolt. "He who exalts himself with savages is a savage," cried Anthony Bagnall. I nodded to him, saying in gesture and word, "What I do benefits all." For a moment their angers humbled. The old mariner hissed, "Claim your divinity, take your wounds."

Lush grows my crown of thoughts, in their jewels reflections of an errant sea. Caught by consequence, I stammer to the act, signing to the Susquehannocks. *Exalt me if you will but I am but a man. The Massawomekes are my enemy too. In that, our bond is deeper than blood.*

"Such an easy chance it might have been to have your gift and now the moment lost," whispered the mariner in disgust. "Two damnations but for a yes."

Would the mariner wound my soul to have his own salvations? What theology is this, that damnation is the prize? Will I ever call myself a god to gain the illusion of a gift?

The air turned parchment. The clouds scrolled in ciphers, as armed in our conclusions we each cursed our premonitions into the drifts of the other's imagined fate.

END OF VOLUME ONE OF

In the Land of Whispers